D1125863

UPGUNNED

Also by David J. Schow

DAVID J. SCHOW

UPGUNNED

For James, locked & loaded...
" " J. Schow

THOMAS DUNNE BOOKS
ST. MARTIN'S PRESS
NEW YORK

THOMAS DUNNE BOOKS.
An imprint of St. Martin's Press.

UPGUNNED. Copyright © 2012 by David J. Schow. All rights reserved. Printed in the United States of America. For information, address St. Martin's Press, 175 Fifth Avenue, New York, N.Y. 10010.

www.thomasdunnebooks.com
www.stmartins.com

Library of Congress Cataloging-in-Publication Data

Schow, David J.
    Upgunned: a novel / David J. Schow.
        p. cm.
    ISBN 978-0-312-57137-5 (hardcover)
    ISBN 978-1-4299-6248-3 (e-book)
    I. Title.
    PS3569.C5284N44 2012
    813'.54—dc23

                        2011033769

First Edition: February 2012

10 9 8 7 6 5 4 3 2 1

UPGUNNED

PART ONE

ELIAS

I had just wrapped up having sex with my best friend's ex-wife, after shooting naked pictures of her, when I heard a slight entry noise from the elevator end of the loft, and looked up into the face of a man holding a gun.

"Hi, Elias," said the man, whom I had never met.

The gun was formidable. I didn't know from guns. For me, shooting meant taking a photograph, and none of my other definitions had anything to do with firearms. I only knew that this pistol had a bore so big it looked as though I could stick my index finger in there with wiggle-room to spare. That was all the convincing I needed.

I thought, *Maybe Clavius is pissed off at me, for banging his wife. Ex-wife.*

My mental camera-eye framed the intruder. Backswept blondish hair (what used to be called "dirty blond"), blond brows, eyes the color of melting dry ice. He appeared too aware to be a cop, a creditor, or a politician as he looked around my workspace with the kind of non-smile that imparts zero warmth—a slit showing teeth.

"You do good work," he said. He was pointing at some of my blowups with his gigantic gun. He wasn't afraid to lose me from his line of fire. The sheer presence of the gun was threat enough.

"The perks aren't bad, either, I bet," the man said. He mimed oral sex at me—tongue poked into cheek; fist pumping near mouth.

Great, I get it, okay?

Then he *did* smile, and I wished he hadn't.

This man had nothing to do with Clavius, the ex-wife, or any sexual indiscretion that may or may not have transpired. If he had, he would have begun a punitive speech by now.

I was so damned tired I completely bypassed the expected stages of shock and fake outrage, the programming that makes people say stupid things like "What the hell do you want?" or "Who the hell are you?"

His suit was too snug and about five years past the style curve. What mattered was the physique inside that suit—tight as a race car. Thick rubber-soled shoes; practical. Silent.

"I don't have any money," I finally blurted out.

He laughed then, and that was worse than his smile.

"Then have some," he said. He plonked down a stack near my light table. Thick as a slice of old phone book; all hundreds. "Ten thousand, for your trouble," he said. "Do what I tell you, when I tell you, and convince me you can keep a secret, and you win. Even more exciting than that, you get to keep breathing. With me so far?"

Thus did I watch a long, exhausting day become an even longer, more exhausting night.

The older bank buildings and department stores at the intersection of Hollywood and Vine had undergone a tediously long rebuild into overpriced loft space. I had been fifth floor for little more than a year. I had never been burgled or bothered until now. It was late June, that period where the sun takes its time going down. Almost 9:00 P.M.; there were still threads of sunset to the west.

His gaze kept straying to my stuff on the wall. He vacillated between two in particular: *Petroglyph,* an up-angle on a row of bridge supports that dwindled with a Mobius infinity effect it had taken hours to capture (due to the light and shadow shifts in time-lapse), and *Targets #5,* which was unfortunate, since it was one of a series of painstaking double exposures of naked people superimposed on silhouette targets with the eyes, mouths, nipples, and groins shot out. I had hired a champion marksman to do the bullet work, since shaping was key. Tiny reports from a pistol that sounded more like a cap gun. Tiny bullets made perfectly circular, tiny bullet holes. My version of pointillism had rendered the subjects weirdly androgynous.

"I really do like your work," the gunman said. Then he made a come-on motion with his fist and two more guys with guns entered the room.

The reason I had been photographing Nasja with no clothes on had to do with Clavius—my mentor, her ex-husband. Photography *is* sex, as Clavius is so fond of saying.

The uglier reason was that Clavius had sloughed Nasja onto me as a consolation prize for some other manipulation, a hand-me-down, as if I were destitute or needed to be reminded of my second-string status to Himself. His most recent divorce had been mere preparation for jettisoning her entirely.

Worse than that, Nasja knew this, too. On some elemental level she realized her lifeline was withering, so she tried to hump me through the lens during the entire shoot. It was embarrassingly obvious to my assistants—Brady, the queen of cosmetology-under-fire; Joey, my loader and all-around gofer; or the anonymous reps of *Clique* magazine who all loitered like gargoyles on parapets, unblinking eyes on their text messages and tweets while they butted in to make sidelong creative "contributions" in harsh whispers designed to connote where the real talent was, here.

I had no idea what the *Clique* vampires actually did to justify their salaries, but there was a flock of them around every shoot I had ever done for the magazine. They were supposed to be assistants, handlers, intermediaries. They relayed messages from people with actual power. They always got in the way. They crossed the frame line and stumbled over cables and drove Joey nuts by leaving their lattes sitting on expensive

3

equipment. They were too featureless for us to bother learning their remora pecking order. I finally had to clear the room . . . that is, I had Joey clear it, since I knew he'd enjoy rousting them. The persnickety photographer, you know. The tormented artist. When in doubt, blame the talent.

Inside the frame, it was just me and Nasja. Her with her meager heat and me trying to commandeer this depleted sexuality, hoping to extrapolate it into something vendible for the mutual benefit of everyone's bank accounts. I did the best I could to shoot around the scars from her last surgery. I had been in the room for the surgery. In fact, I had photographed that, too.

As the sun started to set outside, I knew the messages from Char would be piling up on both my answering machine and mobile voice mail. The hominid lurking deep inside me already knew how this shoot was going to end, so I ignored the pings on purpose.

Human language had not evolved a term appropriate to Char's status. "Girlfriend" was a total atavistic cringe. "Significant other" cued the gag reflex, or should have, for anybody with a brain. "Partner" always made me think of somebody with a banjo. Anyone who did not marry conventionally to reproduce indiscriminately was stranded with nomenclature a century out of tune. Somebody needed to devote federal grant money toward researching a better term.

Char knew I had to spend the afternoon with a naked Nasja. Char knew these things always ran late. Always. Char at least suspected that Nasja was desperate enough to try jumping my frog. Char knew what I thought about Nasja's decaying orbit with Clavius. Premise, conclusion. So all this unspoken stress was venting into voice messages logged as innocent inquiry but dripping with single servings of guilt and accusation in equal measure.

The sort of lanyard around your neck that compels you to go, *Yeah, why the hell not?*

For four hours straight my neck had been clenched as tight as a boxer's fist and I had cultivated a muscle tension headache that could force grown men to turn over their entire families to the Spanish Inquisition. I could smell my own sweat coming out foul and poisonous. When Joey reset the surge protectors on the big lamp transformers, I retreated to the bathroom just to get the press of wanting eyes off me. A tiny moment to unclench, in order to reclench anew and get the job done.

Sure enough; fourteen messages stacked up and blinking red; a personal best for Char. I ignored them. We were doomed anyway.

I locked the bathroom door. I did it rarely; it was not necessary; everybody knew this was the one-stop for blow, Visine, speed, Ecstasy, tampons, and a variety of prescription candy from Doc Ostrow, my overmedicated guru of all things in pill form.

The mirror told me nothing was wrong—that would be too obvious. I ran the tap to cover any noises I might make unduly, like bursting into tears for no reason. Two blazing lines, three Vicodin (the 600 series; not the wimpy ones), a whole bottle of lovely Alpine spring water (to offset the constipation), B-12 and vitamin A, with decongestants for dessert. The stainless steel sink was my font as I gave silent thanks to Doc Ostrow. Deep breath.

The undistinguished fellow in the mirror stared back with his doubts. I could not describe him; I'd have to show you a photograph. If I mugged myself the only description I could give to the police would be brown eyes, about six feet, tamed goatee, black medium-length hair gray at the temples, dark clothing—er, it all happened so fast I didn't get a good look. I mopped my face and the nubbled cloth came away yellow with toxins. My spiritual effluvia.

"Ah, but don't get me wrong," I told the mirror. "I love my work."

Sunset relaxed me. If a day scorched my skull, dusk offered

an opportunity for a general reboot. For me, bald daytime, especially early morning, just looked *off*. Shadows fell in the wrong direction. Unremitting light was the quickest path I knew to headache-land. The rods in my eyes were brimming over with rhodopsin, much more romantically known as "visual purple," which was responsible for my acute night vision. Doctors and astronomers called it the "dark-adapted eye." Sunlight destroyed rhodopsin. This provided a great excuse to wear dense sunglasses while most of the working world was doing whatever it is they did when awake. It added mystery. I preferred working at night anyway. Less ambient lunacy at night, if that doesn't sound paradoxical to all you moon fanatics. And moonlight never caused anyone to get skin cancer.

I could see shades of gray where your eyes would perceive only dead, uniform black. I could distinguish shapes in an absence of light.

Ninety minutes later, I was distinguishing the shape of Nasja's disarrayed coif bobbing up and down in my lap, thinking this is what fascist fellatio must be like.

Joey had shut down the shop and the creatures from *Clique* had withdrawn to their busywork cocktails and dish-laden natter. Nasja and I downed some vodka, our usual toast to another completed session.

Her idea, originally. Vodka. Russian. End of debate.

Ex-pats from the former Soviet Union share a peculiar prejudice when it comes to Americans. They insist they are better educated, more cultured, worldly, and aware—*endlessly,* as though to compensate for the fact they bailed from a cesspool of economic privation as little better than social whores, usually via some form of scumball baksheesh. Or the commercial emigration realities of a fine-boned face and a thoroughbred body. They even brag—endlessly—that the Russian Mafiya are better *criminals* than Americans. They perceive the land of opportunity with unearned contempt as a boundless midway of suckers, dupes, marks, and norms just begging to be plucked . . . which wasn't far wrong.

Which is possibly why I could barely work up a mock of passion, a simulated performance based on ballistics, hydraulics, and friction. What transpired down at my groin was a mercantile exchange. My eyes kept seeking the clock on the Blu-Ray player. Every time I looked, the number clicked by one. It became a sort of side game.

Nasja had been quite a looker not so long ago; a high-fashion version of that ingénue from the summer tent-pole comic book movies, the one whose name nobody can remember now. I couldn't bring myself to grope her too much. Her breasts had been burglarized by implant removal and her flesh was mealy on the bone from anorexia. Whenever she glanced up with her too-big, greyhound eyes I tried to look like I was enjoying myself. Someday, I thought, I'll reflect that I actually fucked this woman, with an odd sense of accomplishment, but it was more fun to *have done* than to actually *do*. I had never considered that perhaps Nasja wanted to fuck me; she just would.

I was thinking about Char.

She would arrive around midnight or one. She would deploy a watertight lie and avoid kissing me at first, and I would smell the mints on her breath and confirm that she had been in her idea of a better world, fucking Clavius—my "superior"—the whole time. This thought, this story-yet-to-unfold with unerring predictability, had the strange perk of stiffening me just as my penis was going on the nod in Nasja's mouth. Nasja interpreted this signal as the excitement preceding a volcanic curtain-ringer of a climax, and went up-tempo. We were done pretty quickly after that—one more vodka, icy-cold—and she was out the door within fifteen minutes. She didn't kiss me, either.

Char herself aspired to the editorial chairmanship of some edgy magazine, partially due to her refreshing lack of the new

Victorianism. I suppose we lasted two years or so because she was one of the very few women who did not come to me directly from the Clavius pipeline—that hit parade of soulless beauties unattainable by the rank and file. She did not know Clavius. We met at an event that had nothing to do with Clavius. We ate dinners and clocked social events completely unrelated to Clavius, and frankly I had begun to feel like a freed man, or at least a kid willfully staying up past bedtime. The first time we spent a night together, we talked ourselves hoarse and got so tired that we did not burden ourselves with the performance obligations of sex. We actually slept. Feel free to jam your finger down your throat, but it was true. Most newcomer pairings lard too much urgency onto a first copulation that is supposed to "feel" spontaneous. Char and I bided our time and were rewarded for our patience and insight, or at least that's how I like to enshrine it in memory. At the time, I thought, *I chose you,* and thereby deluded myself that the world wasn't so dire. I guess it was inevitable that Clavius would charm her. He had won me over the same way—seduced me without any sex.

When the guy with the gun showed up instead of Char, you can imagine how derailed I felt.

My two newest visitors had also come bearing sidearms. They walked in, scanned the space, then very politely holstered their weaponry. One tall, one small, with the laser eyes and disposition of enforcers—the guys who hold you while the main guy punches your internal organs to puree.

The main guy kept his gun out, still gesturing with it.

"These are your two newest assistants," he told me. "You point out what you need for a decent photo shoot and we all take a short ride across town. You get to shoot some pictures—kinda like what you were doing in here—and you develop 'em for us, and then we go away forever unless you try some kind of foolishness, in which case I will put this gun in your mouth and pull the trigger until it's empty, and this holds nine hollow points, which means a great big ole mess and no head for you no more. You copy?"

I had said maybe five words since he first walked in. I looked around as though suddenly teleported here from a nice barbeque or a chummy funeral.

"Whatever you say," I said.

These men wanted to take me out of here. Char was coming. Char could be spared this madness. Our personal soap opera paled next to the threat of death. I did not want anyone to die. Like everybody, I thought black thoughts but I didn't want to precipitate anyone's death, not even these intruders who had come to change my whole life.

That, in retrospect, was my problem: I didn't care enough about anything to kill it.

There on the table: ten large, tax free, for a quickie. Forget the guns.

"Figure an hour," my new life advisor said.

"What do I call you?" I said.

"Why?" His gaze went flinty. "Why does that matter? Do you care? You think you're going to Google me or something? Friend me? Do you honestly believe a *name* is worth a dry rat turd? What fucking planet do you live on?"

Automatically I felt the urge to apologize, which was even more stupid. Instead, I pointed out a good package of minimal, transportable equipment (something I knew how to do on autopilot) and the two heavies geared up.

If I could pretend this was just a normal, eccentric gig, I might survive to continue wearing my own body.

The northern freight elevator was actually installed in the building during the reconstruction to add bogus veracity to the concept of loft living, in a space not originally designed as a loft. It was a sell point. We rode down in silence and wound up packed into a rental Crown Victoria, me in the backseat with my gun-toting guide.

He was still irritated.

9

He seemed to boil over; he pressed the muzzle of his pistol against my temple.

"My name is *headshot,* you rich dick!"

"I'm not . . . rich . . ."

"*Shut the fuck up!*" he yelled. "What *is* that?" He mimicked a puling weasel voice: " '*Euuuw, what do I call you?*' Is that some kind of hostage bullshit you learned from HBO? Humanize the assailant so he won't fucking kill you? Did I ask you who *you* fucking were? No! Am I going to blow your fucking face off if you don't shut the hell up and do as you're told? Yes!"

The shaved apes in the front seat were glancing backward, as though concerned for their leader's calm.

He blew out a harsh sigh. "Jesus, you guys make me fucking mad."

I risked answering. "Uh—me?"

"Yes, you, moron! All you privileged horse cocks with your faggoty little photo shoots and goddamned hot models and little fucking cocktail parties and receptions and magazines and *christ* you piss me off!"

We dropped down to Sunset and headed west, toward Beverly Hills.

"I'm not saying anything," I said.

"You don't have to. It's oozing out of your skin. Fear. Pure animal panic. Because tonight the real world suddenly butt-fucked your little dream existence."

He seemed satisfied with that—or at least mollified—and we finished the trip in silence except for a few directions. *Turn here. Pull in there.*

Below Sunset off the Strip there existed a number of big-ticket hotels not on the paparazzi map, hidden-panel sybararies that catered to a clientele who paid large for guaranteed privacy and excellent room service with no questions asked and no request too outrageous. Security was plainclothes and omnipresent.

As we debarked in the parking garage my captor advised:

"Signal. Shout. Do anything and you're all done. Be business-like."

I nodded. Without a title or pseudonym to mark him, I had shortformed him in my mind as Gun Guy.

Suite 240 rated a presidential subtitle and came with polarized blackout glass. You could fire up a searchlight inside and no one outside the building would see a hint. My new crew and I entered the largest room of four in the suite, lavishly appointed. Cigarette smoke unreeled in lazy webs across the air. The occupants of the room had butted about half a pack in waiting.

Gun Guy steered me around for introductions.

"Elias, say hello to Cognac."

Seated on a wingback sofa was a brassy, implanted redhead who resembled whats-her-name, that British soft-core celebutard. She had on steel-tipped spike heels, about two parallel miles of nylon stocking, a garter belt, an extremely constrictive bustier, and little else except her work smile. I noticed her jade-green eyes were contacts. Several pounds of burnished hair like a four-alarm blaze. She waved perfunctorily. "Meetcha."

With an exaggerated stage whisper my keeper added, "I don't think Cognac is her *real* name, do you?"

There was also a birdy older man wearing John Lennon spectacles. Hair plugs marched in a straight line across the top of his face like a row of shoe polish–brown cornstalks.

"Cognac there is a prostitute," said the gunman, "and this fellow here we'll call the Professor, because he'd pop a clot if I mentioned *his real* name."

Indeed, the Professor immediately turned crimson at the fleeting notion of exposure, and coughed artificially to cover his panic. I realized I was probably looking at another ten grand each, for these two.

"And in here, you'll find our special guest star."

He led me into the master bedroom. On the California king was a large vinyl body bag containing either a person or two hundred pounds of really expensive appetizers. He unzipped it and unfortunately, *shazam,* dead man. My gut plummeted.

Nobody I knew, but somebody I could recognize, and put a name to.

You've seen Clavius's work everywhere. If you lived in New York City, you might decide to attend a party or elite gallery function based on whether Clavius might actually show up. If you worked in an upscale office there was probably a Clavius print on the wall, framed in brushed aluminum, and if you're upscale enough, it would be numbered and signed with his distinctive scrolled "C." Celebrities queue to his favor. Souschefs fawned and prepared off-the-menu vegetarian dishes for him. He occasionally surfaced among luminaries on the news; more rarely on pop rot like *E!* or *Entertainment Tonight.*

Touching the finer things by proxy has always been a big deal in America. Who's-who has cash value, like getting your hair chopped and dyed at Talia's in the 90210. Bonus points if Talia comped you.

Of course, Clavius wasn't his real name, but that was de rigueur for men of his stature. His few approved photos depicted him as a florid Teuton with a severe crew cut and the penetrating gaze of an ocean carnivore. We met about five years ago at a place called the New World Inkworks, which no longer existed in Los Angeles . . . as did most things in Los Angeles.

New World Inkworks was not one of those 24/7 Xeroxeries, but an actual publishing time warp that reeked of the old school: hot glue guns, rubber cement, rubyliths, pasteups, X-Acto knives, and real, live physical layout done on light boards. Its professed specialty was high-end lithographs and limited edition art prints on special acid-free stock, many done for the Getty Museum's gift shop. The owner, kommandant, and chief ramrod was a man straight out of a Broadway road show of *The Front Page* named Harry "Boss" Wiley who—yes—actually wore the visor and arm garters you're thinking of right now.

Due to the looming specter of digital everything and the need to keep the lights on at New World, Boss had neatly divided his profession to address both high culture and low. He had doggedly cemented a reputation as the go-to guy for artsy-fartsy print work while cultivating an after-hours relationship with more mainstream media. In other words, by day he actualized canonical art for the masses, and after dark he kept his staff comfortably busy with porn, for the *real* masses. More American than Boss you just didn't get, as an entrepreneur.

My own lack of a studio, facilities, portfolio, repute, and walking cash brought me into Boss's orbit. In one of three back rooms Boss kept a behemoth of a retired Linotype machine, despite the space it absorbed, purely in honor of his romance with print. Next to that Linotype I humped many graveyard shifts running off-color folio pages for the likes of *Pubes!*, *Just Past Jailbait, FunBag, Foxy Moxie, Drip Groove, Nipplemania, Sluts 'N Tarts, Gashette, Hollywood Loaf, Spankers, Grease Man, 2 Young 2 Date, Hot Trotting Tots, Cave Boy, Wet 'N Squishy, Yeast Beasts, Fistful of Udders, The Diary of Gloria Hole, Muff Divas, Great Big Onez, Marine Discharge, Blood Vamps, Gooey,* and a variety of their high-quality sister publications. The sheet stacks were a never-ending catalogue of artificially moistened vaginae, peter-pumped cocks, leering browneyes, and glassy mannequin stares in ceaseless aggro recombination. You get inured to the flood tide pretty quickly if you don't want to start dropping letters from the alphabet soup made of your brain by the busywork or the Mandarin hours.

The payoff, for me, was the serviceable darkroom Boss also maintained. It was all mine when the adult entertainment portion of my shift was completed.

I'd never liked color photography much, although I'd done my share. Attenuated night vision heightens your discrimination of gray tones, not color, which is why I keep the vitamin A in my medicine chest—to encourage more rhodopsin in the rods of my retinas.

Clavius, as it happened, was attracted by the angle of having a porn sweatshop grind out the posters and prints for a show planned at a West Village gallery called Beneath 5th Street. His highbrow reputation was in no way compromised by his excellent nose for sleaze and he needed a confluence of the two in order to maintain street cred and his cachet as an edgy innovator. So Clavius approached Boss with nearly all the ancillary work for the show whose title won him his big-time sobriquet—"C."

It was a gathering of earth-toned, biomechanoid photo studies, post-Expressionist, post-post-Industrial, pre-Millennial; a style that has since become known, in our new century, as Meltdown, to predate it from "mashup." Now, today, Clavius had left all that far behind in the quaint past. I looped all of it in the darkroom at New World Inkworks, and since Clavius was so fussy about quality control, he hung around while the waterfall of porn flew from the presses. We got to talking and it wasn't long before he said, "I've got something perfect for a fellow like you, if you think you're game."

I told him what cameras I had, what equipment. Showed him some samples of my own work. He was already sold—more or less—due to a conflict of schedule, and I was an at-hand solution. He pulled a couple of four-by-fives out of his Halliburton case. Hot-lit full bodies of a woman with bangs, long, straight, flat hair that looked to be the color of café crème, and huge luminous eyes, almost like a siren from Japanese anime brought to physical life. The eyes were the thing. They commanded your attention, sucked you in, and dealt no mercy.

"This is Skorpia," he said, then laughed. "No shit, that's *really* her name; she's Greek. My problem is that I have to be at 'C'—my show—at precisely the same time as her surgery is scheduled."

I was supposed to ask, but I just raised an eyebrow.

"She's having a couple of ribs removed," he told me. "A little brow work and some butt implants to round her off—see?" He flipped up another full-length shot from the rear. Skorpia was nude and about as unsexually posed as I'd ever witnessed. "That's a problem with the taller ones—no ass. Her ass is like the line between two of my fingers when I clench my fist." He demonstrated.

I asked how tall she was.

"That's the miracle. Six foot five, barefoot."

Barefoot and buttless, I thought. Poor baby.

"With the ribs removed she'll be able to corset to fourteen inches; can you *imagine* how she will take the world by storm?"

I was supposed to agree, so I did.

"I need you to photographically document her surgeries," Clavius said. "Every stage of every procedure. I need to see *inside* her as much as possible. What do you think?"

I was supposed to show no more adverse reaction than if he had just offered to open a door for me, which he had. So I nodded. Fine, good.

He clapped me on the shoulder, a conspiratorial brother now. Then he offered the boon he knew I expected: "Do this thing, and a year from now, you will be famous, yourself."

There it was, and I didn't have to sign in blood, or anything.

Now do *this* thing, and presumably, I got to live.

The dead guy in the body bag was not Clavius, which I will admit was a flash-forward brought on by paranoia and my own retroactive guilt about getting jiggy with his recently discarded wife . . . even as he was probably dancing a similar mambo with my girlfriend-of-record.

The dead guy in the body bag was Dominic Sharps, whose face I knew from TV whenever the news was about the Los Angeles Police Department. There was no mistaking his identity; even the news was in hi-def now. I was pretty sure that yesterday, Mr. Sharps had been breathing. His gray eyes were wide open and unseeing.

"That crap you see in the movies where the bereaved survivor honorably closes the eyes of the dead person with the gentle touch of two fingers or the palm of the hand? Total bullshit. Never happens." My captor, Gun Guy, seemed proud of this knowledge.

Dominic Sharps had not been dead for very long. His skin had gone waxy but there was no smell of rotting meat; not yet. His fingernails were white from the blood evacuation; lividity had probably begun on his back and buttocks. His eyes were starting to sink into their sockets. If this was the pre-rigor mortis state, he had only been dead a couple of hours.

"We've got to move before he stiffens up any more," said my gunman. "Set up your lights. Professor, get your ass in here and finish what you started!"

With his makeup and bronzer and hair plugs, the Professor didn't seem that far away from corpse land, himself. He brought in a case full of cosmetics and I realized why Sharps looked so . . . odd. He had been partially made up already by the Professor, which accounted for the weird skin tone. Dead people first turn grayish, then slightly violet. Sharps's dead flesh had the simulated glow of living tissue.

"I want this lighting dead natural," Gun Guy directed me, missing his own irony. "As though the only source is that lamp, right there. Fire it up."

The Professor fully unzipped the bag. The late Mr. Sharps was naked. The cosmetology was to be full body. Then he withdrew a thin metal rod about five inches long with one knobby end. It looked like a surgical tool.

He must have seen my eyebrows go up.

"This is really inconvenient," the Professor said in a reedy voice, almost introspective. "At the moment of death, an erection is natural. That has already subsided. Too bad we couldn't get him sooner."

"I threw this together as fast as I could," said Gun Guy with a snarl. "Get past it."

I think I fumbled my film load when I saw the Professor

slide the rod into the dead man's penis, as easily as you'd replace an oil dipstick.

Now the naked, dead Dominic Sharps had a fake erection to go with his fake complexion, I thought, devoting the rest of my energy to not losing my mind, or gibbering, or bumbling my lips with one finger like an imbecile.

Cognac was standing behind me, also naked except for the stockings and heels. She obviously spent a lot of spin class time keeping very fit.

She squirted a generous amount of Astroglide onto her palms and moved past me, saying, "Excuse me, sweetie."

She greased up and squatted down after the bullyboys removed the body bag and patch-glued Dominic Sharps's hands in place—one on her thigh, one on her forearm, the same as positioning a mannequin. The Professor zeroed in to do touch-ups on the fingernails.

"How's my hair?" said Cognac, looking back over one shoulder at me.

"Ah . . . good," I said.

If this was a real photo shoot, I would have had her comb it straight back and add just a little powder to cut the shine to emphasize a "wild" aspect. I would have ditched the incandescent lighting. I would have dashed to my bathroom and started searching for hemlock.

The Professor pushed the physiognomy of the late Dominic Sharps into different expressions for each photo. The face stayed in position like clay.

"Start shooting," said the man with the gun. "They don't *all* have to be masterpieces."

It will always be difficult for me to describe the ensuing half hour, even though I was thinking, *Well, this isn't the* weirdest *shoot I've ever done.*

Clavius's first assignment was for me to photograph Skorpia's surgeries. Right before my eyes and lens, she was reduced to a mere poundage of raw flesh. Thank the gods her face was covered for most of it. That way she was without identity, the way the mutilations of a splayed car-crash victim are masked by blood. The slicing and dicing of her glutes were yet to come. The main attraction of the first workday was a single marathon session—rib removal, breast augmentation, and brow job. There was so little actual blood flow that, through the lens, it looked surreal.

I had two digital video rigs for coverage on the blow-by-blow, and moved in close with a Hasselblad or one of my Nikons whenever I was permitted. Clavius had specified fast film, high grain, almost no depth of field—no peripheral detail was wanted here. I myself was without identity as well, smocked and filtered, my hands in latex, my feet sterile-bagged, perspiration darkening the HEPA cap that prevented any wayward hair from escaping into the operating environment.

It was almost loving, the way the specialist slit her open and yawned her wide and took things out and put in other things. Certainly intimate. Most major organs inside your body are a sickly pink or a jaundiced ochre, except for the dark purple and bluish vasculature. Other mystery components looked startlingly inappropriate, like bundled white tube pasta. No matter how sweet you smell on the outside, on the inside you stink like a slaughterhouse or killing field. My lenses fogged up more than once.

I shot the row of autoclaves, too. In one stainless steel dish, saline bags with serial numbers. In another, two short ribs, pitted and porous like big fossilized fingernails. In a third, mounds and scraps of shining tissue limned in bright red oxygenized blood. Each stage of Skorpia's transmutation was labeled in black pen on cloth tape. Before, during, after.

The anesthesiologist—the gas passer—was bored to begin with, and nearly nodded off in the middle of the carving and resectioning. I saw his head bob. Skorpia's monitor emitted a dire flat beeping noise and I could sense one of the nurses getting ready to ask me to leave the room. I documented it all. This team was hot, and Skorpia was stabilized immediately. She would wake up in pain, mummified in a chrysalis of bandages from which it was hoped a rare beauty would emerge—rarer still, because it had been created with a knife, like sculpture. So rare that it was a million-to-one impossibility in the real world. In turn, she would inspire millions to covet things they could never achieve, not that it would stop them from buying an array of pricey consumer products based on her physical say-so.

Later, Skorpia married a tycoon of paper products— bathroom tissue, nose-blow, burly towels—and devoted her time to a great many charities. She shunned the limelight because she was getting on in years; christ, she was nearly thirty-five when Clavius threw her back into the pond, and consumers certainly didn't want to look at a spokesperson that old unless it was to siphon off money to save dolphins or build puppy shelters or feed retards in Africa with no fingers or toes.

For an hour in the historical time line, she had been a goddess.

Then, in the hospital, she was my key to the future.

After Skorpia came Nasja, about eighteen months after my first meeting with Clavius. He asked me to shoot the *removal* of Nasja's breast implants, making a sidelong joke about how it could be another triumph in my "series."

Nasja was packing old-school silicone bags that had ruptured and migrated, the material intermeshing with fat and muscle tissue to produce ungainly lumps that were gathered by gravity into the undercurve of each breast. Excision of this annoyance was very time-consuming, very cut-and-paste; the threat of metasticization was very real. What concerned Clavius was not the issue of survival, but the sculpting of the beautiful, or in this case, the resurrection of beauty as he defined it.

Hence, the scarring, which I could not unsee through my

lens, earlier today. The skin under her breasts was as taut and furrowed as beef jerky.

Clavius next sent me to the city morgue to photograph dead people, which is where I learned what little I knew about how the dead should look.

I embraced digital photography at the same time as everyone else, but I maintain my love affair with photochemical processing—light and alchemy versus pixels. Silver gelatin positives from mystic broth rather than output from a printer. Clavius liked that. He introduced me to some people, I got a loft and a studio and a minor reputation, I did some arguably successful shows, and I branched into style spreads for commercial advertising clients, but all of it in Clavius's shadow. I was, at best, a protégé, not to become a fully formed human in my own right until the Master died, or had a gender reassignment, or gave up his materialistic life for Buddha, or something.

Nasja really had nothing to complain about. She had gotten a green card and citizenship out of her deal with Clavius; she would rebound from the divorce and no doubt become some kind of grande dame of fashion opinion.

But back there in my narcotic-festooned bathroom, before the sex, during the shoot, I couldn't kick the thought that I needed something different. I needed a clean breath. I needed out. Maybe I just needed a break from serving the Master, and an opportunity had presented itself earlier the same day.

A movie pal of mine named Tripp Bergin had called to suggest I might experiment with broadening my retinue by taking on a unit photography job on a film that was to start shooting in New York and Arizona in less than a month. The designated picture-taker had been benched, or gotten a better offer. Tripp was what they called the UPM, or unit production manager, one of those guys still waiting for his first chance at directing, which never seemed to come because he was such a good UPM. Bills arrive regularly whether you get paid or not. Tripp advised that there might be a delay, or more dramatically, a push forward for "commencement of principal," which is movie-speak for when they actually begin filming.

I had about forty seconds to mull this over before the shoot with Nasja absorbed the rest of my day. I backfiled it, weighing the flavors of such a new and different assignment. Whether I could be beckoned.

After that, I think you're caught up on what happened next.

I shot eight rolls of Cognac having simulated sex with the late Dominic Sharps. The Professor, who seemed to be some kind of defrocked mortician, applied makeup cagey enough to satisfy the camera. The bullyboys twisted and turned Dominic into various positions, mostly female-superior in deference to the dependent lividity. Dominic was starting to get stiff, you should pardon the expression. And ripe.

"Good?" asked Gun Guy.

Cognac dismounted and hit the bathroom briskly. The Professor lined up his bottles and jars in a carrycase designed like a box for fishing tackle; it was fussy enough to suggest a professional kit. The two enforcers, whom I had named in my mind as Rondo and Mongo, dumped the naked corpse back into the body bag.

The gunman seemed relieved, as though he had beaten a ticking clock. "Take him to the Kitty," he told Mongo. To Rondo, he said, "Give the Professor a lift home." When Cognac reemerged, having added a jacket to her original ensemble, he asked, "You good?"

"Lobby, cab, Hilton, 3500, wait for further instructions," she said. Her coming and going would not be remarked in a place like this.

"Don't forget to douche," Gun Guy said as she wisped out the door.

I was the only asset of this fireteam that did not know the protocol. I had been denied a membership card and knowledge of the secret handshake.

"I'll take care of Elias here," said Gun Guy. It sounded more ominous than his actual intent. He could grab my film rolls and decamp, but I remembered he had mentioned something about being around for the actual processing of the film . . . which would bite major ween, if Char had returned in my absence.

All his obvious bad guy skills aside, my abductor was an excellent time manager. We were in and out of the realm of corpses in under two hours, including the coffee he more or less forced on me to keep me awake.

"Let me ask you a question," he said when we were back in the car. "You ever get tired of shooting all those gorgeous women?" He looked over at me quizzically. "You can talk. I'm not mad. I was just a bit irritated about our time frame."

"Did you kill that man back there?" I blurted.

His lips went tight and flat. "No. You haven't answered my question, and I asked first."

Did I—? If there's a dumb question I've been asked more since meeting Clavius, I couldn't think of what it was. It was a tourist question. Probably best not to spotlight that, for my keeper.

"It's a job," I said. "Technical job."

"Blow job, more like. You get paid a lot of money for this technical job?"

"Sometimes it's good. Not ten grand good for a loan out, but healthy." It was deceptively easy to slide down into shop-talk.

"Those lofts aren't cheap," he said with a glimmer of his previous contempt.

"I do a lot of work for another artist—print jobs, model wrangling."

"Oh, yeah? Who?" He wanted celebrity. He wanted to know which stars I knew.

"Clavius? He's kind of world famous."

He snorted. "Never heard of him. He ever shoot for *2 Young 2 Date?* Now that's some fucked-up photography."

He had just named one of the skin rags I used to pump out at New World Inkworks. Prepubescent-looking teases with ancient eyes. I released a long, slow breath. "Smaller world than you think," I said. "I used to help publish that magazine."

"No shit? For real? Man, you know any of those models?"

Zeus, I thought, *please don't let him ask for my autograph.*

"No, I just ran the printing press. One was pretty much like another. That was a long time ago."

"Kinda makes you a pornographer, doesn't it?" he said.

Well, maybe in the eyes of some froth-at-the-mouth kids advocate, but I just ran the presses and cashed Boss's paychecks. I eagle-eyed the layouts for reproduction quality, not subject matter, and could honestly not remember whether the barely legals had fallen to this season's socially correct side of the fence. The American national hysteria over pedophilia mandated that documents galore be kept on file—such as the infamous "2257," short for U.S. Code Title 18, Section 2257, one of the many uproarious results of Traci Lords lying about her age during the last gasp of videotaped porn. In many other places in the world, this outcry was no big deal, which was why that famous writer guy had moved to Bangkok, because he got sick of being thought of as a criminal. But I wasn't invested in the sociology of it; I wasn't a dad and never planned to be, and I moved in a world where most of the players did not have the encumbrance of children.

"Pornography is in the eye of the beholder," I said.

"So is necrophilia," said my keeper. "You'd better hope those pictures come out kissing fresh."

"What happened to "—I choked on Dominic Sharps's name—"the body? Can I ask that?"

His gaze went pewter. "No."

"No chance I could get you to wait till tomorrow for me to develop the photos?"

The gun was back in his grasp like magic. "Listen, dickhead: I am not your buddy, your collaborator, or your fucking customer. For the last time: you do what I say or I'll kill you. Otherwise, you go back into shut-up mode. Mister Kimber here insists."

I guess he was talking about the pistol. All I could tell you was that it was massive, squared-off, and black as death.

I didn't want to see Mister Kimber upset. Because then Mister Kimber might speak.

I was terrified that Char might have returned to the loft during my witching hour absence, which meant she would be brought into the crosshairs of my one-night-only puppeteer, the man with the scary matte black gun.

The last time I had seen her, we had both been tightrope-walking around the renewed argument about who was fucking whom, and why. Swigging from a oversized mug of herbal tea with ginseng, she was drifting through the studio with her kimono open, aware of the control that gave her.

Char was one of those blond women with brown eyes so dark they seemed almost Hispanic. She often joked about her gene mix as what happens when a nobleman rapes a peasant girl. She had a big round ass like an inverted heart shape. Long slender legs that elevated her rear end in a Bantu aspect, uncompensated by nearly perfect martini-glass breasts that were mostly nipple. No implants for her, no Botox, no laser vaginal tightening, or tummy tuck. No rips to iron out the smile crinkles at the corners of her luminous eyes. *At least she's real,* I used to think. In the time it took "smile crinkles" to become "crow's feet" in her estimation, she began to talk about working behind the scenes instead of in front of the lens, leading naturally to her current aspiration to become one of the arbiters of perceived style. Her self-evaluation was almost cruel.

I had a lot of mirrors in the loft, and any one of them could trigger the Fat Discourse, most of which consisted of rote repetition, kind of like when you learn soliloquies from Shakespeare in school and can't get them out of your head for the rest of your life. Maybe that's why she was cruising around my rooms with her kimono dangling. I thought it was casually sexy; she was looking to score more points in today's round of the Discourse.

"Jesus . . . I am getting so fat; how can you stand to be around me?"

Cunning, that—framing her fear as a begged question.

A word of advice to all you heterosexual males out there: Don't ever get sucked into the Fat Discourse. There is nothing, I repeat, nothing you can say or do that will improve your situation. Even running away is a tacit agreement that your lady-love is, in fact, fat-fat-fat. Never mind that Char was a tight 110 pounds for her height. Never mind that she could turn heads on a water weight day. Do not agree. Do not disagree. And worst of all, don't try to be understanding or honest, because by lip-wiggling in this mode you will condemn yourself to slow death by compromise.

Yes, honey, you are packing on a lot of lard. That one's a no-brainer.

No, honey, you look just fine. Liar, she'll say.

It makes you curvy; I like it. Forget "curvy." Anything you say—soft, voluptuous, shapely, contoured—will only be perceived as a cheating deceitful euphemism for the worst of the world's f-words. If you use words like "Titianesque" or "fulsome," I pity you. If you have had occasion to make comment about her "backyard" or "junk in the trunk," you're probably dead already.

And if you say nothing, you're doomed anyway. If the bout ends in a draw, the tiebreaker will be the sighting of a hitherto unnoticed varicose vein on the back of a knee . . . and the incoming artillery will begin pounding again.

If a varicose vein or stretch mark could send me over the edge, I never would have lasted long enough to tell this story. I would have been history years ago. We were both cowards, Char and I, using easy, flammable deprecations to palliate our own deeper fears. The way Char kept rechecking herself in my many mirrors, seeking outward evidence of her betrayal, basically told me what I wanted to know. I tried to force her into saying it anyway.

"For fuck's sake," she said, firing off the other f-word to shorthand the sentiment that I should grow up and get real. "I'm just working an angle with C. You know exactly how he is. Worse, you know exactly how this fucking business operates and you don't need me to educate you. God!"

Since I hit her in the face with it, she hit back. I can't fault her.

"Besides, what was up with you and little Mizz Soviestski Nasja? Every time she sees you she practically leaps in the air and kisses you with her big flapping baloney cunt. No wonder they call her *Nasty*."

Was it Whistler or Wilde who said we're all whores, and the only difference is haggling over price?

If Char stays over, we won't have sex. Again.

Char doesn't stay over.

Now, when Gun Guy and I reentered my loft, I saw Char's clothing dropped in an errant trail from the doorway to the bathroom. Her bare feet were sticking out of the fresh Egyptian cotton sheets on the foot-thick futon I had custom-built.

"Oh, christ," muttered Gun Guy under his breath. "Don't go all watery on me, Elias. Don't you ever work late into the night? Is that the bitch from before?"

"No."

"Then hop-to, and let's try not to wake her up. You don't want her to wind up in a can of cat food like your buddy Dominic Sharps . . . do you?"

Take him to the Kitty, he had said back at the hotel. My stomach bounced. Dominic Sharps was being ground up into kibble, probably this very moment.

My L-shaped darkroom has a revolving airlock-style plastic

doorway like a tube within a tube. It's about the size of a phone booth—a cramped phone booth. Gun Guy would not allow me to go through alone. Buster Keaton would have loved our tight little rhumba.

I've got filtered safelights on rheostats preset to different light grades. The tanks and trays, rubber and plastic, are ganged in the center of the room, the same place you'd find the main butcher's block in a decent kitchen. The smell of chemicals— Tetinal mixes, from Europe, plus the acetic acid odor of stopbath—and the background metronome of constantly running clean water on a drip-tap are omnipresent and more than a little bit comforting.

This room was my alembic, my alchemist's furnace.

"How long does this shit take?" My keeper was not being properly reverential.

"Develop, stop, fix, wash, dry," I said. "I used faster film to compensate for your lighting; I'll have to push it a couple of stops in the bath."

He grimaced as though from a gas pain. "Whatever; never mind. Just get on with it."

Joey, fine yeoman that he is, had ghosted in and out of the darkroom to make sure my workaday tasks were relatively painless. Some of the earlier Nasja shots were corrupted by what seemed to be a mysterious light leak—one of my stationary cameras needed a new body. Most likely it was the old Nikon F2, which has a senile hinge cover, requiring me to tape up the seams. I couldn't bear to part with it. That camera had been with me a long time.

As had Joey. While Joey was an ambient presence in my life, I couldn't recall the last time I actually looked at him or took note of his passage. He was like those PAs on a movie set— interchangeable warm bodies on call to execute pestersome little missions, up for almost anything because that's their job. I assumed Joey may have desired to surf my wave the way I rode the breaker provided by Clavius—but he had never articulated that to me. He did aspire to direct fetish videos, which was his idea of a dream job. He was spunky and devil-may-care, yes, but also vital in that he provided major support for my disassociative runaround. He was the opposite of the proverbial squeaky wheel; he was the part of my whole machine that worked diligently and did its tasks silently and efficiently, to the point where I rarely noticed him.

I couldn't tell you, for example, how many facial piercings Joey had. A lot. How many tattoos. A shitload, mostly of monsters from classic creature features of the 1930s through 1950s, interspersed with some Celtic and Maori jazz. He shaved his head, perhaps to outfox an already apparent pattern baldness in the making. I did remark once that aliens could use his skull for a landing site. I tried to conjure his face and realized I'd never taken a picture of him. He'd gotten a labret. A stud in the middle of his tongue. Ornaments straight through the hard cartilage parts of his ears. Bars rowed through his brows and one perfectly centered in the squeezy piece of skin right between his eyes, like a bracket on which to mount spectacles.

One of my enlargers was a Kaiser I'd upgraded for halogen lights. Its lens carrier was matte black aluminum and when it pivoted out, a little indicator light came on. For some reason, Joey had unplugged the enlarger, perhaps for some extracurricular work on the sly. No sweat; my lab was his when I didn't need it. I swung the lens carrier out of our traffic zone. Usually it was not in the way unless more than one person was toiling in here.

"What's all this about?" I said as I worked. "I mean, you can't really blackmail a dead guy with racy photos, so they must be for someone else."

"*Hey!*" It came out like a bark. "You don't rate that information, Sherlock, so shut the fuck up and do what you do best, all right?" He tried to find a safe place to lean, and rummaged out a cigarette.

"Not a great idea to smoke in here."

"Really?" He made an obstreperous show of flinking his Zippo lighter. "Ask me if I give a rat fuck." He drew slow sustenance from the tobacco while the smoke curled silver against the red worklight now engaged. "God, where do you get off being so *precious?*"

"Just another rich dick, I guess," I said. His earlier outburst had gouged deeply, because all the time I had to deny being a rich dick—subphylum *rich horse cock,* as he had said—I wondered whether I was devolving into that very organism.

"I've met a hundred guys like you," he said, "and they all whine about wanting to know what's *really* going on, as if that matters. Serfs, fretting about shit that's beyond them. Who the hell cares who gets elected, or who gets bribed, or who shuffles where? You are a component of an operation. The big picture of that operation is none of your goddamned business. The bag is none of your business."

"The bag?"

"The bag of money," he said, enjoying another deep drag. "In hard-boiled stories it's always about a bag of money. Who has it, who takes it, who's got it, and why. It's a MacGuffin, like Hitchcock said. It doesn't matter. It is ambiguous. It used to be called the weenie. It's the stolen jewels or the missing papers. It doesn't matter."

Obviously this man I was prepared to dismiss as a mere thug had an *opinion* about this topic, and he wanted to hammer me with it. It was weird enough that this *criminal* was citing Alfred Hitchcock.

"The bag. The MacGuffin. The weenie. Not your concern. Your concern is surviving this transaction, period. Then your role is played. Done. You win by me not killing you. Or your girlfriend out there. Did you get all that?"

"Got it," I said. "It's a good speech. Who'd you learn it from?"

"Oh, fuck *you.*" He butted his smoke in the runoff from the sink and looked around for a trash can that I pointed out in the semi-gloom. He pitched the butt and rubbed his fingers together.

He seemed mildly interested in the workings of the enlarger, but did not ask parvenu questions while I worked up glossies. There's a stack of file trays taller than I am and each slot contains different paper. He saw my hand hesitate from one slot to the next.

"What."

"It's just . . ." My excuse died in my throat. I had just had a flash thought, a microscopic, potential gesture of rebellion over my enslavement. An assertion that I could possibly have more grit than some quaking tool about to fill his own diaper with terror. This hesitation would betray me; this man would notice apprehension, even if it was only imaginary. I had to cover what I wanted to do with what I was doing anyway.

"It's just this paper," I said, trying not to stammer. "This stuff isn't going to show up on the Internet, is it?"

His expression curved downward into disapproval. "You were supposed to be paying attention, Elias. Digital doesn't work. Digital *cannot* work. This is hard-ass, photos-in-the-envelope, old-skool physical evidence. It's not for some goddamned blog. Digitizing them would mean someone had manipulated them."

While he dressed me down, I drew my print stock from the topmost shelf, what I called my "Clavius paper," because it contained a digital watermark with unique properties. Fanatical about copyright, was Clavius.

It was my sad way of leaving a bread crumb, since I had no desire to engage in single combat with this man who might just as well murder me when my job was done, and if he killed me tonight, he would kill Char too, and nothing would remain to mark the encounter . . . except for my use of the Clavius paper. As a gesture it was as futile and hopeless as it was pathetic, a weak lunge against expert bondage, and I battled to not let the sneakery show in my eyes. Fight this guy? I had seen

30

fights in movies, and none looked like something I could manage without getting mangled.

In the resultant photos, it appeared that Dominic Sharps was having a fairly wild sexual rodeo with a hireling, and that, I assumed, was why Gun Guy had shown up in the first place. Why the Professor had been brought in, too.

"Who was that guy, the makeup artist?" I said, trying to feint.

"Stop talking," my evil overlord said, not for the first time.

What else had my team members talked about? *The Kitty*— where Dominic's corpse was to be taken. *The Hilton*—presumably the Beverly Hilton Hotel on Wilshire where it met Rodeo Drive. *Take a cab to the Beverly Hilton, 3500*—a cash amount or maybe a room number?

Why was I even thinking about this?

When Gun Guy had bundled up proofsheets, negatives, and prints, he paused before we exited the darkroom. "Hold still," he said. "Open your mouth a little bit."

I did it almost automatically, as though he had spotted food in my teeth.

His pistol was out like a striking viper and something hard and bladed on the muzzle clanked against my front teeth as he grabbed the back of my neck and stuck the barrel straight in to sit on my tongue. My eyes teared up immediately. My breath husked and slobbered against unyielding metal that tasted like machine oil. He had me.

Mister Kimber had me.

"Count to ten in your mind," said Mister Kimber's operator.

I shook my head slightly. The gun seemed as big as a breadbox stuffed into my face. My jaw throbbed. No way would I count. He would pull the trigger at nine and a half. He would cheat.

"Count. One. Two. Three," he said, soft as a lover's purr.

He kept counting. I couldn't feel any part of my body below

31

my neck. All my attention was on the heavy steel fucking my mouth—Mister Kimber, all up in my face, preparing to speak.

He allowed for a little dramatic pause between nine and ten. Then he withdrew the gun.

I was sobbing, I think. "*Jesus christ!*" I rasped out, crashing to my knees, upsetting small stack of plastic manual trays and knocking over an old timer that didn't work anyway, but hit the floor with a resounding *ding!*

"Now listen to me, Elias. That's what death feels like. That's what it will feel like for you, your lady friends, and anybody else you know if you fuck with me. If you're smart, keep the money and forget everything about tonight. Or you'll taste this for real. Here."

He pulled the top part of the gun back with a metallic shucking noise and a bullet flew out into his hand—least it was what I took to be a bullet, with a nasty divot scooped out of its blunt nose. My night vision allowed me to see clearly enough in the darkroom to perceive the mechanism: as one bullet jumped out through the side-ejector hole, another one from the clip bumped up to take its place. Gun Guy handed me the bullet he had just liberated.

"That's so you'll remember," he said. "That's the one with your name on it. You played fair so you get to keep it as a souvenir. But, remember."

I was hoping there wasn't snot on my face when an abrupt rush of odor announced that something far worse had happened, lower down. Below the belt.

"Holy shit, Elias," he said, puckering his face.

The smell was distributed by agitated air because the revolving door to the darkroom was moving, too.

Char poked her head in, her eyes sleepy. "What's going *on* in here, you guys?"

After all of the above, now Char wanted to argue.

It was the middle of the night. Both of us had pounded

through the day, had our drinks, had sex—separately but more or less equally—plus I had run off on an extracurricular adventure of my own, and now Char wanted to stoke up the fight furnace. I was completely exhausted, devoid of calories. At this late hour I might have been able to muster enough intelligence to read a page of book or watch five minutes of movie or clip my toenails . . . not *this*.

This ordinarily required skill, preparation, alertness, and energy to burn, and my needle on all of those items was down to E.

"I don't care who your weirdo pal is," she said. "I don't even care that you got the runs from—what, drinking too many White Russians?"

I was glad Char was able to at least amuse herself.

She had, at least, bought the lie that I'd had an unfortunate gastronomic event while talking to an old buddy from New World Inkworks in my darkroom in the ayem. What was his name? *Uh, Kimber.* From there I moved on to the falsehood that my friend Kimber had come to pick up some negatives and a framed print. He caught on quickly and even seemed pleased when I handed him *Targets #5* right off the wall.

"I thought you weren't going to sell those," Char said, pointedly illuminating my fakeout.

"It was a gift," I countered.

"They're misogynistic," she said with her head turned away. She had never liked the Targets series; the few times she did not dismiss them as sexist, she had called them too violent.

I lurched for the bathroom like an automaton and took two showers, trying to scrape off the last twenty-four hours with a hard-ass brush and soap artificially concocted to smell like melons. I had designed the big tiled multijet stall myself. It was still damp from Char's arrival, which had been at about 2:30 A.M.

What usually bothered me was Char's habit of talking *around* whatever bothered her, which was a tactic designed to confer guilt not onto her as the initiator of the conflict, but me as the one who has been goaded into referencing something specific in a comeback. It was lowly point-scoring, beneath us. Tonight, of course, she dived right in and I found out I didn't like that approach any better.

It was time for one of us to check out, anyway. I quickly reconsidered Tripp Bergin's offer of out-of-state movie work—a safe house. When you snipe at each other past a certain point, partners start acting like defense and prosecution, seeking flaws and advantaging strategic openings and making polite war on the people they supposedly care about. Conflict avoidance is not just a skill; sometimes it's a necessity. Right now the tension had hit that phase where, in bioterrorism terms, an epidemic is possible but inoculation is still available.

Char cut right to the chase, which was kind of admirable.

"I saw the fucking *tape,* Elias! For christ's sake, don't play stupid!"

Nasja had this habit of running video whenever she and I—as she put it—"made love." She said she masturbated to it but I didn't buy that for an instant. She was aware of her place in the carnivore conga line and was backstocking ammunition that might come in handy later; the phrase Gun Guy might have used was "load so you don't have to shoot." Sexual metaphors of this stripe tend to make me laugh at wholly inopportune times, and this was one of those, too.

I clenched my teeth really hard to keep from laughing, partially from delayed hysteria. I was naked and damp in a bathrobe and I smelled like melons. What kind of melons? I wondered.

Nasja had left without taking her tape, knowing Char was incoming. There was some piece-pushing afoot on the chessboard tonight, guaranteed. But I just didn't care—about Nasja's little intrigues, my videotaped damnation, Char's rage, or anything. It just got funnier.

"Go ahead, yuk it up," said Char with a sneer. She was naked too, in a robe, smelling of the same yet unidentified melon. For me to laugh—apparently at her—was so wrong there was no cure, no truce, and zero forgiveness. "I'd laugh my ass off, too, because you're so ridiculous."

"No, I'm brilliant enough not to deny it," I said, trying to tamp down my mirth, realizing now I was comporting myself like a lunatic because I was still alive. "Can't you see that it's just part of this goddamned power play with Clavius? Isn't it obvious?"

"What it is, is disgusting, period. I erased it."

My heart deleted one beat, then sped up. "What do you mean, you erased it?"

She stopped, turned to look as though she had been distracted from walking away. "I erased it, Elias. Erased the tape—the mini-DV."

"No, no, no, what I mean is, *how* did you erase it?"

"What?" It seemed I was challenging her technical proficiency. "Are you kidding? I wound it back and recorded over it. Do I look like I have a degausser in my bag? Jesus, you really are hopeless."

I needed this icy clear: "You rewound the tape all the way, then hit RECORD. Did you put the lens cap back on?"

"Shit, Elias, *I don't know!* For fuck's sake!"

Nasja's favorite roost for the camera was in the low crotch of a potted Madagascar Dragon in the main living area. I liked this plant (also called the Red-edged Dracaena) for the berserk convolutions of its branches.

Char grumbled something acidic about me wanting to save my greatest hits for a sizzle reel, then reclaimed the bedroom for herself. She had this monastic ability to compartmentalize, and once she dispensed her anger—or at least transferred it to someone else—she could sleep like the proverbial babe, as though innocent. She might have started this evening with some crippled thought of a reconciliation or perhaps just a calm zone, but now that was shot to hell. Tomorrow morning she would leave me a third of a mug of her leftover lukewarm coffee and a Post-it note, and we would be done.

In most senses, I was already past this.

Sure enough, the camera was still there, aimed at the sofa group in the main living space, and past that, the front foyer through which Gun Guy and I had entered. The lens cap was off. And the little red light, which had a square of electrical tape masking it so as to not give the camera away, was still glowing.

PART TWO

CHAMBERS

Permit me to tell you a story about all the ways a simple job can turn to shit in your very hands.

In my line of work, you are either active or dormant. When you stop, you are either retired—subactive—or dead. Actives are deployed autonomously for assorted gigs through a very secure network of one-way cues. I was dormant when I received a message that three tailored suits were ready for me to pick up. This meant that Mal Boyd had a job for me.

It had been six weeks since my last gig. I improved my diet, started a cleansing regimen, and hit the gym like a spartan. I spent a lot of range time with my newest acquisition, a Kimber Pro Tactical 1911 .45 ACP that had just been returned with modifications by my gunsmith. I worked targets and a walk-through point-and-shoot maze in the dark. The mods worked elegantly.

I switched to the Kimber because of a stovepipe jam problem with my Para-Ordnance 14-45 widebody. I liked the Para's high-cap magazine—fourteen plus one rounds, staggered, versus the usual eight-plus-one—but one failure to feed or eject under duress can stamp you done. Sometimes rough surfaces inside the gun deplete just enough energy so that the action doesn't cycle and your round never reaches the breach. Less than full-power ammo can do it, too. Or your mag follower— the little elevator platform under the spring that pushes the rounds up—can be too short, or plastic. Same problem.

I had known all this, and had the Para's spring shortened by two coils, and the bolt face and chamber polished. I switched to custom mags with an improved follower. Still, the Para had gotten cursed on its last job.

I hated the drug runs. We all did them from time to time, mostly to meet the bills when things are slow. But drug dealers, smugglers, and their customers are unvaryingly batshit-crazy. They especially love firearms they have no idea how to operate, having seen too many exciting fictions wherein machine guns spray endlessly as if fed from a hose. As often happens when you are surrounded by jumpy people jacked on narcotic and packing maximum firepower, somebody shoots somebody for a perceived cheat, or lack of respect, and the night lights up. I had three bozos to knock down and none knew how to aim or control their fire, but the Para jammed when I had bozo number three zeroed. In the time it took this dope to realize he had sputtered away all his cartridges in a noisy, showy, useless display, I was able to clear the pipe, reload a fresh mag, and plant a double-tap through his septum.

Then I got the hell out of there, because the drug crap was none of my contract, and most everybody else was dead anyway.

But even one choked round out of a hundred was not acceptable. The Para was a fine firearm, but superstition had a way of tainting objects. I decided to go with less ammo and better accuracy; to improve myself instead of blaming the weapon.

The botched drug gig paid the bills and allowed me to obtain the Kimber, which I warmed up with a thousand rounds to wear it in after the modifications. I started using lacquered cartridges—you could store these babies in salt water and they'd still fire. I had not yet run this new combo in the field, and the call for a new assignment allowed me to get mildly excited about the possibilities.

I knew when I have a well-crafted gun in my hand.

Mal Boyd would have you believe that his name was an accident inflicted upon him by two drunken parents who had scrawled the words "male" and "boychild" into the wrong spaces on the bureaucratic form used to officialize his abandonment. Personally I think he made the whole thing up to augment the story of him as a poor waif forsaken to find his own way in a cruel and uncaring world, which upbringing became the excuse for his chronic overeating.

Mal is a vegetarian for whom most commercial bathroom scales do not register high enough. He would crush them. I'm guessing he tips between 375 and 400 pounds. He favored those mint-green surgical drawstring pants and tunics. He started shaving his head as his hairline retreated, which made him look more like a gigantic baby, except for his mantid eyebrows, which were totally out of control and sometimes moved independently.

My meetings with Mal usually took place across a huge oaken table laden with fruit, veggies, tofu, nuts, and candy. His sheer intake of growing things accounted for the elimination of a great many acres of arable land.

"I'm thinking of going organic," he said by way of greeting.

"Who might this be?" I said of the eight-by-ten photo, left on the table near my seat.

"That, my dear, would be Dominic Sharps of the Los Angeles Police Department's Special Tactical Wing. Insofar as SWAT teams go, Sharps is the point man for local counterterrorism. Please have an apple; they're Grimes Goldens from West Virginia. A little out-of-season now, but I have a source."

Sure. I crunched and the apple's texture was perfect, its flavor juicy and bountiful. It was the porn equivalent of an apple. "Security for visiting dignitaries, that kind of thing?" I said.

"Well, his charter includes perimeter security, special escort and even more special extraction—that's why we need to discredit him." Mal noshed into some kind of hard-fried soybean thing that looked like a rat waffle.

"We need to make him look bad."

"Yes, well, you see, he is in charge of formulating the security measures when the president visits our fair city. His public views on his own expertise are well known. Now, the people who have come to me are interested in undermining his credibility in a salacious and public way—drugs, prostitution, something seedy."

"Why?"

Mal did not move a lot. His victuals tended to be arrayed within easy reach; in other words, a hand would rise like a fat anaconda and deliver the next morsel to his face, which chewed. Apart from that his most active feature was his gaze.

"Does it matter?" he said.

"It might." I put the half-eaten apple down on the table next to the photo.

Whenever Mal breathed deeply he made a kind of congested, wheezy noise; now he sighed and made the same noise.

"Usually in our business, the less one knows, the safer one is. Do you know what a MacGuffin is?"

"A muffin thing from McDonald's?" Perversely, I was beginning to crave a bacon cheeseburger.

"It's a coinage of Alfred Hitchcock's. You know, the director?"

"Yeah," I said. "Gooood *eeeeev*-ning."

"Quite. Hitchcock told a famous anecdote about the Mac-Guffin, which was essentially a way of telling someone to mind their own business. Today it has evolved to mean a plot element that incites interest or action, but which itself remains unexplained. It's the bag of money everyone is after. The stolen jewels. The microfilm. The missing documents. The Big Secret. As Pearl White used to say during the great old days of the silents, the weenie. Film executives picked it up to abuse writers and directors. They'd look at a story and say 'Where's the weenie?' meaning 'Why should I care?'"

Mal always took his time getting to the point. I don't think he had much social discourse with the taciturn gunmen and social miscreants he also employed. I made a mental note not only to mark his words—I liked the concept—but to grab some Hitchcock DVDs.

"Dominic Sharps is the weenie," Mal went on. "As to the motivations, I'm guessing that in our current moral climate of false outrage and crocodile patriotism, discrediting the man in charge of the president's motorcade, *before it happens,* could have profound repercussions. It throws cherished institutions into doubt, you see."

I nodded and helped myself to some M&M's. There should never have been blue ones. "Don't bother hijacking a jet and flying it into a skyscraper when you can accomplish similar damage with a blow job."

"Yes. I think that is the limit to which you and I should concern ourselves with the *why.* Our job is the *how.*"

"So—something sexual?" I grabbed for my smokes; a cigarette's worth of think time. "Do you mind?"

"Not at all, dear boy, puff away. Yes, I think you could use Cognac for this one." Cognac was a thousand-dollar hooker who worked the Beverly Hills Hotel. She was reliable and discreet, insofar as those conditions applied to the subterranean uses to which we occasionally put her.

"Our backers specified a sex scandal, in fact. Wrongly, I think."

"Really?" I was not used to Mal being this opinionated about practical matters.

"Well, wrong in the sense that I think Sharps should be indicted by using a young boy, not a prostitute, but there you are. The more depraved profile is the more potent. But our backers shied from it, mostly because a charge of child molestation invites too many similarities to the abundant sins of most churches, and they don't want their political statement defused by the pollution of a religious angle."

It was a valid condition. If Sharps's manufactured misbehavior could be excused by one religious mania or another, its fangs might be prematurely pulled before the op could do any lasting damage. Too many criminals fell back on some god's misguidance, and they got away with it, too, in a country where nearly half the population believed in the existence of angels. Of course, another big segment believed in alien kidnappers, so if you inverted the argument you could see how frangible the deception might become if religion was tempted to cloud the issue.

"It doesn't matter if they want a more garden-variety outrage," I said. "They're paying for it."

"Exactly put. Can you arrange it?"

"How much security does he have?"

"There's a full dossier on the table," Mal said, eyeing a beaker of pomegranate juice.

"Budget?"

"How does a hundred and fifty thousand sound to you?"

"I'll have to get some warm bodies. Say, two. Plus Cognac will have to disappear for a while; public eye and all that. Is an incriminating video the sort of thing you're after?"

"That should do, if it is explicit enough."

"Het sex, fairly lurid?"

"Yes—never underestimate the outrage factor of the conventional."

"Okay, so figure five each for the backup men, ten for Cognac, about"—I ran rough estimates in my head—"about fifteen for sequestering—to pluck him out of his shell, steal some hours from his day. Gear is maybe another . . . five. Not counting a workable escape contingency if a tire blows somewhere."

"You pay those costs out of your end. That's why I bumped the extra fifty thousand."

It was fair enough. Past the setup it was maybe six hours active work.

Cognac and I met, as was our tradition, in one of those hot-sheet motels that are gradually disappearing from Sunset Boulevard.

The dingy, perfunctory rooms that rented by the hour, their linens stinking of too much bleach, appealed to some basic need I had for sleaze. Los Angeles itself underwent a daunting cycle of self-renewal—like chronic plastic surgery for the whole city. The current phase was gradually pushing the low-rent, no-name lodges eastward again.

We had sweaty, athletic, impersonal sex and then I laid out the game. Most operations of this sort came freighted with a high-wire sense of adrenaline tension. Since the release of homicide was not to be involved, I knew that I would be high on endorphins and body chemicals once the job clock ran out, so Cognac would make out on both ends of the deal, which both pleased and inspired her.

She looked at the photo of Dominic Sharps from the dossier. "Strictly missionary," she said, tapping enameled nails on a laminate tabletop and sipping a Mike's Hard Lime. "Once we get going, he might even like it because he sure doesn't look like the type to be getting any variety at home. Straight?"

"Like a ruler," I said. "The file puts him as a tightly wired control freak. He's a little bit of a media whore. Likes being on TV."

"Well, *that'll* be over once this is done." She crossed her long, gorgeous legs. Barefoot she was still nearly six feet tall. She had not put her panties back on yet, not that she bothered all that often. She was wearing thin reading glasses to examine the dossier; her green contacts were marinating in their little container in the bathroom. Her real eye color was a calm blue-gray. Stray light from the curtain slit picked out copper highlights in her hair. "How're you going to get this guy alone-at-last? He's gotta have security all over him; I mean, he gets it for free."

"I've been thinking about that," I said. "Not your worry." I gave her a business card–sized note with the target hotel, room info, and a hot-period timetable.

"Oooh, the Chalet," she said. "Cool. I love their room service."

"Just don't eat anything provocative that'll make you fart during the taping," I said.

"Like I said—he might like that. Queefing."

I loved Cognac's sense of humor. "Oh, god," I said. "That has a name, too?"

"I heard a new one," she said, mischievous. "For when you're sitting on the john and you have one of those half-in, half-out experiences?"

"Do tell."

"It's called a fifty-cent."

"Oww." I laughed. "That's worse than a Hollywood Loaf." Which was vernacular for half a hard-on, sometimes the result of "brewer's droop."

That Cognac, she sure knew how to cultivate repeat customers. I wondered what kind of rap she spieled off for the city fathers or wayward clergy in her client book.

I did not have to rifle her bag while she attended to bathroom functions; I'd done that when we first met a couple of years ago. Her real name was Cypress Wintre, which itself might have been a perfectly serviceable handle for a model or adult film celeb. She had come from Nebraska fresh out of high school with a burning desire to act, and indeed was fulfilling that charter in her current wage job. Los Angeles is busting at the seams with beautiful women, and the competition is even dirtier than you can imagine. Movies are heavily invested in trading flesh, and what makes it to the screen in a theater near you is only a surface skim. What's more amazing is what is never seen: for example, Cypress Wintre had a degree in business administration, acquired *since* she had migrated westward. The poor lost junkies and ex-pornies that fucked for a fix or child support didn't stand a chance against her pedigree. Like me, she had never paid taxes in her life and enjoyed being her own boss.

I paid her up-front and we were solid for our "date," six days away.

*   *   *

My rendez with Conover Tilly and Waddell Pindad—a.k.a. Blackhawk and Bulldog—came that same day at a watering hole called Re$iduals in Studio City, about an hour before last call. Its slummy industry charm had been diluted somewhat by the offer of free wireless Internet service, which meant losers sat around staring into laptops and nursing overlong beers instead of getting shitfaced and hooking up with bedmates who slid in under fake IDs. The barkeeps turned up the music to compensate, which made it an excellent venue for not being overheard.

Blackhawk was a rangy ex-stuntman who doled his extracurricular pay toward ranch land somewhere up north. His chipped-granite countenance got him fairly regular film work as a heavy. You know the anonymous bad guy who always draws down on the hero and gets chopped apart, falling spectacularly while still firing his weapon? That was Blackhawk. He was absurdly proud that sometimes he even got a line of dialogue. What the viewing public missed was that Blackhawk's second job—working for me, among others—fed his primary occupation; he had not learned how to act like a tough guy, he *was* a tough guy, a stress-tested badass. I watched him break a guy's arm once, seven times, starting with the fingers, then the wrist, then the long bones of the forearm, then the elbow, then dislocating the shoulder, as easily as you would pop bubbles in packing plastic.

Yet, Bulldog was the more schooled torturer, a compact man of Indian extraction, born in Rangoon, slaved out at age eleven to some oil sheik's youngest son, whose throat he fatally opened up with a fork. After some mercenary work more or less paralleling America's war-dog progress through the Middle East, he came to the attention of Mal Boyd after being in-country for a mere seven days. He still had a price on his head thanks to the oil sheik, who, despite an expenditure in the millions, had never come close to finding him. Mal Boyd dry-cleaned Bulldog's identity—hence "Waddell Pindad"—so Bulldog was always up for any op sourced by Mal.

Blackhawk took a tiny bit more convincing.

"I'm all good," he said, Texas accent lubricated by Mexican beer. "Got me a three-week commit on a dinosaur movie starts in eight days and my property payments are down to fumes. I don't really need the gig, man."

"Pussy," said Bulldog.

"It ain't that way, B," I said. "Six days from now, next Thursday, we're in and out in six hours, max, you're five large richer, and you've still got two days until shooting—hell, you've even got time to wash your socks, not that you ever wear 'em with those shitkicker boots."

"Come on," said Bulldog. "It's not another drug shoot-'em-up. All we have to do is stand around and look menacing."

"Don't diss my fuckin boots, dude," Blackhawk said.

"All right then, your lovely, manly Tony Lama boots."

"Fuck you, Chambers, you fuckin white supremacist Hitler Youth motherfucker with your blond fuckin eyebrows."

"Yeah, what he said!" chuckled Bulldog, turning down the corners of his mouth.

"See, that's the guy I need," I said. "The take-no-quarter, take-no-shit behemoth. You and Bulldog together are the best hot dog and hamburger combo for this type of meet. Plus, one of you gets to pretend to be a journalist."

"I get all my headlines off the Internet," said Bulldog, drawing off half his Scotch in one pull. "Blackhawk can be the reporter."

"No gunfire; I dunno." Blackhawk was playing sullen to the max. He loved the moment when weapons went hot. He signaled for a fresh beer.

"The price doesn't go up for petulance," I said. "Flat rate, period, done. It's the same for me."

"You know how Mal Boyd is with a dime," said Bulldog. "Squeezes it till the eagle screams."

46

"Yeah, between his giant butt cheeks," said Blackhawk. "Besides—there ain't no eagle on a dime. Not for like a hundred years."

"It's a hermetically sealed snatch-and-grab," I said. "No gunplay. You might get to abuse a public official if things get muddy."

Bulldog's eyebrows went up at this. An opportunity to get paid for inflicting pain to extract information or secure cooperation was not to be missed. "I'm in," he said.

"You promise no more than six hours?" said Blackhawk.

"Tops. But you know that—"

"Yeah, yeah," he overrode. "You reserve the right to alter the op according to unforeseen random factors, rah-rah-rah."

"I also came to you first because I'd love to have you two guys ride shotgun on this one. Leaves me less to worry about because you're both solid."

"Do not attempt petty appeals to my vanity." Blackhawk frowned. "What you *can* do is buy me some fuckin hot wings; I'm starving."

After securing a video rig and backpack that could pass muster as a TV news camera, I spent two days logging Dominic Sharps's comings and goings, based on the breakdown provided by the dossier.

In a word: clockwork.

Next came two cars—one identical to Sharps's personal ride, another matching the chauffeured Town Car he sometimes used to get to and from the courthouse downtown when news cameras wanted to grab a bullet quote. The rear windows of both were coated in reflective Black Diamond privacy film.

From Blaine Mooney, master of spyware, I obtained an upgraded blocker box. This is a keen little doodad about the size of a cigarette pack, which Mooney augmented with a self-charging, light-sensitive panel to solve the drawback of battery drain. Push the button and cellular reception is disrupted for a radius of twenty-five feet. I used this thing all the time in restaurants. Mooney's version also jammed GPS, Bluetooth, and homing devices in case your subject was wearing an electronic leash.

But we wanted a leash on Sharps, so we bootlegged a signal tracker to his personal mobile phone. All we had to do was dial him up. You probably already knew, during this period of maximum access, that virtually every cellular phone in use in this country was equipped with the guts of an onboard GPS system the user could not activate—at least, not without a hack and another dedicated cell phone. But it could be cued externally by anyone who wanted to keep tabs on your whereabouts, even if the phone was turned off. This was just another shackle the American public had donned all too willingly, and one of these days, soon, it would embarrass or implicate you, such as when you called your honey and tried to lie about your actual location. That is, until the service providers decided to charge you for an "extra feature" that was already there. It could even provide a grid map of all your movements for a designated period.

Probably all outdated, by the time we did this. More apps, more shackles.

Mooney provided a good pocket Taser and a briefcase full of what he called "roundabouts," latest generation. These were totally bitchin' clip-on reflector units with a sixty-second digital memory. You snapped them over the lenses of surveillance cameras, where they logged a minute of empty hallway, then looped it on playback until the power source crapped out. Problem was, every place used different cameras—some obvious, some hidden; some big and some pinhole—so you must know how to size the array, which is why Mal Boyd provided a decent 3-D map of the Chalet's security system. Mooney also supplied a pouch of six secure cell phones—one shot, throw away.

From Doc Trigger I got several preloaded syringes of

tripaxidine-B—a muscle-injectable sedative with a mildly hallucinogenic finish.

Blackhawk and Bulldog worked the cars for a day to batten down maneuverability, in case we found ourselves in the middle of a vehicular chase. We schemed out emergency dump routes, with backups on the backups.

There was almost no need to consider work guns, which itself was unusual. Normally you need disposable ordnance, but I did not anticipate any shooting unless things got really hairy, in which case I needed my own firepower close at hand. Blackhawk and Bulldog had their own trusty hardware and I had my new Kimber, arguably unique after the several rounds of modifications.

The gun was the classic 1911 configuration created for Colt by the immortal John Browning as a military sidearm, which makes it a large weapon, but with an admirably thin profile much less chunky than my sidelined Para-Ordnance. Sleeved into an isometrically adjustable Sidearmor Kydex vertical-draw scabbard, the Kimber was an easy hide.

Most important among the mods was a carry melt treatment that beveled all edges so as not to hang up on clothing or holsters, a replate of the frame in Teflon-impregnated nickel (to reduce wear), and an overall coating in nonreflective black oxide to kill visibility. The match trigger and skeletonized hammer were out-of-the-box. Kimber loves grip safeties; I didn't. The grip safety is a cumbersome and antiquated solution to a nonexistent problem, so it was the first thing I had removed, leaving a hole in the backstrap that had to be remachined for proper frame weight. That left a perfectly practical thumb safety . . . which I had ground down to a breezy nub.

I had never liked checkered wood grips and so I replaced them with Pachmayr wraparound rubber, trimmed for the Wilson magwell, and used custom magazines (Wilsons again) to guarantee good ammo feed. Slam pads for the mags. The other problem with such a powerful pistol is weight; Kimber solved this by machining the frame from billet aluminum instead of steel. Sustained fire with heavy rounds usually left the gun filthy, but a good cleaning regimen provided a lookout for signs of wear, most critically in the barrel—after a few thousand rounds, your rifling starts to go and your clips wear out. The mind-set was similar to periodic maintenance on your car: keep the beast lubricated and replace the parts as needed.

All that for a weapon I would probably not have to pull. At least not for this gig.

Mal Boyd supplied flawless intel on Dominic's daily schedule changes; he was either wired directly into the secure comm network, or had really good stringers, or both.

This was almost too easy.

This was the point in any game plan where you ask yourself, "What if this is a masque for a different operational objective altogether?" The stalking horse mission that conceals the real mission no one has been told about. Subterfuge of this sort quickly becomes obvious. The break point is the moment where you are reminded that you and your team are completely expendable. That's what happened back at the drug shoot-out six weeks ago, but it was not Mal's failure. The chain of command for the guys on the opposing side decided to cannibalize itself, and when you watch it happen, you do wonder if you are being the patsy for a similar manipulation.

Expendability, anonymity, and plausible denial were built into every gig—that's one reason why they cost so much to set up. But you didn't want to just recklessly sacrifice yourself or your team just because there's no back-end participation. Mal Boyd had given me no reason either covert or obvious to doubt his setup; he never had, which was why I still subcontracted to him.

People in my trade come and go like sports stars, with about the same half-life; it's true. As you age you gain cunning but erode reflex. You also accumulate a lot of stray leverage, which is one reason why the government sends new assassins to kill old ones. I conservatively estimated I was still at the peak of my ability, and had another five years to a decade to free-agent. I corrected that estimate after this whole thing with Dominic Sharps went down.

Once you think of every contingency, it's the surprise that wallops you, and the Dominic job provided a doozy.

Once the Metro Rail project had gutted Hollywood (literally; sinkholes appeared in the streets to swallow vehicles), more marketing geniuses arrived to "revitalize" the area's most famous intersection. That is, scale up to magnetize more tourists. At the same time, decrepit and defunct office buildings of five stories or more were sitting empty, easy prey for developers who opted to retrofit them into elite "living experiences" patterned after the all-in-one mall-world model. To try and straddle the club trollers trapped between seedy railroad bars and newer lounges with door guards and dress codes, some style wunderkind opened the Vine Street Bar & Grill far too early—uptown prices at a downmarket intersection nonetheless famous for crossing Hollywood Boulevard. Tourists in flip-flops and Disney T-shirts were horrified at the prospect of paying twenty-six dollars for a Cobb salad. The joint crashed and burned within months. Presently it was a meat-rack sports bar with pretensions of Irish pubdom. The six-story Equitable Building in which it was housed changed owners several times, then fell under the redevelopment hammer until it could redebut as even pricier condo space . . . the same year the economy and housing market ate shit and died.

The entire intersection of Hollywood and Vine—originally Prospect and Weyse until 1910—had undergone this tortuous resurrection into condos and lofts. The Taft Building on the southeast corner was Hollywood's first high-rise. Charlie Chaplin had offices there. Across Vine to the southwest corner was the old Broadway department store monolith, shut down since the 1980s. The northwest corner was the first to fall. Originally the site of the Laemmle Building (think Universal Studios in the 1930s), it absorbed a half-block in every direction in its prime, then it vanished a piece at a time. By the 1970s, the corner slot had become a Howard Johnson's coffee shop known for the loser actors that hung around its bank of pay phones waiting for callbacks. Then it became a succession of clubs, ending with the Basque in 2008, when it was mysteriously torched (for the insurance), then torn down. Right now—no kidding—it's a parking lot.

I was grabbing a burger at Molly's when I noticed the Equitable Building, bannered as if still under construction, appeared to have occupants already. The contrast was as bold as a rash: Molly's was a magical hole-in-the-wall charbroiler that had been steaming away—if its signage was to be believed—since 1929, still with the best onion rings for miles, served too hot to touch in plastic baskets by smiling Korean ladies. (If you're sharp you might remember Keanu Reeves grabbing a bite there in that sci-fi movie, the one that's not *The Matrix*.) The first Molly, the redheaded founder, had long since gone to glory, her story lost in the mists of ancient history . . . or, in L.A. terms, anything that happened more than five years ago.

Molly's inevitable doom was cast in the shadow of a former bank; it was too unaesthetic to be retro and some invisible someone, somewhere not in Hollywood, would insist it be murdered to make way for yet another wine bistro or chic eatery designed to attract the type of trendoids and scenesters you never want to stop killing. Spaz West. El Place. Some too-cool watering hole that would repel the Boulevard looky-loos trundling along clutching their bottled waters, but which would gladly ravage their plastic with caste-appropriate scorn. Molly's shack only took cash.

Predictably, the freshly minted office space surrounding Molly's was mostly vacant.

I wondered what bogus sophistication might cost these days.

A million, two million, just for a foothold? I gave the Equitable a closer peek.

Me, I had an apartment in Brentwood, another utility lair in Thai Town, and a nicer though mostly empty house deep in the Valley, complete with false walls and a stash safe sunk in seven feet of rebar-strutted concrete.

The only honest entry on the Equitable's buzzer register was for a photography studio on the fifth floor. The sixth, fourth, and second floors were untenanted; this I confirmed with the security desk as I picked up a brochure.

Vacant space in yet-to-open (or already closed) buildings can provide an excellent hide if operations need a cool-down period. Even if they don't have interior walls yet, you got bathrooms and electricity, and nobody can hear anyone screaming.

I filed the data away for future use, thinking to request a status pull on the current occupants from Mal Boyd. You never knew what would prove useful.

We took Dominic Sharps coming out of a press conference, while media stragglers were chasing him down the stairs.

Dominic Sharps was sixty-two years old, a throat cancer survivor who had undergone several knee surgeries and despite medication maintained a cholesterol count that could fell a rhinoceros. He was a diabetic. He had been an Air Force F-16 pilot in the eighties. One wife, bland marriage, five kids—one of whom, Stacy, worked volunteer time for a sex abuse hotline, which was a bullet point in our favor. His eldest son, Rich, was a prosecutor with the DA's office who had reaped some face time on the news for a couple of interrelated cases about film stars, little black books, and sex-for-hire—another big plus. Mal Boyd's homework was specific and enlightening.

Sharps had arrived from his house in the 90210—the flats, not the hills—in his chauffeured Town Car, so I used the backup we had prepared as a chase car. It was identical to Sharps's

BMW, a two-year-old 7 Series that took three days to match to the naked eye.

In the hour-plus absorbed by the press conference, Bulldog appropriated most of his driver costume from Sharps's chauffeur, whom we left duct-taped in his trunk on the top floor of the parking structure adjacent to the ArcLight Theater. His clothes were hopeless—Bulldog was too slender—but the tie, cap, and glasses were useful, and the rest was just dead, boring black-and-white businesswear. Bulldog had actually worked briefly for a livery service sometime in his mysterious past, and knew the rudiments. He had always broken the carry rule for drivers, and was breaking it in theory again today, packing a SIG P250 with a short reset trigger, chambered, I thought, for .40 caliber. Not certain because this gun was modular, designed to pop apart to change caliber at will; I heard the Hong Kong police had courted it when they finally got past revolvers.

Interestingly, in the back of Sharps's own Town Car we found the watery remnants of a huge go-cup of diet soda and a take-out bag from Pinches Tacos on Sunset. Sharps had stopped for a snack on his way to the podium.

Sharps did not have a personal bodyguard for this gig, which was an advantage. The next time you find yourself in an argument over who should be permitted to carry concealed weapons, ask yourself why politicians who don't carry insist that their bodyguards always be packing.

Blackhawk was stationed in the gnat-swarm of reporters with the correct press passes on lanyards, a wholly fake ID for Canal 34 (one of the Metro area's Hispanic stations, which had chosen not to attend this media event), and a heavy powerpak belt that provided handy concealment for his sleek little Colt .380 hammerless. Just in case. Nominally a backup gun, I think it was some kind of Blackhawk family heirloom. Both men had refused to go unarmed and I thought, whatever works. Keep the subcontractors happy.

I was already dressed in a foolproof LAPD officer's uniform.

Unlike many smaller police departments, the LAPD has a two-stripe chevron for the rank of corporal—often for what is called a Field Training Officer. Not lofty enough for Dominic Sharps to realize he should know me personally, yet the FTO pin would tell him I was a cop in charge of other cops.

Sharps emerged in a mild fluster of reporters with residual questions and desperately outthrust equipment. Blackhawk's task was to herd the group by walking point, leading the flow, staying between them and Sharps when Sharps got to his waiting vehicle. At that point I would intrude, tell Sharps there was an emergency, he needed to get in the car immediately, and escort him inside the rear. He would wonder what was up and allow me to board behind him while Blackhawk body-blocked any stragglers. As far as Sharps knew, he was hustling into his own car with the full rear cover of a uniformed officer.

That part worked smooth as glass.

When the black-masked door closed, Bulldog leaned through in his chauffeur's getup and shot Sharps in the chest with the Taser. All his blood sugar converted to lactic acid in a single spasm, and he became a floppy toy.

We were off and running.

While Sharps lolled around in the seat, drooling, I hit him with the first of the tripaxidine B hypos and he slumped quietly into semisleep. I frisked him and tossed his mobile phone out the window.

"Time," I said to Bulldog.

"Two minutes ahead," he said, meaning we had beaten our own rehearsal schedule.

About now, Blackhawk would be picking up the other car—the clone of Sharps's BMW—to rendez with us at the Chalet, which was *not* the place you're thinking of. This was the *other* one, not available on Maps to the Stars.

Three hours earlier, Bulldog had installed a total of eight runabouts on the Chalet's ambient video cameras, which would cover our preplanned path from the parking garage to the suite where Cognac awaited us. I had arrived with her at noon and swept the rooms for bugs and hidden lenses, just in case the hotel had provided some nasty extras not on the menu of services.

"*Ngg,*" mumbled Sharps. "*Gahh.*"

"He okay?" said Bulldog, eyes front.

"Yeah, for our purposes." I checked Sharps's pulse and it felt as though the vein was trying to jump out of his skin. He was sweating like a gym monkey on a treadmill in a sauna.

We were twenty flat road minutes from the hotel.

"B-dog, I think this guy's going into cardiogenic shock."

"*What?!*"

Sharps was haddock-pale. He was having a heart attack. That was not supposed to be a risk with the Taser, but here it was, happening anyway. It could have been his shitty diet. Maybe he had the flu. It could have been his diabetes. It could have been a witch's curse, for all I knew.

"He just stopped breathing!" Dammit to hell, I was probably going to have to give this slob mouth-to-mouth. "Keep driving!"

Bulldog kept it rock-steady and did not distract me with chatter. That's one of the reasons I hired him.

I quickly got Sharps horizontal, opened my Boker Magnum stainless blade with a flick of the wrist, cut away his necktie, and ripped his shirt open.

He had gone into arrest. His heart was not beating.

CPR was simple. Everybody should learn it. Chin up, clear airway, pinch nose, blow twice until you see the chest rise. Two one-second breaths. Then thirty pumps, right between the nipples, slightly faster than once per second.

CPR was tough. The leather seat cushions gave visibly every time I pushed down on his chest with my interlaced hands. There was not much space to get Sharps's feet elevated. He was, as they say, unresponsive.

"Hospital?" said Bulldog.

Even if we jacked a convenient ambulance—which wasn't

around anyway—the EMTs would see us and possibly recognize Sharps, which meant we'd have to hogtie or kill them, leaving a spoor trail someone might follow.

"No, keep going!"

I continued CPR until *I* couldn't breathe anymore.

Sharps was dead by the time we arrived at the Chalet. Dead Dominic was no good to the smear campaign. If his body was found, he would assume martyr status no matter what his sins.

I grabbed the first of my disposable cell phones and called Blackhawk, who wanted to know what was up.

"Change of plan," I said.

Cognac raised a brow when we entered the room hauling a body bag like a tote of heavy gym equipment. Sharps must have weighed around 250.

Blackhawk, per instructions, had brought the bag, empty. Another contingency that had to be set up and paid for in advance. Ops tended to burn through a lot of materiel you never used. Better to have it and not need it than vice versa.

We had sweated our cargo along the planned route into the hotel, trusting the roundabouts on the cameras to hide our improvisation.

Then I had to call Mal Boyd.

"Everything on schedule?" he asked in his wheezy voice.

"We're right in the middle," I lied. "Tell me, Mal—will still photographs do instead of video?"

"Our sponsors did not specify," he said, aware enough to keep the conversation hermetically nonincriminating. "I suppose that will suffice. As long as the photos are not—"

"Digital? Pixels?" I interposed. "So it doesn't look like a pasteup in Photoshop?"

"Precisely, dear boy."

I already had a photographer in mind, but first I had to ring Oz.

Ozzy Oslimov was a failed makeup artist, failed doctor

wannabe, and most recently, failed mortician. His skill sets never seemed to accommodate his recurrent addiction to opium. He preferred odd jobs that financed his apparently endless program of cosmetic rejuvenation and had undergone enough procedures to fill a textbook on how to look like a human Hollywood robot. When I reached him, he wasn't on the nod—fortunately for me—and seemed excited at the prospect of an à la carte gig, right out of the air. I sent Bulldog to collect him and transpo his ass to the Chalet, doublequick.

The printout Mal Boyd had provided on the new loft residents of the former Equitable Building at Hollywood and Vine had sketched a useful portrait of the fifth-floor tenant, a photographer named Elias McCabe. His tax records revealed that someone else paid for his space. His work ethic seemed admirable—more often than not he was up in his studio, grinding away on starlets or models or god-knew-what when he wasn't grinding away on shoot work. He was vaguely noteworthy within his own nest of pretentious culture-vultures for his predilection for shooting on film, old-school. (Hell, even I knew the last roll of Kodachrome had rolled off the line in 2008.) The samples provided from a few of his shows suggested an unmerciful eye for the sculpting qualities of light and photochemistry. I liked his still lifes, his urban studies, especially the examples I saw of geometric patterns in the everyday, which suggested a hidden order to even the most random of assemblies. It was all a matter of point of view.

"This fellow might just save our asses," I told Blackhawk.

"*Your* ass," he said. "This ain't my fuckup, and you have to pay me either way."

If I had pulled an abort, he and Bulldog would get snippy and Cognac probably would have spent an hour kicking me to death with her spike heels for free . . . and not in a nice way.

"So what do I do?" she asked, sipping some Cristal as though she genuinely enjoyed it.

"Just relax and watch some monster trucks on cable or something," I said. "Until we get back. You don't have to bother going into the Bad Room. Not yet."

"Where're *you* going?" She didn't really care. She was getting paid, too.

"I need another hireling."

I did a quick change into my backup clothes and left word for Bulldog to marry up with us in Hollywood.

No way in hell my new plan was going to work. But it just might, and that was the "if" that generally dooms gamblers. It dooms all of us.

"What's he doing?" said Blackhawk.

"I think he's getting head from that dark-haired chick." I adjusted the spotting scope.

"So he's home, then." *Duh.*

As soon as Metro Rail got its Hollywood-Argyle station up a block from Vine, they provided a large street-level plaza with plenty of shade, open-air space, and Deco sculpture. It lasted less than a year before they razed it to remodel the entire block into a shopping and residential complex. The cab stands vanished. The panhandlers were sandbagged. The entire megastructure was still unfinished four years later, its hard hat zone restricted by chain link and plywood. Once Blackhawk and I climbed up, it provided an excellent vantage of the fifth floor of Elias McCabe's studio loft, right across the street at eye level.

"Is there a plan?" said Blackhawk.

"Yeah. We take him."

"Security?"

"I checked; it's a joke."

What nightlife remained was all at ground level and straggling in the opposite direction. Bulldog even found street parking.

"How's Oz?" I asked Bulldog when he joined us.

"Not stoned, happy to work, waiting at the Chalet," Bulldog reported.

"You tell him anything?"

59

"I asked him if he could make a dead guy look alive and he said that was his specialty."

"He creeps me out a little," said Blackhawk. "All that makeup. He uses eyeliner. His own skin tone looks like spray paint."

"Ozzy only falters when he's looking in a mirror," I said. "Or on the pipe." Oslimov was, in his own peculiar way, as reliable as my two backup men. Different skills, different arena, and now, tonight, same objective. The idea that Blackhawk found any other human being weird was itself amusing.

"Is he gay?" said Blackhawk.

"Does it matter?" I said.

He appeared to seriously ponder this for a moment, searching for weakness. "Guess not."

"Why?" said Bulldog. "Are you available for dating?" He let Blackhawk fume for a moment—just a beat, exactly right—and added, "You know, many males that fancy themselves flaming hets do so because of a bad same-sex experience."

"Shut the fuck up."

"You ever have a threesome with another man?" Bulldog was alight with mirth. "You touch the other guy? You ever say 'I'm just fucking with you' and sort of really mean it, deep down?"

"Boys," I said. "Smooch later. If you'll pardon the expression, we're looking at a rear entry."

"I love ya, but I don't think of ya that way," Blackhawk grumbled.

We watched as McCabe and his orally talented ladyfriend shared a post-beasto toast that looked like straight vodka. She was leaving. Their every movement said so; we didn't even need subtitles. Right about now by my watch Dominic Sharps would be in the earliest stage of rigor mortis. We were still inside the three-hour window before oxygen starvation causes enough calcium to back up in the muscle fibers to initiate stiffening. I hated losing minutes but we waited until the woman left the loft.

No kidding, we gained access via a fire escape. Mal Boyd's map of the Equitable's new architecture was precise to the inch, and Elias McCabe's plate-lock door system was mostly for show. Bulldog tickled it open in under thirty seconds. There was a keypad inside the foyer but the alarm system was easily hornswoggled.

Included in Mal's info skim was a copy of a magazine photo depicting McCabe at work on some arty fashion shoot. It did not provide the sort of biographical insight I needed: dark hair, dark eyes, kind of skinny, straight posture. He did not look like he would put up much of a fight.

The loft flooring was hand-scraped Brazilian walnut, sealed and joined so that it did not creak under our footsteps.

"Hold here," I told my men. I needed to see how far I could intimidate this Elias McCabe fellow solo. If he waxed macho it would be simple to soften him into acquiescence—another advantage of both Blackhawk and Bulldog, with slightly different yet overlapping specialties. If he could be bullied, I could save my guys for a punch line.

Mister Kimber led the way, racked, cocked, and spoiling to rock.

McCabe's entire field of vision seemed to fill up with the sight of the gun, and his mouth popped into a fairly comic O shape.

"Hi, Elias," I said.

He sucked air like a suffocating goldfish while I let Mister Kimber lead me around his display space. He was taller than my estimate, almost wiry, or feline. I put him at about 170 pounds to my 190; he had the reach but I had the power. I saw more of the still lifes and structure studies I had liked.

"You do good work. The perks aren't bad, either." I mimed the fist-to-mouth pump that is the universal language for getting sucked off.

Elias turned bright red. He still had not said a word. I gave him a knowing grin and that just made everything worse. He looked like a man whose entire universe had just come unhinged and flopped into the nearest toilet.

His voice clicked dryly when he finally stuttered, "I-I-I don't have any mon-money."

So I laughed, to push him farther down the well. He frittered as though grease ants had invaded his clothing.

Banded currency comes in fifty-bill stacks. I pulled out the master stack I had assembled—a hundred $100 bills—and plopped it on the nearest glass tabletop. "Then, have some," I said. "Ten thousand, for your trouble. Do what I tell you, when I tell you. Convince me you can keep a secret, and you win."

He was flushed and sweating. His eyes could not decide between me, the gun, or the money. His knees got watery.

"Even more exciting than that," I said, "you get to keep breathing. With me so far?"

Now I spotted a picture I really liked. A naked lady superimposed over a range target with bright white bullet hole patterns instead of pubic hair. Or eyes, or a mouth, or nipples. This man had turned gun work into art.

"I really do like your work," I said, telling the truth.

Blackhawk and Bulldog came in right on cue, and I knew Elias was all ours.

They covered the open space with a three-point spread anchored on my position, then stowed their guns because we had confirmed control.

I laid out the details of Elias's next few hours of existence, and he seemed to dimly catch about half of it. We needed lights, camera, for proper action. He numbly directed Blackhawk to some cases on the floor including a tripod sleeve and a ding-proof lighting chest with a small transformer. Bulldog covered our new acquisition as he shuffled to a glass-fronted refrigerator and plucked out some rolls of film. There was no food or anything inside, just film.

But Elias's gaze kept dogging the entryway. He was expecting a new face to come through that door any moment. As if we did not already have enough good reasons for haste.

"Figure an hour," I estimated, not counting drive time.

He seemed to stir from his logy daze. A tiny point of light came up in his eyes. "What do I call you?"

He was going for the erosion of familiarity—the tiny spilled detail, the foothold to be advantaged later. It was lame and obvious. It needed slapping down. I wanted to heat up the fear receding from his gaze.

"Why?" I said, nailing him like a laser sight. "Why does that matter? Do you care? You think you're gonna Google me or something? *Friend* me? Do you honestly believe a name is worth a dry rat turd? What fucking *planet* do you live on?!"

That cowed him. He was running the Kübler-Ross grief cycle in his head, slightly out of order, switching ANGER with DENIAL. Asking for my name was the leading edge of the BARGAINING play. That failed, so he jumped to DEPRESSION—as in, "Oh, why is this happening to me?"—and was butting up on ACCEPTANCE in record time.

Geared up, we packed him down the freight elevator without another word and into Bulldog's rented Crown Vic.

But I needed to slap him even harder. Keep the terror in his eyes to convince him not to fuck up. Sucker him into remaining meek and behaving himself, and to give him a hair trigger to stay afraid of.

I thought: *This guy does fashion spreads. Everybody hates the privileged. Use it.*

And I went off on him in the backseat, totally without preamble, seating the Kimber's muzzle against his head and hollering like a lunatic. I tore into his station, his status, his perceived wealth, and his misconceptions of how real criminals comported themselves. It came out Method enough to impress Blackhawk and Bulldog, who both considered me as though my brain had just exploded. Elias was completely sure he was within seconds of a messy death.

First the kick—the artery-popping high—then the chaser. I had to reverse his own sad psychology and follow with a tiny dollop of mercy.

"*Jesus,* you guys make me fucking mad," I sighed.

He was curled almost fetally into the tuck of door and seat in a whipped-dog posture of submission. His voice came out miniscule: "Me?"

I gave him a barracuda smile, then I ripped into him again.

My roundabouts were still dutifully beaming misinformation into the Chalet's security system when we arrived and trooped to our hush-hush rendezvous.

Cognac was watching an Oprah late-night repeat on the flat screen and slowly filling an ashtray with butts—slim 100s, smoked halfway and discarded. I didn't mind lending her a name because it was fake anyway. On Tuesdays, she was Sapphire. Fridays and weekends, Valentina. To the DMV she was Cypress Wintre. Recycle as needed.

Ozzy Oslimov presented a different issue. I decided to call him the Professor—a cute jape since he lacked a formal degree in anything, and his subterranean résumé was not likely to improve his chances.

For the grand finale I showed Elias the corpse of Dominic Sharps, set up in the bedroom. Elias's mouth went arid.

Ozzy had already done preliminary dry runs for skin tone. Every moment that elapsed brought Sharps closer to the onset of first-stage rigor, which would lock him up for twenty-four hours and make him a lot harder to adjust into the positions we wanted. Lividity was already a problem.

I allowed Elias to have one extra light for clarity. I did not want to risk reflections or anything that might tip the deception in a photo.

Elias's mouth drooped open when Ozzy twisted the metal rod down into Sharps's penis. He dropped a roll of film on the floor and hustled to snatch it up. His mouth was still open.

Cognac moved past us with a polite excuse me, gave Sharps's dead dick three strokes with her gelled hands, then swung her magnificent ass around as though riding a horsy and mounted him with a slight sucking sound of compression. Bulldog and Blackhawk positioned the dead man's hands using wax-based mortician's glue. Ozzy had lined Sharps's teeth with denture adhesive so his mouth would not hang open (kind of like Elias's was, still); there was no need for a more permanent fix, like wiring the gums. In death, Sharps's features were as malleable as putty, and Ozzy repositioned them to simulate effort and ecstasy. The faces some people make during sexual congress can be pretty frightening. Women howl or bliss out. Men sometimes look as though they are shitting a high-heeled clog. The balance Ozzy achieved was another kind of art. Then, perfectionist that he was, he touched up Sharps's fingernails, which had begun to go ghost-white.

I could have hugged him. We had a flea's asshair chance of getting away with this.

Elias was convulsively wiping his mouth like an alcoholic.

"Start shooting," I told him. "They don't *all* have to be masterpieces." As the bromide goes, film really comes together in the editing stage, and I got to pick what got left out.

We were golden for the moment, unless the body chose that time to purge.

I kept a running count on Elias's exposures with one eye on my watch. When I thought we could do no better, I called time. The late Dominic Sharps was ready to travel to his final tour stop, and Blackhawk was more than happy to "take him to the Kitty."

The place we called the Kitty was actually the headquarters of FFF Corporation—FelineFeast Fancy Cat Foods in Long Beach, makers of Kitty Konnoisseur (a brand you may have seen advertised in those obnoxious commercials with the talking kitten, which I would have loved to shoot, just once, and not with a camera). Among its ancillary products were things like bone meal and fertilizer. It was adjacent to a privately owned, dedicated slaughterhouse with a killing floor, hiding pool, and blood pits; it also featured two large bin-style meat grinders. We had used this facility several times with great success on our own version of the midnight shift. Dominic Sharps would become just another of the carefully selected and USDA-approved ingredients in Southern California's most popular snob brand of kitty chow. I had to suppress a laugh when I imagined the label: NOW WITH MORE CRUNCHY TOENAILS!

Elias was beginning to zombie out on me, drained already. I got him an espresso loaded with sugar and he downed it without protest.

Ozzy received ten thousand, same as Cognac. It was killing my budget but these were expensive circumstances. Bulldog ferried him back to his lair in the Crown Vic and Blackhawk took Sharps for his final ride to cat-land. Cognac understood she was to await my pleasure at the Beverly Hilton for one of our usual post-mission stress relievers. That left me to take Elias homeaways and vulture over him until he finished earning his take.

But I could not resist bouncing his brain around some more, so in the car I started interrogating him about his work. Mal Boyd's dossier had shown me the light insofar as Elias's night-shift job printing skin rags, and I quietly amazed my captive by citing one of them—the illustrious *2 Young 2 Date*.

"No shit? For real?" I said with a goofy fanboy expression, as though I was impressed. "Man, you know any of those models?"

He gave me back weary dismissal, as though that abrogated his own culpability in supplying wanking material for the sexually disadvantaged of our fair nation. So I hit him back with the old pornography argument, which distracted him into thinking of a gang of rote defenses and alibis.

My nonspecific point was that just as we all have baggage, we all have shame and dirty little secrets. Past indiscretions best left unplumbed. No one is immune, therefore no one is innocent.

And no one got away with thinking they were better than me, because Mister Kimber had a swell answer for their delusions. That's why a gun was called an equalizer.

In the loft we found a bread crumb line of shucked clothing leading from the door to the bathroom. Someone was snoozing on Elias's big futon. A female someone.

"Is that the bitch from before?" I whispered.

Elias said no. This was someone new to the mix. Someone he cared more about than his earlier conquest. For me, this was optimum. Now he would do whatever I wanted without even a token fight.

His darkroom was claustrophobic and science-fictional, with a pronounced alkaline smell. I smoked and watched him work and felt a microscopic stab of professional admiration. Then he fucked it all up by asking yet another question about what had befallen him, so I brought out Evil Me to remind him to stick to the job at hand.

Mal Boyd had been damned near clairvoyant. Elias was one of those guys who wasted his life trying to figure out the Mac-Guffin. The developing process seemed to take an entire geologic age, so I whipped the speech on him more or less as Boyd had given it to me. It felt good.

And goddammit if he didn't ask *another* question.

It was time for Mister Kimber to help me with my side of things.

I had just withdrawn the pistol from Elias's mouth when his girlfriend peeped in to ask what the hell was going *on* in here.

Actually, it was about thirty seconds after Elias had shit his pants in panic. I gave him a round from the pistol so he would always think about that steel-jacketed lead penetrating his skull. Stainless cartridge, no fingerprints.

His guest was adorably half asleep. Blond hair, brown eyes, maybe five foot seven, A-plus legs, and an ass to die dreaming of. Her lips were agreeably natural. She was not breasty; her chest was contoured in a beautiful swell centered around large nipples that declared themselves through the sheer silk of her peach-colored jammy top. I had slept with some spectacular women, but never anyone of this grade. People fantasized about fucking her when they saw her photo in magazines, or saw her move around in TV commercials. She was from a world entirely alien to mine—I supposed that was what always prompted the fantasy.

Elias stammered some excuse so he could run off to clean his butt, which left me and the woman named Char alone for a moment in the gallery.

"Sorry if we woke you up," I said. "Elias had some proofs for me and I couldn't get away any earlier. Have to catch a plane." I shrugged.

"I know what that's like," she said, hunting around for—I guessed correctly—a cigarette. I lit one of mine and passed it over. Then she lighted on a leather sofa and tucked up her legs so I would not comment on her lack of undergarments. "Shoots can be murder."

Ho, sister, if only you knew.

"Well, I also wanted to pay him for the print," I said, my gaze finding the two pictures on the wall I'd liked.

"Oh? Which one? *Petroglyph?*" She seemed to scrutinize it for the first time. "It's not worth *that* much money."

She had come in and spotted the cash on the table. Counted it. *Caution.*

"No, this one," I said, getting close enough to read the title. "*Targets #5.*"

Char rolled her slightly almond-shaped eyes. "*That's* worth even less. It's sexist crap."

"Not to me," I said smoothly. "It's the sexlessness of it that appeals to me. Look closer and you'll see that gender identity is left largely up to the viewer. No, really, I'm not kidding. It's the perfect answer to the sexlessness of advertising—the shaved pubes, the boy bodies. Most of the billboard people don't even have heads anymore."

"That's because all the damned fashion designers are gay men." She frowned. "They want the six-pack and the cut butt and no head to talk back to them."

I stayed on the photo. "This says 'to hell with all that.' In death, everybody is equal."

She cocked her head, tossing down a wisp of hair so that a single eye reevaluated me. "I'm not quite ready to say you might have a point there. You used to work at Inkworks? Elias said you were an old compadre."

"Yeah, for Boss Wiley, believe it or don't," I said, once again thanking Mal Boyd's dossier.

"Yeah, he poured toner into the Photostat machine and Boss nearly decapitated him with a paper cutter blade," said Elias, freshly emerged from his ablutions.

"I'd rather forget that dark day, thanks," I said. Now we were collaborators. I had to think fast to catch Elias up on the falsified story. "I was just telling Char about how I overpaid you for *Targets #5* so you would think about running me an entire series for Hofmeister's gallery."

Which gallery, I also knew about from Mal Boyd's dossier. Elias blinked fast several times. "Uh, right."

"You didn't say anything about a gallery show," Char said. "Hof's gallery? Seriously? You mean—*without* Clavius's help?"

"Yeah. It's not cast in stone yet." Elias nervously considered how compelling his own feet were.

"Anyway," I cut in, "since I've kept you kids up and since I'm here right now, why don't I just take it with me?"

"What?" When he looked up I could see his eyes. There must have been some very entertaining chemicals in that bathroom.

"*Targets #5,* Elias," I said with a hint of happy. "That picture. Right there. That you sold to me. So it's mine now. Correct?"

He smacked his head. "Ah! Sorry! Right. Sure . . . you need it wrapped up or—?"

"No, it's under glass; it's fine."

Elias actually handed me the framed artwork off the wall. Oddly, it made up for the extra money I'd had to waste tonight. He seemed tormented enough for one workday, and I speculated that Char's easy manner would evanesce as soon as I was out the door. These two were going to have a fight. You could feel it in the ozone.

I made a little thumb-and-forefinger gunpoint at him when I bid my farewells. "Remember," I said.

"Copy," he said, and I found that surprisingly apt.

Cognac was asleep when I arrived at the Beverly Hilton just before dawn. I left her that way and consumed a gigantic breakfast with plenty of stout and whimsically stray shots of white rum. Then I awoke Cognac just in time to inform her she could sleep in, since I was buying her for the entire following day. Some of the things we did ought not to be recorded.

I thought a lot about recorded data in the next few weeks, when I wasn't sneaking in and out of hospitals. That part came soon enough.

There was a remarkable tension-release flow to the sort of work I do. Sometimes the setup involved weeks, months of prep, playing roles and living in assumed skins; other times the action was fast and fatal. There was no artificial high quite like this sensation, and once the mission was closed, release flooded every nerve ending. This required the discipline of learning to eat stress the way ordinary people crave love. It was almost a regressive state, taking me and people similar to me back to jungle law, to sleep when tired, eat when hungry or instead of being eaten—raw Darwinism with a dash of Nietzsche. It put me beyond the clock of regular citizens and out of reach of their law enforcement. Planning stages were so comprehensive that police interference was always accounted for and factored in, so officers of the normal-world law represented mild deterrent potential at best. Hell, half the time I worked for some shadow-ops government agency that guaranteed my immunity as a deal point—I could always escape custody with a single phone call. A fifty-two card deck of alternate identities didn't hurt, either. Nor did secure drops, safe houses or the finest modern weaponry military and black market subcontractors could provide. Tax free.

I had just pulled off the subterranean equivalent of winning the lottery. A sealed and delivered deal had taken the worst turn imaginable, and instead of folding, my team and I rebounded with solid improvisation. Money was always more fun when you feel you have actually earned it. For "money," substitute "all the things you desire" if you're not a complete capitalist.

About ten o'clock that evening I got a secure cell message that three tailored suits were ready for my pick up. Bad timing; I did not know whether Cognac would elect to stay past midnight.

When I arrived at Mal Boyd's aerie, I found him ashen. Not eating.

"We're severely compromised, dear boy," he said. "Your face and crimes are all over the Internet."

PART THREE

ELIAS

Char left me without even a contact number. If I had been paying closer attention, I would have seen she had been moving her stuff out for weeks, piecemeal, in increments too small to be remarked.

Yes, you could say I had been distracted.

Gun Guy had labeled me a pornographer. That was conditionally true. Most of my catch for the past year had come from shooting fashion spreads instead of nurturing my own tentative idea of art. There's a reason they're called "spreads" and they're generally more obscene than anything featuring split beaver or pink-think or the anal avenging found in the newsstand sections you always pretend to avoid.

We've all become street whores for the fashion industry. It barks trends and we lie back and spread our billfolds, queuing up in a desperate grab for this season's insane idea of faux class. Wander over into that *other* section of the magazine racks, you know the one I mean. Where the bedsheet-sized glossies beckon with empty promises of style and cool. Where they'll teasingly tell you about this season's ten essential must-have accessories, or how howlingly ridiculous parkas are the in thing, why *all* the hoi polloi are wearing them this week.

It makes celebrities of people who have never accomplished anything apart from being celebrities, and offers them to you for worship. You already know the brand names and labels and their snakepit pecking order, because you still believe you can buy pedigree for the cost of a stupid magazine.

It's not your fault you're such a sucker for this garbage; hell, we've *all* been conditioned . . . or I never would have let Nasja delve my crotch after that last shoot. There are some kinds of candy that don't permit the word *no*.

Insiders would attempt to dazzle you with a fireworks display of dropped names, feeding your mad lust for dirt, the real scoop, the hot gossip. Or they'd blind you with the glare of trivia; the chewy argot and insider jargon of the mavens of high style.

Your lust object has butt implants, a face full of botulism, a vaginal tuck, a penile implant, fake pecs, surgically mutilated eyes, a decalcifying skeleton, two or three serious drug monkeys, a coyote's sense of entitlement, a head full of bees, and is so utterly devoid of human emotion he or she might as well be from another galaxy.

But now, used, scared, and abandoned, having filled my pants like a toddler and quaked like a sissy, minus a picture on my wall that I really liked and was compelled to give away to avoid being handily murdered, you may forgive my abrupt and uncharacteristic introspection.

Listen to me: It's not the Year of Gloss. Buzz can eat you alive. You don't care about the A-list party animals or Fashion's Best Catfights, or which supermodels are courting which labels. The Foot is not the New Face; trust me. It doesn't matter what look is the talk of the runways, or how some daring doyenne turned a gallery opening into an all-night bacchanal.

There are other things going on besides the political peccadilloes, breathless soap opera, and empty calories fed us all by a world where advertising has gone berserk. Remember that the next time you find yourself tempted by a logo.

Right now I knew what I wanted more than anything was to kick that whole steroidal designer monster in its warty asshole as far as my boot would sink. Or at least give it a good poke in the eye. It had made me a slave. It took Char from me. It showed me what a naked coward I truly was.

There was a whole other universe out there where Gun Guy operated, invisible in plain sight. That was the fulcrum of genuine power.

And I wasn't a part of it until that night.

Thanks to the speed from my medicine cabinet, I couldn't slip into bed on the far side of the no man's land across from Char. So I dumped more tequila down my neck and replayed Nasja's "erased" spycam tape.

At about the fifty-minute mark, it showed me and Gun Guy entering the loft. The audio was crisp:

Is that the bitch from before?

No.

Then hop-to, and let's try not to wake her up. You don't want her to wind up in a can of cat food like your buddy Dominic Sharps . . . do you?

I've never swooned before and don't know how it feels. Probably something like what was jacking my metabolism now, punching my heart, husking my breath, making the room swim as dust motes in the air ballooned to the size of asteroids.

Then I remembered I had purposefully used the Clavius paper to run the prints for Gun Guy, in my own covert attempt at rebellion.

The Clavius paper is thick archival bond with a hidden watermark asserting copyright, about which Clavius has always been dictatorial. If you were to digitally scan the photo—say, for illicit reproduction—a huge diagonal bar appears across the image face advising you not to do that. Neue Helvetica type across the bottom edge of the bar provides a Web site address where Clavius blogs about twice a year. Its main function is to employ a platoon of nitpicky workers who keep constant watch for violations of intellectual property rights as detailed in the Digital Millennium Copyright Act. Plagiarisms. Unauthorized usages or postings. Anything actionable.

He won a whale-choking settlement from Google just last year as the distribution apparatus for "free first looks" at items that were not free. Clavius had enough of a war chest to paper *them* out, and the details of the accord were sealed under a strict gag order. It was a very large numeral, following a dollar sign.

As a result, Clavius found himself in the unelected position of a popular media figure with a boner for creative rights, which is a rarity on the order of finding a still-breathing Tasmanian wolf raiding your larder's stash of sorbet. Daily hits skyrocketed. His Web site was much-followed and often-commented upon.

So I uploaded the video to it, without fanfare, in the MEMBERS section.

The only reason I had thought of this was because Gun Guy had kicked such a stink about the photos not being digital manipulations. What he was really talking about—although he didn't know it—was presenting pictures that could stand up to forensics on the fractal level.

The Clavius watermark on the paper would autoreference any Internet upload on prohibited material, including the photos I had shot. To this red flag system I added a footnote, which could be done using an access code and a phone, as long as the message was fewer than 140 characters. I sheltered it using a "dead pixel" protocol so that it would not appear unless those specific photos were uploaded. This was possible because every single piece of Clavius paper has its own registry number; you just entered the appropriate numbers.

SHARPS SEX PHOTOS A COMPLETE FRAUD
BY BLACKMAILERS RED FLAG REPS
FOR DETAILS AND EVIDENCE

If the machinations stayed underground, no worries. But if they came anywhere near the Internet . . . fireworks. And my ass was covered. Without the photos, the video would mean nothing to the average Web surfer.

76

This kind of control was made possible by the world-girding monoliths that really control the airflow of digital information, like a slipknot around your throat and mine. It is an ongoing global contraction of ultimate domain. The more devices you have connected to satellites, the more freedom you've already lost, not to mention privacy. Sign up, log in, don't forget your password, and they've got you by the guts. And most people don't mind at all. Why should a budget be wasted on intelligence when the subjects willingly spy on themselves? Convenience is king, and if you're not willing to live a full-disclosure life 24/7, then you must be hiding something.

I don't wish to sound like a tinfoil-hat-wearing conspiracy theorist. But Clavius told me that the surge in liquid crystal and plasma monitors was encouraged by our hidden overseers because each new screen had the built-in capacity to passively watch and listen back at the will of some faraway keyboard jock. It was exactly like the TV that watches you from Orwell's *1984*, but generations more subtle because it did not matter if the unit was on or off; now reconsider that STANDBY light that always glows. I don't know how true the story is, but ask yourself if you think it is *really* that far-fetched.

If you don't believe, you might change your mind if you had met Gun Guy and his pal Mister Kimber. They were supposed to be untouchable but I had managed a limp form of fight-back. A hidden dead-switch bomb.

Nobody was more shocked than me when it blew up.

Tripp Bergin called the next day to pester me about the movie gig. I told him I was in a transitional phase and would get back to him.

Joey, my assistant and facilitator, had been MIA all morning, probably snoring off an Ecstasy binge and subsequent water bloat, after having left my loft for a club that did not open until midnight.

Nasja called twice. I erased her messages without listening

to them. I already knew she would be hectoring me to see photos too soon. Or worse.

Clavius showed up around sunset. Himself, in person.

Which was not usual. This was no rare in-the-flesh visit to cement our bond, or a publicity op, because no media were lurking. He either had a grand new scheme to hatch that mandated my labor . . . or something was seriously wrong.

His limpid eyes scanned the loft with approval. He'd gotten none less than DeMarco—yes, *the* DeMarco—to redesign the living space with a bias toward photography—a lot of glass, flat angles, minimalist work zones and polished wood, yet practical for the sprawl a large shoot can prompt.

"You've done well for yourself," he said. He should know: he picked out most of this stuff himself, or his creatures had. I had become a spinoff of him.

"I've also done well for yourself," I said, uncertain of his tone. Was he angry at me for Char? For Nasja? For an unspecified sin, as the parent who smacks the kid upside the noggin and when the kid yowls, "What'd I do?" the parent says, "You should know."

Clavius seemed calm and ready to be distracted. I already knew this was his war face.

"Char," he said simply. No adjectives, no qualifiers. It was his way to drop a topic like a rock into a koi pond and let others handle the splashing and ripples.

It was also a relief that I didn't have to inchworm my way toward the subject. I dove right in: "She's been moving her stuff out for weeks. I just realized that this morning. I'm not mad at you . . . well, maybe a little."

Clavius waved that off; a trifle. "She's staying at HawkNest, you know."

HawkNest was Clavius's elaborate penthouse-style New York pied-à-terre. He owned the entire twenty-sixth floor of a building on the Upper West Side. In most places, Clavius liked to be up high and on top. Quite a few people could be said to be "in residence" there at any given time—models, guests, celebrities holing up incognito, assorted grotesques. Clavius had an entire wing of apartments for visitors. That way, women from all over the planet could stay there, yet none could claim they were actually *sleeping* with Clavius.

From what Nasja had divulged, Clavius rarely had sex conventionally, which was just too boring. There was a ritualistic introductory phase where he might call upon five acolyte women to each perform different aspects of a single erotic collage. Like A-B-C: Abby does a hand job designed to last an hour, then Barbara replaces her for an anal penetration of one single thrust, then Cathy rotates in for other kinds of stimulation like climax hovering, Doris arrives for vigorous fornication and a precisely timed number of ins-and-outs, and finally Elsey dashes in to swallow the flow of genetic material.

To mess with the orchestration of Clavius's labyrinthine sexual scenarios was to squander spiritual energy like some brutish, low commoner. Why, that would just be *fucking*.

I had no idea what part or role Char played in all that. I only knew she had left me when we seemed evenly matched, sexually, spiritually, and in terms of knowing the same puns and finishing each other's sentences. Her departure did not confirm anything except my single status, because if you were a total boor and lost it and screamed at Clavius, "Are you fucking her?" He would smile and answer, "Yes, I am fucking her emotions."

"No, goddammit—are you having sex with her?" He'd say, "Some might call it sex." And so on, same as the child-whacking parent.

Which was why Clavius had noted that Char was now at HawkNest.

"She's flown across the country already?" I said, a bit stung by her haste.

Clavius ran his hands through his indestructible iron hair and steepled his fingers. "Yes—this morning. Where is the *Targets* picture that was hanging there? Did you sell it?"

"So to speak," I said. "Is this about Nasja?"

Another wave. "Do with Nasja what you will. She has citizenship and a bank balance; I'm done with her."

I tried to stay as honestly on track as I could, even if it seemed coarse: "Is Char her replacement?"

"Not at all," he said. "What makes you think that?" It was the sort of question only Clavius could ask and get away with.

Then a teeny lightbulb zapped on, somewhere, and he added, "Let me tell you a little something about our dear friend Charlene. Do you remember when you met her? Back when you were still moonlighting at that droll print shop?"

I nodded and Clavius indicated that he would deign to imbibe a sparkling water of the appropriate brand.

"Do you remember your mind-set then, what you were thinking?"

"I was thinking I was really lucky to have met you," I said.

"Yes—fortuitous. Profitable for all. But you thought of yourself as an underdog, and still do in many ways. You hated feeling beholden. Char was the answer to that emotional stress."

"Yeah, that's how I felt at the time."

"No—you mistake my meaning. Char was *my* solution to your distress."

"No." I could not backtrack it. Char and I had met at a book signing that had nothing to do with Clavius. She acted as though she had never heard of him except in a distant, peripheral way. But she had never said it outright, in so many words.

"It was simple to follow you outside my purview," Clavius said. "I aimed her at you and she accomplished her task, which was to bring you out of yourself. Look at how your work has matured and flourished."

My vision began to spot and plunge again.

"She has simply flown home, you see? Now I can explain it to you, safely and without guilt or rage or reactionary hostility. Do you agree?"

I sat down rather heavily, sloshing my drink.

Char had been a plant. Even for her, I owed Clavius.

I tried to tell Clavius the story of what had happened to me. I had no other confidants at hand. He found it amusing.

"That's a fantastic confluence of nanochance," he observed with a twinkle. "The hairsbreadth timing, the implied derring-do. Are you thinking of making this a series?"

"I didn't make it up," I said. I showed him Nasja's tape. He was less than convinced. I was right—without the photos, the tape meant nothing, and I didn't have the photos.

"Is it the assignments?" Clavius asked. He moved to the stainless bar sink near the kitchen island to wash his hands, which he did thirty or forty times per day. "Are they becoming tedium for you? The magazine layouts? Tell me what you want."

He was asking if I had snapped into fantasyland because my daily workload was so mind-numbing, and offering deeper debt.

"We can easily alter that," he said with the surety of a man who always gets what he wants. "You've been my champion. I don't wish to see you unhappy."

Really? Then work some sorcery on Char so she never met you.

I was being petty and cranky, resenting the control held by people more powerful than me. Same as with Gun Guy. If I would just face my low position on the totem pole, the food chain, I would at least enjoy the refreshment of an honest panoramic look at how my life sucked.

Yeah, I spent most days sobbing over my unfair lot: I had an upward-bound profile, a killer portfolio, a million-dollar crib, the freedom of determining my own hours, a Jaguar, enough stray dollars to feed my antique camera fetish, a chorus line of lovelies, and an all-access pass to realms a TV watcher can only dream about—all the stuff I had idealized before Clavius walked into New World Inkworks that first time. Yeah, yeah, my life was a bitch.

"If little Nasja fails to divert you," Clavius said, "then Aja had indicated an attraction. You know Aja—the Norwegian?"

This was getting worse and worse. Even the *names* on the sex parade were starting to blur into one another. Aja. Amanda. Natalia. Nastasia.

"I need to fuck my work right now," I said and instantly regretted it.

"Quite. I think you've already sensed that Nasja is a dead end. Bought Russians have few desirable qualities beyond the initial attraction; they're just too mercenary. One can't blame them but one does not have to let them bulldoze you, either. Remember our friend Hofmeister, the fellow with the gallery? Lately he's gone for mute Koreans, purchased through Chinese brokers. I find them so thankful and servile that they're amazingly dull. But they were a godsend for Chinese men, and we in the West are only just catching the cultural coattail."

He paused to see if he still had my attention. True, my mind was on the wander due to larger and more pressing events. He held up a finger, ever the calm academician. "This does have a point," he said, "and it relates to your feelings about Nasja and Char in regard to my participation."

"Sorry." I said that too much, to nearly everyone.

"Bear with," Clavius said. "Chinese cultural preference and dogma has always held that female children were undesirable. The one-child-per-couple mandate only made the situation more heinous. Where before, female children were simply abandoned, now they could be aborted if ultrasound revealed them to be the wrong sex. As a result, available Chinese men began to outnumber available—that is, marriageable—Chinese women. Bond slavery was the result. The border between China and North Korean became what they call a 'wife market.' Female Korean refugees fled their economic distress by seeking Chinese husbands. One out of every three was fated to be sold by Chinese gangsters, if they were not collected by the even more predatory gangs of 'wife hunters.' The good ones cost less than $2000.

They receive the birth statistics of a dead person. The Chinese men, who would never admit to having 'bought' a wife, in return get someone especially pliable, hard-working, and most important of all, submissive. And everyone makes out along the way—border guards, identity brokers, all the needed intermediaries. Many of these people also thrive within the adoption sector. Business is booming, and bureaucracy charges by the hour. Serving up Chinese babies for foreign adoption has become an industry, and an irresistible windfall if you happen to be stuck with a female child you couldn't otherwise give away."

You may have noticed the cost of having Clavius's mostly undivided attention: Every question is the start of an opera.

"The point being—?" I asked.

"Just this: what I do for the women who come under my umbrella, so to speak, is not bond slavery, nor indentured servitude, nor blackmail. Nor is it the addiction-and-prostitution paradigm. Nasja and Char and all the others like them do what they do voluntarily, and are free to leave anytime they choose. I'm not some kind of black-hearted puppet master, pulling internecine strings to make your life a living hell. I just want to help people. I cannot save the world, but I can choose those I wish to help."

You may have noticed Clavius's ego is one of the few things larger than his bank account.

"Fair enough," I said. But it was not fair at all. What Clavius had, the rest of the world lusted for. Between that and capitalism was a lot of wiggle room.

To be honest, how could I really blame Clavius for any of this? He had marched right over and told the truth. I think.

I pressed him on the matter of the photos and video. He did not seem too hooked.

"Frankly, I don't spend a great deal of time online," he said. "It's too frustrating. All that advertising."

We shared the same pain. When I said I "uploaded the video," that was the short version of the story. It was more like three hours of keyboard-punching and teeth-gnashing. Unless one had the latest computer—and yours is outmoded by the time it leaves the factory—navigating the nation formerly known as the World Wide Web was an exercise in sheer self-abuse. Simple pages took ages to load because they were piggybacked onto advertising. Nine times out of ten, the "apps 'n' feeds" incorporated a video, animation, or god knows what to bog down the load time. On my computer this molasses-retardation frequently prompted a browser crash. Start again. Then the load times for what you wished to disseminate threatened to overflow the cup again. Pop-ups were scotched only to be replaced by sneakier pop-ups that circumvented the filter while tons of attached spam sniffed for your in-box. Start again. Ad clicks, widgets, and error messages sucked up entire minutes until they forced another restart. Repeat as needed until you're in a padded cell.

"Dude, just get a new computer," my fireball Joey would advise. I admit I murdered my first one by punching it off the desk. After that I tended to keep them until they died from their own obsolescence. With Joey, the concept of upgrade was an urgent minute-to-minute reality. He could probably do more with his phone—"mobile device"—than I could with all the devices in my home.

"Personally, I think Char was quite taken with you," Clavius said.

"But she had other goals."

"As do you," he said. "Try not to be morose for more than a day or two. *Transcendency* magazine wants a fashion model spread using my surgical studies as big poster-sized backdrops; we're making the giclées right now. Call Willeford Whats-his-name to set it up, yes?"

Clavius had said "his" studies but I had shot them. I felt a large boa constrictor around my neck taking an interest in me as food.

* * *

Google the word "kitty" sometime, just for shits 'n' gigs. You'll get seventy million choices.

The bullet Gun Guy had left me stood like a little pewter-colored sentry on the desk as I uselessly cruised online, looking for a clue that might expand what Gun Guy had meant when he told his enforcers, "Take him to the Kitty." "The Professor" was useless—nobody had come close to mentioning the mortician's real-world name. If I wanted my sad clues to mean more, my best option would be to stake out the Beverly Hilton and wait for Cognac to breeze through the lobby. Or whatever her name was.

You don't want her to wind up in a can of cat food like your buddy Dominic Sharps . . . do you?

"Kitty" meant cat food. That didn't narrow the field much.

Kitty Comfort, Super Kitty Cat, Royal Kitty, Kitty Dry-Blend, Kitty Kat Club Casserole, Kitty Kafé , Special Kitty, Kitty's Favorite, Wild Kitty (recalled for salmonella, I noticed), Kitty Weightloser, Kitty Liver Heaven, Kitty Gourmet Select, Malchin's Private Kitty Reserve . . . my eyeballs were about to melt and cascade off my face.

"I smell the boss's cologne," came a voice from the foyer, followed by the traditional door slam. Joey was in da house, yo.

"Shitty Kitty," I murmured.

Joe clapped me on the shoulder. "Hey, my brother used to say that to his girlfriend: 'Tough titty, shitty kitty.' Or, like, 'One in the kitty and one in the shitty.'"

"*What?*"

"You know! One in the pud and one in the mud. One in the pink and one in the stink. *You* know—DP."

"Director of Photography?" I said. Dom Perignon? Dr Pepper? Diet Pepsi?

"Double penetration, dude—DP. Try to keep up." He shrugged as broadly as a Catskills baggy-pants comedian, which should tell you something about the disparity in our ages.

"Oh, yeah, that classic payoff to porn film structure," I said. "Silly me."

"Don't laugh." Emotions on Joey's pierced face were always amplified, fluid, then gone in an instant. "People who use porn expect a certain progression. First the phony make out, then blow job, then twat-licking, then missionary, doggie, horsy, then two chicks, then a guy with two chicks, then maybe sometimes a chick with two guys, then freestyle, then roll credits."

"That sounds like really hard work to keep track of."

He gave me the finger and grinned. "Fuck *you*. As if you're interested in any of that shit; I know where the duck shit on the wood."

(I thought it best not to correct him.)

"Hey, what happened to the picture on the wall?"

"I wish everybody would stop asking me about the picture on the wall," I said. "The picture on the wall went bye-bye."

"Where'd you get the bullet?" He already had it in his hands, marveling.

"Not bullet," I said. "Cartridge. Round." I had learned a few rote factoids, too, before "kitty" jeopardized my sanity. "The bullet is the nose, the slug, the projectile. The casing is the brass part, but this one is some kind of special mint. The gunpowder's in there. The primer that sets off the powder is on the bottom— the little silvery disk in the middle. Primer ignites powder, big bang, bullet flies off to do mayhem." I had never fired a gun in my life, let alone held one containing live rounds.

"That's funny," he said. "No headstamp. Looks like a .45." He saw my reaction and pointed. "Here on the base. There're usually numbers for caliber and abbreviations for maker, stamped around the primer. The letters mean all kinds of shit—who made it, what it's for, what arsenal it came from, if it's military. This one's naked. Where'd you find it?"

"Literally in the street," I said. "It caught the light. So no numbers and stuff means what?"

"Could be a custom load. Could be a reload. You know— bang-bang, the shells fly out?" He did an action-movie panto-mime. "Guys reuse that empty brass all the time. Saves money."

Put a pin in that thought: Joey knows a tiny something about firepower. Right now it was time to divert his attention into the kitty zone. "Here. Maybe you can help me with this fruitless quest."

I sat him down in my place and gave him the parameters. He was wearing a Cable T-shirt with the sleeves cut off, to showcase the Celtic and Maori stuff on his arms—almost full sleeves themselves, now, I noticed. A good full-color inkwork of Karloff as the Frankenstein monster lowered at me from the back of his neck, peeking from behind the collar.

Just the potential number of clubs and restaurants with the word "kitty" in their names was threatening to stormfront a migraine.

"Okay," Joey said. "Cat food only. Manufacturers. Probably not Chinese, then. There can't be that many."

"Los Angeles area," I said. "Figure not more than an hour's drive from the Strip."

"Good, that gives us a radius." He squirmed around as though bioconnected to the computer.

I was best-guessing, relieved to have an assistant to hoist the burden. "Just be a genius," I said.

"Dude. It ain't rocket surgery, okay?"

Joey helped me keep one foot in the current world of things. He was aware of this intermediation, but instead of clubbing me with it or treating me like an antique old fart lost in the mists of over-forty, he acted and reacted as though I were a nonhostile older sibling of the same tribe—that is, an older iteration of himself. He performed this kindness countless times, at least to my face. In return for this, he asked nothing. Beyond the mentor-apprentice dynamic we could have been any two guys hanging out.

With the usual qualifiers.

For one, Joey was priapic as his carefully cultivated persona suggested. He was a demonstration of what Clavius meant when he said all human congress is based on sex, and in this we are no different from bacteria, which is why it is called a sex *drive*. Eat, excrete, and make more. Our entire culture and civilization was a by-product of the be-fruitful-and-multiply mandate. Power devolves to sexual dominance; ditto success. We had more pretensions than amoebae, but when you boil away the snow we were all just organisms hardwired to keep procreating. And what do happy little microorganisms do besides eat, excrete, and reproduce? If they have enough spare time after those depleting activities, they kill each other. Then they die.

One day Joey and I were plowing through especially strong espresso, seated at an outdoor table ostensibly so he could smoke. It was also a much better vantage for the flesh parade outside a designer gym in a plaza containing the Newsroom restaurant, on Robertson, near the Ivy, where paparazzi loitered around with the mien of hunters who didn't care about stealth. This was back when New Line Cinema's offices were still upstairs in the plaza. So we had actresses, celebutards, and workout tarts in abundance doing the in-and-out platelet flow. For every single one that cruised past, Joey asked me, "Would you? Would you? Would you?"

No. No. Sure. I guess. Maybe, if she has a job or isn't really a man. I read them differently than he did. As a game it was tiresome. Joey could not see the baggage, just the containers. Safer to detour him onto another topic. Music. He begrudgingly acquiesced while keeping one eye on the make.

"Redhead," he snorked. "Awesome. Hope the curtains match the drapes."

Was Joey even aware of what he was saying, half the time? In a former life I would only have said the word "awesome" if I was staring into an erupting volcano or a nuclear explosion. But I understood what Joey meant whenever he said it, which meant we were still capable of communicating, sort of.

Now that I had a premium audio system, I rarely listened to

music on purpose anymore. The interesting stuff was there as always, but it was harder to give a damn. Joey found this to be sacrilege, but I felt the same way about books, about films, current affairs, topical news, politics, religion, in fact everything except the minute focus of the job at hand. To generate anything artistic that has meaning, you had to proceed without distraction in a universe devoted to breaking your concentration. Sometimes stress yielded surprises, but that was not dependable, and if you were a professional you had to consciously invoke the mind-set more and more, and hoard privacy in which to apply it.

Yet at some mysterious juncture in the past couple of decades, I became aware that as far as most things are concerned, I was suddenly outside looking in, observing. This was notably different from the glandular reactionary verve of my twenties, where every pursuit had been a passion and every emotion overwrought. I saw that in Joey still. His art—even if it was fetish videos or nudie shoots—was his lifeblood; he felt he would die if he could not participate, even to the point of using his own flesh as an ever-evolving free-form canvas. I felt the incipient danger of becoming one of those people that does not have time to read books, or listen to music, unless it directly impacted the latest job. And I already knew the contempt in which I held *those* people, those pedestrian droids . . . even as I felt the tug of becoming one myself. To pinpoint the stage at which I had parted company with the flow of the world was futile. It just happened, somehow, while I wasn't looking.

Part of it was a disinclination for the been-there, done-that. The world rehashes new art in terms of old, generationally. Nostalgia for the 1990s? The 1980s? I had been there and didn't feel the retro charm. (Disco sucked in the seventies and still sucks now, thanks. And don't get me started on the Beatles, those kings of supermarket muzak for the twenty-first century.) Sturgeon's Law held that ninety percent of everything was shit, and that included ninety percent of the ten percent that was worthwhile. Without filters in place you would simply drown in the overflow of crap.

Then again, my idea of perfect harmony pretty much began and ended with "Don't Worry Baby."

During the course of one beery late-night discourse on such things, I told Joey that part of my retreat had to do with the human brain, which switched him right on. In brain-land, the ninety percent was the portion we still did not comprehend. Brain-mapping scientists had determined that there was a specific part of the brain devoted to memory for music. We carry all the music we have ever heard in that unfathomable little quadrant, accessible at will, and indeed I could "hear" it any time I wanted without the cumbersome physical requirements of cueing it up or putting it on. Joey loved the idea of the "built-in Nano" and would have sprung for an implant that moment.

Then he played me a song by Nerveblock that sounded like Inquisitors torturing Pygmies to death with flamethrowers during an airline crash into a mental hospital. I didn't know if it was one song or three, and had no idea of the titles, but I did like the energy and urgency of it. If it was too loud, I was officially too old, and I always liked my music loud.

You should do pictures to some songs, Joey had said. Visually represent them. See what plops out.

Lacking that, I could get kidnapped by gunmen and made a post-facto accessory to murder for a huge payoff I assumed was some kind of dirty money.

And see what plopped out.

I did not tell the abduction story to Joey. Not yet. I talked around it because telling Clavius had worked like a busted flush. But Joey's angle might be valuable if I waited for the right time. Never discount the opinion of someone who carries so much steel in his face. All that made me think of was my bullet. In my face.

There were other bullets just like it, and although I did not know it, they were looking for me right now.

In the time it took to hook up with the improbably named Willeford Grimhaven for drinks that elongated into dinner, I lost most of my loft. The door was ajar when I returned, and in spite of traffic neither I nor Joey would have left the door hanging open.

Every single framed picture—there were more than a hundred—had been smashed, or yanked down and *then* smashed, probably with the fireplace poker left behind in the crushed-ice fragments littering the floor. The glass tabletops, likewise. The furniture was overturned, legs up like snipered dead beasts. It was the first time I had ever seen the inside of my hard drive, now strung across the floor like freed guts. My swell stereo had been angrily eviscerated from its niche. The flat screen had become unlikely Cubist sculpture by being impaled on a plinth meant to hold an oil lamp. My shelf of antique cameras had been volleyballed into broken debris. The stainless steel fridge was lying on its side, its interior light still on. Splashes of red wine bloodied everything where hurled bottles had disintegrated. The whole place looked hit by an explosion or a passing hurricane, vandalized in the time it had taken me to order dessert.

When I lifted the house phone to notify the security desk, the line was dead.

Not a single residual sound. Whatever had transpired here was over. On my way to the darkroom—fearing the worst—I found a Post-It note from Joey on the floor. It read: Try Kitty Konnoisseur FFF Corp Long Beach later dude, J.

Okay—at least Joey had missed the party.

Outside the revolving door to the darkroom the red En-GAGED light was on. I could smell cigarette smoke.

"It looks worse than it is," said Gun Guy. "It only took about five minutes. Ten, tops."

Maybe he wanted his bullet back.

The darkroom seemed yet untouched, which meant he was saving it for something extra special. The red light could not pick out his gun; it was a black blob in his hand.

"Couldn't leave it, could you?" Gun Guy fairly snarled. "Had to poke your dick into it." He spoke like a bar drunk itching to start a brawl but I could see he was dead level, decanting his anger in clipped bursts.

"I was scared," I said. "You scared the—"

Boom. The cannonade of his single shot fairly blew all the air out of the darkroom, creating a vacuum in which I was deaf and trying to suck my own limbs into an armadillo ball in a full-body flinch. The intercom unit mounted next to my head came apart as though dropped six stories, puking plastic shrapnel. It was totally destroyed by the bullet; almost vaporized.

"Scared *now?*" he asked. "No—stay down on the floor. Mister Kimber says *stay.*"

He was lurking behind the Kaiser enlarger. Joey had left it unplugged again, so the swing-out lens carrier was the only thing between us. It swings by itself unless you clip it down. Gun Guy moved forward a step out of shadow, which was not an improvement.

"Do you have any idea how difficult my little missions are to set up?" he said. "The planning, the expenditure? You just sent all that swirling down the loo. People who pay me money not only want it back, they want to know how the things they needed got fucked by a simpering nobody like you. You just shit on my reputation. You don't do that. *You,* especially."

I started to object but Mister Kimber advised I stay mum.

"Pay attention, Elias: you don't have the right to just sail on as though nothing happened. You have not earned that right."

"What do you want?" My knee was bloody; gouged by frags on the floor.

"*Want?* I want to put a bullet in your skull, set fire to this little workshop, and go have a nice steak. That's too quick. Too easy."

He *wanted* to pound the bone marrow out of me, first.

After other forms of torture.

"You know the first time I shot a guy?" He blew a plume of smoke that coiled in the crimson light. "I was nervous. All that crap about seeing your victims' faces until you die; the wrongness of taking human life. I shot him right in the face with a wadcutter, point blank, so what he had could never be remembered as a *face,* at all. It looked like a dropped pan of lasagna. It felt *good* to put that fucker down and I liked the way it felt. I liked it so much, I couldn't wait to do it again. That was like twenty years ago. The only time I ever cut slack was when I used a smaller caliber once, to shut a baby up. So forget all that shit about talking to me to humanize yourself—I don't give a fuck. I like doing this too much. What I fucking *hate* is doing cleanup jobs for free. I didn't get *paid* enough to kill your ass. So I'm doing this because I like it."

I returned his glare, my eyes large and wet. *So do it already.* He wanted me to protest, to offer conditions, to grovel. I decided not to.

"*Why* did you do that?" he said. "I paid you. Everything was fine. When I kill dicks like you it's for a *reason,* and I want to know the reason."

He wasn't up for a moral debate; I could just tell. Whatever excuse I offered would only fan his flame more.

"Fine. Die stupid, like the rest of the world."

He was so intent on coming for me that he failed to see the lens carrier hanging in midair at head level. There is a flange that juts out for handling the unit when the lamp is hot. It's matte black like the rest of the carrier body. I could see it—thank my rhodopsin, my dark-adapted eye—but he could not. He walked right into it in the red gloom and the flange hit him in the face.

I sorted it out later. The flange must have gone straight into his left eye like the edge of a metal spatula. That's the only answer that can account for what happened next.

He howled. He dropped his gun. He sank to his knees clutching his face. The sounds he made were more of fast terror than simple pain. He screamed obscenities to vent his fear and the unfairness of it. Then he started groping in wide arcs, seeking to recover Mister Kimber, to latch onto me. He could not see either one.

I grabbed the gun by the still-warm barrel and scuttled backward out of the darkroom. He would hear the door turning; know what that meant.

"Goddammit, you sonofabitch motherfucker, no, no, no!"

The cruel universe was cheating him. It had been simple, direct. Until.

I threw a bolt to immobilize the door, which was glazed plastic veneer and fiberboard, to keep it lightweight. He could punch through it but maybe he would be stymied for one running moment.

I scrambled, still crab-walking, into the living area. Chunks of glass and metal embedded into my palms and I dropped the gun.

Point of order: the gun.

I could point it at him and shoot him and he would stop. Lasagna.

Was it loaded? Probably. Ready to fire? Who knew? Did it have a safety? Was it engaged? How did I switch it on or off? The thing seemed to weigh ten pounds. Was that normal?

I was still holding it by the barrel. Gun Guy was still hollering, wrestling his way through the darkroom door. Heavy thuds, as he started ramming through.

As I gripped the gun there was a tiny click and the clip fell out to clatter on the floor. There at the top of it, a dull-nosed bullet—cartridge—the same as the one I had been given. Had I just broken the gun? If you reinserted *this* thing into *that* little slot, did it still operate?

I snatched it back. Maybe I could just throw the bullets at him.

Maybe he would chew off his own arm to get out, sink his teeth in my throat, wrest the gun back, and shoot me anyway.

His fist came through the door paneling, violently dislodging a square chunk. It made me jump.

I found my legs and beat it for the front door.

Ricky at the desk downstairs could be swiftly advised to call in a SWAT team, K9 dogs, poison gas, armored support. I did not have to be here. Ricky, true to form, would not have heard or noticed anything amiss. I tried to remember whether I had tipped Ricky last Christmas. Yeah, better to warn Ricky to get out, too.

Because I had no idea when I'd be coming back.

I called Joey to warn him away from the loft. He met me at Bourgeois Pig on Franklin, a caffeine dive across the street from the Scientology Celebrity Center. I sat in the back where windows could not give me away. I had scooted north and east from the loft in a pattern similar to the knight's move in chess.

The inside of the Pig—the belly—was painted dark blue, and past the serving counter and a single pool table there was a back room entirely swathed in cheap East Indian draperies. Low tables, lots of pillows, like a downscale pasha's love tent. Couples frequently made out back here while getting caffeinated.

Nobody who works barista at Bourgeois Pig could tell you why it's called that. There are like-named cafés in the East Village, Chicago, even Kansas. I always thought the term—it's redundant, if you think about it—came from Clopin's "Charivari" in *The Hunchback of Notre Dame,* where he sings of Topsy Turvy Day, when the devil in us gets released.

I bolted a Mexican Coke from the bottle, for the sugar—it's made with real cane sugar, not the high-fructose corn syrup that perverted the taste of every soft drink ever made back in the 1970s. Now people did not know any better. That whole New Coke–Classic Coke fiasco had been an advertising dodge to smokescreen the transition.

Joey plunked down near me with his usual, a latte with four shots of espresso. "It figures," he said. "A coffeehouse in L.A. that doesn't serve actual coffee." It was true. You came here for rocket fuel, not pallid brown water.

"I want you to take this." I showed him the gun.

"Put that away!" He blanched like a school yard monitor who has just spotted a child molester. "Jesus, dude!" His eyes darted to test our space. There were no witnesses back here just now. "Okay . . . lemme see it."

With a maximum of dope-deal lookaround, he extracted the clip and pulled the top part of the weapon back. It locked and I could see the space inside. Then he closed it all up and concealed it in the cushions at his crotch.

"I can't take it, dude," he said. "It's beautiful but I can't. I got popped for concealed carry a couple of years ago. Just a shitty little junk gun, but I got nailed. Imagine me walking into a courtroom. It's a felony if they don't like you, a double misdemeanor if they do—'concealed weapon' *and* 'loaded gun.' I pulled a fine that made me broke and summary probation only because I didn't have any priors. Now, man . . . I mean, *shit.*"

I was still wrestling with the first part. "You were carrying around a, a—" I was afraid to say the word.

"Yeah. Don't ask. Flaming youth. Not now, no way." The votive light in the back room sparked glints off his piercings.

He had to ask, so I had to tell. His first question was, "Why didn't you just tell me in the first place?"

"Because I didn't know it was going to bounce back this hard. Listen, Joey, I'm going to need you to explain it to Clavius. To Grimhaven. To everybody on the dance card. Be vague. There are probably cops all over the building by now and I don't know what happened to this guy, but maybe he's in custody. That would be lucky for everyone but me, because he made me an accessory to a crime. I need to vanish for a while and nobody can know where."

"You mean like, lay low? Dude, you can stay at my place."

"No. Thanks, but no. No place predictable. Just until I sort my head out. Until I know whether that guy is not coming back again. If you go there, you might get hurt."

"What about Nasja?" he said.

"What about her?" Char was relatively safe in New York, at least for the next foreseeable few hours, and Clavius would have his entourage. I had not heard from Nasja since the photo shoot and subsequent roll-around.

"I tried calling her all day and nothing but voice mail," Joey said. "You know how she always calls back in like five minutes."

"What did you want Nasja for?" I knew almost the moment I asked.

"She was gonna help me with my little video project," Joey said, a bit sheepishly. "Hope that's okay. She found this shithole studio in Silverlake and got this fetish chick named Serpentina, who can't fucking act to save her soul, 'cos all's she done is these German things where she just licks her lips and sticks a high-heeled shoe into her cooch, right?"

"Too much information," I said.

"Naw, wait, it gets worse—the rigger supposed to tie her up gets stuck in traffic, and Serpentina or Snakerina or whatever her fake name is can't knot for sour owl shit, so Nasja said she'd do it and we're supposed to set a time, and she doesn't call back, which is why I'm here instead of downtown grinding Hi-8." His brain speed-shifted once more. "Oh, and sorry about the enlarger, dude."

"What do you mean?"

"The Kaiser. Halogen burned out. You know how we thought it was a short? Well, I replaced the bulb and that sucker was hot—too hot, like the fan wasn't working. So I forgot to plug it back in. It's too easy to walk into that thing in the dark."

"That quite possibly saved my life," I said.

He was still trying to wrap his mind around the intrigue of it all. "But where're you gonna be?"

"Tripp Bergin had a gig for me. Out of town. I think I

might take him up on it. But not as me. I tell you this so you'll know . . . but you don't know anything, okay? As far as you're concerned, I just took off."

"Copy that," Joey said. "But what do you need, like, a fake ID or shit like that?"

"I'll figure it out. I've got a lump of cash and I can get more on my cards as long as I do it tonight and don't use the cards again. Speaking of which . . ."

I handed him several thousand in a wadded roll. He didn't know where to stuff it; his crotch was occupied. He finally manhandled it into a coat pocket, as though afraid of being caught with it, his eyes brimming with more questions.

"No, don't," I said. "That's for you. I might call you; I don't know. Later. Just do this for me now and don't worry about the gun. Here." I indicated he should slide it back to me surreptitiously.

"Safety's on," he said. When Joey tries to look serious, he just looks like a tattooed madman. "Kimber. Goddamn, that's at least a thousand bucks worth of gun, right there. Funny, though."

"It's a funny gun?"

"Kimbers nearly always have grip safeties." He showed me. "Like here; you have to squeeze the grip before the gun will shoot. Looks like this one's been removed by somebody who knew what he was doing."

"You mean like by a gunsmith?"

"You hit the nail right out of the park."

The only thing I had noticed about the weapon was that it was stamped YONKERS, NEW YORK U.S.A. on the right-hand side where I supposed there should have been a serial number.

"*How* do you know this shit, Joey?"

"Misspent youth, like I said. You're sure you're okay with that thing?"

"I'm good. Now get out of here. Go, scoot, now. Okay?"

Quite without warning he gave me a fast embrace, one of

those manly hugs with three back pats exactly. "Take care of yourself, dude. Let me know what happens when it happens."

He rolled without further misty leave-takings.

It was the last time I saw Joey alive.

PART FOUR

CHAMBERS

I had Elias's framed print, *Targets #5,* with me when I checked out of the Beverly Hilton. I wanted to give it wall space in my Valley hide, where I could sit and stare at it if I wanted to. It was the first piece of artwork that I had ever acquired, not that I paid anything for it. Monetarily, at least.

Money, I had. Less ops budget and unforeseen expenses I scored a clear $94,000. Secretly I hoped the next job might involve gunfire, which would make Blackhawk and Bulldog eager to join up for reduced rates. More hazardous, yes, but I viewed this less as drawback and more as practice under combat conditions.

Then Mal Boyd called and my whole day slid straight down to hell. That's when the time delay of coded contacts and protocol can drive you buggy, waiting to find out what went wrong.

What a difference a few hours can make.

I was seated in my usual spot across his massive eating table, but Boyd was not eating. I had a Perrier to settle my stomach.

"I used to joke about my size," Boyd began, expecting me to shut up and listen. "I used to say things like 'mass is divine.' Even though my employees made little jests about it. 'How much does Mal Boyd eat?' they'd say. 'Lots—parking lots.' Or 'Mal Boyd eats for two but nobody has ever seen the other two, because he ate them.' Or 'Mal Boyd is dong his part to make okra and avocados extinct.' That sort of light humor. I tolerate it. I share in it, sometimes, because it promotes a better all-around working environment."

The light in his eyes pinpointed down to ball bearings, like those of a water moccasin hiding in bank mud. "What I do not tolerate is operations going public. Derailing. Becoming useless as leverage. What I do not tolerate is my best and brightest field men not doing their job. You owe me $150,000."

"Hold it," I said. "I did the goddamned job. I did it *twice*— one plan had to become another plan. You think just another gang of trigger-happy fuckwits could have finessed that?"

"At least they would have killed everyone,' Mal said sourly, "and we would not have this problem."

"No. Wrong. I fulfilled the contract. I delivered the photographs to you. You never said anything about the contractors putting them online, and the photographer did not have copies, negatives, or anything. I made sure of that. I had no way of knowing about the special paper, Mal—there was no way I could have checked that."

"Unless you had bothered to go online and take a look at the Clavius Web site," said Mal. "He's all about the legalities."

"I didn't know Elias and Clavius were connected."

He pinned me down again with the weight of his gaze. "You're *supposed* to know that sort of thing." In his mind he was still playing "find the fuckup." His glove-sized hand gravitated toward a plate of fried calamari and he munched a piece with an expression that said it tasted like dogshit.

"Doesn't that count as meat?" I said.

"It doesn't have a face," he said. His wayward eyebrows sampled the air for pheromonal lies. "You picked this photographer at random?"

"Yeah, outta thin air." Usually it was better that way. It left no associational links of logic or acquaintance . . . that is, every time but this one. It was the dread exception to the work rule. "Remember, Mal—when the photos were done, the deal was done. Now, if you want to make a *new* deal . . ." I was tired of being the principal's whacking toy.

"I understand why-the-photographer," said Mal. "You wanted first-generation images that could withstand examination by people who would insist they were doctored up."

"They have labs now that dissect photos on a fractal level. I wanted no evidence of any kind of photo manipulation."

"And in that you succeeded."

"But?" That big invisible "but" was hanging in the air between us. Mal thought it, so I voiced it.

He let out a huge sigh that might have filled a hot-air balloon. "The campaign was to be viral," he said, clipping his words as though biting them off. "When the prints failed to scan correctly, they used the negatives you supplied. The images were unstable. They turned to mud. I don't know how and don't really care. Nothing we gave them was usable. And within a day, it was all rendered worse than useless by the Internet, and that dead-pixel message thing used by your patsy."

I didn't know what Mal was talking about, so he showed me.

SHARPS SEX PHOTOS A COMPLETE FRAUD
BY BLACKMAILERS RED FLAG REPS
FOR DETAILS AND EVIDENCE

"Why, that pusillanimous little shitbird . . ." I can't say what shocked me more: the "secret message," or palpable evidence that Elias McCabe might have a dram of actual spine. I immediately cleared my dance card for a new date with him.

"We are in a very bad position, though that was clearly not your intention," Mal said. At least he had begun saying *we* instead of *me*. "As to the video, you really should have been more circumspect in your language. I was surprised, to put it mildly. Ambient security was one of your specialties, I thought."

"I didn't know his Russian whore had been making humpy tapes," I said.

"Fortunately for you, you are so backlit that it is difficult to distinguish you . . . for anyone who had never seen you before. I knew. Others will know. That makes it a risk to field you, which is another deficit for me, and as you know I dislike being in the red."

Cleanup or reparation, if there was any, was going to be completely on my head. That's what he was angling toward. He slid a digital blowup across the table. The picture was me, definitely. Ill-lit, fuzzy, but it would not save me in a lineup unless I had very expensive legal representation.

"That's the maximum enhancement and resolution of which the police are currently capable," Mal said.

"Mal, the whole idea was *not* to digitize the damned photos! If your backers hadn't rushed so fast to put them online— which I didn't know they were going to do—and if Elias Mc-Cabe hadn't planted that flag, the job would be solid. I did the job I was supposed to do."

"There is no job," Mal said, grimly considering curly fries drenched in non-meat chili. Everything would taste terrible to him until his difficulty was resolved. "The whole abortion has to go off the books. This never happened. It was a brain fart. I cannot be connected to it. Documentation connects you, therefore you cannot be connected to me. There are more serious questions."

"Wait a minute. What are you saying? Plain English."

"Our world is full of wannabe killers," Mal continued. "Every spermbag standing dreams of being a hit man. They do slapdash work for lousy money and usually leave a train wreck of incrimination behind them. That's why I hired you—for your excellence and professional standard. Part of your job is to relieve me of the burdens of exposure. Which you have done, for, what—?"

"Over a decade," I reminded him. A decade without a slip, until now.

"Yes. Which compels me to ask you about burnout."

A while back I had been kidding myself about being at the absolute peak of my ability—the perfect confluence of skill and experience. Now Mal Boyd was suggesting I had already passed my spoilage date. My throat stayed dry no matter how much of his Perrier I sipped. I pointedly replaced the tumbler on the table. I was getting angry.

"What'll it take, Mal?"

He sniffed. "Sharps is dead."

"Nobody will ever find him." Not unless they were browsing the pet food aisle at a Ralph's supermarket.

"Our leverage is useless. My backers are completely dissatisfied. Your cover has been outed. To run you at all now means a complete change in your identity which I will not underwrite. You left witnesses."

"Only because there was not supposed to be a death to witness," I said. "My crew is all solid. No leaks there."

"Except for the photographer, and now, anyone he has told. Instead of a viral campaign of discreditation, we now have an equally viral wild hair that only gets more toxic."

"Elias McCabe will not go to the police," I said. "He is a kept boy, a walking definition of denial."

"Not good enough. The police are, as usual, nuisance value; I'm not concerned with the police. I buy and sell them the way I eat grapes." So saying, he ate a grape as punctuation. *Crunch.* "I'm talking about *your* options. You don't seem to have any."

He had not called me "dear boy" once during the exchange. This was serious. I had to demonstrate that I was worthy or be put out to stud, which was a euphemism for early retirement achieved by moving my own death forward on the cosmic time line. I had to choose my next words with caution.

"I'll expunge the entire op for free," I said. "All loose ends."

It was the sort of thing he expected me to say. What were my options, other than falling on my own sword? He pretended to think it over.

"Even to the extent of your own crew?" he said.

"Their performance was solid, top to bottom," I said. "Don't punish them for my screwup."

"Don't tell me you've gone soft to the point where you would trust a prostitute, a drug addict? That doesn't say a lot to recommend your method."

It had worked just fine for me, for numerous operations, up until a day ago. Now every single factor would be dissected to death. I didn't like the idea of punching ticket on my own employees, but it was preferable to looking over my shoulder constantly for a new set of cowboys dispatched to punch mine.

It happens, sometimes.

"Mal," I said. "You want it done, it's done."

He took a huge bite of garlic bread and chewed it for a very long time.

And the moment I left, he must have picked up his phone and called Conover Tilly and Waddell Pindad—a.k.a. Blackhawk and Bulldog.

I drove directly to Ozzy Oslimov's rathole in Tarzana, jumping over the hill to the Valley on Coldwater Canyon and taking surface streets west. Tarzana is actually named for Tarzan, thanks to Edgar Rice Burroughs—there was a booklet you could get from the Chamber of Commerce outlining him as the township's first citizen. He originally owned the land, christened it Tarzana Ranch, then sold it to developers who kept the name, officializing it sometime in the late 1920s. The flats have a lot of good Persian restaurants and Armenian delis, and a few low-rent celebrities live "above the salt" in the foothills.

Ozzy answered his door in bare feet and a bathrobe, his pupils grandiose from pipe time. Apparently he had been sitting two feet away from a sixty-inch plasma screen, working his way through about two hundred TiVoed episodes of *Jeopardy!* I killed him just as Alex Trebek asked a buoyant female contestant about an important document of the thirteenth century that was obviously the Magna Carta. She got it wrong.

I wrapped Oz's head in a towel until he suffocated to unconsciousness, then I overdosed him with brown heroin, leaving cooking gear scattered around. He settled into death as though sleeping, without a kick. I lingered long enough to watch Double Jeopardy, but Final Jeopardy was about biblical trivia, so I left. Far more often than it should be, Final Jeopardy was about religious hoo-hah.

Targets #5 was in the backseat of my Mercedes E Coupe, the meatier V8 version with the seven-speed tranny, adaptive suspension, and bigger brakes, wheels, and tires than its siblings. Zero to sixty in five flat. This was my personal car, not a job car; no one knew this vehicle as having any connection to me, with the possible exception of the clerk at the gas stop on the 405 Freeway where I tanked up and bought smokes, and that did not matter because I saw to it that the plates were fluid, ever-changing.

I knew Ozzy's lair was not that far from my own Valley secret—my house in Hidden Hills—and I liked being able to accomplish two jobs with one trip. Los Angeles County is laid out so that everything is forty-five road minutes away from everything else, and nowhere is the sprawl more pronounced than in the Valley; people waste a lot of time and generate too much road rage from being in traffic for significant portions of their lives. That stress could eat you alive.

L.A. was as provincial and prejudicial as what block you're from in New York. Beverly Hills turned up its nose at West Hollywood, which would never deign to soil itself by visiting "the other side of the hill." Hollywood residents mocked the outbacks of Glendale and Pasadena while the denizens of Burbank, "safe" in their postwar crackerbox houses just on the other side of the mountain with the Hollywood sign, shunned

Hollywood as a war zone. Los Feliz residents almost never ventured downtown unless they had to go to traffic court. Koreatown and Thai Town and Little Armenia all had invisible walls. Venice and Santa Monica were universes distant.

"Hidden Hills" suggested seclusion, which charmed me (Shadow Hills was a close second). No streetlights, few sidewalks. It began as a gated community that overflowed. It courted a happy-family aesthetic but the real passion of the overwhelmingly white population was a fanatic devotion to minding its own business. Its last high-profile murder had been in the 1960s. When the whole Robert Blake thing went down he was arrested in Hidden Hills but the crime had been done in Studio City. People kept horses here. When the seasonal wildfires incinerate large tracts of the county, Hidden Hills was rarely in danger though you could always see the smoke from there.

I had scored a ranch-style as-is foreclosure with zero "curb appeal" at the terminus of a dark rural block, and had screened all windows while installing a perimeter and motion-detector system with the help of a pair of Afghani contractors who were in the States illegally. They also helped with the fortifications, safes, and a false wall of my own design. Nobody missed them.

I hung *Targets #5* above the cast limestone mantel over the brick fireplace. I never liked gas fireplaces for the same reason I disliked outdoor gas grills—pointless and too phony. Plus a real fireplace was terrific for burning shredded documents. I toasted Ozzy's memory with some smoky single-malt and sat down in a fat chenille recliner to contemplate the artwork, and to determine how best to ruin what was left of Elias McCabe's smug little life.

Just because your team was expendable doesn't mean you had to enjoy the idea, because it means gratuitously confronting your own mortality. In all likelihood, Mal Boyd was stewing in similar juices right now, because he was too practical not to consider ending me.

I hated to lose Cognac. Seriously. She did what was required, never panicked, and stayed wired tight. Just look at how unhesitatingly she fucked a dead guy for me. No funny faces, no goofy protest; she jumped on and rode that pony, took her fee, and decamped. Plus she was a sexual adept, and those were getting harder to find in a world where the most sordid perversions have gone white-bread and mainstream. Past scat and torture and slavery for real—not the precious pretend slavery of safe words and mistresses by the hour—there weren't many extremes that could compare with the imminence of death.

So I made sure she had a top-rail, expensive dinner—a real date. We had fabulous sex. Then I killed her and dumped her body in the Lake Hollywood Reservoir. Most of it, anyway.

I halved her carotid artery with the Boker Magnum and she bled out in minutes without a sound. I was quick and merciful. She slid down into the still black water minus her teeth and fingertips.

I wrote it off as rehearsal for the Russian chick.

I added another charge to the tab that Elias McCabe was going to pay. I did his Eastern Bloc fellatrix out of momentum and sheer spite.

Nasjandra "Nasja" Tarasova was most likely Ukrainian since her given first name was anything but Russian. She was probably culled from some Lugansk cattle call because she was "linguistically capable," a big plus in the world's second most popular sex destination after Thailand. Perhaps Clavius bought her at a bride auction. Apart from his sphere of influence, she was easy enough to vector upon because I had cloned the chip from Elias's cell phone. If you know how, anyone can do this in five seconds; I did it while Elias was shooting the commingling of the late Cognac with the late Dominic Sharps.

Nasja claimed to be married to Clavius—or maybe it was the other way around—but I could find no paper support for this. Out of his sphere she had a satellite time-share in Marina del Rey. The mail delivered there was all junk; apparently having the place was more important than using it. Tracking her own cell phone was kid stuff if you have the extra bucks and hours, and utilizing that as my own GPS told me she was headed there today. And not taking calls, it seemed.

I knocked, smiled, cut her main tubes and left her to slowly fill her clawfoot bathtub. She would read as an obvious suicide. She had ugly scars from multiple surgeries beneath her breasts, which I guessed were implant removal. Breast reduction is even uglier, especially when done by a hack, leaving a circle around the nipple, a vertical line, and fishhook curves that all resembled a cartoon anchor.

Her dreary ocean-view hole up was devoid of individuality to a degree I thought impossible. No snapshots, knickknacks, or personal gear more than six months old. All the clothing was new and from what I could see, yet unworn. Her shoe collection barely had scuffs on the soles. Once you subtracted the pictures (of her, every single one) the CPU data from her laptop hardly filled a thumb drive. Her nonpersonality had the telltales of someone on their way out. Clavius had finished with her, Elias was unenthusiastic, and she had a mirror cabinet full of prescription antidepression meds. Tailor-made. Nobody but nobody would check on this woman, here, until the smell hit.

I cut her with a straight razor I found still in its gift box (also in the medicine cabinet), and left the blade in her cooling hand. A tool is no better than the person wielding it, so I had to mess up the incisions to make them look tentative and unschooled, as though she had tried, hesitated, chickened out, tried again.

I was aware that I was saving the Kimber for my encounter with Elias. I had left him the cartridge; it was now a matter of form to finish up by gunfire. I should have just killed him straightaway with that bullet. But I had misjudged his diffidence. I should have gone with my gut feeling, and instead I gave him unearned slack because I actually liked his picture of the lady with her bits shot out.

Maybe I *was* losing my edge.

I showered and changed and dogged Elias's ass for most of the next day to scope his movements. He had some kind of business dinner that would hog-tie him for at least an hour, so that's when I went back to his loft.

Everything I saw there reminded me of my own failure. He was another guy who'd had it too soft for too long, and all he did was complain about it. It was time for Evil Me to let out the beast. I went utterly caveman on the whole place, working up a good clean aerobic sweat that would settle my pinging metabolism when the time came to show Elias how angry Mister Kimber could become.

After Elias, next stop was to find the blond chick, then maybe take out Clavius as well before confronting the more bitter problem of Blackhawk and Bulldog. Mal Boyd would only be impressed by a clean sweep, and perhaps some leniency would trickle down when he saw I would stop at nothing. No employee is so motivated as one who craves reinstatement.

And to be perfectly candid, the expungements performed thus far had my blood singing.

If the crimes were ever connected by the associations of the victims, media hysterics would think that a new serial killer was loose in the land. Yes, that was intentional.

But Mal had been right about another thing—my face was blown. There was the strong possibility of plastic surgery in my near future. I didn't feel like chilling out and opening a taco stand.

The break point is the moment where you are reminded that you and your team are completely expendable, I had thought not so long ago. But it takes the biggest balls of all to confront that reality and enact it methodically. I killed Ozzy and Cognac first so that I would not hesitate or falter for all the rest. Mal Boyd would be frankly astonished and maybe even do a spit-take. He would recant his impugnation of my professional ability. It would be fun to watch him consume such a big roasted crow, vegetarian or not.

I could smell Elias's welling panic as he entered his formerly sacrosanct space to find it raped. The worst thing about home invasion is the idea that strangers have moved through your space without your permission, which is why, as with rape, the feeling is one of violation. I wanted him to tour the destruction of his own life, then die in the darkroom, his dingy womb, the place where he had tried to play superspy.

Which is where he found me, right on cue, on my third cigarette, because he had run late by my clock.

"It looks worse than it is." I shrugged. "It only took about five minutes. Ten, tops."

Elias was already trying to back away but the revolving air-lock door to the darkroom did not permit that kind of retreat. I made sure he could see he had Mister Kimber's full attention in the lousy light.

Instantly, he tried to dissemble. To waffle. To yammer his way toward some lie that would disqualify him. So I put a slug in the wall next to his face and he folded up like a lawn chair. He was probably going to poop his pants again.

"Scared *now*?" I asked. His pre-death job was to listen, not talk.

Invigorating, it was, to slap his brain around with the complexities of setting up a job and pulling it off smoothly. Surely he could at least comprehend the idea of a job, a schedule, responsibilities.

"Wha-what d-d-do you want?" he stammered.

What I wanted was for him to stand up, face the hammer, and die like a man. Yeah—hold your breath.

"What I *want* is to put a bullet in your skull, set fire to this little workshop, and go have a nice steak." And that indeed was my basic plan for the rest of the evening.

But my verbal thrashing made me feel better. It was emotional vomit and I needed to purge, so why not purge all over pussy boy? He wasn't going to stay alive long enough to fret his bruised feelings. So I spun him a recollection about the first time

I ever killed a man for money. It felt good then, and it was going to feel even better now. Plus it drew him a picture that frightened him more—the remorseless taker of life, the stone-cold killer. His entire world was aloof and jaded, "mildly amused," stylishly unimpressed. I needed to see him care about something enough to fear it.

The real question was why had he gone and fucked it all up? I had only borrowed him, and paid for the inconvenience. That was standard in America—cash absolves. I returned him to where I got him in more or less intact condition. There was absolutely no sane reason for him to try to fox me.

But now he was going into shock. Some beaten animals fight to get in that one last slash or bite, to take a piece of their tormentor into the next world. Others just lie there tharn, resigned to more pain. That was Elias now, glassy-eyed, breathing shallowly, unresponsive. He was not going to utter another syllable.

Which pissed me off even more, that he would not protest.

I was so close I didn't need a two-handed combat grip on the Kimber—handguns were never originally intended to be shot that way, but everybody picks up bad habits from the movies. I needed my free hand to shield my own face from backspatter because hollow points tend to be unsubtle. I took one step forward. He was going to die gibbering in a puddle of his own shame.

Something penetrated my right eye in the dark.

There was a brilliant white flash of impact lightning inside my head and I instinctively jerked backward to prevent the offending protrusion from sinking deeper into my soft tissue. I dropped the gun. My flailing arms swept the counters clear as I fell on my ass, immediately thinking—

—*You just put your eye out.*

Panic did the rest.

I clutched my face and roared like a savage, more scared than hurt but the idea of what just happened nearly immobilized me with that fear, that pain. I had a lifelong terror of screwing up my eyes or hands. Now that terror flooded me, and made me a child again.

I could already feel some kind of wet dribble on my cheek.

I spread my wounded eye wide with my fingers, absurdly trying to *force* it to see. There's a blurry wash of vague color and knifing pain; when I looked at my fingers with my other eye—my *good* eye, I was already thinking—I saw dots of watery blood.

This was bad.

I couldn't wear a pirate patch or have a vacant hole in my face for the rest of my life.

I couldn't see Elias, couldn't find the gun, couldn't deal with the ominous lancets of pain in my head, and had to grope my way toward the door like a retard. My plug had been kicked out well and truly, surely as Achilles' own heel did him in.

I was thinking, *Ice pack wet cloths boiling water telephone. Kill him.*

I got halfway to my feet and my viscera plunged as though I was going to puke. I fell into the inner curve of the darkroom door—I had to deduce this by touch alone—and started punching my way through the fiberboard. Every time I blinked it felt as though a cube of razor-edged glass was buried in my eye. Something was flopping around beneath the lid. Sliced nerves, ripped cornea, whatever; it blanched the shit out of me to even consider it.

And Elias had gotten away, or was getting away. I couldn't see so I didn't know.

It felt better to vent my panic in violence, so I kicked my way through the rest of the darkroom door. I could already tell by the room ambience that Elias had fled. I had to evacuate this area myself, posthaste. Get out while not being able to see; retrace my entry path while blind.

I pawed out my mobile, trying to think of who to call. Mal Boyd? Not a good choice. Friends? I didn't have any.

I knew some doctors, dentists, veterinarians and busted paramedics, though, and I fought to imagine what keyboard patterns their numbers might form. 1-2-3 was A through F. The right-hand side of the keypad was 3-6-9-#.

I couldn't let anyone find me. I had to get out and far away. I couldn't see a damned thing.

Crouching in a pool of water, I knew not where, shivering with the *potential* for the damage done, I tried to punch numeric sequences on my mobile and got them wrong because I was incapable of watching what I was doing. I had to be self-sufficient in this. Finally I reached a guy who could get a doctor, off the record, and that doctor got a specialist. Circumstances and security dictated that I wait more than an hour to be picked up, and it was very possibly the worst hour of my life.

The first doctor was named Albright. I had used him once for a gunshot wound. My last memory was that he looked like Falstaff, from Shakespeare. Round spectacles, neat gray beard. I couldn't confirm any of this. But his voice sounded the way I remembered. He acted as though he had been treating this exact injury all night and I was gushingly thankful for his businesslike efficiency; his patter was intended to impress and reassure, and that racked great points with me because he said things I wanted to hear—past the horror show in my head, that is.

"There's a triangular flap of your cornea sticking out," he told me after droppering Alcaine into my eye to anesthetize it, then adding UV-sensitive fluid and locking my head into a metered steel gadget for a close-up inspection. All this was going to cost me a fortune, which is maybe why he was so avuncular.

The pain, the flinchy horror of my eyelid exacerbating the damage every time I blinked, magically evaporated for a few precious minutes. He tried packing my eye in antibiotic salve and taping a dressing over it. No go; the pressure was worse than the pain. He jabbed my arm with a tetanus shot and referred me immediately to an ophthalmologist whose office would not open for another eight hours. A third of a day ahead of me, during which I could barely see enough to stagger to the bathroom, gulp painkillers in an attempt to remain semi-comatose, and try, try not to think, every second, about tearing, blinking, or being practically blind.

Oh, and I couldn't lie down. I had to sit upright in a chair with my head between two pieces of duct-taped foam, and "try not to look at anything," and avoid blinking if I could, and seek counsel in my own thoughts for the next eight hours. Rising to recharge the curative gunk in my eye (from two bottles and one tube) proved a bit more difficult than Dr. Falstaff's prestidigitation; he just shot it in there and it somehow stayed. When I tried to do it, my eye teared instantly and flooded out all the medication. I finally smeared lines of ointment on my lower lid and dragged my upper lid over it to transport the salve onto the surface of my eye. I could see in the mirror that the sclera was totally crimson. The goo had the fringe benefit of cementing my eye shut, a microscopic blessing for which I was nonetheless thankful.

Falstaff planted me in his living room until the drop-off time. By now, if Elias had called the cavalry, policemen were checking the hospitals. I could not even tell you what Falstaff was wearing, or what his living room looked like.

I was extremely grateful to Dr. Falstaff, miracle worker, until the Alcaine wore off.

I was very tired—exhausted—but knew I'd never capture anything like sleep.

"The good news," as I was told by an impeccably manicured and groomed Dr. Frankenfelder in a significantly more upscale medical environment, "is that corneal tissue repairs comparatively rapidly."

The subdued light in his examination bay was much easier on my headache—my imagined pain, so I hear, from the trauma, because like the organic brain itself, the eyes possess no nerves to transmit pain signals. The "optic nerve" is a signal carrier akin to coaxial cable, uninterested in broadcasts not having to do with visual information. Hence soldiers on the battlefield could reinsert their own eyeballs, popped out under combat duress, feeling (one presumes) only such "imaginary" pain. My imagination had gotten pretty explicit, though.

I went ahead and asked for the bad news, since Dr. Frankenfelder was still waiting for his cue.

"The bad news is that until then, it's going to hurt like hell. I can bump up your scrip for painkillers, but it is vitally important that you do very little over the next couple of days. Apply the meds religiously. Be back in here day after tomorrow unless there's an emergency; you've got the number for that."

I just couldn't *see* it very well was all.

I blinked. *Flip-flop.* The protruding, pie-wedge shape of gouged cornea opened and closed its yawning mouth, feeling like a cockleburr trapped under my madly flapping eyelid. This boded to be a whole amusement park full 'o fun. Perhaps the pasty consistency of the antibiotic would help glue down this ocular hangnail?

Good news is always bad news for somebody else, and vice versa.

There was really nothing I could do apart from waiting for it to get better. Memory of the real world, prior to the accident, seemed a week or more distant, but it had only been a few agonizingly protracted hours.

Nervously, I asked if I'll have to wear glasses from now on.

"Maybe. We'll just have to wait and see."

Glasses. Goggles. A helmet with a visor. Anything, so long as it got better. From this point until the end of my life, I would be jumpier about objects near my head. Treasure your eyes, and for fuck's sake, take care of them. For this first time ever, there was a *difference* between my two eyes. Smoke, cold, allergies, pollution have all assumed an amplified status of threat. Just what I needed—a reason for being *more* paranoid.

The first day of sitting in my modified chair, like Frankenstein's monster waiting for a jump-start, completely sprung my back and neck. Add an orthopedist and masseuses to the menu. Poor old monster; nobody ever got his name right; he was hounded and abused; he wanted a girlfriend and *that* didn't work out; then he educated himself and kicked the ass of his own highborn "creator" . . . which is more than humankind has managed to date, as a species. The Frankenstein monster should be on our currency as an example to emulate.

He didn't *ask* to be here.

I stupidly attempted to go online and within seconds tears were coursing down my face (rinsing out the medication) and I won a very unimaginary migraine. I ate tasteless food and eliminated it. I became one of those stock-schlock brains in an aquarium, the kind in black-and-white movies that bitch about having nothing to do but *think*.

I had never felt so thoroughly neutralized, and would have willingly taken several bullets to avoid all this.

I requested and got enough powerful meds to keep me asleep through most of the waiting. There was literally nothing else I could do, except perhaps listen to music, or maybe books on audio. And wait. Wait for an entire week to pass as my laggard cornea tried to heal itself.

Frustrating, it was. I ate essentially nothing but soup and lost five pounds.

The sole advantage was that nobody knew I was in Hidden Hills, especially not Mal Boyd. Any attempt to track my cellular movement was doomed to be shunted into tail-chasing frustration, which is why you always sweep for bugs, especially after job meets.

If I contacted Mal Boyd now, he would merely advise that I keep as far from him as possible. If Mal Boyd held back and played it smart, he would begin to perceive my architectural pattern: Ozzy Oslimov overdosed, Cognac simply vanished (as hookers often do), and Nasja Tarasova had been a clear suicide. There were no connection among them, and the window for theorizing such links was shrinking.

Similarly, if Elias McCabe stuck to a fable about interlopers and murder, he would be nakedly available. If he ran, he would graduate to being a Person of Interest in Dominic Sharps's disappearance. It was very possible this here photographer fellow had just snapped and trashed his own place, say, prior to becoming a fugitive.

I wondered if Elias would wise up and cut his cellular leash as I reviewed the data from his phone chip—or tried to. My left eye kept hanging up like a shopping cart with a bumpy wheel. The only position that felt neutral came from rolling it upward all the way. Every movement of my good eye brought a parallel movement of its injured twin, and another stab of pain and phantom light, just as the doctors promised. If I tried to ignore this very real handicap I was adding wear and tear that would delay healing. Try it sometime: try looking at something with one eye while prohibiting the other from following. It cannot be done unless you were Marty Feldman, Kevin Pollak, or a chameleon.

Elias's top five contacts included the blond lady, CHAR, who had seen me, JOEY, his gofer, NASJA, who didn't matter anymore, somebody named BRADY, and at the top of the list, CLAVIUS.

Char and Clavius had left for New York, which did not put them high on the list of informants. Mal Boyd wanted a total slate wipe—his usual response to compromise, a downside I had never presented to him before—which meant Char had to be checked off, definitely, and Clavius, maybe.

Then there came Blackhawk and Bulldog, both utility sub-contractees. Three options there. Mal Boyd would have them killed independently. He would wait for me to kill them as part of our new deal. Or, most practically, he would aim us at one another, send them to kill me, and deal separately with the last man standing.

This disaster was still containable. I hoped Mal Boyd could see that. I hoped I would not have to take Blackhawk and Bulldog out, because they were essentially blameless.

I was functionally blind, but at least I was not hospitalized, IVed, and sedated. That's sitting duckery.

It was crazy-making. I could do nothing except watch time elapse, and I had people to kill.

Blackhawk and Bulldog showed up to kill me on the third day.

A word on the topic of security: Never assume you're safe.

I watched my exterior perimeter system go passive on the little readout screen as somebody de-lased it outside. Okay: my uninvited visitors were aware of the system and outfoxed it without a noise. They couldn't lick the motion sensors, though, and came in hot, front and rear, simultaneously.

How they found me . . . well, I just assumed they would.

I had to keep wiping tears away from my left eye. It was devilish, constantly baiting me. It acted completely normal one second, then went "chunky" the next—that's the only way I could describe it. It was hypersensitive to cold, allergens, air, every goddamned thing, responding like a jumpy point man sending his fear back to infect an entire patrol. I could not depend on my vision for split-second options. My answer was stealth and overkill.

Blackhawk worked frontally—of course—and Bulldog handled the rear. They each had a backup man with them, and I marveled at Mal Boyd's cold-bloodedness. My own guys had come to wax my sad crippled ass . . . and then get killed by their own backup. I wondered why Blackhawk and Bulldog had not seen this. Then again, I had no idea of what they had been told. A survivor might be informative if I could make the idea of a double cross clear. That would be sweet if I could manage the more urgent task, which was keeping my head on my own body.

God, they were good to watch. Both teams came in high-low with maximum coverage of unknown space, and they were immediately aware of the trespass sensors, which one man would fog on a clear signal from the other. Light by telltale light, I watched my sensor grid go to sleep.

Good thing I wasn't in the house. Not technically. I wasn't in any part of the house they could see.

The false wall built by my late Afghani contractors? It was right behind my gun safe, and it would stop a speeding car, so I could not be shot through it. The only vulnerable spot was a horizontal firing port, built so as to be invisible until actual gunfire had to commence as a last resort.

Which was pertinent since the backups both had shotguns—cut-down Benelli SuperNova smooth-bore shorties, from the ugly profile they presented. With no stocks, sights, lasers, or any real way to aim, they were abbreviated weapons strictly for close-quarter carnage, and I knew on discharge they'd kick like a kangaroo with a shock stick up its ass. Probably loaded with fletchettes encased in sabot rounds to spear right through body armor, which all of us were wearing.

I had a fish-eyed view of them via pinhole camera as they rallied in the living room near the fireplace after checking and clearing all suspect space. They seemed a bit befuddled, almost disappointed.

"Nice place," said Blackhawk, taking in the framed print of *Targets #5* above the fireplace. He gestured idly with the gun in his hand, which looked something like an old Beretta M951R because of the wooden front grip and extended mag. Another close-quarter lead-sprayer.

Bulldog had his trusty SIG. In concert with the shotgunners, they were going for a rapier-and-mace combo assault. "Gun safe," he said, pointing down the hall toward me, or rather, the room I was hiding behind.

"Booby-trapped, I bet," said Blackhawk.

"So?" said Bulldog, wiping his face. The first jittery flush brought on by their armed breach was past already. "Aren't you curious?"

"You open it, then."

In fact, there were stacks of cash in there. To attract the greedy eye long enough for a directional mine to detonate.

"Where's our boy?" said one of the shotgunners.

Blackhawk shrugged and pinched the bridge of his nose. "Maybe he went out for a burger. Maybe he's banging that high-priced whore, whats-her-name, Saki, Chardonnay . . ."

"Cognac," said Bulldog.

"Yeah, whatever. Well, we fucked up the security system already so it would be stupid to just leave for nothing. There any brew in the fridge?"

"I'm not going to open it. You can."

"Dog, it's a *fridge*. Jesus fucking christ."

Not bad—I should have thought of putting a mine in the fridge.

Together they drifted toward the kitchen. Blackhawk selected a bottle of Amber Bock and decapped it with his gun.

"Maybe this is sign," said Bulldog. "Nobody home."

"Ain't no sign," said Blackhawk after a long pull. "Maybe he's just flown. I would."

"It's not right, amigo."

"I hate it too, but it's him or us. Pick one now if you're not decided. This is a real nice kitchen, ain't it?"

"You thinking panic room?"

"Yup." Blackhawk finished the beer. "Gun safe."

Before, they had merely cracked the door for a sneak-and-peek. This time they came into the gun safe room ultra-hot. One of the shotgunners kicked the door full open for a clean field of fire.

That was my cue.

Sometimes the simplest mantraps were the best. One of my

favorites was a plain double-aught buck round lodged against a cement nail as a trigger. The shells were cut-downs, inside the door. The nails were in a parallel vertical row under thin spackle inside the wall. I had removed the doorstop so the door would impact the wall, and when it did, the array went off all at the same time. The topmost two shells caught the first shotgunner right in the head, splashing Blackhawk with brains and teeth. The disintegrating door provided extra shrapnel.

There's only one way to outdraw three expert men with automatic handguns and shotguns, and that is with a bigger shotgun.

My AA12—Atchisson Assault Shotgun—is a drum-fed nightmare that can spit five rounds per second on full auto, and my loads were Frag-12s, high-explosive antipersonnel armor-piercers with a burst radius of nine feet. Some maniac in Britain had modified a standard three-inch twelve-gauge shell to deploy tiny rocket fins for stabilization, arm three meters from the muzzle, and detonate on impact. The drum holds twenty of these bad boys, which should inspire your awe. Great if you have to pulp a roomful of terrorists through a window from a hundred yards away; not so great for close quarters, where there was a danger of eating your own frags . . . unless you have a specialist mess with the fusing and were prepared to deal with the consequences. My rounds came from the same fellow who custom-loaded the cartridges for my long-lost new Kimber. The AA12 has such a controlled kick that you can fire it one-handed, Arnie-style.

Or one-eyed.

I opened up on them chest-level, destroying the fake veneer on the gunport. The drum of explosive rounds took four seconds to empty, and after that, all three were down and the room was on fire.

I slid out from the panel behind the safe with an extinguisher.

Not only the gunsmoke, but the CO_2 fumes made my bad eye chunk up. The entire left side of my head felt abscessed and swollen. I finished putting out the little collateral fires and turned on the room air.

Their body armor shredded by tiny grenades instead of buckshot, the men were lewdly butterflied and voiding. Blackhawk was already dead. The second shotgunner was blinded and braying, pawing around, trying to find his face as his half-cooked innards aired out. I knew how he felt, not being able to see the end of his own life. Bulldog was similarly opened up and exsanguinating all over the place, but still dimly conscious.

"Nice place," he said, gagging on crimson froth. "Nice trick."

"Sorry, B-Dog. You know how it is."

"Yeah." His lungs were collapsing. "Do me a solid?" He made a thumb-and-forefinger pistol pointing at his own temple. The rest of his fingers were gone.

"No problem," I said, picking up his own SIG .40.

"Then shoot that fucker Boyd, right?" His eyes were fogging over. "He wants your ass."

"I gathered," I said, taking up his uninjured hand. He squeezed back. "Go easy, buddy."

Bulldog closed his eyes. I seated the SIG into his temple and fired once. I didn't care about the backspatter.

I was still holding his hand as he clicked off. My injured eye was dripping. Irritation or unfairness; you call it. Now my safe house had been violated. I was not ready to leave but it was time to go.

PART FIVE

ELIAS

*T*ime to go, time to go! There was an imp poking my brain with a fondue fork. All it ever said was *time to go.* I stared at the tiny photo of myself. Blue background, bad lighting, the way I'd look in a mugshot.

"Julian Hightower?" I said.

"Yeah," said Tripp Bergin. "That's you now."

"Where the hell did you get a gay name like Julian Hightower?" I said. Then I emptied the skinny Russian vodka glass, in memory. The vodka was subzero and caused an instant brain freeze. It made me crave an equally poisonous Eastern Bloc cigarette.

"Just watch the end credits of movies," said Tripp. "One from column A; one from column B. Match the first name of a stuntman with the last name of an accountant. Take a bit-parter from the beginning and a thank-you from the end. Voilà. Cheers."

We were warming a booth at LAX's Terminal 5, waiting for the New York flight to JFK. LAX is called that solely because airports came to need three-letter designations; before that it was just called "LA."

Tripp was one of those film industry lifers who wanted to demonstrate how aggressively he did not care about losing his hair. By this time next year he would be shaving his pate, and probably polishing it. He must have had four hundred gimme caps with assorted film logos on them—some on which he'd worked and others he'd been comped—and wore a different one every day. You could gauge the emotional temperature of a set by following Tripp's succession of hats. It was an obscure skill on the order of reading tarot cards. He wore action movie titles on heavy stunt days and jolly comedy titles when it was time for the martini (the last shot on a working day). If things were tense on a set he'd show up in a Merchant Ivory sort of cap, all business and no fooling around. If he was between jobs he'd don the title of his most recent biggest title, to remind people he'd worked on the best. He liked it when people saw his hat and asked him if he'd worked on *that* movie, so he could aw-shucks them.

Right now he wore a crew hat bearing the title *Confirmed Kill,* which did not make me feel any better. Big tent-pole action flick, big-time commitment, big paycheck. As it went on to break domestic box-office records last summer, the economy took its grand diarrheic dump, and Tripp was happy and proud to just keep working. They had not made crew caps for his latest venture as unit production manager. His job was making all the deals for below-the-line workers—you know, those people you don't care about when end credits unreel.

He had answered my call answering *his* call; that was the important and life-saving thing.

The film was called *Vengeance Is,* and as Tripp had predicted, its date for commencement of principal photography had been moved forward, which was why he had made me the original offer to be a unit photog—that is, the person who documents the production and captures the whole clanking machine in action, also responsible for the earliest approved press shots.

"No other cell phones, BlackBerries, crap like that?" Tripp asked, sticking to beer.

"Like you told me." I had called him from a pay phone. That's not as easy as it sounded, not in L.A., not anymore. Actual phone booths had faded with the previous century, and the surviving phone carrels usually looked as though they had barely made it through some apocalypse. People would not use them because they feared nasty diseases lurking on the handsets . . . if the handsets had not been ripped out. The proliferation of cell phones also helped the carrels become an endangered species. Blind people kept walking into them because they jutted out from walls and poles with no clue on ground level. Bums still checked them for change, religiously, but they were dying out.

Tripp had told me how my mobile phone could be turned against me, if people such as Gun Guy were interested in my location at any time. I had tossed mine in the reservoir, keeping the chip on his advice.

I had gotten rid of my watch, too. Most of my clothes were new.

The bulk of my ten large windfall from abetting the postmortem framing of Dominic Sharps had been eaten up by new camera gear. I needed extra-heavy straps, because I would be wearing cameras virtually all day. I needed a blimp—a soundproof box to encase the camera and make it noiseless during a take. I needed a digital rig that could shoot photos as RAW files, which gobbled up computer memory on the order of something like three hundred megabytes per picture. This necessitated a new laptop to log and coordinate each day's picture file. Tripp got me a single-owner, aluminum unibody Mac-Book, the kind with the wide screen. I think he handed it down in order to upgrade his own laptop, but it was certainly up to the job.

"Do I really have to add, no e-mail?" he said. "The laptop ISP will come up as the production office if anybody checks it, but do me a favor and don't start a blog or send kissy notes to old girlfriends or something. Every single time you go online you start leaving footprints. No personal shit."

"What about as Julian Hightower?" I said. "Not as—you know, the Artist Formerly Known as Me?"

"You might slip up. What are you, an expert at deep cover?

No. The stuff online is just too tempting; it's too easy to make one wrong click. What I told you about the cell phone's GPS capacity? That goes double for the laptop."

He was undeniably right. Gun Guy had the resources to sniff out a pseudonym if he spotted anything suspicious. I had a good cold trail working and no desire to wax cute.

"Oh, and lose the whiskers—it's the twenty-first century."

I almost rankled. But Tripp was correct. It was the cheapest, quickest change to my face that I could affect.

"How do I get paid?"

"You get a check every week from payroll," He told me. "Per diem, expenses, processing, all that happy crappy. If you need an advance I'll spot you."

He had paid for the fake ID, too. His idea.

"Listen, I've had to cheat documentation a million times," he said. "You always get actors with visa problems, or somebody's working off the books, or union bullshit. I've got access to the best propmakers and digital manipulation guys in the world; they do this stuff for laughs on their coffee break. Press passes, IA permits, all access, secret agent shit." Half an hour after he told me this he was sitting me down at a Kinko's for a passport photo featuring my new hairless face.

"It works," said Tripp. "Thank god you've got a jawline."

My chin and upper lip felt naked and sensitive. They were actually a lighter shade than the rest of my face, from what little sun exposure I did get. I saw my father's chin on my face. Thanks, Dad. When he had been my age now, he had already been daydreaming about retirement, a good pension. He died still railing against the way President Reagan had fucked over legitimate war vets.

Tripp had specified the same blue background the California DMV used. Then he told me to lay low at my hotel until he could work his magic.

The driver's license he provided was letter-perfect down to the hologram, UV stamp, bar code, and bogus Social Security number, which I think he had matched with an obituary record somewhere. Dead people received government checks all the time. Another finesse matched my new name to the number and as Tripp said, voilà, I was a wage earner.

A dead wage earner, fittingly. Just like the nice Korean ladies with new Chinese husbands.

That was miles better than being a dead fashion photographer.

Light-years better than dying in my own darkroom by being shot in the face by Gun Guy with a slug so powerful I would see pieces of my head raining down before my consciousness evaporated.

I could become Julian Hightower *voilà tout*.

Nasja's fate was all the encouragement I needed.

After Joey left me at the Bourgeois Pig, I was afraid to walk outside. The average citizen appears on more than two hundred surveillance cameras in L.A. on a normal day, and there was little need for Big Brother now that your fellow civilians would rat you out so willingly. Everybody photographed everything now, and the life of the art was leaking slowly away while I tried to stand in defiance of that attrition. I was becoming a crumbling relic of the previous century.

But my nondigital, noncomputerized, nonmodern enlarger had saved my life, with Joey's help. He and I ducked around the wayward lens carrier all the time; it was second nature even in the dark.

I sincerely hoped Gun Guy had gouged his fucking eye out. That way, I could be on the lookout for somebody with an eye patch. My equipment, the tools of my trade, had spared me.

Allowed me to run.

I kept thinking of Dominic Sharps, ground up into kitty kibble, probably at a plant in Long Beach. Of how I could have just used standard photo print paper, just let it all ride, and try to be a false do-gooder some other less fatal way. It made me avoid my own countenance in the mirror. Call it phony bravado or a miniscule gesture of defiance, but what I had done was mine, and I owned it, and it had returned to correct me. I had seen Gun Guy play angry to keep me in line, then glimpsed his genuine anger, then recoiled from his nuclear bellowing rage. I did not want to linger for what came next in his escalation.

I had lost Char and now, my place. Clavius had unmasked as my master manipulator without a care. Think about how wonderful that would make you feel about yourself. I had been slacking off and drugging myself into the robot zone just to get by. Emerson said the reason we lie is because the truth hurts so much. My truths had roosted at great cost.

Why *not* change the channel?

Here's an alternate scenario: I report to the authorities my part in the Dominic Sharps case and then sit, and wait, and rot, in protective custody at best, for $50,000-per-year cops to locate a man whose specialty is not being seen.

Or: I get implicated and wind up eating mushy food and dodging dicks in jail as my entire professional standing slowly turns to sewage, with Clavius's help.

Or: I do nothing and sit holding Gun Guy's weapon, waiting for him to return again so we can have a true standoff, all Western. Gee, guess who would win?

I wanted the freedom of being Julian Hightower, who had no such encumbrances. Hell, I craved it.

But the breaking point was my last-minute decision to go to Nasja's place in the Marina. Surely Gun Guy's knowledge of her had only encompassed a few seconds while playing Peeping Tom. Surely his web was not cast so far.

It made me even more of a cad that I had a key.

I tried to look back on all this and convince myself I had the best of motivations—apart from self-preservation, the topmost one. The one I strayed from by not minding my own business, which rule I broke one more time by going to Nasja's with the intent to do a right thing.

I wanted to warn her about Clavius, tell her whatever she did not already know. Advise her against the bad men loose in our world. Maybe cadge one more night on her sofa or in her bed. Just for a caesura, a moment of calm.

The air inside her place was tight with wrongdoing.

I found her dead in her own bathtub, eyes rolled up, arteries cleaved, floating in a sea of red water.

I vomited, just like they do too often now in the movies for realism's sake. I mean, who wants to watch that, really? I missed the toilet, which was closed. Then I entertained a fleeting fantasy about being implicated by DNA or something in my own throwup. I mopped up with her Calvin Klein Lush towels and took them with me when I left, remanding them to a trash bin at a fried chicken place.

Then I threw away my cell phone, spent twenty minutes trying to find a grungy pay phone, and called Tripp to tell him I was phoneless, per his advice. I tried to hide the panic in my voice as I asked him what was next.

Poor Nasja. I was probably the last person she'd had sex with.

It turns out that Tripp had sold me extra hard to the director of *Vengeance Is,* likening me to a Rolls-Royce instead of mere rental. One of his responsibilities was the procurement of the unit photographer. The guy who had signed on wound up in the hospital getting emergency LASIK surgery on exactly the worst dates for the production. But however I could help Tripp was nothing compared to the favor he was doing me, and once I told him a bit more about my predicament, he fairly lit up with the chance to do intrigue.

"We're in the last week of prep, and I really shouldn't be playing hooky," Tripp said. His bright crimson cap featured an embroidered logo for a movie called *Spyscope.* "Fortunately the other guy was there for preproduction, and got shots of the sets being built and the first costume fittings for the actors. We're covered, just barely."

The first two weeks of shooting were in New York City—the real one, not Toronto. Then there came what Tripp called a "company move" to Arizona for four more weeks. As typical with the madhouse musical chairs of moviemaking, the last scenes in the script were the first to shoot since they were in and around Manhattan, front-loading the project with permits, crowd control, and the usual baksheesh needed for shooting exteriors in a densely populated urban environment that had a valuable and unique recognition factor. The Arizona part was more about interiors (sets on soundstages, for the New York part) and exteriors without the whirligig crush of Big Apple streets.

At first I holed up in a beach hotel on the Pacific Coast Highway—never mind which one. The cash I pulled down from my credit cards in the one-day window before I shredded them had helped. I called Tripp from my barely working pay phone every day at 5:00 P.M. EST. I developed a relationship with that pay phone. It became my mute ally, an old soldier still standing, perhaps to be uprooted after it had served me.

Tripp's sense of obligation and friendship was grounded in my old life. He had lived in my loft for a month while his third marriage fell apart on account of his wife's enthusiastic search to find her inner lesbian. Hayley had hit age forty and was desperately trying to hone a new edge to prove she was still part of the world, and her own woman. Too desperately. Whatever. She had treated Tripp like a predictably dull life choice and dumped him as though he were the jerk. It was immature and pointless, compounded by the fact that Tripp actually loved her.

Ouch. This sounded uncomfortably familiar.

I also did my best to matchmake Tripp with a few of the less-toxic models I knew, which sounded oxymoronic. In return for their version of kindness, a couple of them reaped walk-on bits, day player gigs, and one of them, Inocencia Sanchez, lasted nearly six months. Inocencia was doing Bloomingdale's spreads now.

Tripp had a single off day as general of his multilimbed production juggernaut, and he used it to fly out and run a quick face-to-face with me in hopes of getting the true story, the one not for public consumption. The unrated cut. Once I filled him in, he demonstrated how involved he was by extending his stay—distance is the best excuse of all, and can work miracles—long enough to work out the alternate identity scam, and now we were both headed back east.

I had forgotten I had friends of this caliber.

As Joey might have said, it was a mute point.

Time to go, time to go.

I worried more about Joey than any other person on the West Coast. I hoped his street smarts would keep him clear of the firing line, if Gun Guy chose to probe that deeply or become that insanely petty. I hoped my entire catastrophe passed him by like a jet skimming perilously close to the earth before crashing, changing Joey's life no more than a tragic news item from a foreign country. If I could get through the next six weeks and make a properly professional showing of myself, then perhaps I could risk a single contact with him to find out whether any flaming debris had landed near him.

Calling him right now was against my new set of life rules.

Then there was the puzzler of the gun. I had it and Gun Guy did not, which was another motivation probably sufficient to expedite my death. I tried to dispose of it like the cell phone, but it lingered in my grasp until I began to enjoy the weight and heft of it; its implicit guarantee of protection against harm. It was somehow karmically wrong to merely abandon it. Now I understood the mass and lure of killing hardware, the easy seduction of its mechanics. This was a thing designed to extend your reach and knock down those who would imperil you. And it was a lot better reminder than a mere bullet, which I had taken to keeping in my pocket.

I know—stupid, wrong, dumb. File a lawsuit if you care.

I found an online diagram and after several false tries, I

succeeded in making the Kimber's two main sections come apart—the slide and the frame. Push a release and it's done, not dissimilar to breaking down a camera for cleaning. The clip with the bullets was a third yet equal part. That came out when you pressed a little button on the right side of the handgrip. With the slide off, you could remove the mainspring and the barrel. The online guide said you should change the barrel every 800 rounds but I was not sure what that meant. There was no need to take out the spring or the barrel. I just wanted to break the weapon down into smaller pieces so I could adequately conceal it among my camera gear, which totaled two large pro cases I could safely check. I always used Pelicans, which were airtight and waterproof, like little indestructible safes on wheels. Practically everything in them looked like a weapon, and Tripp and I had the added sanction of special dispensation for movie folks in a hurry.

I was especially proud of the way I hid the ammunition.

The cartridges were coated in some kind of sealant. During coffee at an internet pit stop with rental consoles, I found out that such lacquered ammo can prevent bomb dogs from sniffing the gunpowder. With a bit of coaxing the bullets fit into a tube support for the case feet (if you have seen *From Russia with Love* you know what I'm talking about; that's where I got the inspiration). They would not rattle around and were now invisible to X-ray. They totaled nine; Gun Guy had come packing a full magazine plus one in the chamber of the Kimber. The argot was "nine is fine." He had fired that bonus round at me in the darkroom. I replaced it with my souvenir slug, preserving an oddly pleasant symmetry.

Smuggling an undeclared firearm onto an airplane? I was already learning new skills. To get caught with the gun inside Manhattan would be a pure felony. Hell, even having the bullet in my pocket there was a crime. But I needed and liked the sense of the weapon and ammo near to hand. I chose not to tell Tripp about it. Mine; private.

The outright relief of leaving L.A. behind me buffered my head as though an anvil had just been lifted away. I got drunk on the flight and slept through most of it. Waking up on the other side of the country, despite the wrongness of the hour, was very much like rousing from a bad dream.

When I first met Andrew Collier, he was pointing a gun in my direction. Actually, he was staring through the empty chambers of the cylinder on a formidable revolver. At least it was unloaded.

Collier was British, pink-cheeked, and tousle-haired, his manner that of a big kid set loose to play in the fields of celluloid. He resembled an aging Beatle. The production offices for the New York leg of *Vengeance Is* were set up in a building between the Battery Maritime structure and East River Park. The director's sanctum was three times bigger than it needed to be and everything was crowded toward one busywork corner with his desk as the hub. None of the chairs matched. Production drawings and photographs were pinned and Blu-Tacked to the walls but with no sense of organization because everybody was set to vacate in two weeks. It was typical for an on-site combat office.

"Colt Navy .36, converted from cap and ball to a revolver," Collier said proudly. "Look at this thing. It's almost an Expressionist gun."

"Is this a Western?" I said after Tripp had introduced us. I could not tell if the pistol was real, or a prop. Today Tripp's blue cap had an iron-on logo for *Covert Reprisals*.

"No genre," Collier said with an air of rehearsed speech. "If you like, an urban Western crossover. I wanted no fixed time or place; I tried not to have any character make conventional phone calls or watch television."

"Drive the product placement folks bananas," said Tripp, who had changed into the workwear I would see on him for the entire shoot: jogging duds, an old garrison belt adangle with a fanny pack, a sling for his water bottle and a holster for his walkie, which was wired to a headset I never saw him without. And of course, one of his bazillion crew hats.

"Yes, I wanted all our brand names to be invented," said Collier. "Labels, signage, that sort of thing. Makes for a better created reality."

Collier struck me as the sort of fellow who had all his day wear tailored, but had fourteen identical sets racked in a closet somewhere so it always looked like he was wearing the same clothes, with minor variations in pastel tones. A lot of "creatives" affected this shortcut system attributed to, I believe, Albert Einstein: don't squander valuable thought or waste time by selecting an ensemble. Yet Collier's dunnage was another peculiar form of rank: the director was always well-dressed, but not overdressed, his starched cuffs folded to mid-forearm to indicate he was already ready to work.

I smiled. This would drive fashion hounds berserk. I had entered a different realm for sure.

Yet much of the basic playbook was the same. The schedule was the gang boss of all that unfolded. There was never enough time for anything. You had to be nimble enough to adapt and improvise on the spot. Hot lights, cranky subjects, and an eternity of waiting for the right light or makeup rescues followed by activity that was often fast and frantic. As Tripp said, you have to be able to jump out of the chopper and start shooting, hence the term "run and gun."

Vengeance Is was run and gun because the studio had amputated a week off the original shooting schedule for budgetary reasons, which meant Tripp had to hustle in order to make the six-day weeks add up. Two of his most important jobs involved Gordo, his highly caffeinated first assistant director: at the end of each day, they had to somehow juggle and rejigger the schedule to fit the *next* day of madness, and they worked in concert to keep the lurking producers off Collier's back so something useful might actually be shot. The whole system was elegant and hair-triggered; one had to account for every variable from runaway egos to unforecast rain.

I was introduced to roughly seventy people over the next twelve hours. I did not have a hope in hell of remembering every crew name when I was having trouble remembering my own.

Gordo's job description was more akin to master sergeant or ramrod on a cattle drive. Just look for the person on the set with the bullhorn, the khaki shorts, and the climbing boots, and that will usually be the first AD, especially if he or she is yelling into the bullhorn or requesting a "20" (seeking some crew member's location) on a walkie.

In Gordo's company Tripp and I trooped around the production offices and met everybody from the DP to Crafty. The former was Konstantin Vendredi, the cinematographer, the guy who shoots the movie. I resisted calling him DP for director of photography because of Joey's whole double-penetration anecdote. The latter was Molly Bellerose, reigning diva of craft services—the snack-and-drink watering hole that is the second-most valuable thing to locate on an active set, after the nearest restroom. To a person the crew all greeted me warmly—as Julian Hightower—and eyed my camera with suspicion. Tripp had just finished a dustup with the fellow responsible for video documentation, whose name always slipped me; Collier did not want him on the set during shooting and the faraway gods of executive production had decreed otherwise.

Video documentarian, I learned from Tripp, was possibly the lowest form of life on a film set, below even the screenwriter . . . practically under the floor. This hapless individual was charged with intruding camera-first into every aspect of filming on behalf of the eventual DVD making-of supplements. Nobody really liked him yet everybody tolerated him as an inevitable engine of relentless surveillance. Nobody wanted to get caught on tape disparaging work conditions on tough days or bitching about another crew member. Everybody tried to pretend a lens was not always in their face—yet, months later, they got irritated if they could not spot themselves in the behind-the-scenes footage. One frequent accusation was that the guy with the roving camera was actually a spy for the higher-ups. All I knew was that I did not wish to inadvertently appear on some podcast done for an online diary about *Vengeance Is,* which would be counterproductive.

So naturally it fell to me to share office space with this fellow.

Then, as Tripp had to catch up from going AWOL, I was remanded to my hotel with a copy of the screenplay that was joyous with multicolored revision pages.

I hated screenplays. There's a lot of argument over whether their manufacture constituted an art or a craft, similar to the artistic caveats targeted at photography. The debate held that pictures and movies (hence, moving pictures) were documentation, as opposed to paintings and prose, which were supposed more stylistically representative. The conflict was basically good for wasting time in a coffeehouse if you're an idiot college student. Making a living at anything remotely defined as an art form could straighten your priorities out superquick.

A script is essentially a blueprint for visual storytelling— without any pictures. The agreement between scenarist and reader is to imagine angles, tone, whether characters have distinguishing marks or not. A lot of people can't suspend disbelief in a fictional movie narrative anymore, not even when all the work is done for them. Their capacity for dreaming awake has become that atrophied. The lack of visual augmentation in any film script irritates me in a bemused way. At the same time, I knew I was being asked to help interpret a production visually, to convey my own sense of attitude and composition in regard to a larger work controlled by outside forces. It was like being a war correspondent on some foreign front. My job here was to file dispatches and fabricate a historical record; not a notion that charmed me. But I was able to enjoy the sense of disengagement from my previous life as Elias, that poor dope still stuck in the merry-go-round clusterfuck that was the world of Clavius.

Vengeance Is had to do with a sheriff in an Arizona frontier town at the turn of the last century. He gets lynched by bad guys who kill his wife and daughter. As he strangles on the hanging tree, the boss (a dapper J.F.K. type) shows up astride a mule and tricks the sheriff into selling his soul for a shot at revenge. A hot, unpleasant century passes in hell, after which the devil guy calls our hero up out of the pit to make another proposition: a gang of five super-badasses have escaped. Our guy's job is to round them up "topside," in present-day New York, using special bullets supplied by Hell's Armorer, one for each bad guy in the cylinder of our guy's modified Navy Colt six-shooter. If our protagonist succeeds, he gets his family back. He is monitored long distance by a vulture who happened to be on the hanging tree where he originally died—the eyes and ears of the boss on earth.

As Tripp pointed out to me, vultures are carrion eaters. They only go after what's dead.

Naturally, Collier wanted to know what I thought of the script.

"So you could call this a horror movie?" I asked, while shadowing him around an airplane hangar in New Jersey, then an office building with a vacant floor in the lower Thirties—a structure that would be condemned after filming. I nabbed about two hundred shots of Collier pointing at things. Peeling paint on a wall. Old architecture for a backdrop the crew would not have to build. Framable space.

"God, no," he said. "Don't even *say* that word. It has, shall we say, a supernatural element. Like *Field of Dreams*."

"So, *Field of Dreams* with a high body count and gunfights, then."

"No, more like *Heaven Can Wait*"—he grinned evilly—"with a lot of gunfights. Call it a meta-Western if you like."

"Why not a horror movie?" I enumerated from my fast over-view of the story as I understood it. "Guy goes to hell, comes back, there's a devil, there's escapees with supernatural powers, there's zombies."

"Zombies?" Collier seemed genuinely taken aback. He was incredibly camera-aware and always froze his pose when he thought he looked good. I nailed him with that observation, though, and captured the first photo of him that I really wanted.

"Yeah, at the end, when the bad guy's crew rises from their graves at Boot Hill."

He stopped and blinked several times. "You actually read the script to the end?"

"Wasn't I supposed to?" Snap. Move. Focus. Snap.

"Unusual," he said, shaking his head. "That puts you ahead of most of the crew. Anyway, in our film they're not really zombies. Not *zombie*-zombies, anyway."

I had heard Tripp employ this weird real-world, fake-world dichotomy. For a night shot, he'd ask is it night or is it *night*-night? For rainfall, is it rain or is it *rain*-rain? For fake-real or for real-real? It made everyone sound like a five-year-old speaking code only other five-year-olds could register.

"Most horror films are . . . horrible," Collier said. He was pleased with that. You could see him storing it for later sound-bite use. "Call it a mainstream film with perhaps a horrific ele-ment." He was apparently changing his mind about the bones of his movie every four minutes.

He was eager and nervous, manic and resigned all at once. He wanted to get past the first shoot day. He needed to plant that flag, get rolling, because the entire cast and crew comple-ment would not settle into any kind of routine for the first six days or so. He had to marshal them through the wear-in pe-riod. He had to spend more time pop quizzing the actors, since the end of the film would shoot first. Tripp was somewhere knocking his brains out right now, so they could shoot scenes with the most warm bodies early and the fewest later. Sort out how much time to spend on each location and set, as I said, and prefigure backups if anything upset the plan. This would all wind up on a document called "day out of days," I learned, as in "Day 1 out of 36 Days," not counting pickups, second units, or overshoots.

"No, not horror, at all." His British was showing as he said "atoll." "I mean, we've got Mason Stone." He said that as though it was the cure-all answer to everything.

Mason Stone was a piece of work. His hairdresser got screen credit. His personal trainer got credit. He had his own chef, his own wardrobe lady, four assistants, a hovering minion of private security, and on location he lived in a two-story, trilevel "mobile estate" designed by Ron Anderson. Built around an eighteen-wheel rig, this ultimate "trailer" provided 1,200 square feet of living space that included a removable state-of-the-art recording studio, a lounge that could seat twenty, a fold-out exterior deck (really), a master bedroom, a baby playroom, a lush gallery, and marbled bathroom all with electric-thermal privacy glass. Flat screens everywhere. Double-soundproofed, satellite-capable, and a bullet- and bomb-proof Cocoon security module.

The very rich are "different" than you or me, as Fitzgerald wrote.

But since he was visiting New York, Stone was also billeted crow's nest–high in the Jumeirah Essex House, with a million-dollar view of Central Park South.

Mason Stone had hair implants, and I needed to figure out a way to shoot close-ups that did not brag this fact to the universe. Mason Stone had plastic surgery scars, fine as threadlines, that I had to decide how to deal with in high-def. He had a clause in his contract that prohibited my taking pictures of him when he was wearing his glasses, and another in his general deal memo that specified that no one, but nobody, was to interview his hairdresser, trainer, chef, wardrobe lady, on-call physician, analyst, bodyguards . . . or photographer. While the lens rarely forgives, I had to pretend to be forgiving.

Mason Stone was half a decade away from sixty years, and his leading lady, Artesia Savoy, was not even half his age.

(You may recollect Artesia's first movie, *Kiss in the Dark* [2001]. She was the sassy cousin. I remember her earlier, actual debut before a camera—as Cherry Whip, in a video extrava-ganza titled *Bungholers 6* [1998], but the supermarket rags had yet to sniff out this tidbit for point-of-purchase consumption. Neither had the dirty-drawers Web sites twigged. So far.)

Mason Stone was nearly fifteen years older than me, and I could've passed him off as my little brother.

Mason Stone had weathered hits, flops, strikes, scandal, ad-diction and recovery, celebrity marriage and tabloid divorce. He once tried to diversify with a show-off directing debut: a cash-stupid vanity project for which he actually *sang* the title theme. After his one-and-only directorial flagship crashed and burned like the *Hindenburg,* he was now comfortably reen-sconced in his primary duty to society—leading man of the cinema, one of the ten people in the movie industry with the power to help green-light a project by signing on the line. A "tent-pole" star who had successfully evolved from winsome to craggy without losing his audience. When in the public eye he was gracious and giving; at his rates, he could afford a faux interest in commoners. He was not bad or evil. He was the sort of working actor who inspires wannabes to sign up for drama classes, so don't ask if he owned a considerable ego. In the book of Mason Stone, every paragraph began with the words "Mason Stone."

A phalanx of PAs—production assistants, like Joey—deflected diversions and held at bay eager beavers who all just need a tiny piece of Mason, right this minute, so I was able to fire off some pretty decent frames of him posed in costume against elements of the lynching tree set built outside the airplane hangar in

Jersey, close to the Meadowlands. That is, after Mason waved away his bodyguard, who pricked up like a pit bull on my approach. I got some up-angles that were shadowed a bit ostentatiously, but for this movie, melodrama played. Later I found out the setting sun threw an interesting glint into his left eye in the last shot we grabbed by the tree, which was a gypsum-and-plaster fake, apparently from a haunted house yard sale. Mason Stone bid adieu and promptly forgot my name when an effects assistant stopped by with what looked like an enormous stuffed vulture to chock into the tree. It wasn't dead or taxidermied but was instead fabricated by the makeup department, which promptly nicknamed their creation "Lurch." The faux vulture was used for setups and focus-pulling; it looked dopey and I opted not to use it.

Later I got to meet several real vultures, trained—insofar as scavengers could be "trained"—to food-based commands by a genial guy named Hunnicutt who told me that at one point, one of these monsters would soar into frame and land right on Mason Stone's shoulder without clawing his star face off or pecking out his eyes for hors d'oeuvres. I tried to imagine the rehearsals. It would be like trying not to flinch while a helicopter tries for a two point on your shoulder. None for me, thanks. They trained falcons; I guessed they could train vultures. Hunnicutt had three, a hero and two backup birds in their own spacious travel caddies. Like wardrobe and props, even the scavengers in this movie came in multiples.

The optical and digital effects team had the entire movie already on an animatic, prearranging scenes that had not been shot yet. An animatic is basically a moving storyboard, like a cartoon, that can impart a crude sense of movement within a shot and changing camera angles. These omnipresent keyboard jockeys also had lockdown plates of the bigger exterior Arizona sets—like the period Western town—they could factor into their compositions. They had a wireframe model of the fake plaster tree they could shrink, enlarge, rotate, and plug into their pictures. The little flying vulture in the animatic was wearing aviator goggles. They showed me a shot of the vulture swooping down to light on the tree and sit there, glaring. The cartoon vulture hunched forward and little black lines shot out of his head, just like Sunday funnies. In fact, the caricatures provided by the effects team put me very much in mind of that old Tom K. Ryan strip, *Tumbleweeds,* a kick in the pants to everything Western and clichéd. The actual shot would not see live film for another four weeks.

On another monitor they demonstrated how treelines, mountaintops, and green-screen sets could be made to match lighting in postproduction. This same midnight-oil magic could also put your head seamlessly onto another person's body, or erase your limbs to order in case you're playing a cowboy who lost an arm or leg inside a mine collapse or dam explosion. For the climactic throw down where the ex-sheriff faces off with his old enemy of a century earlier, the CGI guys were removing a third of the bad guy's head so you can see the exposed skull and a few convolutions of brain matter. From there, I met the antagonist of the piece.

Garrett Torres had a trademark toothy sneer and a complexion like indifferently mixed concrete. You've seen him bite the big one in a dozen movies, and he loved his status as a bad guy character player. His voice was chipped ice, raspy, from the back of the throat, and bespoke visions of whiskey and cigarettes. In the feature film of my regrettably short life, Garrett would have played Gun Guy. He was currently trying to bed one of the camera assistants, a woman he met four days ago named Aspen DeLint. She wore cutoffs and work boots that molded her legs in a showy way; the way her set tool belt was slung around her hips was an angle most appealing. She was obviously a runner *and* a climber. Burnished chestnut hair cascaded in a horsetail from the gap in her gimme cap. Possibilities, there. The left ridge of Garrett's skull had been shaved to allow the makeup guys to glue on a partial skullcap, bright green with coordinate pips—tracking dots—to aid the computers in later removing the appropriate section of his head; Garrett was concerned his weird haircut might make him look too freakish as he pursued his mission of getting into Aspen DeLint's cutoffs. But he was game enough to allow me to shoot pictures of him on his absolute worst day for photogeneity.

No one busted me. When I awoke the next day, I felt better, as though I was now part of this movie, on the job, ready to work and in full command of my senses. Never mind that I knew where Char and Clavius were holed up, across the city. I would be leaving in two weeks. It would be child's play to avoid them. At least, until my first and only day off.

"No, it's a kick, you should see it. In fact . . . hey, where's that fucking photographer, whats-his-name?"

Mason Stone was cranking up the charm and firing it straight toward costar Artesia Savoy's all-too-willing wide eyes. She was working with an icon, so she nodded attentively, and went "um-hm," and encouraged him to say more for as long as he could stand talking to her without having an actual conversation. Inside of two weeks her conditional misgivings would crumble and she would be rocking Mason's world with a live replay from another of her early video successes, *Cuntfinger* (1998). Right now she was still working up the nerve, knowing that their affair would last exactly as long as the shoot—six weeks, if that. Mason was already playing her like a Stradivarius, maybe a Stratocaster. He already knew how this dynamic worked, what the unwritten rules were, and was so good at cherry-picking young talent that he could probably circle, on the call sheet, the soon-to-come date at which he and Artesia would mix fluids.

Next Thursday was my guess.

I came up on Mason from behind and told him my name

again. Not my real name, but my *name*-name. His face went all friendly and he clapped me on one shoulder like an old war buddy. Artesia's expression shifted into neutral, vaguely hostile, judgment pending. Mason told her I was the unit photographer and her face changed channels so she could invest some of her energy into guaranteeing I'd flatter her with my camera. She nailed me with her frank brown eyes and cornered me into the Man-Woman Standoff—you know, when you maintain eye contact and jabber away until your gaze finally drops to her chest and back, at which point she "wins." It's not my fault the female breast was composed as a bull's-eye; three concentric circles, breast, aureole, and nipple. Targets.

Conversely, I zapped energy directly into her eyes, determined to outlast her until she dropped *her* gaze, not to look at any part of me, but as the more primitive submissive response to direct scrutiny. I won this time, because it was my job to look at things.

"It's called the Salon Fantastique du Exotique," said Mason. "I was just telling Artesia. Just the 'Salon,' for short. It'll be somewhere in the Village. It's at a different place every time. Very expensive and strictly A-list."

I told him I'd heard of it. Poor Artesia didn't have a clue, but by god she was willing to learn.

"The Salon hasn't been in America for nearly seven years, but things loosened up once the Iron Curtain fell down."

"That was like recently, right?" said Artesia.

"They stuck to Russia and China," said Mason. "Picked up a few new members in Xiang Province—at least, that's what I read on the Salon Web site before *that* ate shit and died. And they're finally coming back to New York. And when they do, I think we should go, and see if we can get Jules here to shoot some pictures, right?"

Jules?

I allowed it, seeing as how Mason Stone could buy my entire family tree several times over, or shitcan me because he disliked the cut of my jib. I asked him how he has come by this information, which usually classed at about the same stature as an urban legend.

"I subscribe to their newsletter." He pulled a broad reaction so everyone would get the joke and Artesia laughed politely. "Naw, you know how it is—I know some people who know some people. Who know."

Artesia had a dragon tattoo encircling her left ankle, something that Makeup would blot out for the camera with a special matte base cream and a layer of powder to match her skin tone. A removable mask for permanent ink. They used this stuff on some of the models I had shot, the ones shortsighted enough not to want a career.

Mason cut to the cookie: "I can get us in. Maybe even you," he said, meaning me.

"Only if you promise it's as weird as you say," said Artesia, in full coax mode.

"Weird is the word," said Mason. "Double scoops." Nearly everything he said was convincing. He had once played the president of the United States. Viewers *wanted* to believe everything this man told them. But his talent was the artful depiction of human emotion, and I wondered what he was really feeling behind the firewall of his broadcast persona. I let him know how to find me if I was not at hand, and if he turned out to be for real.

Then I snapped the first photo of them together ever printed, one that later did good traffic on wire services and Web sites. Mason turned his head so his profile was emphasized. Artesia lit up as though on a hot switch. She could carbon copy that smile any time she spotted a camera lens. She derived energy from exposure.

Artesia was not wearing a bra, and had nipples the size of the crown on a Tootsie Pop. She caught me looking. I lost.

My so-called office was one floor down and on the opposite side of the building from Andrew Collier's spread. Somewhere in the maze between was my benefactor, Tripp, crunching schedules with first AD Gordo. And three feet away from me was Arly Zahoryin, videographer.

Not "playback." That was a more essential cog in the modern moviemaking mechanism: the person with the video links to all the operating cameras, who supplied instant playbacks for the director and thereby kept hard evidence of every take. That guy's name was Sinkevitch (I think) and we had traded cordialities, but nothing real. To him I was a glorified paparazzo. But if Arly Zahoryin could befriend him, I could too.

"Sinky's invaluable," said Arly. "Especially if you need fresh batteries on the fly; he's got a whole drawer of them. I get a spare set of phones and a radio hookup to the audio feed from him every day, if the actors don't hog them all. You might wanna try that, too—when you can eavesdrop the feeds off all the live mike channels, it's a heads-up on where to be."

As long as I didn't cheese Arly out of the set of headphones on which he had permanent squatter's dibs—that was pretty clear.

We were in a ten-by-ten afterthought of a room mostly consumed by a very large and apparently decommissioned ceiling duct and two big desks, the old, drab, metalwork, military kind. Both desks locked, which was an advantage since both of us could store valuable gear here. Arly had four cameras that each cost about five grand, not to mention two computers and a bewildering array of auxiliary gear, including a double-handled stabilizer that, when he wore it with the camera, made Arly look as though he had been in a serious automobile accident since it was a square frame of metal that fit around his head and neck.

Arly himself was endomorphic and gawky, with a prematurely sloping neck and a notable degree of pattern baldness for one so young—he could not have been

age, but could probably have passed for

genetics really fuck us over. Arly was de

all at the same time. Yes, he wanted to

idea what. He had been prepared for op

nearly a decade. Yes, he would tell you a

you did not flee. That boy was a talker.

"Studios keep trying to do all the su

now," he said as I shucked gear in the office,

tryman dropping pack and rifle to catch s

"But I've done Andrew's last three movies ar

The budgets for add-ons to the DVD are dry

age for video is already over. But people war

have extra stuff, even if they never watch i

more bang for the buck but the studio gets it, n

There followed a lengthy and complex expl

gets for such things. Arly seemed deeply org

very inspired.

"Tripp probably told you that rap about how

pher is the lowest form of life on a set. That

started." Arly clearly did not appreciate the lor

humor. "See, I'm one of the few people that has to

every single person on the set, because even the cate

me move out of the way. The camera crew doe

know the grips except when they need something

The effects guys don't talk to the actors unless the act

a peek at the green screen stuff on monitors. The stunt

know who the gaffers are. But I have to know every

depend on their tolerance. Then there's Tripp an

who'll come along with that little wave that says 'do

this,' y'know, when somebody pitches a fit or things g

on the set and I'm there, recording. I shoot it anyway 'c

the hell, I'm not gonna betray them and stick it on You

something. That guy, Richard? Mason Stone's bodygua

"Black trench coat," I said.

aring. Richard Fearing—Dick Fear-
opriate? He comes over to me. 'Wha-
t for?' he says. 'Nobody wants to see
ked behind a flag to change his shirt.
video because it shows Mason is down
ippity enough to have to go back to his
shirts, right? But now I got Dick Fearing
otecting his client from exposure, like, lit-
ow, I can pussy out and run to Tripp. If I
lo will make that face that says I'm wasting
can come back at Dick, who is a foot taller
t out for Dick: all my footage has to clear a
approval, one of which is Mason Stone's.
that the company doesn't want out. And I
s like, yesterday, that he can look at anything
ck anytime he wants. I'm supposed to be here;
crew. And he backs off, man, and goes, 'Naw,
like a friggin' *test* or something."
ial was clear as vodka, too: *I took on Mason Stone's*
on. These were the kind of hurdles jumped during
of actual production. Arly's fervent hope was that
nobody would care if he was around; he would

hinds me," I said. "I'd prefer not to be visible on
, if you know what I mean. It's a tax thing. I'm not
okay?"
's inevitable that you'll be on some footage. But I
it for a podcast or anything. It'll be on my log and
e office, but if you don't want it out there, it won't

o trust him that far. He gave my proposition a swift
he did not want to be distracted by the main thrust of
point.
ve basically got the same job, y'know," he said. He was

constantly trying to upgrade his own status, even tacitly. He felt pilloried and unappreciated. Deeper in the resentment lobe of his brain he knew that perfectly acceptable hero shots could be culled off his video, but I had the "photographer" designation and he did not. More than once I would probably position myself in what he saw as his roost for a shot, and in a very real sense, I outranked him.

Which was itself strange because I was used to being the boss of my own set during shoots. Here on the flip side of the country, I was part of a team and much more vulnerable to the opinions of others as to what I should or should not be doing. Yet within limits I was relatively free-range. I still could not shake the feeling that at any moment a grown-up would wander in and say, "What do you think you're doing here? Who said you could be here?"

In the most oblique way possible, I asked if I could use Arly's computer to check some stuff on the Internet. Generally, if you claim some software foul-up, people will accept your need even if you are standing there with a laptop in your hand, due to the common acceptance of technology as evil. Every such "deal" I made with Arly was based on a polite lie—my imaginary tax bogey, my non-fouled-up laptop, which worked fine. We were all trapped in this big machine together.

"Sure, no prob," Arly said. "I'll make a log-on for you. What do you want to be called?"

I thought about it for a minute. "Mister Kimber," I said.

That Sunday it was Mister Kimber who staked out Hawk-Nest, Clavius's Upper West Side base of operations, hoping for a glimpse of Char. I wore a Panavision gimme cap (courtesy of Arly Zahoryin's coat rack) and big sunglasses, feeling like the idiot I was. The new Mister Kimber had no class at all when it came to disguises.

Knowledgeable producers call it "film jail"—the removal of

yourself from the world at large while a production is shooting. Calls don't get returned, bills stack up, friends and lovers go unanswered . . . unless they are inside the hermetic universe of the movie, which demands to be the only thing that matters for a large chunk of time. Urgent world news items had only the vaguest echoes here, akin to village rumors. Stepping beyond the boundaries of *Vengeance Is,* even for a single day off, felt like a loss of rhythm. Smart crew members slept and got drunk (or vice versa) and never "left" the persistent bubble of the film at hand, even on their days off. For overtime days there was a thing called "turnaround," which was supposed to guarantee a worker eighteen hours before the next call-time, but this margin got cheated more than the unions would like to admit. One of Tripp's solutions to last-minute schedule trims was to admit we had to go to six-day weeks when he had originally planned for five. That made the whole shoot more intense, but also more exhausting, overtime be damned. It solidified the chain-link limits of the *Vengeance Is* universe. Active movies were very much like cocaine. You accomplished a staggering amount in a short moment of time; then, when the hot period passed, the slowdown felt deadly, like walking in sudden hypergravity.

Usually, by then, you were exhausted enough not to care.

Very quickly on that Sunday, my first day off, I found myself circling and twiddling. I thought I'd bomb down to St. Mark's on the C train or the #1 and grab a slice at my favorite East Coast pizza dive. I thought I might drop in to see what was new at the American Museum of Natural History, which still has a calming, cathedral-like atmosphere, and was not very far at all from Clavius's pretentiously named bastille, HawkNest.

Who was I kidding, really?

A blessed breeze had agitated the hanging humidity, reducing the ambient city odors of seawater, garbage, and soot to background accents. HawkNest was below Columbia University on the Hudson River side of Broadway. I stationed myself in a nicely grungy black-painted storefront called Espressoholic, got rocket-boosted on very strong Cuban coffee, and proceeded to spy on the building's doorman with my telephoto lens. He stood sentry about a block away.

It took about two hours before Char emerged, solo. She was wearing a vested leather outfit, a beret, and had seemingly also gotten the "big sunglasses" memo, but it was her. I knew her stride, her carriage when in heels. Nobody else has Char's legs.

I tailed her to Maxilla & Mandible, where she tarried among bones and fossils (it was a good choice for offbeat gifts), then she snagged a cab downtown. I snagged another, resisting the urge to say, "Follow that car." She spent about half an hour inside a chain drugstore near Columbus Circle, then headed for a lunchtime watering hole on Amsterdam. She seemed to be working her way south toward the garment district, where I knew I'd lose her. She probably had a fitting, or wardrobe approval, or perhaps Clavius was underwriting some nascent idea of her own spinoff apparel label.

What was I thinking, really?

I supposed I could have handed a cryptic note to the doorman: DANGER. WARNING. *Crazy Elias, who just trashed his own loft in L.A., needs to warn you about crazy people crazier than himself.* But Char did not have an escort, and acted blasé enough to indicate that she either did not know or did not care someone might be following her.

What I should have been wondering instead was the possibility that someone might be following *me*. But I thought I was the secret agent here, the man in control of his asset but not his own ass. Sometimes I got that nape-tingle that said eyes were looking at me. But this was New York; everybody stared. I whipped around a couple of sneaky times but never caught anyone looking.

I was still worried about Gun Guy. I had given him superhuman powers in my mind, which is one of the first warning bells of outright paranoia.

Little did I know I was right on the cusp of meeting the *real* "gun guy."

I got my wish and saw Char one last time.

And least predictably of all, I was about to fall in love with a mutant.

PART SIX

CHAMBERS

I had to cash in a six-year-old favor just to get a spare dead body to tuck among the four dead hit men in my Hidden Hills house. Elias was causing me to use up fail-safes I had stockpiled, hoping never to become that desperate. But the extra corpse was essential. It would satiate or misdirect Mal Boyd's interest, ideally long enough for me to cure the disaster that had become my life, which in scant days had gone from clandestine ops to open warfare.

I deeply hated to lose the house, but since the safe room was a total charred loss and full of dead guys, I decided to roll in the chemical drums and torch the whole setup. As a hide it was blown, and useless to me now.

I fell back to my Thai Town way station, a two-room "apartment" nestled above a scurvy bar called the Black Hole on the east leg of Hollywood Boulevard, near Normandie. I was pretty sure Mal Boyd had not sneefed this one out, but then I had been wrong about my supposedly secret house, so I took extra precautions. The biggest advantage was that I had not used the Thai Town place for more than three months. Had not visited, had not unlocked the door, had not been there. The keys disagreed with the locks, which needed some WD-40. I had brought a trunkload of arms and devices, plus all the emergency cash from the Hidden Hills safe. I had to rally my materiel in order to transmogrify. If I could steal a couple of hours to sleep and regroup, I could be out of the apartment and into a completely new place before anyone might notice my traffic here.

It took a solid week for my injured eye to fool me back toward normalcy. One moment it felt fine, rotating in its cushioned socket without incident. The next, it would suddenly "jam"—that's the only way to describe it—and seem to swell in my skull like a cartoon thumb struck with a mallet. A normal blink would be followed by another blink that aggravated my still-healing flap of cornea against my inner eyelid. The sensation, trust me, would make your entire body contract every single time it happened.

To be honest about it, my options sucked. My eye interfered with any optimal response reflex; it needed tending and I had to make time for it.

Option one: just kill Mal Boyd and get it over with. It was inevitable. It was life in our subterranean food chain. Complication: now that Mal's play with Blackhawk and Bulldog had failed so spectacularly, Mal himself would be on maximum lockdown, a very hard target indeed. You couldn't even sequester a hostage, because Boyd did not care about anyone enough to permit that leeway for leverage. In Mal's view, I was stacking up charges on an invisible bill the same way Elias was accumulating debits on *his* tab—the one I was keeping.

Option Two: Elias. Just find him and kill his ass deader than owlshit, which might curry favor with Mal Boyd, or at least get Mal to call no harm, no foul and stay off my dick while I wrestled with . . .

Option Three: cut to the chase. Throw my old identity overboard and get started on the New Me, right now, chop-chop. I had to do this anyway because as Mal pointed out, my hangdoggy blond mug was all over cyberspace. But even if I went to a plastic surgeon in Rio this instant, Mal's watchdogs would be on the lookout. More complications.

My tentative bargain left not only Elias, but his goddamned sleepy girlfriend as hangnails. Quite possibly Mal was still piqued because he knew they were still walking the planet and wasting everyone else's oxygen. Quite possibly Mal would shrug off the loss of his hit men—they came cheap and abundant at any rate—if I performed up to the standard of my brag.

"I'll expunge the entire op for free. All loose ends."

Jesus, did Mal think I'd kill myself, last, just to be a completist?

"Even to the extent of your own crew?" he had said.

Bingo, gin, Yahtzee, hands down—he had *expected* me to kill Blackhawk and Bulldog. They had been part of the crew along with Ozzy Oslimov and Cognac.

I still had a dog in the fight.

Complication: Elias had evaporated. Gone under. He and I had begun thinking the same way and making similar moves. I did not wish to appreciate that irony long enough to actually start *liking* the sonofabitch, who, after all, was the cause of all my problems *including* my punctured eye.

Plus, the motherfucker had purloined my brand-new gun.

Nasja Tarasova had known less than nothing and was worse than useless. I had to reconsider the data from Elias's cloned phone chip.

If I had known Joey, his assistant, was in fact at Elias's trashed loft at the moment I opened up his name file, I might have saved some valuable time.

Back at my crow's nest in the construction across Hollywood Boulevard from the former Equitable Building, I focused my spotting scope on Elias's fifth-floor windows just in time to see a remarkably hot goth chick get busy with a straight razor.

My crippled eye chunked up suddenly and I had to grab for my eyedrops. Everything smeared to a fever-dream wash of desaturated color. A pop-up replay of Nasja Tarasova bleeding out into her bathtub fast-forwarded across the inside of my brain. If my eye got worse, I had a semi-illegal bottle of proparacaine hydrochloride, the miracle numbing fluid.

The loft was still a post-tsunami mural of my temper tantrum, most of which had been swept up (all that broken glass) or shoved aside to make way for what appeared to be a down-and-dirty adult film shoot that looked more like a party with occasional video. An inner circle of lighting equipment was focused on the sofas, which had been rearranged into a crescent. Beyond that, several people loitered, swigging beer from green Beck's bottles. The auteur-in-charge sported a goofy crop-circle haircut, full arm sleeves, and a bunch of facial piercings. That would be the intrepid Joey.

Installed on the couch was a woman made fairly anonymous by being mummified in evenly spaced coils of bright yellow bondage rope. The goth chick, sizzling in very little clothing apart from six-inch spike heels, was slowly shaving Mummy Girl's exposed pubis with the razor. A degree of struggle is mandatory for most good bondage scenes, but Mummy Girl remained as stiff as a statue when the blade came in contact. Her job was to keep her eyes wide and terrified; I watched Joey zoom in on her face several times. Then she got repositioned like a bendy toy for some bloodplay—shallow incisions between the winds of rope, leaving thin crimson trails that would soak into the rope fibers in an interesting way. Then a rather large tribal fellow in assless chaps folded her like a fuck pillow and proceeded to slowly penetrate her from behind with his long, skinny cock, which was so weird-looking it appeared to be a prop itself. Its entire length vanished into her like a serpent down a gopher hole. This went on for a while as Goth Girl expertly freed a single loop of rope from Mummy Girl's mouth so Tribal Guy could slide his dick in there, too—maybe Mummy Girl was a sword swallower. The tip had to be down between her lungs.

The tableau compelled the eye. My eye. *Both* eyes. It was impossible not to watch.

Mummy Girl was gradually unveiled. Her tits were insouciant. Each freed loop of rope was resecured to a lockdown point until she was half-exposed and spread out on the sofa like a buffet, still immobilized, after which three people, including Goth Girl, descended on her like hungry vampires.

This ate up another half hour or so while Joey interrupted the action to move lighting or give direction. There were many more unpleasant ways to lose surveillance time compared to this—most of them, come to think of it—so I held my position as an audience of one for this special sneak preview. Hell, you never knew; you might learn something new.

Mummy Girl turned out to be an extremely pale, waiflike nymph with white-blond hair and no tattoos whatsoever; apparently this had been critical to her casting. Not even colored nail polish. My focus could not pick out whether she had scarification patterns, but that seemed a safe speculation. Goth Girl lovingly helped her blot the incisions, then Mummy Girl cloaked herself in a thick bathrobe for some well-earned break time while a woman in black gym sweats—obviously the rigger—proceeded to wind up Tribal Guy's broomstick penis in black rope of a thinner gauge. After the thirteen loops traditional for a hangman's noose there was still a lot of penis left to restrain.

Goth Girl's ink suggested she was with Joey; similar patterns, similar coverage. You know, like when you see a couple walking along wearing matching T-shirts or exactly the same running shoes, which they obviously bought together and at the same time. A couple.

She was a dark beauty that the style conceits of goth fashion only made more compelling, and my summary was confirmed when the shoot wrapped, everyone hugged and kissed in that very touchy-feely wolfpack way, and she remained behind. I was hoping to see her naked, and got my wish.

I put my gun to her head just as Joey mounted her.

The two hours or so of fascinating video shoot had provided

another gift: by logging the time on the scope I was pretty sure there were no extra uninvited players around waiting to kill me. Tonight it was just me and Joey and his goddess.

"Hi, Joey," I said.

They froze, doggy style, maybe waiting for someone to hose them down. A drop of Joey's sweat hit the large Maltese cross tattooed on her back.

Her kohled eyes sought me with an angry "what the fuck" expression.

Joey, speechless, with a similar expression, tried to back out.

"Don't move," I said.

The gun made the rest of my argument for me.

I wanted something visually intimidating, so I had added a nine-inch nail—glasspack silencer—to Bulldog's reliable SIG P250, which he had upgunned with a Jarvis match barrel threaded to accommodate just such a suppressor. (I was right, back at my house; Bulldog had chambered it for .40 cal.)

Goth Girl's eyes tried to see the gun pressed against her temple and in that moment I think she experienced a minor orgasm. Good for her.

I put a hardball round through her skull. I saw the full-metal-jacketed slug come out the other side. The report was comparable to the cough of a large dog. She went rigid, then relaxed, still gripping the arm of the sofa. Then she voided while Joey was still inside her.

That was the face I wanted to see on Joey—total bugfuck terror.

He scrambled backward like a punched cat on a slippery floor, his penis bobbing free with a wet catapult noise, naked, defenseless, and freaked-out. I was on him like the Black Plague.

I straddled him and slapped him to semicognizance with my free hand.

"Hey. *Hey!* Look at me. *Look at me!* I just did you a big moby favor. You know how many people get to experience that?

"*Haaaah?*" Joey gasped. Tears were running out of his eyes and I felt my own uppity orb twinge.

I jerked my thumb toward the dead woman on the sofa. "You put one through their head at the right time, and they contract like you won't believe. Did you feel it? It's the ultimate squeeze. Life shoots out through the groin. Did you feel it?"

"*Oh my god oh jesus fucking christ—!*"

I had to slap him some more. "*Stop. It.* Look at me." I wanted to be as clear as possible. "Where did Elias run off to, Joey?"

"*E-E-E-El—?*"

Okay, maybe I had gone too far. If he went into a spastic coma or something he would be of no use whatsoever. His eyes were joggling in and out of focus.

There was a big equipment pad on the wood floor and I used it to cover up Joey's late paramour so he could not look at her.

"Joey, it's time to collect your shit and lift it. You spazz out on me now and I'll just leave your dead body on top of hers the way I found you. Do I have to keep slapping you? Fuck, it's after midnight and I've got places to be."

"You fuckin . . . *shot* her . . ." he said in a big husking gulp.

"Correct! And I'm going to shoot *you* if you don't tell me where Elias went." The SIG's chamber was full up, trigger cocked. I spotted the spent brass cartridge on the floor and pocketed it.

"Elias—?"

This was going to take more time than I thought. It was like waiting for a monkey to evolve. Or explaining politics to a third grader.

"Your boss, Elias, ran away. He stole my gun. He should not have done that. I need to find him. You will help me."

Joey's sanity found a microscopic foothold. "That Kimber," he said.

Right answer, wrong detail. His mentioning my gun by name made want to kill him five or six times in a row. Evil Me battened on my suppressed rage. Joey was one of those Tattoo Savages who dreamed of living in *Mad Max* land but had never killed for food. He was the same as the Boulevard punks of the 1970s who affected cartridge belts but would melt into complete pussies if you fired off a live round anywhere near them—poseurs who would be the first to die in some idealized zombie apocalypse theme park.

I had to rein myself back, a courtesy I don't normally indulge. Damn, but this was getting overcomplicated.

"You saw the gun? You saw the Kimber?"

Joey suddenly seemed to spring a word leak. "Yeah, yeah, he wouldn't tell me where he got it I saw it big gun customized gun he wanted me to take it but I-I-I-I he said he said *you're that guy he talked about—!*"

"He *talked* about me?" This was news.

Joey was sucking fast, shallow air. He was going to faint from the blood rush.

"He wouldn't tell me," Joey mumbled, his eyes still darting. "Had this gig, this trouble, he had to take off, he said. *Awwwww—!*"

"Joey, please don't pass out on me. It's all shock and adrenaline and it'll make you sick. So puke if you have to. But you're going to tell me. If you drift, I'm going to start yanking those Christmas ornaments out of your face to keep you awake.

I watched him struggle to regroup mentally. "I need a cigarette," he said. "He just took off. I need a drink of water."

"Sure."

"Varla," he moaned, veering back toward incomprehensibility.

"Varla has left the building." I presumed he meant Goth Girl. "You're next if you don't *focus* for me."

He mumbled what sounded like a chant or mantra while I got him a Crystal Geyser and one of my own smokes, which I lit for him. It was a bizarre parody of interrogation by a movie Nazi. *You vill talk, ja? Zigarette?*

Joey killed half the cigarette in one pull.

"Elias said you kidnapped him," Joey said, still blurry. "I'm not supposed to tell."

"No, Joey, that has changed. You *are* supposed to tell. Tell me. Now."

I had been in Joey's position a couple of times—long story—and did not envy his options. It was all about seeing one's way clear to the truth.

"Movie job," he finally said. "In New York. That's all I know."

"What kind of movie job?"

"I dunno. Got it through some pal of his."

Oh, swell, *another* warm body in the mix. Another bystander Elias might have told. "Well, what's the *name* of the movie?"

"I dunno. I don't." He was shaking his head.

"Elias went to New York?"

He wrestled with it. "Yes."

Char and Clavius had also gone to New York. Okay.

"When?"

"I dunno. Soon. Like, right away."

"What did he do with the gun? The Kimber? Is it still here?"

"I dunno. He wanted me to take it; I couldn't."

My eye throbbed. Now I was going to have to risk more exposure and search this dump again.

Maybe I was hallucinating, but I could have sworn I saw Elias at the airport, Delta terminal. Just a sidelong glimpse, but I pursued the vision and saw nothing. My handicapped eye was generating wish-fulfillments. I was more concerned that it might pressurize and explode when I hit 30,000 feet. I was wired and tired.

Elias had fled to New York. Where Char had gone. With Clavius, who was easy to find.

That was all I had really needed out of Joey, although in the end he volunteered a great deal of useless peripheral intel—his backhanded "permission" to use the loft in Elias's absence, for instance, or that Mummy Girl's name was Gwynne. I covered his desperate eyes with my hand before I shot him, collected my brass, and dug out the slugs, including the one that had terminated Varla, which was stuck in the wallboard not far from where *Targets #5* had once hung. I stripped all the ID I could find from Joey and Varla. Two fresh Does on a previous crime scene would make law enforcement very interested in speaking to Elias, who would become a person of interest. That might drive him further under . . . or cause him to bolt into the open where I could scoop him.

Back in Thai Town—less than a mile from the Equitable Building—I broke down Bulldog's P250, plus adequate ammo, into an aluminum kit I had devised specifically for travel, a showy road case for a set of pricey paintball guns. I swapped trivia with one of the baggage rats about leakproof valves, custom volumizers, in-line regulators, and best of all, "reballing." A high-end paintball gun cost more than some actual firearms, capping in the $1,500 range. All so dimwits could pretend to kill each other. The checked-bag examiner snapped my case shut and wished me a safe trip. You don't hire geniuses for twelve bucks an hour.

Similarly, I had a laptop carry-on modified to conceal my bank.

I scarfed some airport pizza. I had always thought the concept of "terminal food" to be amusing.

My wonky eye did not burst, although I kind of hoped it might, since the in-flight movie was a crapfest called *My Best Senior Prom,* about two rival cliques of airheads who become serial prommers. It was a prom-rom-com, espousing the idea that life is all downhill from high school. Even with no headphones, it was excruciating, constantly veering into my peripheral sight even if I tried to ignore it, and I could not utilize one of those little sleep masks since its pressure exacerbated my left eye. If you ever need a justification for going on a killing spree, watch this film or one of its many clones, which always feature a scene where some ingénue sings along to a pop hit while nursing a glass of white wine in her underwear, and always ends with these mouth-breathers getting married or reproducing. This was a dastardly life template that provided impossible aspirational ideals to people who had no lives to begin with. It predefined happiness for people who needed to be told they were supposed to be happy. It was like seeing a documentary about life on another planet. I wondered what aliens might make of the film as anthropology. Like that classic story about how the only evidence left of life on a long-burned-out Earth is a Donald Duck cartoon.

It was *charming*. It was *delightful*. It was worse than drinking barium. As I slouched in my miniature seat I felt the glassy gazes and toothpaste smiles of the other passengers crowd in on me. When had airlines downsized the seating to fit the average petite Japanese? I did not belong here, among these benighted idiots. Ignorance really *was* bliss, it seemed from their vacant expressions and vapid laughter.

I was happier than civilians could ever fantasize. Because I had a talent, something I was good at. Few were better. I needed to prove that to Mal Boyd and all the phantoms who stood behind him, judging me. I wanted to stay in my world, off the grid, not transition to this shallow pastel purgatory, which was the one-and-only life goal for many of our fellow pedestrians.

But then, I've always thought Thanksgiving could be improved by initiating a lottery system whereby a family can elect one member to kill. Carve the bird, add fresh whipped real cream to that pumpkin pie, and stone Uncle Carl to death because he's a fucking pedophile.

I wondered if Elias had smuggled my Kimber along on his trip. If he was working a movie gig he had probably zipped east in a private jet, a thousand feet higher and a hundred miles faster than my lumbering commercial heavy. No such thing as baggage checks on those sporty Hawker 800s and Gulfstreams.

You could toss a bag of M-16s and plastique into the cargo bay and nobody would blink.

Also riding clandestine class with me, disguised in a diabetic kit, were several ampoules of tripaxidine B, the instantaneously acting knockdown I had used on Dominic Sharps. Did you know that airlines permit a diabetic to board with unlimited syringes? Too late, I thought of jamming myself into unconsciousness to avoid the damned movie.

Airport security was a fool's illusion, administered by amateurs. If I had to remove my shoes for a walk-through scan, I wanted to wear six-day-old socks. I had a phony passport and ID, a custom gun, plenty of ammo, two completely nonlegal knives and a complement of deadly drugs . . . but no gelignite up my ass or beauty products, so I was permitted. I recalled the story Cognac had once told me about being detained for her nipple rings—that must have been festive.

Poor Cognac; I did regret killing her a little bit.

Five years ago, before Cognac, I had become enamored of a woman provisionally named Dawn Marie Sonderhoff, an independent contractor, same as me. She was technically married to some beard in Las Vegas and her cover job was as a substitute teacher in some elementary school. I never saw the school or the husband, but I saw quite a lot of Dawn Marie on weekends when we could both work it out (via another poetry ladder of coded phone contacts). We had a lot of sex in the best hotel suites subterranean cash could buy, after a lot of big-ticket meals in the restaurants most avoided by frugal tourists. She pulled me into her with an almost feral hunger and you could sense these interludes were a lifeline for her. Any and all stress generated by her double life, her white picket fence, and her elective assassination jobs got sweated out when we joined up. She was a true sensualist and we were both grown-up and smart enough not to complicate what we had, inside our safe little bubble, by splicing on the shackles of a *relationship*. We had what we had inside a safe zone where the rubrics of the dull, conventional world outside did not apply. It was comforting enough that we achieved a fundamental connection that could never be disrupted by time or the background players in our separate lives.

One single time, I went to Dawn Marie's home at her invitation. Her happy lumpen hubby was state-hopping or business-conferencing, or as she put it, "off screwing Asian hookers because he's adding stomach and losing hair." Her house turned out to be a characterless McMansion in some development, with all the right cars in the garage, a rarely used yet overremodeled dream kitchen, and a depressing abundance of beige. It was the sort of norm paradise I would have pegged as a halfhearted cover house. No dust would ever accumulate here, nor history.

Exactly three family photos were strategically positioned in the cubbyholes of the living room's prefab entertainment center—one stilted, ultra-stiff wedding pose that did not bespeak any sort of fulfillment, and one shot each of the branch tribes. Hubby's crew was a sprawl of relatives whose generational pride resided in their breeding capacity. Dawn Marie's similar gang shot said two things: Dawn Marie's family did not get together very often, and Dawn Marie had gotten the best of their gene mix. Her two sisters looked like horsy failed experimental iterations of her. It had taken Mom and Dad three tries to get it right.

Hubby, of course, had invested considerable effort in impregnating Dawn Marie without knowing it was foregone. Without offspring or teacup humans to impress his tribe, he had been written off as a failed branch of the tree and left to channel his frustrations into work, long hours away from home, and Asian call girls. Problem aborted.

By moonlight we swam naked in her pool and made love in her Jacuzzi. It was very important to her that I occupy—for one single night—the bed she shared with hubby (she took his side; I took hers), a bed that appeared brand-new and utterly unused. She wanted to remember me in that bed, even though after I had gone she would restore it to its usual undespoiled state.

That's when it struck me: Dawn Marie was completely comfortable within this asphyxiating suburban death trap, because it compensated for the other half of her life as a contract operative. It was her safe house, her fallback, which was why it had never developed as a home in any meaningful way.

Then—also one single time—I saw her work. I watched from a distance. It was another of those drug-monkey sausage parties. She did not trust her hand-to-hand skills and stuck to gun work, triple taps to three targets in a couple of seconds, chest-chest-head. She was using a Kimber then; that's where I got the inspiration.

That was when I saw the *true* light: she needed both lives, the frantically covert and the dunningly dull. They were her balance; her yin and yang. My own "normal" existence was spent waiting for the next job. I had nothing like what she had already found.

Dawn Marie was the only person who ever called me on my birthday. Granted, I never told anyone else the date, and granted, she used secure phones and never identified herself, but I knew it was always her, just checking in.

Elias's girlfriend Char reminded me a bit of Dawn Marie— same body language, same flashing eyes, hints of a similar attitude.

I never found out what happened to Dawn Marie other than she got killed in a complex operation involving Mafia goons, but in the private rooms of my mind I always maintained the fantasy that her death was a firework, a showy display to mask an identity switch, just like mine. In my version of the story, Dawn Marie was still out there, and one day she would make contact again.

If she was really, truly dead—*dead*-dead—then there was always the chance we'd be reunited in some warrior's Valhalla when I finally bit the big one.

I snapped awake uncomfortably to the stench of burning in-flight coffee, thinking (just for a nanosecond) that I was on approach to Vegas instead of New York. My eye was gelid with gut-wrenching lumpiness.

Air travel had lost so much of its getaway allure.

Clavius owned an entire floor of a building up in the Seventies, West Side, and was simple to stake out from the Lucerne Hotel on West Seventy-ninth, dead center between the river and Central Park. Using the next card from my deck of IDs I got the highest room I could, but it was still a radical up-angle view from my roost to that of Clavius. I could sneak onto the rooftop for a more level vantage, but it would still depress a sniper. Looking down, though, I had excellent coverage on street level.

Each of my identity packets had an ID for differing states of origin, a passport for same, and four credit cards with astronomical limits for which I would never see a single invoice. The bottommost identity was nearly two years old and I was leery of testing it to see if it still played. What I really needed was a refresher session with my prince of documentation in L.A., a grizzled cowboy named Rook. But a stop at Rook's would be on Mal Boyd's checklist, so I spared him and rolled with what I had already.

Today I was George Walker Boult, an insurance claims field adjuster from Chicago, fresh from a one-year around-the-world cruise that explained his lack of recent air travel.

It didn't take long for George to fix a 20 on Elias's runaway ladyfriend, Charlene Glades. She strolled out of Clavius's highrise looking like about a quarter-million bucks on the hoof, a walking *Elle* cover in soft brown leather and cashmere. Over-the-knee boots with dangerous heels whose lift brought me another sharp memory jolt of Dawn Marie, my lost Vegas compatriot.

I cornered Char in the elevator at some garment factory in the mid-Thirties between Seventh and Eighth. The district was a sad shadow of its former fashion glory, and had been ever since the Gambino trucking slap-down forced out most of the designer crème in the early 1990s, leaving millineries and cutting shops to be redeveloped into retail space and condos. New York, of course, wanted to reverse the en masse flight, but zoning and sky-high rents hobbled the rebirth, which was still dodgy and under radar.

Char immediately recalled me as "Mister Kimber," and that just made me madder. She smiled hesitantly. I smiled back with grinding teeth and set the lift for the top floor. She bridled, so I stuck a gun in her face and changed her expression superfast.

"There is no Mister Kimber," I said, close enough to breathe on her. "I'm Mister Boult. You can call me George."

The eighth floor was stuffy and abandoned, still waiting in dusty silence for its face-lift. I sat Char's ass down inside a room full of dismembered mannequins, ancient wire-frame body forms, and decommissioned office equipment; empty desks with drawers rusted shut, broken chairs exuding the smell of rat piss from chewed and sprung stuffing, several stacked tons of obsolete paperwork, and the moldy blanket miasma of water damage.

"Where's Elias?" I said.

In any sequestration scenario valuable time was always wasted by the subject, who felt the outraged need to establish her own bona fides. Yes, I was that man from the night in the loft. Yes, that was a real gun. Yes, I knew what I thought I was doing. It was so ingrained it had become a bore years ago. I needed to see a bright, wet spark of fear in Char's almond-shaped eyes, since she was practically begging to be roughed up. Yes, I had killed—

"What the fuck do you mean, Elias said I *killed* people?!" I almost shouted. I could see flecks of my own saliva in the dust-moted air between us. "When did you hear this from Elias?"

"Today!" she shouted back at me, higher volume. "About an hour ago!"

I got sick of bulldogging her back into a busted chair every time her body tried to lunge for escape. The chair was minus a wheel and listed to port. "You keep this shit up, I'll tie you to the chair and roll your ass right out the window," I said. *"Where?"*

"Right here in the city!" she said. She was only just getting the idea that her life might depend on whether I believed her. "Like an hour ago!"

Holy shit with a capital *shit*.

I had tailed her for longer than that. She had moved in and out of five or six public places, the longest layover being at a pub on Amsterdam with a terminally bad view through the front windows. I guessed lunch and kept my distance. I had guessed wrong.

Then I remembered. Dude in a baseball cap and sunglasses who came out of a coffeehouse right after Char had grabbed her first cab. His collar had been up and his face, mostly obscured. No goatee. Just another cabber in a city of taxis. He had to tail her that way. Me, I had already taken Char's cab number and hacked into Yellow's GPS destination base, so I didn't haul ass out the door on the mark, which is what I should have done.

"He didn't *say* where he was; I only saw him for about five *minutes* and he was acting totally *insane;* he said you killed Nasja and now Joey's *dead* and and and—"

In fact, she was starting to babble the way Joey had. Backhand slap, left, right, snapped her trap in midrant. The floating dust was already harassing my weak eye.

If I went ballistic on her, the way I had on Elias that first night to subdue his protest, Char would just dish that anger back in equal measure. Yelling would not work with this woman. I kept my voice low and steady. It creeped some people out, that flatness.

"Listen to me, Char: none of that matters. It's a long story you don't have time for. Concentrate. Simple answers to simple questions. Yes or no would be splendid."

She wasn't crying, not yet. She'd fight the impulse to run off at the eyes because Mr. Boult was manhandling her.

"You *saw* Elias at that pub?"

"Y-Yes."

"He came all the way to New York to tell you I killed somebody?"

"*He said you were framing him!* Yes!" Her pupils were down to pencil points, I realized. I was getting an erection.

"Why, Char," I said, keeping my tone avuncular. "What are you *on*, sweetie?"

She shot me the "fuck you" look. Whatever Elias had told her back at the pub had stirred her up enough to grab for the blow stash.

"Where is Elias now?"

"I have no idea!"

"Does Clavius know?"

"No, no, no!" She shook her head like a child with increasing velocity. "Clavius doesn't even know I saw him. Clavius got a call from the police about Nasja. Then about some Internet thing. Then about Joey, because of the loft. Clavius says somebody is trying to frame *him*. That's all he told me. Really. I swear to—"

I overrode her silly and futile desire to convince me I could trust her. Just a tap, for emphasis. Really, why do people *swear* so vehemently when they're lying their asses off, seeking to deceive and dissemble?

Dawn Marie had been all about the bottom line. Char had reminded me of Dawn Marie from first glimpse. Staring at Char now, it was easier than ever for my damaged eye to make the substitution. Close up I could see her boots were Hussein Chalayans, with straps. Expensive.

Her voice clicked dryly. "What-what are you-you going to—?"

I sighed. What did it matter, what I was going to do? Jeezo-pete.

"What is the name of the man Elias knows in the movie business?" I said.

This seemed to take her completely by surprise, which meant

her previous speech was most likely true. I saw the squirrel running rampant in her brain stop and focus for a moment.

"What . . . do you mean Tripp?" she said as though I had just asked for a cupcake recipe.

"Not a trip. A person."

"No, no, Tripp *is* a person, I mean, his name is Tripp. Bergman. Bergen. Something like that."

I suddenly felt sorry for anybody stuck with the name Tripp. But Char thought she had lucked onto an escape hatch with flashing lights. EXIT HERE. Then she had another brilliant idea.

"Are you going . . . to rape me?" she said, voice tiny.

That drove me back a half step. "I hadn't really thought about it," I lied.

"If you can fuck me, will you let me go?" She was wiping off her face, trying to reorder. Hopeful. The expression was sickening.

I shot her through the heart and then fucked her anyway.

PART SEVEN

INTERMISSION

The first week of production on *Vengeance Is* occupied significant portions of Central Park (two days), and couple of square blocks in Midtown involving explosions and nighttime gunfire (three days). In one hellishly compacted run-and-gun session, it shut down the George Washington Bridge for four hours in order to record the quintet of escapees from the infernal regions riding motorcycles across the span as traffic disappears in front of them, courtesy of green screen and process plates.

It was called a shoot "day" whether it was high noon or *night-*night.

Tripp Bergin was alerted by his location manager, Bobby Katzenbrigg, that repair work was planned for the GW, and they could take advantage of the lower span at night. Andrew Collier wanted the upper span, to show off the iconographic structure of the bridge, but Katz informed him that was a no sale because some city ordinance decreed that one lane had to be kept open on the upper span at night for the transportation of "hazardous materials" not permitted on the lower span. Collier's gaffer had planned on illuminating the upper span from the top of the bridge, now impossible. The lower span was a demon to light properly.

It was Tripp Bergin's job to fit an entirely new operation into the old schedule. As he told Elias while wearing a gimme cap for something called *Fart! The Movie in 3-D!*, "An idea is not a plan."

Elias caught some terrific shots of Cort Ridenour—the gaffer—backlit by the magnesium flares he tossed around in abundance to provide ambient light for the Steadicam shots. He factored in car headlights and cherrytops from the police cars and emergency vehicles, all of which had to vanish on cue. He grabbed as much background glow from the mercury-vapor streetlamps as he could, which played off the green tones of the bridge structure. He deployed punchy 6K Arriflex parabolic reflectors to light the center of the bridge from the Jersey Shore; their powerful beams threw two thousand feet, or almost exactly to the center of the superstructure, so he positioned fill lamps of equal power on the New York side to dimensionalize the bridge for the long shots.

Elias was enthralled by the sheer effort that went into every shot, every setup. He remembered what Tripp Bergin had said about film being war; perhaps that was why Production was called a "unit." Vast resources were mobilized to distant locations. The fight was against time, against money, against weather, egos, competitors and the script. The players were dog soldiers, officers, old warriors, fucking-new-guys, conscientious objectors, mercenaries, seasoned vets, and heroes. Some were grunts. Some were like Patton. Sometimes there were casualties; other times glory. A lot of the time there was shellshock, exhaustion, and aborted missions, none of which hampered the relentless pursuit of victory. Brotherhood bonds were forged from pressure, innovation, and necessity. Battlefield romances waxed and waned. At the end, everybody got to Go Home. Promises to keep in touch were never fulfilled, and this was routine, based on the if-come presumption that perhaps you would rejoin your platoon mates again on some other project, in some future location, for some other war.

Of course, Tripp had reeled off his favorite metaphor while wearing a cap from a film called *Mud Grunts*. Grunts got shot up in the trenches while the leaders sat at some faraway teatime with their pinkies out, talking of art and trophies.

Elias McCabe might have been a KIA. Julian Hightower had better odds.

Every single location required multiple release forms and permissions, which had required Tripp to be on the job days earlier with Cody, since such paperwork is not the sort of thing that clears in a day. You had to factor in bureaucratic lag.

Not to mention unpredictable delays, such as when Hunnicutt's hero vulture, Vlad, flew up to the top of the bridge and would not come down for an hour and a half. Crew members had to watchdog Vlad while his understudy Borgo was quickly uncaged to substitute. Vlad eventually got hungry and descended home; it was very nearly the same as an uppity actor refusing to leave their trailer.

The Midtown gun battle where the resurrected cowboy takes out two of his enemies with his special Colt was diverting.

The conceit of Mason Stone's character, the cowboy, was that he could intuitively spin his revolver cylinder to the exact shell needed to demote each of the hellriders. These cartridges were each inscribed with the name of the recipient, literally a bullet with your name on it. But the cycle psychos all came with state-of-the-art modern killware—miniguns, auto shotguns, and a Milkor grenade launcher with a six-shot cylinder that made it look strongly like Mason's Colt, as reimagined by invading extraterrestrials. The armorer, "Cap" Weatherwax, told Elias that the Milkor had been especially popular with Blackwater operatives in the Middle East.

The movie crew had their permissions from the city duly executed, of course, and officers were stationed appropriately. The reams of paperwork required to stage a fictional gunfight in the middle of Manhattan would choke a blue whale, as Tripp Bergin ruefully knew. You had to get all kinds of sanction to discharge a weapon, even a prop weapon. But Andrew Collier's idea of "gunfire" in the middle of the night exceeded what the city fathers had thought to be one or two shots per take—*bang, bang*, done. His plan had bad guys shooting at Mason and

Mason shooting back, surrounded by police and SWAT teams shooting at *all* of them while five cameras captured the action.

The first take of this throwdown blitzed through three thousand rounds of ammo at two o'clock in the morning, and phones all over the city started ringing.

The cops on site just grinned at one another. In their pockets were authorized documents saying all this was okay.

Worse, it took twenty minutes for Cap and his crew of gun handlers to reload everything. That meant if you were a local just awakened by this doomsday salvo, you decided it was a onetime disturbance and put your head back down just in time for the next take.

Of six.

Some citizens thought World War III was on. The shots were heard five miles away. In Jersey. On Staten Island.

It was all written up in the papers the next morning as MASON STONE'S NIGHT OF THUNDER!, which was not fair because Mason had not been present for most of it—only the close-ups and cutaways. His camera double, Trent MacEvoy, stood in for the wide shots. When in doubt, blame the celebrity.

Or sacrifice the nearest warm body, which was Katz, the location manager, who was forced to lay low for a day while the official smoke of outrage cleared.

Elias—Julian—logged killer hero shots of Mason and the baddies, and managed to sneak one good picture of the evident joy on Andrew Collier's face at the mayhem he had created. Even Cap cracked a tiny grin of awe. Elias nailed another primo shot, regrettably destined for the "do not use" category, of a SWAT extra discharging a shotgun too close to a fellow extra (right by his head, earplugs be damned), for which he got reamed out at length by Cap. The extra was not fired or dismissed, merely deweaponized. Nevertheless it was this disgruntled individual who got quoted in the morning news about how the film shoot was "excessive," implying "out of control."

From what Elias could see, Cap was all about control. When

actors were faced with a set armorer or military advisor—always called the gun guy—they generally expected some abrasive, abrupt warhound vet who yelled a lot between flashbacks, twitches, and tics. Cap was firm and for real. He knew set etiquette and made sure his distinctive cargo vest was visible for anybody with a question. As a supervisor he made damned sure people understood weapons on set were his responsibility and covenant, and if you wish to call that a dictatorship, so be it, because nobody could outvote him where firearms were involved.

Cap's "cap" was a rich iron-gray flattop trimmed so precisely that every hair seemed to be exactly the same length—if you asked he'd tell you he thought it was still the best haircut for a man. It would have been easy to call his alert gray eyes "metallic" but they were more the tint of thunderheads. Not tall, but solid and big; not heavy, but squared-off, a man who could plant his feet and absorb recoil. He had retired from the Airborne Rangers as 1st Sergeant over a decade ago and had been a trainer for SOCOM, SWAT, and hostage response teams. He took his calling seriously because too many people like to clown around with weapons, especially people who have never fired one and don't know the first thing about them.

Cap could drill neophytes faster than any wrangler Elias had ever seen. He spoke with authority, backed up by four of his crew to cover all the extras Collier needed to see firing weapons. His sterling record of stewardship over violent action movies had made his company, Fire When Ready, the first choice of A-listers all over the globe. Supposedly his arsenal truck did not contain a single live round, but since Cap was licensed as a federal firearms dealer and held carry permits for nearly every state in America, Elias doubted his signature sidearm was a prop. His gun was a visible expression of his rank and power.

It was natural for Elias to start tracking Cap on set with his cameras, because Cap was usually where the good stuff was. Every time he caught up with Cap, Elias learned something new.

Real guns had to be coordinated with prop ones. If Mason Stone had to run down a hallway with his Colt visible in the holster, a fiberglass or rubber dummy was used because it weighed less. Same-same for scenes where a gun got knocked out of your hand; you slap the mock-up and shoot an insert of the real piece hitting the concrete (less damagingly) later. Many of the guns in Cap's arsenal truck could fire but not shoot, meaning they had arrestors (metal Xs) blocking the barrel. They were good only for blank rounds, but there was a hazard there, too. Blanks feature gunpowder tamped in by paper or plastic wadding; the open end of the cartridge where a bullet would seat is crimped shut. Sometimes the crimp could fragment under the force of the igniting powder, blasting forth little triangles of brass that could take out an eye. The actor Jon-Erik Hexum had been famously killed by a piece of paper while goofing with a gun loaded with blanks. The wadding hit him hard enough to push chunks of his skull into his brain.

Six out of ten of the modern commandments of movie gun safety existed because of Brandon Lee's accidental death on the set of *The Crow* nearly twenty years earlier, and Cap had known Lee.

Always assume a weapon is loaded or "hot"—first and foremost, the "prove it" rule. No such thing as "kidding." Finger off the trigger and muzzle up (or down) on "cut." Wait for a Fire When Ready man to clear a jam or misfire. Know your backstop. Never point the muzzle at anything you are not willing to destroy.

Through his own viewfinder, Elias saw how this last rule, the "offsides" principle, worked on film. If you were plugging some evildoer and the camera was on your right, you aimed slightly to the left of the target, and so on. Depth of field could not tell the difference. Collier had specified full-powder blanks for the practical guns—real weapons that could shoot real bullets—in order to see brighter muzzle flashes on film, and Cap had agreed since quarter-charge blanks often failed to cycle the automatics.

And an extra's ear had gotten singed.

One accident was one too many. Make-believe could become serious business in many ways, and Cap was dedicated to keeping every single warm body on his watch from harm. As he told Elias, he thought of Brandon Lee every day of his life. If Cap had been there . . .

"When you think about it," Cap said, "it's all about common sense . . . which too many people don't have."

The disassembled Kimber back in Elias's office was starting to chew a nag-hole in his brain. Cap's other commandments involved more familiarity or intimacy with the weapon itself: *Know your gun. Use the right ammo. Don't depend on safeties. Will it richochet?* And most obvious of all, don't pick up a weapon if your senses are dulled by chemicals, lack of sleep, or stupidity.

Cap also had a great spiel on movie gun sound effects, which were beyond his control, much to his displeasure. "I think it all started with John Woo, at least, the *modern* age of stupid gun foley," he said.

Whether you called it "automated dialogue replacement" or "additional dialogue recording," ADR was still looping—actors in a booth rereading their lines. Foley was the sound effects equivalent, named after Jack Foley, a sound editor at Universal back in the day. If you've ever wondered what a "foley walker" was, now you know it's a person who makes footstep noises to order for any postsync footage.

Gun foley, however, gave Cap a pain every time he watched a movie; more pain if it was his own gun work that had been polluted in post.

"Back in the forties, fifties, sixties, everybody had the same track library of the same five gun noises," Cap continued, "and we knew them all from TV and the movies, same as we knew the same car crash noise or artillery boom repeated from film to film. Warner Brothers cartoons used the same gunfire sounds in cartoons, Westerns, and Bogart movies. Then ole Sergio Leone spliced them howitzer noises on to pistols, and by the time the Man with No Name turned into Dirty Harry, well, ole Clint's Magnum had to make its own unique noise, didn't it? It probably happened first somewhere else, but these are the examples that stick in my memory. They were okay by me even if they were inaccurate to the firearm. But by the time John Woo's first movies got dubbed over for Stateside distribution, I nearly lost my freakin mind—here were guns that made all kinds of, I don't know, *clickety* noises every time you touched them. Drew them. Looked at them. Had nothing to do with gunfire! Chow Yun-Fat pulls out a Beretta nine, and it makes all kinds of weird clicking sounds in his hand, like somebody winding a busted watch, like the gun is full of loose parts!

"Then these foley motherfuckers started getting cute, because once you get away with something, an escalation always follows, right?" Cap would then draw his sidearm, a fancy-looking .45 that had probably been a thank-you freebie from the folks at Para-Ordnance. "See? Gun left the holster with nary a whisper. No little cricket-clicks. I wiggle it around in my hand, it doesn't make a sound. I cock the hammer and it's a very soft two-stroke, *ticktock*. Then a foley guy gets ahold of it and all of a sudden I hear a triple click of a hammer that sounds like a ratchet or breaking celery, followed by the sound of a cylinder rotating on a weapon that has no cylinder. If guns made as much noise before being fired as they do in movies, you'd never be able to sneak up on anyone with a gun because they sound like some half-wit scratching an eight-ball shot."

Elias had no doubt that Cap's personal sidearm was not loaded with blanks, and that helped him make up his mind about Mister Kimber.

Back in the City of Angels, a housekeeping employee of the Laguna Negra time-share complex discovered Nasja Tarasova's decomposing body after about half the water in the tub had evaporated. The pathology was consistent with suicide. Pornographic videotapes were found on site. The artist Clavius was notified since she was found to be a "companion" of indeterminate status, possibly an illegal alien, despite her paperwork.

Five unidentified male bodies were found in the smoldering meltdown of a Hidden Hills home, sniffed out of the wreckage by police-trained cadaver dogs who came equipped with little boots to keep their paws from getting burned. Evidence at the scene suggested a private meth lab crew had gotten into a violent disagreement, and in the process of shooting one another had ignited unventilated ethyl ether fumes. The conflagration had burned long and blisteringly hot. The home's owner of record, a man named Jules Vanderheiden, had been listed dead since 1991.

In Tarzana an ex-mortician named Oslimov was found dead of a self-administered heroin overdose. His plastic surgeons identified him according to the serial numbers on his many implants. Accidental death was the ruling.

At the Beverly Hills Hotel a popular prostitute named Sapphire had vanished without a trace, whereabouts unknown, which was not unusual for women who fell into the life.

The burning house with its drug angle made the news for one day. None of the other deaths rated coverage.

Slightly more newsworthy was the disappearance of spokesperson Dominic Sharps of the LAPD Tactical Wing. His empty BMW and limousine were found parked outside his home in the 90210 bearing no signs of foul play. His bound-and-gagged chauffeur could not identify who, or how many, had waylaid him. Sharps's eldest son, Richard, a prosecutor with the DA's office, took to the TV screen for an appeal after allegations of sexual impropriety were put forth as the reason for Sharps's abrupt and unexplained leave-taking. He emphasized that no Internet smear campaign could be thought to be legally credible, and his sister Stacy, a counselor for a sex-abuse hotline, added real tears to the public request for decency and understanding during this bleak time.

Because of the cyberconnection to Clavius, the viewing

public naturally concluded that Sharps and Nasja Tarasova had been involved in some sort of illicit affair. It was obvious to anyone with eyes.

Clavius himself turned his formidable legal juggernaut to the task of denial. Nasja's suicide was a tragedy. The Internet scandal was the result of a smear campaign by a rogue ex-employee who was possibly implicated in other misbehavior, no further comment.

Over in Hollywood, two homeless kids had vandalized the loft residence of a photographer named Elias McCabe, then got murdered when they returned to either squat in the residence or trash it a second time. A drug deal gone bad or illegal sex trafficking may have played a part in the two deaths. No associates had come forward to identify the pair and Mr. McCabe, apparently on assignment in Europe, could not be reached for comment.

Charlene Glades (yes, the model) was spotted in New York City in the company of Clavius at one of the latter's gallery shows. Charlene Glades was known to have associated with Elias McCabe. More questions.

Then McCabe was name-checked again in regard to the subsequent murder of Ms. Glades homicide in the garment district, a shocking ritualistic homicide involving grisly postmortem mutilations apparently derived from or inspired by examples from a past photo series by McCabe. Where previous speculation and circumstantial evidence might have led to McCabe as a possible lead or suspect, his very disappearance pointed to the more gruesome possibility that he, too, had become a victim.

Chambers had no way of knowing he had missed spotting Elias at LAX by about seven minutes. His body count for his "unilateral expungement" stood at nine, not counting Dominic Sharps.

PART EIGHT

JULIAN

My previous romance prior to meeting Char had been the kind of crazy-making miscalculation that makes you reorder your entire view of yourself.

For one thing, Rebecca Effner was a fellow photographer. That alone kicked the pins from beneath most of the social fencing intended to get people either hired or laid. For another, her work was staggeringly good. Like me, she had preferred film over digital, raw light over pixels. I met her at a gallery showing of hers called Old Bars—almost Weegee-like photo studies of tarnished dives, barely hanging on as the new century crushed them.

I asked her what she did at the old bars.

"Get shitfaced," she said. "See who fucks, who fights. Waste my time in the jaded pursuit of empty thrills and try not to see my existence as a hollow lie. You know—the usual."

She was attractive instead of pretty, smart instead of glib, more willowy than thin, with all-seeing violet eyes and raven hair so dark and thick it seemed Indian. Her face was an inverted teardrop with a bit too much forehead versus chin, yet organized around those fascinatingly shaded eyes. Falling for her in the moment was too easy—sometimes it just happens that way. So everything I could conjure in the way of monopolizing her time sounded like just another lowball come-on, which I guess it was, because then I could plead being blindsided.

Once she backtracked to study my work she felt a reciprocal

connection, and we encountered each other socially but never privately. There was always some obligation, mission, or relationship—hers or mine—in the way. We were rarely in the same city at the same time, and so for nearly two years we compared notes via phone and e-mail on all the ways love can firebomb itself. And the deeper we got, the more pointedly the lowering specter of sex between us went unremarked.

That unspoken tension meant that losing the distance was inevitable. It was just a matter of time. It was an attraction to hold in reserve, like a secret crush. We had to come to a day, sooner or later, unless one of us died.

We shared nervous drinks in the bar at the Mark Hopkins, unsettled by each other's physical nearness. We were meeting each other on neutral ground, unchaperoned, and could not have been more gunshy and uncomfortable. It was shaping up to be the worst first date ever, since we already knew so much about each other without . . . you know, that other thing.

Finally she said, "It didn't hit me until I was at the airport. I am flying to San Francisco to sleep with this man. Then I thought, do we make out? Are we brotherly sisterly? Just one of the many reasons I held off for so long. But late at night, we're both thinking about the same thing. I hate the tension and don't want it to spoil the other things we have, rare things, valuable things, and at the same time I hate the 'let's just be friends' speech worse than anyone."

This was not the Rebecca I had grown to cherish for her caustic wit and unflinching vision. This Rebecca was scared and uncertain, and if I rang wrong she would shield herself with icy formality . . . because I would do the same thing.

"In the lobby?" she said, eyes downcast. "When we were ten feet away, then three, then we went into that automatic hug like it was the most natural thing in the world? Then I knew we'd been having the same damned thoughts, and I wasn't totally loopy. So here's what I think: the best and simplest solution is to just hold hands and jump. If it's a disaster, then it's a disaster and we shake hands and stay amigos. But if there's something else there—anything else—I'll torture myself for the rest of my life if I don't find out. Feel free to tell me to shut up at any time."

We were so apprehensive that we'd gotten two rooms. I wound up in hers. It was a temporary vacuum in which we existed only for each other, separate and away from every other concern in our individual lives.

Everything that could have gone wrong, did.

Which is why there had been no ravishment on my first night with Char. Then again, now I knew Char had not been real, either.

Rebecca still got in touch from time to time, but much less frequently, her messages and talk either brightly superficial or guarded and wary, her verve adulterated. We never spoke of San Francisco, had no cute snapshots or souvenirs, and a shroud had settled over what shreds of bonhomie we had left ourselves. I knew for a fact that she had been in and out of L.A. at least ten times in the past three years, but we did not kid ourselves by trying to do lunch. Until we talked about it, nothing would improve, and I could imagine this stalemate being one of my few regrets if Gun Guy ever caught up to me the way I imagined he might.

I successfully followed Char to a pub on Amsterdam called OMFG, where I knew exactly what she would order—salmon salad and two glasses of Pinot Grigio with a chaser of seltzer, no ice, yes lime. Bubble water always cranked up her pee meter, so she would probably hit the Ladies'.

Sleazy? You bet.

I could not simply accost her on the street; too many variables, too many watching eyes. A tell-all at Clavius's was out of the question. I could have babbled some of this via a long-distance call from L.A., but imagined how much more deranged it would sound to someone who had the option of hanging up. I needed to *see* Char, see her with my eyes, in person and without

Clavius, and try to tell her as much as I could to her face. She was in danger but would wrongly think distance from me would neutralize that threat. It was the only day of the week I would not be missed from the *Vengeance Is* set, and right-now-this-minute was the best of a bad field of options. Or *no* options—who knew when I would get another opportunity, if I lived?

Pissed off, was Char? You bet.

I had to bracket her in the restroom. She yelped as though goosed by a pervert before her eyes slowly took me into focus, sans goatee. I never wore hats and now she needed a beat to figure out it was me under that brim.

"God*dammit*, Elias!" Her face blushed luridly. Her heart must have been racing.

"I know, I know—everything about this is wrong, but I need you, I need you, I *need* you to listen to me right now!"

She would start hitting me any second. I had my palms up passively. To grab or restrain her would waste our time.

"I'm not a screamer, Elias, you asshole, but I will scream my tits off. This is not fucking funny." Her eyes had gone mine shaft dark.

"Please just listen," I said. "That's all."

What better time for another patron to enter the Ladies'? Just like in the movies, I crowded Char into a stall and flipped the latch. She was trying to meter her breathing, looking at me as if I were a dog pie on the sidewalk, while we enjoyed the aerosol noise of someone else pissing. What the hell, right? Passionate drunks copulated in toilets all the time. There must be something about the smell of excrement, air freshener, melon hand soap, and composted tampons that turns some people on, I guessed.

"Do you remember Mister Kimber, from that night at the loft?"

"Do you know that you're eyebrow-deep in shit?" she snapped, harsh. "They think the Soviet killed herself."

"I know."

"*Joey* is dead."

I did not know that. My gut bungeed.

"At least, I'm pretty sure it's Joey, from what I heard. Clavius is out for your blood for involving him. And you look a lot like a jerkoff trying to run away from the police. That about cover it?"

She blew her nose on a streamer of toilet paper and dug in her pocket for her coke vial. She tapped out two lines on the back of her hand. "Disapproval is not allowed," she said, then aspirated the cocaine.

"Kimber is the guy who set me up," I said. "I have no idea what his actual name is. He set me up to frame Dominic Sharps with blackmail photos. Sharps died. But Kimber or whatever his name is went ahead with the scheme anyway. I used Clavius paper for the photos as a sort of SOS. When you left Nasja's camera on RECORD, I got video of Kimber talking about killing Sharps. It all went viral and now the mysterious Mister Not-Really-Kimber is killing everyone I know, everyone who saw him. Everyone."

"Jesus *christ*," she said, still sniffing. "I'll have whatever *you're* on."

"I don't understand it, Char. All I know is people are dying. Kimber saw you. Worse, he saw you on that night."

"The night he took that stupid framed print of yours."

"Please, please—this isn't about you and me. Just get yourself safe. Get behind Clavius's walls and surrounded yourself with bodyguards and don't come out until it's over."

She was still weighing me for telltale signs of madness. "You're not joking," she said more slowly. "You believe in this *fantasy*." A quick stab of pain at her temples caused her eyes to mist as she tried to massage her head. "The loft was wrecked. I told the police *you* wrecked it, because I left. Clavius said he had explained everything to you. You're not doing anything to prove you haven't gone batshit; I mean, *look* at you."

Post-urination, our guest had left one of the taps dripping. It echoed.

"I had to call Tripp," I said. "Get under. Get out. New identity."

"Stop it," she protested. "Just shut up!" She left the stall to lean on the sink and watch me over her shoulder, in the mirror, weary, as though the marrow had been drained out of her while she wasn't looking. "I heard about the tattoos and piercings on the people they found in your loft," she said. "I'm pretty sure that was Joey and his girlfriend, Velma—"

"Varla."

"—but nobody could tell because their *faces* were blown off!"

Lay low? Dude, you can stay at my place. Gun Guy had nailed Joey, I was sure of it, and Joey hadn't been involved at all, except by knowing me. And inadvertently saving my bacon with the enlarger. Tickling the information about the cat food planet from the Internet. He had gone so far as to offer me a fake ID before I went into Tripp's witness protection program.

Even Joey had paid the ghastly price for being my friend.

Char turned back from the steel lip of the bowl sink. "You said, when it's over. When is it over?"

"When I'm dead, I think."

"Well, be sure to let Clavius know when that happens. He needs his giclées done on time."

Her body was making those preparing-to-leave movements.

"Char, I—"

"You *nothing*," she said. "You never know when you're *over*; you can't amputate anything even when it's killing you. You just wait for gangrene to rot it off. I'm going now. Don't follow me. It's been fucking hell knowing you. Best of luck with your career. Asshole."

She hadn't even gone to the bathroom. At best she would have managed three drops. All the rest had vented as superheated steam.

I wanted very badly to talk to Rebecca Effner, but I had no idea how to find her anymore.

Day seven was mostly second-unit motion control shots at the airplane hangar in New Jersey. Hunnicutt brought his birds and Garrett Torres, antagonist, was holed up in his hotel room in the city, front-loading orange juice and antibiotics to head off an impending cold that made his distinctive voice sound as though he had been inhaling helium. Collier was also doing pickups on angles of various gunfights, which required a lot of costume changes—bits and pieces from all over the movie. Most of it was MOS—"mitt out sound"—but the sound cart was present so I brought my new camera blimps.

Shooting during shooting, so to speak, required the blimps—big soundproof boxes in which the cameras were imprisoned into silence on the set, so I can capture an image or two you might glimpse as an eight-by-ten in a press packet, or a saucy shot in an advertisement a year from now when the movie is being marketed. Film magazines, coming-soon Web sites, and suchlike hungry for the skinny on production had to go through the publicity liaison to get their mitts on my images. Spooky Sellers—that was really her name, supposedly—was the PR person responsible for setting up interviews and spin-doctoring all media access to the production in progress, and it was a new feeling to have somebody at my back that way, like Mason Stone must have felt about his personal soldier, the imposing Dick Fearing. Spooky was short, round, blonde, bobbed, blue-eyed, and flirty. We played at getting her to stand still long enough for me to get a decent photo of her (with her clothes on, I mean), and quickly developed a shorthand signal language. When she cocked her hand into a sort of bird shape, like Lurch or Vlad, that meant "get over here and cover this." A little wave behind her back meant "stress alert—don't shoot this." And so on.

She, too, was trapped in constant doubt over her own im-portance, and came off a bit needy when she tried to peel me free for an after-hours cocktail. The way she put it was, "I hope you don't mind me asking, but . . ."

No way I could risk it, so I begged off, pleading work.

My job was to stealth around the main unit all feline, unobtrusively; most often I bumped into Arly with his video camera, trying to do the same, always two steps too late. *Click*: here was Mason Stone joking with the grips, Styro coffee cups all around. *Click*: here was Collier framing a shot with his hands; that would be good for the profile *Cinema Sleuth* would run on him, eight months later.

I was invisible. Nobody ever shot pictures of the unit photographer. The routine was soothing. Elias McCabe had major problems; Julian Hightower did not.

Before lunch I dumped my RAW files into my laptop for logging and hijacked Arly's computer to dredge up something more on what Mason kept calling the Salon, making it sound like a fleshpit he just had to experience.

The clues online were vaporous. The full name was the Salon Fantastique de l'Exotique, with just the right pinch of phony, feelthy French leer, which made it hard to Google since I couldn't read French (although the translation software could still provide hours of hilarity). One brief bit compared the Salon to the Grand Guignol, others likened it to the freak shows of carnival days gone by. Freak shows were technically illegal in our highly moral age, which is why the Jim Rose's Circus Sideshow did not deal in deformity. Most of the orts I clicked had not been updated since 1999.

You probably don't remember a notorious short story titled "Spurs." It was the foundation for one of Tod Browning's most notorious films, the 1932 MGM version of *Freaks*.

Alternate title: *Nature's Mistakes.*

Which became my doorway to finding out about the Salon.

Supposedly, the Salon Fantastique de l'Exotique came into being when sideshow freak tents and exhibitions of "oddities" on carnival midways were forced into extinction by political correctitude. One army of do-gooders erased the visible means of support for rubber men and alligator women around the world, while another wave protested that "those people" should be able to earn a living. While the social outrage swam round and round, freak shows were banned, outlawed, and finally obliterated in the 1970s and '80s. Now the only place you could find pickled punks or two-headed calfs were in remote highway stopovers, removed from civilization in most other ways as well. It took longer to happen throughout Europe, but gradually, the ogre of civil rights shot itself in the foot there, too. Social propriety disenfranchised them even more, when most *wanted* to exploit themselves, and preferred working to poverty and marginalization. Even calling them "freaks" became a no-no, despite the fact that's what they comfortably called themselves.

I could see where this was headed.

The Salon started in Russia or somewhere in the Ukraine. Nasja may have even mentioned it once or twice. Strictly underground, members only, a combination of traveling speakeasy and Algonquin Round Table of human oddities who had banded together and learned a very important trick from the world of porn.

I used to know a fellow named Moonshine who ran a burger and biker bar called the Kickstand in Nevada. Since he wasn't inside the boundaries of Cook County where prostitution had been conditionally legalized, you had to know about his bungalow of sex rooms in order to ask for them. It was a little maze of chambers outfitted with big showers, towels, lube, toys, a dentist's chair, a mechanical bull, suspension racks, torture gear, cuffs, masks, rope, a wet bar, and a handy take-out menu for food delivery. Renting the rooms for play purposes was illegal, but allowing their use for free was not—provided you paid what Moonshine called a "beverage charge," an appropriately astronomical fee that got you the same booze he served at the bar inside the Kickstand for real-world prices. You paid the beverage fee by the hour and were served through a discreet airlock slot (like a miniature of the door on my now-defunct darkroom back in L.A.) which, just by happy coincidence, fed into the sex rooms. You then enjoyed your refreshment inside one of these rooms, which, by sheerest chance, just so happened to be loaded with gear designed to enhance the fornicatory experience. You weren't obligated to utilize any of those nasty contraptions, of course. You could ignore them if you wanted to.

Just as the Kickstand had, the Salon discovered a template for resurrection and commerce in the loophole of the "beverage charge." Problem was, their clientele was so high-class that groundlings were never able to enjoy any placard-waving outrage. It was a mythic tease, a fancy having everything to do with the jaded tastes of the upper crust, just like the legendary strip bar in Hollywood where you can, it is rumored, be serviced in various ways by TV and movie actors on the wane.

Except I knew that place—That Obscure Object of Desire in Brentwood—was real. That hottie teen Jezebel from the *No, I Don't Think So* series? She could be found at the Object, ten years older now, and would suck you off for a fast fifty. So the stories I'd heard about the Salon were probably not far from the truth. Next problem: no one could get in, get news, or get a clue. No one except celebrities like Mason Stone, who had just invited me to tag along with him, schedule permitting. With my cameras. As "Jules."

Ever notice how much time people spend talking about food? Was I the only person who found this weird? Maybe it is one of the reasons for America's much documented all-time high in obesity; or perhaps just one of the few common grounds for communication left to a culture in which fewer and fewer citizens can accumulate any sort of shared experience.

There's no such thing as "watercooler conversation" anymore, if you follow. Coffee came from a boutique at five bucks a pop, and mass culture had devolved to YouTube, reality TV, and movies derived from toys and comic books, leaving only a stubborn minority who did not need that whole "reading for pleasure" thing explained to them. Those that still read (or could read), all read different books. But everybody had to eat.

Across and three down at the lunch table, grips were talking about what they'd eaten, where they ate it, how it stacked up against other things they'd eaten, personal food bests, what they anticipated eating next. It filled the air almost like an actual conversation, or the "how are you, I am fine" rote that fills a page in a holiday letter from, say, one's grandparents. Empty calories of talk. It was almost as bleak as hearing new parents blather on about their offspring. Listen:

"I had them pork chops yesterday. This snapper is good. But them pork chops is better."

"I like the caraway seeds on 'em."

"Yeah, only pork chops I had was as good was on a set in Texas."

"They have barbeque sauce on 'em?"

"Naw, they was just pork chops, but they was good."

"They have the seeds on 'em?"

"Naw. But these are pretty good. Well, they're not bad for pork chops."

"I like pork chops every once in a while."

"Yeah, you dunk 'em in applesauce, they're not bad."

Just so you know, these were union men talking. And I was being an elitist snob, dissing classic American table conversation.

Crew lunch was a brisk forty-five-minute window. Andrew Collier rarely ate at the catering tent, but when he did, he always sat down with the crew, as did Mason Stone. More often Collier sent his assistant out into the wilds of Manhattan, where there are arguably more good restaurants bunched together than any place in the world, for take-out. Every Friday, Mason Stone picked up the check for an à la carte surprise meal for the whole company. One week it was a fleet of trucks from White

Castle; the next, a platoon of sushi chefs. This magnanimity endeared Stone to the crews, at least when he was not having one of his prima donna furniture-smashing episodes.

If Stone could afford that extravagant mobile home, like a yacht on wheels, he could easily absorb the tab for all the crab roll and unagi ninety-five people could wolf down, but it was his willingness to make the gesture that provided a huge portion of his public persona. It was all written off as PR. He kept encouraging my tag along on his sortie to the darkly mysterious Salon, so I wondered at his true agenda.

Meanwhile, I had other crew members to collar. Michelle Bonaventure, a hairstylist attached to the makeup key, had agreed to trim and color my hair. Char's news about Joey and meeting Mister Kimber had discombobulated me enough to seek a deeper disguise as Julian Hightower, no doubt about it. On impulse I cited Cap Weatherwax as a model, and we compromised on a sort of brush cut. When we were done I completely did not look like me anymore. My mustache and goatee had been on my face for more than two decades, and I still missed them. Men looked more like men with facial hair, and less like the corporate Aryan wet dreams of fashion photography, at least to my dark-adapted eye.

Then I had to work up the testosterone to broach my illegal gun to Cap. The smuggled Kimber was still in pieces. I had taken it apart but was unable to puzzle it back together. I brought it up on the heels of a barter arrangement with Cap to provide a detailed photo inventory of the contents of his arsenal truck, which he had mentioned he needed for insurance purposes— a lot of extra work for which we had to steal time minute by minute as *Vengeance Is* rolled into its second week.

Every weapon in the truck needed several shots. Left profile, right profile, and a dynamic three-quarter orthographic view, usually in Cap's hand for scale. Cylinder out; action open. I opened a new project file called Guns and began to fill it. Many of the weapons were flashy in accord with the need of movies to show new and interesting things first, and in the gun subcategory there was a not-so-subtle race to be the first movie to feature name-checked weaponry.

To elaborate, Cap held up a subnosed pistol. "Nickel-plated .32 caliber Colt Police Positive—Charlie Bronson in the first *Death Wish*." Then I photographed a gigantic hand-cannon revolver. "Smith & Wesson Model 29 .44 Magnum with an eight-and-a-half-inch barrel—Clint, in the first *Dirty Harry*. Beretta nine, model 92F with a fifteen-round mag, a fucking classic— Mel Gibson in the first *Lethal Weapon*. It's supposed to be the premier appearance of the Beretta in an American movie, but John Carpenter got there before Dick Donner. And John Woo got there a year before either of them.

"Point is, movie guns become iconographic. People see 'em in movies and want to buy them, and sales for that model surge, and when that happens, sometimes the gun companies comp your whole stock, just so you'll use their brand name."

"Just like Coke and Chrysler," I said.

"They give you freebies, too," Cap said. "Check this out; it's insane."

He hoisted up a scary configuration that looked like Dali's idea of a flowing, Surrealist table leg with a trigger grip only a Martian could grasp properly. "Fabrique Nationale Project 90," he said. "From Belgium; the U.S. Government version. Bullpup design makes it shorter. It's ambidextrous. Special fifty-round mag sits flat on top of the gun instead of poking downward like you're probably used to seeing. Spent shells drop out the bottom so they don't bounce off your face. Shoots a NATO round slightly better than nine mil. I thought this looked pretty distinctive, wanted to use it for the bikers from hell in this movie, but some other guy working some other movie already beat me to it."

Slowly, I was catching on. "What was that gun Pacino had in *Heat*?" I said.

"Which one? His duty gun or the rifle?"

"I remember the rifle." Nearby everybody did.

He put the Dali gun down so I could shoot profiles of it. "Same make as this—FNC-80 with a shortened barrel and some-body added a birdcage flash hider, like an M-16. Not that it hid anything. Directors like muzzle flashes, especially the starburst kind. They put 'em in digitally if the camera doesn't read 'em. Persistence of vision, y'know."

Hence the full-powder blanks, during Mason Stone's mis-credited Night of Thunder. At twenty-four frames per second, conventional film could miss the flash, which sometimes came "between the frames," so to speak. Persistence of vision is what allowed you to perceive twenty-four still pictures as one sec-ond of movement.

"Did those Bank of America robbers use the same guns when they hit that place in North Hollywood?" I said. "You know, the robbery Heat looks like a training film for?"

"No way," said Cap. "Those guys had AKs, a Bushmaster, and an illegally converted Heckler-Koch. Their ordnance and footwork were good but their marksmanship sucked. They cheesed away over a thousand rounds but ignored the rules of shoot-move-and-cover—actually, they should have paid more attention to the movie. The guy who blew his own brains out used a Beretta nine. What a miracle, he actually hit something."

If Cap was ever to be warmed up, now was the time. I slowly brought the components of the disassembled Kimber out of my work pack and lined them up on the display table. "Can you tell me about this gun?" I said.

He narrowed his eyes at it first, me next.

Then, just to show off, Cap assembled the Kimber in about ten seconds. He snapped the action dry—no clip—and then knowingly said, "This thing isn't papered, is it?"

Guilt made me look everywhere but at the workbench in the truck. "Papered?"

He pointed to the stamped Kimber legend on the slide. "Should be a serial number right there," he said. "But there isn't one scratched off or etched by acid. It was never there to begin with or this was refinished by an expert. See this? Skeletonized hammer. Match trigger. Those are the sort of mods you get from a custom shop. Now see this? There used to be what's called a grip safety there, but it isn't there anymore. This thing has been through several rounds of customization, and not all by the same shop." He weighed the pistol in his hand. "The loaded balance bears me out. This is a professional's gun, and I don't mean a professional target shooter. Hence, unpapered. It doesn't exist. I should be calling the cops about now, because this is live ammo and we're connected to a film shoot. Liability."

"Somehow I get the feeling you're not going to call the cops," I said hopefully.

"Several reasons." Cap rubbed his face and raked his hand over his scalp. "First, we're *near* the set, not on it. Second, we're *in* the truck, not outside. Third, nobody can see us doing this. I have the right to have live rounds in my own personal sidearm." He patted the Para-Ordnance .45 strapped to his hip. "I can take this on a commercial flight if I want, but I don't. Concealed carry and a smaller gun works better for travel."

I saw a quick flash of the fate of hijackers on any airplane where Cap happened to be among the passengers. "You're skipping over something," I said.

"Should be obvious," Cap returned. "I'd like to buy this from you if you're willing to sell it."

"I'll make a deal with you," I said. "Strictly outside *Vengeance Is*. I'd like you to show me how to shoot it. How to strip it, load it, use it with a purpose. I'd like to be able to hit a target. I've never fired a gun in my life. I'm not planning on boosting liquor stores or becoming a gunslinger. Totally for my own protection."

"Yeah, I kinda got the feeling that you might be in some kinda trouble."

"There's a man looking for me I think wants to kill me."

"That why you dyed your hair?"

"Partially, yes."

"Color looks weird," said Cap. "Too yellow." He offered me a diet beer from a little fridge beneath what I took to be a gun-cleaning station in the truck. "This is swill, this lite-beer crap, but I've got to skin off a few pounds."

I took the chilly can gratefully. He destroyed half of his in one gulp.

"Okay," he said. "First thing we've gotta do is get you out in the boonies where we test-fire all the practical guns. My schedule is limited for that sort of thing so you're gonna have to adapt. You might have to jump when I say so, agreed?"

"Done," I said, having no idea whether I could make the time fit.

"Foremost thing is you do every single thing I tell you, when I tell you. Questions are okay but in matters of handling I am God. Good by you?"

I nodded, remembering what Char had said: *Disapproval is not allowed.* I was pleased Cap had cut me the same slack.

"Next is: you leave that thing in the truck," he said. "Don't carry it around, don't flash it, don't talk about it."

"It doesn't technically exist," I said, resisting the urge to pick it up one more time. That would be bad. Amateurish.

"See, I told you and you did it. Good sign. All right, you've got a conditional deal, Mr. Hightower." He winked. "If that really *is* your name."

Somewhere out there was a world where people had families and families were enough, because that was what people "did." I was beginning to prefer film jail to the civilian realm of the ordinary.

Now Char would haunt me for the rest of my life. She had used her body like a rental car to ascend the career ladder, and now someone else had used it as a canvas, plagiarizing me. It was all over the shit-sheets, luridly printed, suggestive in its blotchy splash spreads and bargain-basement pulp paper re-pro: CRUCIFIXION HORROR IN GARMENT DISTRICT.

Gun Guy had followed me to New York City. He collected Char on the same day I had spoken to her, and used *Targets #5* as the framing scheme for her death, substituting stab wounds for bullet holes. Traces of commercial lubricant were found, which meant that sometime during the horrific ordeal he penetrated her the other way, using a latex condom to preserve his anonymity. My throat closed up. I hoped Char had not been alive for that violation. Hope was a joke and Char was dead.

I had known her; made love to her. Loved her, in fact, for whatever that cheap sentiment was worth now. Char would have hated her death to evoke a work of mine she so disliked. Now they would be linked forever. It was a matter of heartbeats before some snoopy dirt-hound found reference on *Targets #5* and made the match . . . then Elias McCabe would have one more offense to answer for.

Julian Hightower did not know Charlene Glades.

If I had kept the Kimber with me, reassembled, locked and loaded, I might have stuck it in my own mouth at that moment. But even that sentiment, far cheaper than my delusion of romance with Char, was soiled and untenable because Gun Guy had done *that* to me, too. Humiliating, all around.

I sat in my little office, not knowing what to do. My tubes were all plugged with remorse.

Arly Zahoryin rattled in, sloughing off his orthopedic-looking camera rig. "Tripp just banned all personal cameras from the set," he said, making a victory fist. "Yeah, baby!"

"What?" Arly's face was a white blur to me.

"Too many leaks," Arly said, jaunty. "A shot of Garrett Torres in makeup showed up on a coming-soon site and Collier had a shit meltdown."

"How're you going to stop people from taking pictures with their phones?" I asked.

"You can't. So, you do it and get caught, your ass is totally fired. The memo will be in everyone's boxes tomorrow morning."

In the main production office, heartbeat central for all things related to *Vengeance Is*, was a honeycomb of cubbyholes for such directives; I even had a slot bearing my new name and job designation. Half of them (not mine) were stuffed daily with rainbow-colored script revision pages. That seemed strange because there was no actual writer on the set I could perceive, which meant the sheets were being modified as shooting progressed, most likely by Collier, or in committee with the line producer and Gordo the AD. Locations changed, sets were reconfigured, dialogue was altered, whole scenes were dropped, and already shot scenes (or changed text) were denoted by a vertical row of asterisks. Scene 42 became Sc. 42-A-B-B(i)-C. The revisions followed a rigid color code—blue, pink, yellow, green, goldenrod, buff, salmon, cherry, tan, gray, all the way back to white, and started all over again. By the end of production the script resembled an unwieldy catalogue twice its original length, holes punched in the wrong places, some pages jutting out past the trim line (like a mad composer's fever-dream sonata scribbled while on a laudanum binge), as varicolored as a peacock. When the script was at last in its most complete and final form . . . nobody needed it, because the project was done.

And nobody in the outside world gave a damn, either.

Arly unhinged the tiny monitor screen on his camera and treated me to some playback of his stalking activities. It was less than reassuring.

The frame was afflicted with the shaky-cam jitters, and underlit in a sodium-yellow monochrome, heavily artifacted, but starring center screen was Andrew Collier in his pastel shirt, wearing a bandana, with goggles perched on his gimme cap, smashing a Bluetooth on the floor near Video Village and then stomping on it like Scrooge McDuck, screaming about gag orders, nondisclosure, his vision, and who the fuck are you anyway? He was beet-red and spluttering with rage. His voice cracked.

"You fucking pillock! Who the fuck do you think you fucking are? Do you think we're spending a half-million dollars a day so you can put pictures on some goddamned knocking-shop fucking Web site when I specifically, specifically *said no shots of Garrett Torres under any fucking circumstances?! Who are you, anyway? What the fuck do you* do? *Gordo, take this arsehole out and fucking shoot him in the head!*

The nondescript crew member was swiftly escorted away while Collier continued to vent for a full thirty seconds more. It was not the director's brightest moment, but it did become one of his most infamous.

"Is that *classic*?" said Arly, pleased with his combat photography skills.

"But you can't use it, right?" I said.

"I already used it." He smirked. "I pixilated it to look like cell phone footage. Because earlier, I got a shot of the guy, I think he was a grip, shooting Torres in makeup while he was sweet-talking some camera girl. That's what I showed to Gordo, right *after* I posted the Collier rant-and-rave anonymously. Gordo showed Tripp and Tripp came unglued. Now all cameras are banned from the set—except ours."

"And you're a player because you exposed a spy," I said. "Don't you feel bad that you just lost that guy his job?"

"To hell with *him*; he's a donkey," said Arly. "Those guys fart around all day and all they do is bitch about overtime and talk about getting shitfaced and going to the beach. They don't care that they're on a set. They're always wandering into a background or making noise when they're not supposed to, chatting and texting instead of doing their job. They lug lumber and should be fed gruel and chained up at night. They act like its this huge imposition to do anything. They don't feel honored to be here."

Now I saw the lightbulb: what Arly *really* wanted to do was *direct*. His camera and mine would be the sole live lenses for behind-the-scenes . . . at least until Spooky Sellers showed up with an EPK crew, which didn't actually count to Arly in the universe of cinema.

Electronic Press Kit shooters came in under the wing of the publicist—Spooky Sellers—usually on celebrity-heavy days, to shoot all the froth and nonsense important to shows like *HBO First Look*. They monopolized the talent, strictly grazing inside a two- or three-day window. They set up canvas chairs and a backdrop and lights and grab face time hosted by some ex-weather girl who pretended she had a deep personal bond with actors who did not like her. They were not part of the crew tribe and the crew disdained them as a necessary nuisance. Aware of their status, they tended to flaunt their privilege, tripping over C-stands and generally pissing off anyone below-the-line. Then they were gone before anybody could really sabotage them.

Andrew Collier and his stars grinned and bore it the way one would an embarrassing relative. It was part of the promotional game. Arly hated them because they had better equipment and even they, too, could make him get out of the way. If Arly ever got one of his own projects going, he had the makings of a total martinet, a monster who would make everyone pay someday for all the wrongs done unto him. Then he would get his turn at a similar *Candid Camera* blowup, all in the name of his creativity and vision. People would grumble, "god, what a jerk" . . . and then ask to work with him. That was Arly's dream.

Andrew Collier never would have indulged his tantrum demon if the EPK crew had been hanging around. Set drama was supposed to stay in Vegas. That was before the new century whisked in the new surveillance, causing everybody to double-check their emotional reactions. It's tough when you can't even slam your steering wheel and call the tourist cretin ahead of you in traffic a dick, because somebody is capturing an image of you doing it—an image that could wind up on TV or in the hands of a prosecutor. To most civilians, TV was still reality, not the other way around. "Look, he did it, I saw him doing it, it's right there on the screen, he took his hands off the wheel, he was probably texting, test him for alcohol, test him for anger, he's probably got a gun in the glove box, check his jacket, because nobody is innocent."

Now Arly's squalid subterfuge had breached the sanctity of film jail. If I thought I was safe here, I was nurturing a comforting lie.

Somewhere in the New Jersey marshland, in an automobile graveyard, a forsaken potter's field of junked cars. Me, Cap Weatherwax, and Cap's 4Runner full of ordnance. The 4Runner had a police chaser engine, a built-in roll cage, nondeflating tires and bulletproof glass—the whole Severe Service Package.

Lined up for target practice: gallon jugs of colored water at twenty-five paces. Not glass, which might come back at you.

Cap's initial drills involved not gunfire, but handling. Pop the clip, lock the action, check the barrel. Reinsert the clip, release the action, thumb on the hammer, you're hot. Do this several hundred times. Get to know the gun, the weight of it, observe how its parts work in concert, and "what the fuck are you doing touching the trigger, newbie?" A fucking gangbanger amateur no-no. Align the finger alongside the trigger guard and don't even think about it, not even casually, unless you're committed to the pull.

Next, paradoxically, you get to touch the trigger. Dry-firing on an empty mag. Forty pulls in thirty seconds. Try it sometime; it's harder than it looks. Now with the other hand. Now repeat. Hundreds more times.

This is your ammo. Forty-cal hardball here. Nine-millimeter Parabellum there. Do not confuse the magazines. Load them with your thumb. Unload them with your thumb. Push each cartridge down hard against the spring. Learn the wiggle. Build a callus. Over and over. Do it until your hands stink of brass and full-metal-jacketed rounds; nothing else smells like that.

It was a lot like good old-fashioned film grinding. Prep, load, lock, point-and-shoot. This is not digital. Know how many shots you have. You've cleaned your cameras, now clean this gun. Now clean it again. Break it down, put it back together, give it a shoeshine and a little attention and it will never fail you. That's good, you got most of the crap off, now do it again. Again.

"Where the fuck do you think you're pointing that cock? What are you, Wyatt fucking Earp?" This end goes bang and knocks people down. Always know where it is pointed. No such thing as a casual move with a firearm. Be aware.

My hands were aching and sprung after the first session, yesterday, in the truck, late at night. Cap had lent me a SIG SAUER .40 with a blank adapter and neon-colored plastic dummy rounds. Every time you look at that gun, do it again, he said. Break it down, clean it, reassemble it, dry-fire. Shave your personal best for timing. Then shave it some more. Lock the action, check the barrel, do it again.

Now do it blindfolded.

It's a simple configuration, basically four parts. Barrel assembly, spring, slide, frame. Know its weight, its feel, its balance, its attitude. Do it right and the whole deal works. Never be not sure.

Now do it blindfolded while I pitch crap at you, make sudden loud noises, and force you to recite Marullus's speech about blocks and stones. "Knew you not Pompey?" And don't you dare get it wrong.

That night when I cleaned and loaded my film cameras, my hands were shaking. Tactile discipline had been biased. New muscle memory was being shaped.

Now, in the auto junkyard, Cap had a workstation built out a door across two sawhorses, tableclothed in vinyl. Boxes of cartridges, fifty each snugged in foam or plastic, lined up like building blocks.

"Now," he said. "Show me what you've learned."

I had still never fired a live round from a gun.

I broke the SIG down and held the barrel in the air. Don't blow in it—moisture is the enemy of every firearm. A soft cloth rubdown for powder residue; the cloth should come clean, the white-glove treatment. Reassemble with the action open. He handed me a magazine. "Load that, release to chamber, and decock," he said.

"Wait," I said. "This is the wrong clip."

"Good," he said, taking back the Beretta clip of nines and handing back the SIG clip.

I seated the magazine. You always feel for the click of engagement. I hit the slide lever and eased the slide forward "into battery" with my free hand instead of letting it snap. The movement hoisted the first round into the chamber. You could look for brass by inching the slide backward just a degree, to verify a loaded chamber, which Cap called a "thumb check." Index finger alongside frame. Do not engage trigger. Right thumb down on the decocking lever. One soft click as the hammer rests in the intercept notch. Now the firing pin is locked. No such thing as an accidental discharge possible. SIGs don't feature safeties on the theory that no safety is foolproof. Instead they have the decocking lever, intended to put the gun in neutral and allow law enforcement, for whom the pistol was designed, to get off a fast first shot. You thumb the hammer full back—one click—and the whole package is hot.

"You switched guns on me, didn't you?" I asked.

Cap almost smiled. "What makes you think that?"

I didn't look at the SIG at all. It was a copy, a substitute, not the weapon I had manhandled through primary gun school. I just knew. "This feels different," I said. "I'd know it even in a dark room. I think you swapped out my stainless steel SIG with the blank adapter for an identical SIG without. I think you just handed me a mag of live rounds and I just loaded them into a hot gun."

"Well, if you're so fucking smart," said Cap, "why don't you take a shot at one of those bottles over there?"

Behind the row of bottles was a stack of junkers. This would prevent wild shots from flying off into the troposphere, or maybe landing on some poor civilian's skull a town and a half away.

Cap handed over shooting glasses and a set of bright red headphones. He donned a pair himself. We had used these on the set to adumbrate the noise of movie gunfire. We had worn them constantly on the *Night of Thunder*. I had doffed them a couple of times just to hear the palette of noise for real.

Now Cap's voice was muffled and distant although he was speaking louder to compensate. "We can lose this later so you can get used to live fire."

The last time I had heard a live round go off—as Elias—was in my darkroom where it had converted me into a snail-ball on the floor.

"Ready on the firing line," Cap said. "Hot range."

I stepped up to the line Cap had etched in the dirt and lifted the gun in a two-handed grip.

Before I could thumb back the hammer, Cap said, "No."

"What?"

"That's really adorable," Cap said of the aggro way I held the piece. "That's called a 'cup and saucer.' See how your left hand is underneath your shoot hand? Cup and saucer. What's that for, to keep you from dropping it?"

"I thought—"

"No," he overrode. "Are you in SWAT? Do you know the two-step? How not to cross your legs in front of each other? No. Shoot it one-handed. Full extension of your arm. The gun is a method of reaching out, long-distance."

I had practiced this during my dry-firing. Now the weight of the gun at the end of my arm was nothing at all. Muscle memory accommodated it.

"That sight is zeroed," Cap said. "Just line it up and drop it just a hair to compensate for the top of the sight because you're looking at the dots. See? There's a microscopic difference. Pull it to full cock. *Then* aim, the way I just told you."

"Trigger?"

"Just kiss it with your fingertip. You know the pull already, about four pounds. Squeeze, don't jerk. Whenever you're ready."

I shut one eye and might have even stuck out my tongue tip, real Western.

"Don't do that," said Cap. "You ain't fucking one-eyed Pete or something. Try to keep both eyes open. You won't be able to on the first shot, but you can learn how."

Binocular vision seemed to veto this, so I just turned my head a bit.

"Fire when ready."

"Very apropos," I said.

Bang.

The SIG nearly jumped out of my hand. My wrist felt slammed as though I was sparring with a boxer and had just caught a good punch.

A sad little wisp of dust spiraled into the air behind the bottles, which the bullet had come nowhere near. I held the extension; the gun was ready to fire again, so I did not drop sights or wave it around as if it were spent. It was ready; I was still owlishly awaiting permission to fire again.

"Correct your aim and fire again," said Cap. "Don't drop your arm until you're out." Out meant empty.

The second shot was easier. Now I anticipated the recoil, even though it completely spoiled my aim. The third shot came faster and easier.

"Don't rush through it," said Cap. "Aim. Otherwise you're just pissing on a hot plate. Don't crush the trigger. Don't snap it."

The gun seemed to beg to be fired. That was its purpose. Each shot flowed more smoothly into the next. *Bang, bang.* The air seemed to evacuate from around my head with each discharge; that was something I wasn't used to and did not expect. I regained control of my arm quicker, and compensated for the up-and-down bob. *Bang*.

Bang. The action locked back. I knew it would, but it still seemed odd to see it do that all on its own. The gun was ready to be fed again.

I hadn't hit a single thing except the backstop of junkers.

"Barrel down, finger off the trigger," Cap said. I had forgotten to do that. "Now, in competition, speed-reloading is a big deal but we're not gonna worry about that right now. Here." He lifted the SIG from my grasp and dumped the empty magazine.

I stared at the inviolate row of bottles. "Jesus," I said. "I *suck*."

"Naah, you're just getting started," said Cap. "First time you shot a picture, was it a perfect picture?"

"Anything but."

"Well, there you go." He unsnapped his Para-Ord .45, pulled the hammer to full cock, and emptied his mag in about three seconds—nine shots. Each bottle sprouted a wide mouth and collapsed or began spewing water. Nine bottles, nine bullets, nine hits, no waiting.

"Okay," he said as the air spiced up with gunsmoke, "now it's your turn again."

A little later—after I had hit two bottles out of nine in, I don't know, thirty seconds—Cap lined up a set of different targets at the same distance. Smaller.

"What are those?" I said. "DVDs?"

Yeah, they were. Nine copies of *Die Hard 2*. I had to ask.

"Worst offender of all," Cap said. "You don't just pull a clip of blanks out of a goddamned MP5 and substitute live ammo. That gun needs blank adapters to cycle blanks. First live round would make the fucking gun blow up in your hand."

"You mean there's no such thing as a porcelain gun?" I said, paraphrasing Bruce Willis.

"There no such thing as a 'Glock 7' *at all*," he said with unveneered contempt. "They made that shit up. The guns in that movie are Glock 17s with lipstick on 'em, as I like to say. Tarted up. But they're not porcelain, or plastic, or any goddamned thing because they'd blow up or melt if you shot them. Glocks have polymer parts, sure, but there's plenty of steel or the gun *would not work*. And the ammo would show up on X-ray. And they're not made in Germany; they're made in Austria, for fuck's sake."

Another mag for the Para-Ord and four seconds later, all nine copies of the special edition had burst apart into plastic shrapnel, disabled from spreading their untruths.

"And don't even get me started on how a round from a Beretta nine can't punch through a mahogany table and still have enough velocity to kill a guy," he said. "Maybe one round in twenty."

He handed me a Beretta 92F and a magazine. "You don't believe me, see for yourself."

PART NINE

A MAN CALLED JACK

I watched Clavius speak to the detective from my secret hiding place. It took a fair bit of setting up, but I needed a read on Elias McCabe's mentor before I decided whether he was worth killing.

Prior to that trick 'r treat I found out a bit more about the Clavius empire. The "C" Corporation was diversified into things ranging from paper products—like the watermarked photo paper—to a hand sanitizer called ElGel, marketed under the company division named Illium, after Marlowe's poem about the siege of Troy. At a glance it did not appear that Clavius spent as much time on art anymore as he did on being Clavius; his last big show of note had been titled "9/11.5." He had invested much more time in becoming his *own* artwork.

I settled into my hide to observe as the artwork spoke to the cop.

Detective First Grade Hanson Stoner Jr. was admitted—gradually—to Clavius's offices on the power of his shield and ID, representing Manhattan South borough, Fourteenth Precinct, also known as Midtown Precinct South. His gold shield bore no number (lieutenants and above being identified by their tax registry numbers instead) and the laminate ID card's photo featured Stoner against a red background, indicating he was commissioned to carry a firearm. The photo looked about two years old; Stoner had threads of gray in his now slightly longer blond hair and brush mustache. A lot of New York cops had cookie-dusters like his.

Clavius was clad in a loose white cable-knit sweater and worsted wool slacks, and tended to keep the air conditioning on his floor about five degrees below comfortable. Right behind Stoner an attendant wheeled in a full service coffee tray and parked it at the edge of a vast Persian rug, a Herez Serapi with 180 knots per square inch, a steal at $40,000. There wasn't a mote of dust in the room, which contained a twenty-foot curve of glass desk piled haphazardly with things needing Clavius's attention, several mammoth modernist canvases (slightly disturbing in their implied chaos; I did not recognize the artist, but then, I had only recently acquired my first piece of what could be termed "art," myself), and a museum-framed Picasso ink sketch hung in an obvious place of honor. Clavius was washing his hands in a small wet bar sink when Stoner was escorted in. As always, his complexion was rosy, as if he had just vigorously scrubbed his face. He had some green-toned aloe vera concoction he used to cut the red whenever his image was to be captured by nontechnical photographers. White brows, white hair, cut medium short and combed straight back. It was completely unfair, yet impossible not to see him as the privileged scion of some woebegone ex-Gestapo guy. He ignored Stoner completely until he had finished drying his hands, then regarded him on silent standby, forcing Stoner to cross the rug, to come to *him* for the pro forma handshake, which was three dry pumps followed by a grab for the nearest bottle of ElGel. He had on Japanese paper slippers and requested that Stoner remove his shoes prior to crossing the expanse of rug.

This guy Clavius was all about power games, and had obviously taken Sun Tzu far too seriously.

"First Grade Detective Stoner," said Clavius, glancing at the card on the glass tabletop but not touching it. "That's an odd notion, isn't it? A detective of first grade would be in charge of, what? Recess? Ah, please disregard my pathetic little jokes, Detective. Wordplay is one of the few things that stimulates me anymore." That was obvious from his cutesy company name, designed so his single letter "C" would appear right after the copyright symbol, another "c."

His limpid, colorless eyes evaluated Stoner. "Are you a lieutenant or a sergeant, or—?"

"No, sir, that's a TV thing," said Stoner, his eyes still taking in the huge office space. "I'm an investigator—about the same pay grade as a lieutenant. The investigative supervisors you see on TV, the guys in charge of all aspects of a job, are only a small percentage. I can't even give orders to a uniformed officer, when it comes right down to it."

"Fascinating," said Clavius, indicating that it was anything but. He stationed himself in a Humanscale Liberty chair on the boss side of the desk so Stoner would not try to touch him again. The Liberty chair was the fashionista answer to the Aeron, which had become so popular with the commonweal that it now appeared antimillennial and dated. Clavius was already offended that this man, Stoner, assumed he, Clavius, was the sort of person who sat around watching television. Stoner looked for another chair; or wherever he was supposed to sit. There was no other chair.

"Have you come to ask about Charlene Glades?" asked Clavius. "Hideous, what befell her. Barbaric. Grief like this is draining."

"Actually, sir, I've come to ask you about Elias McCabe." Stoner had begun a tight circle pace on the far side of the desk, like a prosecutor summing up. "You said that he was acting erratically the last time you saw him."

"Detective, 'erratic' is one word. It is *a* word. It does not adequately encompass how upset McCabe seemed to be, how wild and distraught. It immediately seemed to me that he was losing his grip on sanity. He babbled, quite frankly, about an internecine plot to implicate him in . . . what? A blackmail? A murder? I'm still not sure myself—*that's* how crazy he seemed. It was as though he was confecting a melodrama: He was abducted, forced to take photographs, bribed, then attacked in some arcane retribution, so he said. The sole proof he had of any of this were some obviously staged photographs and a bit of muddy videotape, which he put on my Web site, thereby implicating me. Worse, he cast me into an uncomfortable position with a magazine by failing to do his job. Then people began to die. It looks very bad for him, doesn't it? Running and hiding. Elias was never the bravest of men, Detective, if you'll pardon that observation."

"Where would he run?" asked Stoner. "Where would he hide?"

"Well, that all depends on his measure of guilt, yes? If he has lost his mind to the point of taking people's lives, who can say? If he is innocent and is merely cowering in some squalid hideout, who knows where he went? He had an obvious alcohol and drug dependency. His lover had just walked out on him. Perhaps he was despondent to the degree he would make harsh, rash, impulsive decisions you or I could not even theorize. He wasn't always that way. He was talented and reliable. But now . . ."

"What happened to Charlene Glades was clearly done by a lunatic, sir," Stoner said, withdrawing a legal folder from a vinyl folio case he had brought in. "Patterned after one of McCabe's own photographs. Would you like me to show you the pictures?"

Clavius got redder. "No, sir, I would not."

Stoner was good—he had laid back and let Clavius do the talking, then ambushed him with crime scene shots he knew Clavius would never look at, all to gauge his reactions. He shot that last "sir" back at Clavius like a bolt from a crossbow.

"This is all very upsetting to me," added Clavius, unable to keep from filling dead air. "Char was a treasure. Tell me, can you with your discerning eye make anything of the fact that the artwork that provided the template for her murder—it was called *Targets #5*—was missing from Elias's loft, when the atrocities that were committed there were discovered?"

"We don't know that it was in the loft at all," said Stoner. I could tell the detective was jonesing for a cigarette up here in the sterile bird's nest.

"It certainly was the last time I spoke to Elias."

"Hmm. Did *you* take it?"

Clavius permitted himself a small, lipless smile. "No."

"Then where is it?"

"He may have sold it. It's useless as a direct link anyway, I think. You see, several articles were done on that showing; the image was available in a number of places, even my own Web site."

Clavius folded his hands on the desk. He seemed to be taking inventory of his fingers. Yep, all there. "Detective, I need to know if I am suspected in any aspect of this crime. Public speculation has already proven most damaging, and my legal team is very costly. They require me to submit to little interrogations, just like you're doing now, and this absorbs very valuable time and wastes further time in the processing of extreme stress. So, if you please—am I to be accused of anything? If so, then arrest me. If not, and I am very sorry, but I don't think I can help you. I last saw Elias over two weeks ago. He was unstable and semidelirious. I've since had to waste an enormous amount of time getting those troublesome photos off the Internet, and that in turn has caused me to fall grievously behind in preparation for a very important show."

Yeah, Clavius was really broken up about Char, all right. I was amazed he could still remember her last name. What he was hoping was that one more week would erase the whole Internet embarrassment to the attention-deficit world at large.

"The photos are not the issue," Clavius went on. "The special paper makes them unviewable online. But they were linked to my Web site, and hence that distressing video clip. I am being involved totally outside my own control, don't you see?"

"That's it," said Stoner. "You saw him. I did not. All I need is the benefit of your eye, don't you see?"

"I wish I *could* tell you more," said Clavius, already looking for other things to do. "Who really knows, Detective, what happens in someone's mind when it goes wrong? You would be more of an expert than I. He may have suffered some sort of traumatic break, changed into some schizophrenic alter ego."

"That's not schizophrenia," Stoner said, just politely enough to make me start hiccupping with suppressed laughter.

Any thoughtful police work generates metric tons of paperwork. Everything has to be written down. There were three damning points of connection in what was turning into a cross-country case: Elias McCabe's association with Clavius, the loft that Clavius paid for out of petty cash, and the damning fact that Elias had been screwing both Clavius's ex, Nasja, and her replacement, Char. Both were now dead, among others, and Elias had chosen to run. It appeared Clavius's primary concern was scraping Elias off his shoe, but not to the point of killing anyone. Accustomed to calling the shots, Clavius had found himself mired in a scenario over which he had no control, and he was obviously afraid for his life. It must have been driving him buggy.

I had wanted to redefine Clavius in my own mind as relevant enough to kill as part of my unilateral expungement of the Dominic Sharps abortion. But no one in the real world gave a damn who Clavius was. And Clavius barely had any facts at all, and most of those were thirdhand, so what he had said was the truth as far as he knew it. I could feel Stoner's dilemma: it would be hard to make Clavius a suspect even if he *was* guilty of something other than being an asshole, which unfortunately was not illegal.

The meeting was already over. Stoner redonned his foot-wear and left his card. Once he was out of the building, I came out of my hiding place.

I stowed Stoner's mustache and wig in my vinyl folio along with his fake ID. I thought the gun had been a nice touch, though it went unappreciated. Most members of the largest police force in the United States, or "MOS" (Men in the Service) to the NYPD, were authorized to carry nine-millimeter SIGS, Smith & Wessons, or Glocks, all adjusted to a twelve-pound trigger pull. Bulldog's SIG filled that bill perfectly.

I was sorry I had not gotten the chance to make Stoner re-ally bitch-slap Clavius with the photos of Char, which I had taken myself. Not bad shots, either, for a beginner.

Clavius wasn't worth killing. A bloated, egomaniacal, purple-veined Nazi helmet boner, yes, but not worth the bother of killing. Unlike the others, his death would draw serious atten-tion. Unlike the others, he was not relevant in the least to my inquiries.

That left Elias.

Being an artist, I had discovered, was no great leap. Elias did still lifes. I did "stilled lives," or perhaps could call my photos "steal lifes." Elias's work had inspired me and I would liked to have thought my work as good as his. We were both artists now.

Once Joey had blurted out that Elias had fled to New York, Joey did not need to be alive anymore. When I shot him in the head, his face detached from hydrostatic pressure and skinned above his brows in a single flap, held together by all his little pins and studs and things. It was an anomaly; I don't think I could have done that on purpose in a thousand more tries.

Once Char had blurted out that Elias's movie connection was a man with the laughable name of Tripp—"Bergman. Bergen. Something like that"—all I had to do to find him was look him up on the Internet Movie Database. Under *in production*, but not *rumored*, was something titled *Vengeance Is*.

Currently filming in New York and New Jersey, with a unit production manager named Tripp Bergin.

After getting nothing out of Clavius, just noodling around sniffing for causal links, I linked onto a hot item about some British director's temper tantrum on the set of *Vengeance Is,* currently a busy YouTube tidbit. It was not luck—I don't believe in luck—so much as thoroughness.

If Tripp Bergin was hiding Elias, and Elias had changed his appearance—no goatee when I think I spotted him stalking Char, too late—then Elias could be any of the hundred-plus warm bodies on that film crew.

Elias could run, but not from me. It just made the chase more interesting. And I had never been on a film set before in my life. Neither, from the look of it, had many of the people working on the movie. It seemed as though twenty-odd bystanders did nothing except mumble into mobiles or text message the entire time. Which was good, since it meant I stood a better chance of blending in unobtrusively.

I kitted out for this excursion in jeans, running shoes, and a thick denim work shirt. If nothing else, I looked durable. A small hardware-store work belt pendent with a cell phone holster, a web water-bottle sleeve, and a utility pack (weighted down with Bulldog's SIG) made me appear hipslung. I later found out that many of the crew wore steel-toed footwear—sandals or anything open-fronted was prohibited because of the perfidious mantraps that litter a working set: cables, wheeled frames for flats, unexpected sharp edges, and camera dollies that could crush bones with their casters. If you try to navigate this maze in the dark you might as well be dancing through a minefield.

The ID lanyard was a tiny bit more complicated since there was no time or opportunity to forge crew cards. Set security was perpetually on the lookout for signs of your legitimacy. At first I thought to plead guest status. I had prepared an identity as Jack Vickers, a New Jersey public safety officer assigned as observer to prevent a repeat of Mason Stone's Night of Thunder. One phone call would obliterate that façade, so I snaked around for options and soon found the cramped trailer command post for the first, second and third ADs. Most of them had to be on set, so watch duty in this overstuffed capsule of phones, walkie chargers, fax and copy machines, usually fell to one or two busy souls who stepped in and out for coffee, smokes, and bathroom breaks so often that the door was never closed. I stood around smoking until a guy who looked about fifteen, belted with three walkies, battery packs, and three phones, answered his nature call. Then I ascended the aluminum drop steps into the office as though I expected to see someone there.

I snatched a lanyard from a hooked bundle of about twenty. It was not a key card—no mag stripe. All I needed to do was emplace a trim of one of my utility ID shots and seal the front with clear packing tape from my kit. The background would not matter; most of the card pictures of the crew looked like candids.

This was before I realized that so long as you *appear* to know what you are doing, practically nobody would question your presence anyway.

I saw several uniformed Jersey cops, all overweight, moonlighting as set security, dallying near the craft services table and trying to chat up anything remotely female. They hovered, unconcerned by interlopers. Another knot of people in bike wear and logoed jackets hung together in a clannish circle of portable chairs near the big doors to the hangar like a tribe protective of their campfire. These were an element of the stunt team, awaiting their various summonses.

An AD outside the hangar called, "Rolling," in a town crier voice. The background noise of circular saws and hammers terminated and everybody stopped talking. A lot of people froze in place as though waiting to be reactivated. I became absurdly aware of the crunch of my shoes on gravel and decided to hold still. There was a roar like an aircraft engine emitting from the hangar, shouting, and the unmistakable sound of gunfire. I'm not sure how the microphones inside were vulnerable to the sound of me walking, forty yards away from that cacophony, but it was just how things were done.

On "cut" the peripheral activity resumed. Good to know. A billow of brown dust was roiling out of the big hangar doors.

Inside was a piece of Manhattan street, stoplights and all, crowded with lights and cherry-pickers and several enormous Ritter fans about eight feet across at the blade. A trashed ambulance was on its side, plowed into a mailbox, newspaper vending machines, and a tilted light pole, its flashers still cycling. A collapsed gurney in the middle of the road. As I got closer I noticed I was stepping on spent shell casings. Somebody wailed on a bullhorn, calling, "Back to one, reset, quickly now."

"Hi!" The voice behind me came with a light touch on my arm. In here, people really had to stay aware in a three-sixty sense—semidarkness, workers ghosting through with ladders saying, "Watch your backs," tricky footwork all over the concrete floor. "Who might *you* be?"

I turned to meet a short blond woman with wide, guileless eyes of cornflower blue, lozenge-shaped red-framed glasses, a high-wattage PR smile, and a slightly hefty, saucy, low-slung carriage that said she could easily prop her heels behind her head if she thought you were worthy.

Defensively, my hand sought my lanyard. "Jack Vickers," I said. "I'm with Public Safety."

"Oh!" Her brow furrowed—adorable—but she quickly grabbed my handshake. "You were here yesterday, right?"

I nodded. Sure I was.

"We're not in *trouble*, right?" Her grin was semiconspiratorial.

Put her at ease, I thought. "No, no, it's not that, it's just . . . I like watching. What was your name again? I'm so sorry; my brain for names is like a wicker sieve."

"Spooky," she said. Again the eye-roll, as though we were sharing a confidence. "I know, I know . . . it really is Spooky.

Spooky Sellers, how's that for fake Hollywood? Except that I'm probably the only person here that hasn't changed my name. And weirdly enough, I'm not the only publicist named Spooky. How likely is that?"

Her sped-up patter made it clear that if one did not inter-ject, she would quickly fill the conversational gap with more fragments attached to spin-out phrases.

"Well, how's it going so far today, Spooky?"

"Light duty." She sighed. "Had the EPK guys in yesterday. Actually it's a slow day for publicity. Meat and potatoes." She shrugged as if awaiting a better offer. She was wearing a logo cap that read ANTI-AUTHORITY.

"What part is this?" I said, indicating the urban mayhem setup.

"Oh, umm . . . that would be . . . shoot-out, second guy from hell tries to take the ambulance Walker is in, postcrash, second Hell Guy summons a dust devil from 1848 to help him, that blows the pedestrians back, and Walker and Hell Guy number two draw down in the street. Hmm. The hydrant is supposed to be gushing."

As if on her cue, the decapitated fire hydrant beneath the wrecked ambulance began to emit a plume of water. Some-body on a megaphone said sardonically, "Thanks for coming to *work* today, Bernie, *love ya!*" General laughter.

"And Walker is Mason Stone?"

"In the flesh. He was here this morning; I think they're do-ing reverse angles now."

Walker had also been the false middle name of the nonexis-tent person who had polished off Charlene Glades's life.

"Why aren't they just shooting this on a street in the city?" I said.

"Better control of the dust cloud," she said. "Outside, dust and fog are the worst; your clouds just drift away; control of the light is more consistent."

Now I could see, through the haze and gloom, that most of

the crew were bandanaed and goggled, or wearing paper filter masks. Several guys behind the big fans had the duty of shoveling dust *into* the fans to blow around from large dumps on the floor.

"You mean they just blow *dirt* all over their high-priced actors?"

"Actually, it's peat moss," she said. "Better 'granularity' for dust. Healthier, too. For actual dirt, ground cork. Hey, be sure your mobile is off if you're in here."

"No worries," I said. Then a guy with a live vulture on his arm walked right past me.

"Vlad hates the dust storm, as it turns out," said Spooky. "Animals are always a bitch to work with during physical effects."

"Is that a *real* vulture?" I had never seen one up close. It looked like it wanted to kill everybody.

"Yeah, Hunnicutt has got three of 'em."

"So the vulture has two . . . understudies?"

"Oh, yeah, if one won't work, you can't just stop."

I got the clear impression that Spooky the Publicist was grateful to have somebody to talk to today, which meant that the main unit probably blew her off unless they needed something.

It did not take her long to fasten on her real interest.

"So," she said, "Despite all the logistics, big scene and all, they're actually going to wrap on time today. And I hope you don't mind me asking, but . . ."

Recent personal history had it that Spooky Sellers had confessed an attraction for Garrett Torres, the second lead in *Vengeance Is*, who had been more interested in delving the girly parts of one Aspen DeLint, a clapper-loader, which itself just sounded like a dirty joke. Ms. DeLint had a *boyfriend*, she had lugubriously announced, slapping Mr. Torres's down harder than she had intended, in front of several other crew members. In retaliation, Mr. Torres had recently begun to impugn the professional abilities of Ms. DeLint in the hope that Tripp Bergin might fire her worthless, though hydraulic, ass. Now they had escalated to eye-daggering each other during every setup.

Some sets are all business, some are divertingly flirty, and some are downright horny. Spooky had flirted off and on with Torres, but he wasn't interested in a mere publicist, so he froze her out. Spooky admitted to me she had pointed the set videographer at Torres during the unfortunate makeup moment that turned up live on the Internet. Of course she had not intended for it to go *that* far, and still felt a bit guilty about it.

This was her version of budding intimacy; now I was supposed to tell her a secret, too.

Naked and randy, Spooky's nerves were all very close to the surface; she orgasmed easily and often, and was in fact so limber that she almost *could* put her heels behind her ears. Sexually she was hungry and grabby, moist and vocal, and she knew how to perform oral like an adult—no hands. Her skin temperature seemed to be redlining when she came and she exuded the scent of her coconut moisturizer, which was actually quite pleasant.

"I don't usually do this," she said, gulping air as though famished, pinpoints of sweat dappling her upper lip.

"Call it animal attraction," I said. It was better than saying "My last date was a corpse."

Every daquiri had made her more chatty about the secret underpinnings of *Vengeance Is*. We landed at a dark Asian restaurant called Rain near Eighty-second and Columbus and I had stuck mostly to bracingly cold Thai beer, just listening. The bar mixtress here made 'em strong, and Spooky was a fountain of information just waiting for an excuse to gush.

Rain closed its doors not long after that.

I padded naked around Spooky's smallish room. She had picked the Hotel Beacon for reasons of budget, but it was smack on Broadway, strolling distance from the restaurant. Her accommodations were colorful and efficient. Not much of her work gear was here; it was just a temporary roost. No copies of the crew lists, for example—featuring names and contact info for a crowd of people, any one of whom might be Elias McCabe.

But now all I had to do in order to legitimatize myself on set was defer to Spooky. I supposed it had been too ripe to hope that I would just drop in and collide with McCabe, and my new inlet, in the form of this compact, sturdy blonde, would obviously reward cultivation.

Spooky was already snoring lightly.

I treated myself to a stingingly hot needle shower that scoured my senses and left me warm and dopey. A nap would not hurt. She did not budge when I crawled in next to her. About two hours later, I awoke with a start and found her going down on me.

Even more surprisingly, my penis was giving her every co-operation.

She mounted me, her face shadowed in the semidarkness (the bathroom light was still on), and we slowly melded through a bout of that hypnotic, half-awake, sleepy sex that can totally divorce you from your senses. It can't stop time, though, no matter how healthy it is. In four hours or so she was going to bound forth to report for duty and I wondered where she got the energy; I certainly had not spotted any speed in the bathroom or in the contents of her shoulder bag, although I did find most of the more popular prescription antidepressants—Lexapro (twenty milligrams, about three bucks per tablet), Wellbutrin, Cymbalta, no generics, all from different doctors.

She even kissed me on the head when she took off in the morning, radiant with scented soap and light perfume. Rather, she kissed Jack Vickers, quaintly believing him to be asleep. Her speedy trust was depressing; it meant that nothing of value was left behind in her hotel room.

I wondered if I might wind up slitting her throat, just to be thorough.

That day I met the production videographer, a doughy, perpetually flop-sweated kid named Arly, who acted more harried than he was and lent every distracting task a bogus air of do-or-die dedication. He was next to useless. The unit photographer, somebody named Julian Hightower for whom I could find no contact information on the call sheets, was either playing hooky or out for the day. Arly described him as a clean-cut, blond-haired guy—"you know, a guy." Like I said, next to useless.

Hightower's desk was locked—file that one for later investigation, when nobody was looking—and the detritus left in his corner of the office bespoke nothing about him, except that all of his gear seemed to be brand-new.

But this guy was the *photographer*. Right-to.

Spooky had asked Tripp Bergin, though, and gotten the story that Hightower was from Chicago, off the books because of some union thing. The gloss-over was vague enough to suggest it had been invented.

That was when I saw the baseball-type hat on Arly's messy coat rack. *Panavision*. Same as worn by Char's briefly glimpsed stalker.

If Julian Hightower was Elias McCabe, why wasn't he here?

Answer: *because he knows you're here too, stupid.*

I should have just left Charlene Glades in a Dumpster. I had to lose control for that one little moment, and show off, and re-fuck my shot at Elias. God, maybe I *was* past my prime in this game.

Having no other true virtues, I reminded myself that patience was a good one. I lost most of the day in waiting but consoled myself with thoughts of the hunt. Skilled woodsmen knew the least breath of wind could expose your presence and blow your hide to creatures who could smell your anticipation.

A twig snap, an eyeblink at the wrong time, and you were made. You had to be able to squat or statue up in a single position for hours, until your fingertips got numb and your feet froze and your legs fell into tingly sleep. You had to be able to consume the discomfort like snack food, and process it into resolve. The best snipers know this pain, and embrace it, because the kill is worth every sacrifice. After all, *easy* tasks can be done by anyone.

All I had to do was be patient, and wait for that motherfucker to waltz right into my sight picture.

That evening I got the use of Spooky Sellers again. She claimed not to have gotten laid for the better part of the year, and sexual stress was the *worst* thing to hoard, didn't I think so? I said it was easy for work to take precedence and overwhelm other considerations. She said, yes, that was true, but most human beings were designed to have sex a *lot*, and if you didn't, well, that was just like pulling a random wire out of your distributor and expecting your car to function. It just wasn't *optimal*, she said.

"I tried that post-relationship flameout thing," she told me as we demolished a pretty good chophouse spread. "You know, where you just *don't*, because you're so full of resentment and don't want to feel cheap? Where you convince yourself you're waiting for something better? Well, there's waiting and there's *negligence*, if you ask me."

But wait—there was more.

"I mean, these bitches, these fucking twenty-five-year-old cunts on set," she said, her tone sharpening. "They all so goddamned predatory and act like they're saving themselves for somebody in a cape and tights. Why? So they can pick his bones, like maggots. They think they've got a million years to dither and choose some rom-com idea of Mister Right, while they're constantly scanning the room for something better."

Spooky was still obviously upset over her perceived rejection by Garrett Torres.

"I mean, I don't come on like a whore or anything. Do I?"

"No," I said. "You come on like a man, and I mean that as a compliment. You know what you want and you're not afraid to ask for it."

"Damned straight, amigo."

In twenty-four hours I had become Spooky's new best friend. She was no siren and she knew it, but she worked what she knew she had. A decade ahead of her avowed competition, she still worried that her years were nothing more than age. Fragile egos came under ceaseless assault by media images of what was desirable—Elias McCabe's former specialty. Today's centerfold or smoking hotness was tomorrow's baggy breeder or burned-out bundle of neuroses, yesterday's wastrel. Once you got Spooky's clothes off, you were dealing not with transient hotness, but genuine fire. Like all of us, she too had been badly used in the past, but instead of whining about how the world had fucked her over, she bootstrapped up and got on with the business of being alive.

"*Whoo*, you're fun," was how she summed it up. "You're not going to go all gummy on me in five days, are you? Tell me you're not."

"What do you mean?" I stroked her thigh absently. She craved the tactile.

"End of the week." She was glazed and cat-happy. "We've got to pull stakes, rally up, and go, lover. Arizona awaits. Period shoot, Western town, setups, showdowns, all the rest of the movie."

I still had not gotten so much as a positive ID, phone number, or make on Elias McCabe.

"Publicists, too?" I said. "The video guy, that Arly Whats-his-name, the dumpling that walked like a dork?"

She snickered. She was the realization of Arly's desperate late-night pud-pounding sessions, and the poor fool would never suspect it.

"What about the photographer, High-britches—?"

"Hightower."

"Does he go, too?"

She focused on me. *Bad omen.* "That's like the third time you've asked about him. What's the deal?"

I would not be able to sluice her off with "just curious"; that would no longer play. *Really bad omen.* I dissembled through a diversionary ramble about wondering *how much* of the crew had to relocate, but it was lame and she knew it.

"Yeah. You want to know about craft services, too? C'mon, I'm not going to tell anybody. What's your deal with Julian?"

Well, I need to put him down like a sick animal, and I've just wasted another whole day without finding him. That was a no-play.

"He owe you money or something?"

I could have kissed her. In fact, I did. "No, actually, he owes me some photographs." Beautiful save, that. The rest I needed to confect in a big smooth hurry. *Open file on Elias McCabe; activate falsehood lobe of brain; hose the room with untruth; and hurry because hesitation will hitch your voice, and her alarms will sound even louder.* It had to seem casual, not freighted.

"He shot some fashion spreads, in Chicago, with an old acquaintance of mine—"

Spooky ribbed me. "You mean like a *girlfriend*?"

That was exactly the detour by which I'd hoped Spooky would be misdirected. Her flaw, from what I had observed, was rising too quickly to ready bait. Now I had to gild the story just so.

"Sister of a buddy of mine. He's getting married in October and he can't find her."

"And you want to find her for your friend in time for the wedding," she said. "That is so sweet, Jack. That is the biggest bullshit story I've heard this week, and I've dealt with some whoppers. Sis is your old paramour, right? And Julian did the nasty with her, something like that? He's some kind of romantic rival, is that your biz?" She grabbed my penis to ensure veracity.

"Yipes," I said, then sighed. "Okay . . . busted."

"What are you going to do? Beat him up? Because you certainly don't talk about him with the warm fuzzies. I notice shit like that."

"I just want to talk to him."

"Lie. You just want to punch his face in, all knightly. What did he do?"

Let Spooky write the story in her own mind.

"Got her pregnant and blew town; no forwarding."

"Wow." She kept her grip and did the cat-stretch on the bed. "That is pathetic. What century is this, again? Oops, I'm pregnant; gee, how'd *that* happen? God, *people*. Fucking ordinary people. Oops, I'm pregnant, golly, there goes my whole life, bye-bye. I had my tubes tied as soon as I could; do you know how *liberating* that was? Half the states in the union, doctors won't allow it until you've pooted out a couple of fetuses. That's terrorism. We've got, what, how many *billion* extra people already? Make more! Because when you can keep people focused on breeding, make it attractive, give tax incentives for family, you can keep their minds off evolving, or making anything of themselves, except more selves."

"That's quite a speech," I said.

"Oh, baby, don't get me started," she said. "I've had too many friends give up on their whole lives because they were obligated to be parents, and it was never a *choice*, but they spin-doctor it like crazy once they're trapped. And they always come back at you with how *wonderful* it all is, how it's the most important goddamned thing they've ever done. Yeah, for *them*, that's true, because they'll never know what they *could* have done. Then their little darling becomes a teenager, rejects you, rebels, wrecks your car, asks for money, and soon enough gets pregnant themselves, same program. Vicious cycle, never ends. None for me, thanks."

She grabbed a little too hard for punctuation. "There is no family. We're all mutts, mating with other mutts." Okay, so she had some mommy and daddy issues, who didn't?

She rolled, still with me in her grasp. "Let's fuck over the churches of the world and have sex for pleasure."

"Isn't that a sin?" I grinned.

"Not in the First Book of Spooky. It's a commandment."

The tactic worked, or would at least hold water for another day. Spooky would not mention me to Elias if she saw him first. If I saw him first, no foul. But if she wanted to sight-check connective data between me and him—not so good. She didn't know it, but she was walking a tightrope, even as we were fornicating like crazed minks. Her own snoopiness could write the end of her life. I did not particularly want to kill her—at least, not right this minute—but that codicil had never blocked me before. She was too inquisitive to leave it alone. Sooner or later she would feel compelled to poke that snake on the hot rock. I wondered if I should grant her even another 24 hours leeway. Reckless.

Spooky made it all academic, without intending to. When I reached for my cigarettes, she reached for her water bottle and one of her fine, lacquered fingernails skinned my damaged eye.

"You have experienced what we call corneal erosion," said the good Dr. Blaine.

We were in the Lenox Hill emergency room; average triage wait, three hours. They had added a special treatment room for opthamology in 2003. The waiting room was full of cops and EMTs. This time of night, half the incoming patients were gunshot wounds or misdemeanor fallout, and half were heart attacks, so any nonlife-threatening distress got to wait. I dosed myself with my stolen Alcaine from my kit to neutralize the hideous hangnail sensation caused by my eyelid prying up my corneal flap. I had only just gotten around to deluding myself that my eye was at least partially healed, good enough to ignore for minutes at a time, and now it felt as bad as it had when I had rammed it on Elias's enlarger. Fortunately Spooky did not quiz me on the drops; she accepted that I had suffered some kind of setback in an ongoing condition.

After an hour I had been installed on a waiting bed in a curtained semiprivate ward, to wait while the gunshot wounds got plugged and sutured, while the cardiac patients fell to one side or the other of their internal equation. The other people in my ward, also waiting, and waiting, were less dramatic than the TV-style action that echoed dimly from down the corridor.

Spooky herself had become an action heroine. No delays and no confusion. She had bundled me into her car, delivered me, and walked me through the sign-in, which was good because I could not see a damned thing. She approached the triage nurse with just the right combination of urgency and understanding; she was, after all, well-versed in PR.

Plus, she got to go through my wallet.

I could not remember if anything incriminating was in there. My gear and my other identities were still stored at the Lucerne Hotel. But I had my key card. If she took it . . . if they anesthetized me . . . if she went there . . . that's all she wrote. She had been an angel and all I could think about was the need to punch her ticket, however reluctantly. You can't leave a trail, especially a trail of people who can talk about you, form memories, and therefore opinions. She had begun as a trifle, a vector on Elias, but with every moment she became more in-volved. Dammit. I was almost certain I could have kept her out of it. Now she was spoor.

Now she was babysitting me.

"Corneal erosion," as described by Dr. Blaine, means that all my nice, new regenerated ocular tissue had slid off the sur-face of my eye like cheese off a pizza slice. Particulate irritants, stress, temperature, blinking too much, almost anything could cause such a setback. I was half-blind again, and in no condi-tion to execute a search and destroy on Elias.

Spooky thought it had been her fault; sexing too vigorously. So I had to calm her down with more lies.

Blaine had that paterfamilias look of the very best, most trustworthy TV doctors: Brisk white hair with lingering refugees of gray, big durable build, slight hunch from overwork, expensive spectacles, spotless smock, silk tie yanked to half-mast. He smelled like fresh laundry.

He checked my eye under ultraviolet light, then let Spooky take a peek. "It's sticking up like a slice of pie," she said. "It's *glowing*."

I thought she said "growing," like meteor-jelly from a blob movie.

It was back to the torture chair, back to the ice packs and the meds, back to waiting for my eyeball to catch up with my schedule. Plus now I had Spooky to hold in abeyance. Back to one.

Bad news is always good news for somebody else.

PART TEN

JULIAN

In the right light, she iridesced. Not from some misty-brained romanticist notion outmoded by a century or two, but literally, eye-catchingly. She was patined in rainbow colors. Her surface was cool and smooth to the touch, not polished like the carapace of an insect, but alive with the tactile reality of human flesh. She was the kind of sight your brain insists must be an illusion, then marvels at how the trick might have been achieved, then staggers at the knowledge that there *is* no trick.

Her flesh was translucent and hyperreceptive. Trace a design on it and it manifested in deep organic red or venous blue, an instant dermagraphic that lasted for about a day. Any touch must be accepted, though; invited and permitted. Punch her and you'd never leave a bruise or scar. Hell, you'd never land the blow. She was quicker.

Her hands and feet were webbed. Bat wings of radiant membrane connected her wrists to her ankles. Not delicate or ephemeral but durable, resilient, practical. She stood about five foot eleven barefoot, a technical albino with silver-violet eyes and no pigment to protect her from the sun. Because of the sensitive nature of her retinae, she had to wear special UV glasses for anything daytime-oriented. I held them up to a light and they were as dense as welder's shades. You could watch a solar eclipse through them with no harm.

Her name was Davanna.

When Mason Stone had said there was an alligator man with Salon, I expected the usual—some guy who resembled a terminal case of eczema or had some facial defects. Jesus god, was I a dope. Erik—that's his name—was the closest I've ever seen to a hybrid, more akin to a monstrosity dreamed up by the guys in the makeup lab on *Vengeance Is*. His skin wasn't superficially scaly, but the same thickness, texture, and corrugation of crocodile hide, though the colors and patterns were a bit more flamboyant. Square-cut overlapping armor plates that could probably deflect a bullet. The front of his skull was pushed into a shape that was a compromise between an elongated snout and a human face. His teeth were blocky and pointed; he told me he had half of them extracted to make room for the others, and they grew like crazy, necessitating periodic filing. He cut himself to prove to me his skin was real; sank a utility knife a quarter-inch into his forearm, cleanly dividing a scale. No blood. He must have weighed three hundred pounds and there wasn't an ounce of fat on him. Watching him eat wasn't pretty. He looked, more than anything, like a really good alien from an expensive movie. Audiences responded with instinctive recoil from insects and reptiles, even amphibians. He was a man-phibian, and if his appearance didn't steal your breath, then his voice would help your nightmares along.

"Isn't this the *shit*?" said Mason Stone.

I was hardly on set anymore, having received special dispensation from Tripp, who was already nervous enough about stray photos in the wake of the Internet exposure of Andrew Collier's bad day. When I was monopolizing Cap Weatherwax's time on our remote gun range, Cap's Fire When Ready crew ably handled the on-set armory chores. The moment I checked back in, Mason Stone grabbed me for his field trip to the Salon.

"Don't sweat it," said Tripp from beneath today's hat, *Plunging Tarantula*. "Today is basically a repeat of yesterday, but without Mason. Second unit, cutaways, reaction shots from extras, green screen, pickups. Rain cover usually drives us toward effects shots." Out in Jersey the hangar was besieged by sporadic sprinkles, and the problem with using an airplane hangar versus a soundstage is that rainfall messes with your sound. "Besides, you'll be seen less . . . yes?"

"Nobody will miss the set snapshot hound for a day," I said, as though reciting primary school gospel or the pledge.

Mason Stone's limo was, of course, ridiculous. Dick Fearing, he of the great Easter Island face, played chauffeur. Garrett Torres had hooked onto a date named Jodi, who I think was one of the day players. At least, I think I recalled her from the New York Street shoot-out, bundled up in business chic with a French twist and glasses, standard library girl, diving for cover—she might have been a stuntie, too. She was decked out quite differently tonight, openly competing with Artesia Savoy in the category of total length-of-leg exposure, and I watched Mason's eyes stray appreciatively. Andrew Collier was supposed to have been with us, but begged off to wrestle the next day's schedule with Gordo and Tripp.

Then there was Kleck, our emcee, ringmaster, tour guide, advocate, and point man. Kleck was a dwarf in a tailored suit with spats. His face looked like a clenched fist. He greeted us as our limousine door was opened by his sidekick, a big powerhouse of muscle wearing a turban and a veil that concealed his entire face, like a footman from *The Arabian Nights*.

"That's Uno," Kleck said.

Kleck wobbled along with his filigreed walking stick, regaling us with the air of an oft-repeated spiel about the special nature of Salon, and the extraspecial privilege we were about to enjoy by seeing its denizens firsthand. Henceforth, he enthused, our lives would never be the same. Along the way he added that he was an hermaphroditic twin, and that he would prove it, since seeing was believing.

"You don't really want me to photograph a bisexed midget, do you?" I whispered to Mason Stone.

He had to divide himself from Artesia Savoy's overly touchy-feely sense of dominion. Affection, to Artesia, was a matter of barrage. But he spared me a glance: "Be cool, Jules; you'll see."

We found ourselves in the middle of a sumptuously appointed, marble-floored megasuite somewhere in the heart of the city, high up. Almost a Vegas sense of overkill, fireplace, full bar, lounge space for fifty and "areas" for every task. I tried to record details since I wasn't shooting documentation, but something about the air in the room seemed different and charged, like the crackle imparted by ozone. I later realized it was pheromones, attraction molecules emitted by the members of Salon, who were somewhat more than human. The effect was thick and heady. You breathed it in and your perceptions changed. All things were suddenly possible.

When potables were distributed, I stuck to seltzer.

"You few come to risk the unusual," Kleck intoned. "You come with open minds, open hearts. You expect disappointment. This is normal. It is the only such normal thing in these rooms. You expect trickery. There is none. You are willing to entertain the idea that perhaps you do not know everything. As you are willing, so are we."

"*Hurry,* hurry, hurry," muttered Garrett, and Jodi snickered. "Step right up."

Mason Stone shot them both a look that could set fire to the ice in their cocktails.

"Unenlightened individuals quite understandably expect what used to be called a 'freak show' back in the day," said Kleck. "If you had come to see obese women, flipper children, geeks, the malformed, or hirsute wolfpeople . . . well, you would not have been invited to Salon. I daresay our beautiful ladies seated before me probably have more tattoos than any of my colleagues."

Artesia and Jodi squirmed appropriately. I already knew about the dragon braceleting Artesia's ankle, and Jodi obligingly rolled over to display a tramp stamp on the small of her back that resembled the grille of a Chevy, appropriate since such ink was also called a California license plate.

Fifty years ago, my former helpmate Joey would have lived in a sideshow, no question. And the Amazing Fat Man . . . well, he was now so ordinary that airlines had to rewrite their seating rules.

When Kleck introduced Erik, the Alligator Man, Jodi's mouth snapped shut like a mousetrap. Garrett's remained unhinged.

Erik came out of the darkness behind Kleck, where lush sleeping quarters were arranged like the spokes on a half-wheel. He was bare-chested but wearing bigass 505 rapper jeans, which he offered to remove. I would never forget his voice, that clicking, froggy glottal that brought its own echo from within the caverns of his head.

"Touch it," he said of his arm, extended toward Jodi, who flinched. "Find a seam, a zipper that says I am not real."

"How did you come to be the way you are?" asked Mason, choosing his words cautiously, ultrapolite.

"Born this way," rasped Erik. "All of us, born this way. Do you have a talent? An expertise? My beauty and power are on the outside for all to see."

"Erik killed a shark once," said Kleck. "A bull shark, the most aggressive, a four hundred pounder. Wrestled it in salt water and killed it."

"They swim in fresh or salt," said Erik. "So can I. He bit me. Here."

He displayed a lightning bolt scar near his kidneys, muted by overlapping scale growth.

"They're manhunters," said Kleck. "Tell them how."

Erik demonstrated with his armored talons. "Tore off its jaw. I drank its blood. It was an honorable death."

Azure light seemed to waft into the room, and I turned and caught my first look at Davanna, the arabesque to Erik's grotesque.

I had described her as a kind of butterfly woman, but that's not completely accurate. She was, in form, more a hybrid of bat and moth, with a symmetry possessed by neither. Faint winkings of flight dust scattered there, like the talc-fine shed scales of moths, the kind old wives used to say were poisonous. Davanna would never, could never fly.

All the bug-bat were-woman nonsense flew away when you saw her face, her body, the absolute reality of her. Moths were hairy; she was hairless. Bats were essentially airborne rodents; Davanna was, as I said, more than human.

"Don't be afraid," was the first thing she said to me. "Take the time your eyes need to accept what you see."

She filled even my dark-adapted eye to capacity. These people were all rhodopsin purists, almost certainly. I wondered how their eyes saw us.

Then there was Mejandra, the tentacled woman. Imagine Cthulhu, only hot, with eyes like mulled cider and real, chatoyant, vertical pupils. Multiple appendages that were not grafts but living tissue, fundamentally connected. They moved with the grace of cilia.

"Think you could do something with this material?" asked Mason, elbowing me.

Tabanga, the Skeleton—not some emaciated derelict, but a living ossuary shrink-wrapped in blue-gray skin about half a millimeter thick, a skinny Visible Man road map of vasculature. Shine a bright light on him and he would probably dehydrate to death on the spot.

When Uno unveiled, I nearly gagged on my bubble water. He only had one eye. It was large, slightly protuberant, sienna-brown, and right in the middle of his face, above his flat and flare-nostriled bullish nose, which had a ring through it. More flashbacks of Joey. This ring appeared to weigh several pounds. Uno looked strong enough to bend it double between his thick fingers. The eye beneath its single brow was no fake, no trick, no illusion, and it did not miss anything.

There was no "performance" as the word is usually understood. This was more like a reception; you drifted around as your interest drew you, and spoke to Kleck's people. Except they did the same thing. Not only was there no performance, there was no performance wall. They mingled. We mingled. Until we were all indistinguishable; one group of people, making conversation.

Kleck introduced his sister Klia, his feminine iteration, wizened and wise. That weird sensation in the air, and the hyper-reality of the Salon, gave each contact the mild blur of an acid pop, until, in a way, it all seemed very ordinary.

Because it was.

Mason compared notes with me at the bar. "So, Davanna, huh. You want to monopolize her. Tell the truth, Jules, you're thinking about banging her. I was. Everybody does. But she'll know, if you think that. Your aura, or something, gives you away. Ole Erik, the Gator Man, can whiff fear just like a bloodhound, and Mejandra is practically a living lie detector—all those limbs, like antennae, she can read your vibrations. Like I said, it's the shit, ain't it?"

Kleck interposed. "Another new friend," he said of me. "Tell me of your life, new friend."

"He's a photographer," said Mason.

"Is it allowed?" I asked Kleck.

"Normally, no," said Kleck. "Rarely."

That was Mason's cue to slam down two inches of Franklin notes on the bar. "*Now* it's allowed," he said. I had an uncomfortable flashback of Gun Guy doing the same thing to me. *Cash,* wham, *now shut up and do as you're told.*

Kleck's gaze danced between Mason and the money. "There are conditions," he said. "No flash. No strobes. No bright light."

Bright light destroyed visual purple. Maybe civilians had lived in bright light for so long, their innate capacity to see the unusual had been curtailed.

"No exposés," said Kleck. "No tawdry feature articles. We do not seek exploitation."

Then Lyle entered the main room.

"Ah," said Kleck. "I feared Lyle might not join us tonight; earlier he complained of a headache, you see. Lyle, please come meet our new friends."

Lyle emerged from the shadows holding his head, and my eyes got a read on him before my companions did. He was holding his head as if to prevent it from toppling off, which was sensible since his cranium was twice the normal size. His features were bunched together in the center of his face and surrounded by a perimeter of pale flesh. Baby-fine, wispy white hairs floated in an atavistic semicircle at the ear line. His forehead bulged up and out; his occipital was swollen backward, but apparently his skull had accommodated all this expansion. The crowding of his physiognomy gave him a perpetually surprised or perplexed expression amplified by his lack of eyebrows. He was wearing a white surgical smock, the kind that buttons up the left side, and I think his collar was reinforced.

"Please except my apologies," said Lyle, freeing one hand to shake mine. "As you can see, sometimes I have problems with my neck, and lying down in a dark room with my supports is the only thing that can ease the stress."

He kept hold of my hand while looking into my eyes.

"No," Lyle continued, "it doesn't handicap me in the way you are about to ask. It's not an Elephant Man thing, if you follow."

Funny; I was just thinking of asking him that.

"Lyle is clairvoyant," Kleck announced matter-of-factly.

Indeed; letting go of his hand was like breaking an electrical circuit.

"Mr. Kleck was not joking when he said I had a headache," said Lyle. "As you can see, it is obvious if someone wished to be derisive." He almost cocked his massive head at me. What was odd was that he had to hang on to his head to do so, as though balancing a full tureen of soup.

"You, too, seem to be in hiding," Lyle said of me. "You worry about it a lot. There are faces in front of your other faces. That is typical with movie people." He spoke of movie people in a tone that indicated he was dealing with another kind of freak show. "All that worry will just eat you up from inside. Better to just process the problem. I like to think of problems as equations with an eye toward correcting the imbalance. Do let me know if you would enjoy discussing this further."

With that, he moved off—carefully—to greet the others.

Kleck toasted me in passing with his flute of champagne. "Lyle has an unsettling effect on most people," he confided with an elfin wink. As though the other members of the Salon were completely prosaic. "He is our only American member. Come, let us get you started with your photography."

Thank Zeus I had brought my Hasselblad four-by-five and thought to pack high-ASA film for the Nikon. The lighting was tricky and demanded a tripod for long exposures. But when I photographed Erik, luridly shadowed in gothic light, he remained as still as a Grecian sculpture. He allowed me to position him. Touching his scaly armor was never *not* going to feel weird.

Fancy that, I thought, models who were not whiny or erratic.

Davanna smiled at me with even, normal teeth that glowed slightly, as though under UV light. She seemed amused. I wanted to amuse her.

"It's a vaginal cleft, Mr. Julian, surely you've seen them before."

I had been staring at her crotch too much. She was so boldly nude that it was hard not to concentrate on her breasts, or her pubis, but then it was just as tempting to take in her startling pinpoint white eyes (not to mention everything else about her), to try and plumb what those eyes saw when she looked at me.

"What are you thinking?" Still, the smile, utterly magnetic.

I was thinking that I could help Salon make four or five million bucks, easy. I was thinking that an opportunity to express my vision, as opposed to my subordinate work for Clavius, had just plonked right into my lap. I was thinking here before me was the perfect confluence of the commercial and the artistic. No compromise, no committee, no editing. There was a clothing company called Serpentine, sort of a halfway house between the Gap and higher-end designer glitz, that had conferenced me not so long ago about finding a way to establish a bold new product identity. In that meeting I had mentioned using a tempting form of promotion that did *not* incorporate the product, on the theory of beguilement—an oblique approach to curry fascination for the unseen. Now all my brain could see were titanic billboards in Times Square featuring the members of the Salon in utterly mundane, casual poses, dramatically lit and without the need for Photoshop or airbrushing, completely honest and real, with the Serpentine logo alone in one corner, that was all. No other text. No cute phrases like "Live in Your Skin" or "Just Wear It." The idea had seeded when I saw Erik's capacious hip-hop jeans, and was now in fast ferment.

Start with Erik in assorted stages of undress, then follow with Davanna, two sets, one with her dense sunglasses and one without . . . my god, it was all so obvious inside of a split second.

"Your hands are trembling," observed Davanna.

"I can't look at you enough. My eyes can't absorb you the way I'd like, as you said. I need the film."

"You are looking at me much differently through that lens," she said as she turned at my direction and her membranous wings caught the warm air like veils. "When you look through that eyepiece, suddenly you're not thinking of sex so much, I think."

"This is a different kind of lovemaking," I said, meaning it.

I thought back to how difficult it had been to ramp up Nasja's exhausted sexuality in the camera. How Joey had wanted to indulge even more groundling expressions of the simplest sexual recombination, artificially spiced with tattoos and rope and leather. It was all mining a depleted vein. You had to do more, and more, to get less and less. That was Clavius's one basic trick—he had legitimatized basic porn for the masses to consume without guilt, then "shocked" them with the surgical reality behind the endlessly augmented images the world was supposed to accept as the baseline for sexual attraction. *I want that, even at the cost of the butcher shop.* And most people *did* want it; just look at what they were willing to endure in the name of hotness. Being hot. As Joey would say, "being a Hott." *Would you? Would you?*

The appeal of the members of Salon was that they were totally unaugmented. You could want it but not have it, although you could buy products to align yourself closer to it, and that was fine because the big 99 percent would never dig having a snout, wings, or tentacles, because that would be going too far. And pushing perceived limits was what the sell was all about.

I had forgotten about Gun Guy for more than an hour. Two. I was distantly aware that the sun would be coming up soon.

"I'll need to see you again," I tried to say offhandedly.

"I know," Davanna said with the slightest imperial nod.

"I mean, all of you." I meant all of *them*, not all of her.

"That is not what you really mean." Again, the half-smile.

Lyle butted in. His head tended to stop conversation anyway. "I think you are formulating a worthy plan," he said. "But you need to ponder it more before you talk to Kleck, yes?"

I did not know whether he was referring to my overpowering attraction to Davanna, or my nascent strategy to make them all famous.

I mean, it was laughable. Meet a mutant and eat the thunderbolt of love at first sight. It was teenaged in its vehemence. It was depressing in its predictability. This probably happened all the time to her. It had to be as real as meaningful eye contact with a stripper. Wasn't the whole game to make them come back for more? It was desperate. It was hopeless.

It was undeniable.

"Some dude wanted to meet you," said Arly Zahoryin, back at his desk.

Nobody was supposed to know I was here.

"What guy? What did he look like?"

"Blond guy, glasses. Some guy." Anyone outside of the purview of *Vengeance Is* held little interest for Arly. "Funny. I described you to him the same way."

"You didn't get a name?"

"Hey, I'm not a secretary, okay? Lighten up, jeezus."

"Some guy with the production?" There was still the morose hope that it had nothing to do with my old self.

"Nah, some guy Spooky was cozening up to. She called in sick today. You don't think she finally jumped Garrett's bones and caught what he had, do you?"

Arly really was remarkably insensitive. I put it down to his immature vintage. My problem had nothing to do with his avocation.

I scanned my desk with a critic's eye, looking for things that might betray me. If Gun Guy had shown up incognito and foxed the drawer lock—simple enough—I was totally made. I looked for scratches around the keyhole and was not satisfied. Every desk in the production office already looked like it had survived demolition. Scratches, gouges, dents, scuffs, skewed handles, crippled track; a *CSI* television series clue crew would go delirious looking for a place to start.

I pulled out a crew list—the one from which Tripp had

omitted me—and ran a finger down to Spooky's vital stats. Hotel Beacon, Broadway and Seventy-fifth. She wasn't answering her phone or her mobile.

This was beginning to feel like a disturbingly familiar pattern ping. *He's here. He knows you're here. He knows you know he's here. Scramble defenses.*

By the next session with Cap, it was obvious that he could read me like a billboard. He slapped one of his swill beers into my grasp and gave me that look like my father used to give me when I'd screwed the pooch.

"I was hoping you'd tell me now," he said evenly. "About what all this bullshit is *about.*"

To cut sharp to a gang of prefabricated excuses would insult this man.

"Tell you what," he said. "I'll tell you a little story. Then you decide if you really want to talk to me."

The implication was clear: *if you don't, no more free lessons.* I had advantaged his love for his profession, something about which he had been more than willing to speak freely, to impart information to demonstrate his expertise. That honeymoon was done.

He dug around in the footlocker he called his "war box" and handed me a revolver—rather, the remains of a revolver that appeared to have exploded. The top of the frame between the sights had broken and peeled upward like parentheses reversed, burned and ragged. The cylinder, too, had butterflied open as though pried apart with pliers.

"Fella I knew had this gun on a range," said Cap. "Fired it. Next thing he knew he was on his back with a broken nose, seeing stars. Care to guess what happened?"

"Gun blew up?" I said, knowing Cap would wait patiently for me to get to the why. "Wrong bullet?"

"Wrong load. Probably double-charged a reload. Some of

the fast-burning powders don't take up much space in the cartridge case. That's why I use bulkier powders. No shifting problems, and if I were to 'accidentally' double-charge a case, it would overflow."

"You have completely lost me," I said.

"Look, not that it matters to you, but here's a bullet."

"Cartridge," I said, remembering my argot fest with the late Joey.

"You fill the casing with ingredients, just like a recipe. Some brands of powder don't fill the case all the way and you get wildly varying velocities depending on where the powder is inside the case. Like, if you point the muzzle down, then raise the gun and fire it, the powder will slide to the front of the case—against the bullet. So it's a good distance from the primer, see? Like sand in an hourglass. If you raise the gun up and then bring it down to fire, the powder slides up against the primer instead. Bang—much higher velocity."

"So you . . . don't do that?"

Cap directed me again to the sundered metal of the revolver. "This guy should've used a Hogden 110—that's a slow-burning powder that completely fills the case. Instead, he blew up a .44 Magnum, bludgeoned his own face, and nearly blew several fingers off. You get less of a pressure spike with slower powder. And that guy thought he knew what he was doing. He was not an amateur. So my question to you is: Do you know what you're doing, or do you just *think* you know, or are you making it up as you go along?

Cap was always rigorous with the tough love. He had caught me eyeing his arsenal when I thought he wasn't looking.

"Because if you only *think* you know what you're doing . . . in fact, if you were to be inspired to, say, lift a piece from my truck to go collect yourself some frontier justice, I would advise a rethink." He popped another racing-striped can of swill and drank half. Two pulls per can was his average.

I had to be exacting about what I said next.

"I have to be able to defend myself," I said.

"So you're in some kinda trouble I reckon is not quite legal."

"Yes."

His expression was that of a man who has received an enormous bill for something he did not order.

"Listen," he said. "I can show you how to shoot, but I can't Rambo you up, if that's what you're fantasizing. Close-quarter battle is a unique environment. It's what I call the cop problem: cops qualify on a range, with eye and ear protection, shooting at paper targets. No gunfight will ever require those skills. The paper target doesn't move. It's in full light. It doesn't shoot back. What about your stance? No stance in a gunfight. Fights involve movement. Safety on a range means you stay inside the shooting carrel. How many armed confrontations are cops going to experience while standing inside a phone booth?"

"They don't even make phone booths anymore," I said with a cheesy half-grin, with nostalgia for my long-lost pay phone, my ally, probably already uprooted from the beach on the other side of the country.

"Fights are about time and stress. Your adrenaline races. Hormones kick up your heart rate. You start panting; lower oxygen level. Your movements get clumsy. As one guy I know said, 'Try to thread a needle in an emergency.' You wind up with too little finger on the trigger. Tunnel vision. A thousand things. And here's what happens: guys have emptied pistols at point-blank range and not hit a single thing, once. I'm talking about firing six to nine shots at arm's length, at a person . . . and *missing*, due to all those factors."

I thought it was impossible to miss if you were close enough. The only "close enough" that existed was to jam the gun down someone's throat. It wasn't the size of the gun or the number of bullets; it was the mind-set operating the tool. My action-hero report card had just gained a fat, red F.

As though he was reading my thoughts—somewhat like Lyle had, back at Salon—Cap added, "Just because you know how to point it and make it go *bang* doesn't mean you're ready to use it."

"I know."

"I don't think it's sunk in yet. And if you bring me trouble, I'll give you back ten times the trouble. If there is gunfire, I don't know you, you don't know me, and we've never met except for you taking pictures."

It was a tough call. Moments after I had gushed my drama all over Char in the city, she had died.

"Is this one of those 'I could tell ya, but I'd have to kill ya' things?"

"Yeah. More or less."

"Tell ya what: you think about it. You come back and give me a decision, and I'll see what I can do. No explanation, no help. Lessons done, photos taken, payment accepted in the form of the Kimber. Yes?"

"I just need some time to sort it out."

"I can't let you walk around packing otherwise."

It really was quite like talking to my dead father. Cap did not say he would or would not enable me, but let the suggestion float. It occurred to me that Cap had faced similar trials before. I needed this man.

"I have to shoot at Salon tonight. After that, I'll come back here."

Cap nodded as though that was the answer he needed. "Not here. The company's getting ready to move to Arizona." He let me know where I could find his truck. Even when locked up, there was a Fire When Ready man on graveyard shift sentry duty. Always. Cap made sure I had his cell number but I had stopped carrying mobile devices around—too risky. Better a gun than an iPhone.

Maybe I could just join Salon and run away with the side-show.

The payoff to *Vengeance Is* was the usual kick in the teeth. Walker, the dumb sonofabitch, crawls up after a century of torment in hell to reap six escapees for the boss, who promises Walker will be reunited with his wife, who would otherwise have died of tuberculosis—they called it consumption back then—in 1848. Except the way the boss saved the fulsome Marianne was by making her his own immortal concubine. When Walker completes his mission, the bedraggled last man standing, his still gorgeous, still twenty-year-old wife wants nothing to do with a hick like him. His vulture overseer wings off into the setting sun, back to the hanging tree. Walker is alone. Fade out.

The final showdown was to take place in the jackstrawed remains of Boot Hill Cemetery, part of the Arizona leg of the shoot that included the period 1848 parts—nearly the entire first act—to be shot at Old Tucson, a standing Western backlot used since 1939, when it was built for the movie *Arizona*, with William Holden and Jean Arthur. It became a bona fide production studio entity in the late fifties, about the time it began to degenerate into a theme park and tourist attraction. If you have seen a shoot-out in a Western, chances are you've seen Old Tucson's main drag.

In the back of my mind I had already accepted the idea that Julian Hightower would face his fate on a Western street in Old Tucson, facing off with Gun Guy for some climactic exchange of hostilities. One bites the hardpan and one survives. The chase would end on a fake cowtown street where the running could stop at last. Ready clichés massed toward such a climax. Slap leather and draw guns, moving from Peckinpah slow-motion to Walter Hill sharp focus. Pure horse opera melodrama. Suddenly and unbelievably proficient, all manly and upgunned, I would rise to defeat a superior opponent against all odds by cutting Gun Guy down with his own weapon in a cleansing blast of powder, cordite, and hot lead, reclaiming my stolen existence through the hard rules of the equalizer, the last man standing. Cut, print, wrap, fade-out for real.

I could not have been more wrong.

PART ELEVEN

JACK

Most people spend their lives just waiting to die; to them, life was a crossword puzzle, a time killer. Most of the same people desired to feel special and apart from the herd. They craved a windfall of money or the benediction of popular culture. They prayed for a transformative event beyond their control and outside their own selves. For a select few, in this life, I was that event. If their life before me was dreary or unremarkable, I changed them. I gave them importance. At least, somewhere, somebody thought they were worth the kill.

The real tragedy of human interaction was that people don't automatically die when you're finished with them. If the divide was bloody, they never go away and they never mind their own business. If they feel hurt, they log you away for some future vengeance that never happens, but feeds their self-pity. They're better off dead, and you're better off, too. They long for some exterior happenstance to make them "right" . . . just so long as it involves no personal risk or culpability. They're the people who call the police to clean up after them, and make them right. A professional adventurer named Jean-Jacques de Mesterton once said, "If you have a problem, you go to the cops. If they can't help you, you go to the FBI. If they can't help you, you go to the CIA. If they can't help you, you come to me."

Nobody has heard of Jean-Jacques, but everybody has heard of Britney. Nobodies spend their lives worrying about cash flow and style blunders.

Which is why the general public's idea of the ice-cold robotic assassin is just as wrong as everything else they cherish and have been programmed to believe. In a world where most people wish most other people dead (remember that the next time you're stuck in traffic), it's not complicated to kill for pay or practicality. We're all at war from birth. The head of a penis is that odd helmet shape because it evolved to scrape out enemy sperm. Spooky laughed when I mentioned that, and she should have. She knew our collision had the half-life of a typical set romance, and she was right about that, too. I did not want her to fret or suffer, so I used her pills. Spoor expunged.

Somebody like that Artesia Savoy hottie I saw on the movie set could reap jobs by simply unveiling "accidental" cleavage or a length of leg. Spooky had it tougher but she knew the truth: all's fair. I probably saved her a lot of emotional pain.

Elias McCabe was another one whose ego bruises would never fade. He could never make himself unaware of the degradations inflicted upon him. He would spend the rest of his existence sniffing for a payback opportunity, even if it never arrived, even if he could never muster the backbone to do anything but run. So far, he had run pretty well—better than I expected. Plus, the little weasel had my Kimber. If I allowed him to slip into anonymity, he would resurge, perhaps years later, in an ugly and inconvenient way. That's when you usually take the worst hits: years later, when you thought the file was long closed.

Assassins cannot change the laws of physics, either, despite what the movies may have told you.

I got a beard trimmer and shaped what I had spent the last two weeks growing. My new hair color was, what? Auburn? Dark mocha? I dug the box out of my hotel bathroom trash bin to remind myself what the manufacturer called it.

That's when I discovered I could not read the fine print on the back of the box. The text was blurred hash, like the back cover copy of a bootleg DVD. I held it further away from my eyes and squinted down, the way I'd seen people do when I had dismissed them as "getting old."

Don't panic.

I couldn't read the goddamned room service menu, either.

Don't panic.

I shucked Bulldog's SIG from its scabbard and sighted it. The front ramp sight was dissipate, blobby. I tried it with my bad eye shut. Same deal. And I was accustomed to sighting with both eyes open anyway.

Time to panic.

My defocused reflection in the mirror suggested that I now resembled Elias McCabe, before he had disguised himself.

My eyes were going. My sight was becoming a handicap. I had already noticed—and denied—that my nighttime vision was becoming hazy. This was an unexpected drawback; it emphasized how narrow my work window had become. I needed to run Elias to ground, and let Evil Me off the chain . . . and soon.

But not if I needed a Seeing Eye dog and a white stick. The prop glasses I had used as Jack Vickers now seemed too cruel a joke.

At a twenty-four-hour pharmacy on First Avenue I discovered that a simple pair of x1-power reading glasses could snap my close-up vision back into focus. I almost felt like celebrating, as though some governor had phoned in a last-minute stay of execution. But it was at a Home Depot on the East Side that I chanced across what I *really* needed: bifocal safety glasses in strong acrylic. They hugged my head (no slippage) and provided side panels to shield my eyes. Look through the uppers for a normal view; tilt head slightly to engage the lenses for close-ups. They were almost identical to shooting glasses, and perfect for gun work. Here were glasses that could not only augment my need to disguise the planes of my face, but were functional. Not a prop. Even better, anyone who glanced at me would only remember the glasses—they were just odd-looking enough.

Getting used to having the things on my face was the ordeal part.

If you have never worn glasses out of necessity, you know what I'm talking about. If you're like most of the rest of the world, you'll feel little sympathy. *Big deal; I've had to wear them since the fourth grade; what're you bitching about?* It was a weird transition. I had to constantly check to ensure they were in a pocket, if they were not on my face. Going anywhere without them became like leaving the house without clothing, or, if you were a teenager, being caught in public without a Bluetooth or some Pod device.

It's easier to move unnoticed when everyone is concentrating on little screens. That's how I sandbagged Arly Zahoryin, videographer.

Where to find Arly Zahoryin? Where else—Skyping from his production office, the one I was fairly sure he shared with Elias McCabe. Holding forth.

". . . yah, *dude*, you know what they say about working in Hollywood: It's like climbing this enormous mountain of bullshit to pick one single perfect rose from the top, only when you get to the top, you discover you've lost your sense of smell. Like, seriously. *No*, I'm not quoting somebody. I just thought that up, just now. Be*cos*, mah nigga, I am just that good."

Arly was not aware I had entered the room until I snapped shut the lid of his laptop, terminating the video link and putting the computer to sleep. He looked up, eyes large and wet, with the frustrated fear of a schoolboy caught fapping to kiddie porn.

"Is this a bad time?"

"Excuse me; what the hah-h-hell do you think you're—?" It took him two breaths to form the word "hell."

"If there's one thing I hate," I said. "It's stupid questions. The ones designed to buy time and express false outrage. 'Eww, who do you think you are you've got no right.' Here's my credentials."

I showed him the business end of Bulldog's modified SIG. A line of drool actually escaped one corner of his mouth before he remembered to shut his trap.

"You stay right in that chair. Sit on your hands. Just like that. Good."

Arly's supersized pores were ripe with amber panic sweat. He wanted to wipe his smudgy glasses but didn't dare. He squinted as he tried to suss me out. Dim awareness, like the dawning of tool use for Australopithicus. "You're that guy. That fire safety guy."

It had not occurred to me that he would not recognize me with my new hair and beard, in Glazelnut, or the lightest cool brown Clairol Perfect 10 could offer, since I went back and read the box again when I could actually make out the text.

"Your hair's . . . different . . ."

"Focus, Arly. The question you need to be asking now is what do I want. I want Elias McCabe. You may know him as Julian Hightower."

"Are-are you some kind of cop, I mean, you're not the fire guy, right?"

"*Focus.* Last warning. I ask, you answer. *You* ask, and this weapon answers for me. Deal? Good."

"I-I-I think that guy Julian is a fake. I checked him out on the IMDb and he doesn't have a single credit."

I wasn't sure what that meant but it sounded encouraging.

"Listen, swear ta god, totally honest truth: my days here might be numbered anyway. I think Julian was the one who ratted me out to Collier about the YouTube leak."

The short version—the bullet version—was that Elias McCabe, in his secret identity, had gotten this pasty boy in trouble with *his* superiors, too . . . by providing the video clue that had led me to *Vengeance Is.* Swell, now we were brothers under the skin.

"That means nobody would miss you," I said, pulling the sig's hammer to full cock, a single soft *click*.

His hands flurried into the air as though he was trying to stop a runaway bread truck. "No, *no, no, no,* wait—*wait!* Wait!"

"Hands," I said.

Arly contritely stashed his hands again. He fell completely silent for a beat, marshaling his next words so he wouldn't stammer. Points to Arly, for that. I didn't think he had the depth.

"Look, I'm cooperating, okay? I didn't see you, don't know you, and can't remember you. You want Julian, or whatever he calls himself, he's been slacking off work for a couple of days now. Shaving the time-card since we're about to do a company move I'm probably not gonna be a part of now. Mason Stone—you know the actor, Mason Stone?"

Not really, I thought, nudging the gun so it kept Arly on track.

"Mason Stone got him into the Salon, that underground freak show."

More Greek, to me.

"No, just wait—follow me now. You want that guy, he's probably at the Salon if he's not here. I didn't get invited. Couldn't. Never mind. But I know where it is in the city." Arly was proud of knowing the inner workings of things, even when he was excluded.

"And you think that's worth your life?"

"Yeah." He gulped audibly. "I'm hoping it is."

Details spilled out of Arly the way loose change falls from people when you turn them upside-down and shake. Details on Salon and its location. He had a copy of the desk key he'd given to Julian Hightower—"you know, just in case." The desk gave me Elias's hotel hide. No Kimber, though. Irritating.

Yet I did not cap Arly the way I should have.

Several possibilities: perhaps I didn't want a body count connected to this movie. Perhaps I didn't want to risk another eye injury by harvesting him. Or perhaps yes, maybe I was losing my edge for real.

Or maybe I was simply fed up with killing people who *weren't* Elias McCabe. For free, just win the next morsel of intel.

Pick any or all. I let Arly live.

He was completely craven and pathetic. He tended to splutter. But at least everything he did added to my knowledge and brought me nearer to the unexpectedly slippery Elias. Dammit-all, Arly had *helped* me. He didn't excuse or lie. I saw him in the grip of his own transformative moment. Waking up one more day to pop fresh zits in the mirror had become important to him. He would torture himself far more, in life, than I ever could with threats of death.

As "Julian Hightower," Elias had become as blond as I had been before Clairol. He now looked like I used to. I now looked vaguely the way *he* used to.

Don't think that didn't mess with my brain. I was essentially trying to find myself . . . and he kept eluding me, mostly through luck, and I did not believe in luck. Coincidence, yes; accidents, yes, but fortune, never.

The dropped ball was mine. I owned the responsibility.

I wanted to bring Mal Boyd the head of Elias McCabe in a bowling bag. I wanted to jam a ballpoint pen into his eye and watch him squirm, as payback, before I did his other eye. I wanted the satisfaction of bearing witness as the life vacated his body. But then what? According to Mal, my face was blown and I needed to start shopping for plastic surgeons if I wanted to stay in the game. Become a shape-changer. New life or not, none of it could begin until Elias was off the planet.

Predictably, the Salon held court in the middle of the night.

I had always liked night shifters, the people who moved between the spaces of the ordinary world. Daytime was noise and bright light and obligations. Mister Sun no longer held Nazi dominion over your existence, forcing you to rise at cockcrow. I accepted that some people are nocturnal, and some diurnal. What I resented was that all the diurnal ones, the rush-hour masses, insisted they were the "normal" ones. When a dentist cannot understand why a 10:00 A.M. appointment is not good for you, and you turn the scenario around and say, well, how about you come 'round to my place and work on my teeth at two thirty in the morning, the dentist would regard you at best as unreasonable, and at worst as a being from some other planet. Because to him, *you are*. You're from Nightworld. You have learned the core value of sleep, because Daywalkers permit you so little of it.

Nightworlders were easier to get along with. Give them a little quiet time and some coffee, and they're good to go. Get in their face before that and you're likely to get your own face peeled off and fed to you.

All I knew was that daylight savings time had always felt skewed and unnatural to me. I felt more calibrated between October and April.

From what I could make out in my spotting scope, the denizens of the Salon were hard-core night people; foursquare on the "night" part, iffy on the "people" part. Either that, or my eyes were now actively deceiving me.

From twenty-six floors up, my vantage was similar to my spy perspective on Elias's loft in Hollywood. The street was wider—Upper Broadway—and penetrating closed buildings after business hours a bit dicier, but nowhere near impossible. The row of target windows as provided by Arly Zahoryin were all obscured by reflectorized shades. Except one: a narrow side casement looking down a blue-lit hallway that apparently led to a bathroom on the north side, after a jog to the left.

This was the waiting part. The excruciating time-crawl of stakeout that can unhinge ordinary minds with its sheer dullness.

On the south side of the corridor were two large archways that fed from a bigger central room, which overlooked Broadway. Intermediate closed door on the south side about four feet in from the naked window.

First up: a big guy, Olympic weight lifter size, in a kind of genie getup with a turban and a veil. His eunuch-pimp carriage hinted that the oh-so-exclusive Salon was just another tarted-up whorehouse.

Next: skinny guy. Either incredibly old or notably emaciated. But for the cut of his clothing, he looked like one of those derelicts found in a refrigerator box after a winter thaw; malnourished and caved-in.

A half hour after that: a topless woman with well-sculpted breasts and a round ass to match. She paused to stretch in the corridor and her arms seemed to subdivide into thinner appendages, making me think of a spider measuring a space for a potential web to trap food. It was a neat illusion. She must have been wearing some sort of harness or appliance under what appeared to be skin. She was backlit by the blue corridor light, so it was hard to tell.

Then: a midget, a dwarf, little person, whatever. A Munchkin in a W. C. Fields suit. This was getting boring.

My acrylic spectacles were carving grooves into the sides of my head. I administered my eyedrops and nearly missed the woman. Ordinary configuration—two arms, two legs, sky-high booted heels. She kept glancing back the way she had come in the manner of someone who needed a bathroom not for cleanup or relief, but to do more coke. She fit the profile of Artesia Savoy, from the set of *Vengeance Is.*

I dearly wished for a decent sniper's rifle. Something built around a Remington 700 bolt-action, a heavy-barrel .308 that could reach out and slap down. Maybe with a recessed-crown muzzle for better accuracy. My gunsmith could have supplied a Savage Model 10 with the AccuTrigger and a Millet mil-dot scope (a gun popularly known as the "Tackdriver")—but that tempting option was on the other side of the continent; out of the country, in fact. Bolt guns are better because an autoloader can give away your position. From cold barrel zero, one shot to break the safety glass, one shot to patch the target, about two seconds from start to finish. I dearly wanted to see what a custom-packed NATO round could do to Elias McCabe's skull.

Artesia came out of the bathroom. Definitely her—I caught her face in the light before she blacked out into a backlit silhouette. At least I was in the right place. She passed a guy wearing a crocodile head.

The whole Salon thing seemed like a pretentious *bal Masqué,* the kind of artifice wealthy pricks needed in order to stiffen. Crocodile men. Spider women. How too, too cutting edge. My contempt for privileged, pampered celebutards like Mason Stone made me feel better about hosing the room, if it came to that. Nobody would miss these fucking ghosts. They'd be replaced by the next up-and-coming batch of superstars to cannibalize. It's been that way ever since Jesus. *Eat me, drink me, I give my life for you. Next.*

I could have gone from trigger pull to target down in one shot, not two, if I'd had the luxury of a Barrett, perhaps an M-107 or an M-40A3, basically the equivalent of a tank without treads, a one-hit kill either way so "stopping power" per round was irrelevant. You had to know what are called "damage multipliers," that is, formulas that balance body mass and general health versus ballistics to yield probabilities for your own success. But I was no mathematician, nor was I a seasoned sniper, really. Mooning about best cases meant I was getting impatient. Drifting was not allowed. In any case, I did not want to dispatch Elias from a distance. Up close and personal was what I truly wanted; dammit, we had only met twice and we had the burden of a *relationship.*

Jerk.

His new look almost threw me. Lightened hair, trimmed differently. Clean chin. I recognized his body carriage first of all, in the blue corridor light. He meandered, as though exhausted or drunk.

Target acquired.

As light as I was traveling, I needed a bulky jacket to hide most of my gear, and most of the mods to the jacket could be done with a complimentary hotel sewing kit. I had Bulldog's SIG .40 with two extra mags in open-top pouches (flaps just get in the way)—thirty-six shots, plus one already in the tube. Sewn inside the lower right front of my coat were sleeves for my spotting scope and a Gem-Tech silencer about seven and a half inches long. The Bar-Sto threaded barrel for the silencer had cost Bulldog about three hundred bucks. The silencer, commonly known as a "can," was engineered to reduce recoil and bore flash as well as mute noise. It was made out of aircraft aluminum, finished in matte black, and featured a little piston-spring combo that decoupled the mass of the suppressor from the gun barrel during recoil so the weapon could cycle properly. In other words, it allowed the barrel to move backward inside the silencer housing while the silencer stayed in place. Without it . . . jam-town.

The in-gun clip and two spares were full of jacketed Hydra-Shoks—picture a hollow point with a tapered post of harder lead in the center. On impact, the post uses clothing, tissue, and body fluids as a wedge to force the bullet to expand. Muzzle velocity of 1,100 feet per second at 445 foot pounds. Sledgehammer hit, then it treated your insides to a weed-whacking.

Glasses and gloves, check. Building security was nothing my LockAid kit could not rape quietly. I stashed my scope after wiping it down. If it chanced to fall out of my coat, it needed to be print clean, like everything else I carried. It was tough to find latex gloves in "nude"—like panty hose—but essential so that some stray or bystander would not remember seeing a man wearing gloves.

Okay: a large subdivided, retrofitted loft space, probably fed by an elevator on the west end, which meant fire stairs some-where in the back of the building on a less-stylish emergency exit route. The interior of the building would most likely be a maze; easy to get confused if you did not know which way was north. Decades of tenants had added or subtracted walls to taste. There might be blind access, or a sealed-off doorway or two. *Probably. Most likely. Might.* The total scenario was what tac guys quaintly called "controlling unknown space."

I could *probably* have waited a day to reconnoiter the space, *most likely* would lose track of Elias once more, and *might* have gone a little more blind during all that wasted time. Or I could attack frontally, demote maximally, and assess threat potentials as I tightroped through that wet worker's version of interpre-tive dance—the run-and-gun.

I had him in my crosshairs. It was time for us to meet again.

Fifty-five-odd stairways and four locks later, I came out into the elevator foyer of the building's twenty-sixth floor. I had encountered four security cameras on the way. I lacked the luxury of reconnaissance, floor plans, or Blaine Mooney's lovely roundabouts. I did not even have pieces of tinfoil and earth-quake putty, which could be stuck to the coaxial collars to make static. So, I smudged the lenses with hotel soap. The water pipes visible in most New York stairways provided my ladder, and when I reached up, I found each camera frosted in dust. Once installed, they were rarely maintained except for periodic checks by the security company—like elevators. Think of the last time you were in a spastic elevator with a duly dated checkup slip. These things frazzed out all the time and nobody called the cops. At most, the desk guy downstairs would whack his mon-itor as if it was an old rabbit-eared TV set, bitch and moan, and then scribble a note to have the goddamned screwed up system checked tomorrow, by somebody else. Security officers in build-ings like this were unionized, and not eager to run into poten-tial life-threatening situations for thirteen bucks an hour. If they panicked and whistled up the NYPD, I had a good thirty to forty minutes to work. Plus, this setup was middle ground, not top skim. The illicit nature of the Salon would require certain bribes and a subradar profile. In English: yeah, the building had "security," but only just.

The other thing I encountered in the twenty-sixth floor elevator foyer was Richard Fearing, bodyguard to Mason Stone. His station gave me the correct suite door, and his manner upon my entry told me he was an obstacle that needed to be put down quickly. He was six foot two of shaved pate, black trench coat, and zero warmth. On my way up the stairs, I had decided I needed him.

"Hey there," I said, all sunny. "Building security. I'm the rover."

"No, you ain't," he said. As last words go, it was sad. He was staring at my glasses.

Like a nightclub magician, Fearing had one hand out to distract me while his other hand snaked into his coat. It didn't work.

One would have sufficed, but I gave him two—throat and forehead—with the already-drawn SIG. Throat to shut him up, head to collapse him. He dropped like a clipped marionette. Both slugs stayed inside him, minimizing the mess. The silencer worked like pure gold; modern magic. No more noise than two loud coughs.

The reason I needed Dick Fearing was for an extra firearm; I wanted one for each hand when I tackled the room. His still-parked gun turned out to be a two-tone Browning Hi-Power nine, a weapon particularly abusive to the web of the hand. He carried it cocked and locked. Interestingly, he had loaded the mag with alternating rounds—Gold Dot hardball and Golden Saber hollow points, all high-performance cartridges. One to perforate, one to destroy.

Fearing was—had been—one of those "lighter and faster" guys who used nines or .357s, conscious of the overpenetration factor of bigger guns and more beefy ammo. You wanted your bullet to stay inside the target and wreck some mayhem, not drill cleanly through the far end. Clearly the man had lent some thought to how best to fuel his firepower . . . and came up with a compromise, knowing that he would probably never have to field-test it. How many times have you seen a celebrity bodyguard actually pull a hot weapon? Not many, if there's a camera around, and there always are. Politicians, yes—they're making a political point, after all. For Mason Stone's club, having an obvious pistol-packin' posse would be counterproductive to image. You had to be in the music biz to get away with that.

The foyer was done in fake marble veneer, black with jagged white veins, floor to ceiling. It was akin to standing inside the brain of a lunatic. The suite doors were done in a gilt-edged, antique style whose sloppy brushwork betrayed them, too, as equally fake. Despite all the brass hardware, you could blow these open with a sneeze.

I gave the double door to the suite three smart, no-nonsense raps, just as Fearing might have.

The door was opened by the midget in the W. C. Fields suit. His eyes and mouth made a perfect inverse triangle of zeros.

"Shh," I said, backing him into the entryway with the SIG.

"Kleck?" A feminine voice caught up with us. Another little person.

"Shh," I said, covering her with the Browning.

My eyeline was hampered. Holding three-foot-tall people at gunpoint was new to me.

They went into fear clinch, grabbing each other, just as another person rounded the archway—Mason Stone.

"Hey, Kleck, do you think it would be possible to—" Stone's mouth stalled at midpoint. To his credit, he reacted quickly, backpedaling the way he had come. If he was going for a weapon I needed to know about it.

"The photographer," I said as I trooped the short people backward through the archway and into the main room. "I'm here for the photographer. Not you." Stone was in a half crouch in front of Artesia Savoy, who was seated on a mushroom-shaped pedestal divan near the crescent bar. The back of the bar was toward the curtained windows. Was Stone trying to shield her? He obviously was not packing.

It was difficult to make out the other occupants, due to the size of the room and the dimness of the light. A big fireplace threw dancing shadows. I was facing a circular sofa that sat between the two archways. It was gaudy and velvet, a giant padded donut with a spire in the middle, like something picked up at a brothel fire sale. Turban Guy had risen from it, and seemingly, kept on rising. He was huge, at least six-five without the headgear.

"Please . . ." said the little man in the W. C. Fields suit.

"What the fuck is this?" said Stone, grabbing for command. "Who the fuck are you and what the fuck *is* this? Where's Dick?"

"Dick has gone away," I said. "Shut up. Sit down. Now." All warm bodies were inside my forty-five-degree cover sweep.

Turban Guy kept coming. His carriage said he would not stop until he grappled me into a headlock. I cross-elevated the SIG and stuck a pill into his sweet spot. He grunted on impact and kept coming . . . so I did it again and he fell face forward, trying to keep his blood inside. Mildly amazing, that he could absorb the carnage of two Hydra-Shoks and keep thrashing.

It also froze everyone in tableau. Peripherally I saw them looking for openings, thinking I was distracted by Turban Guy.

Kleck—the dapper midget—got a half step toward the fallen giant and yelled out "Uno!" before he remembered to hold still. His distaff partner began weeping.

Artesia Savoy had flinched as though bee-stung with each silenced shot. She would offer no resistance whatsoever, and Mason Stone had to concentrate on appearing to protect her.

"Everybody listen. Photographer. I need him. I saw him here. Where?"

267

On the floor, Turban Guy stopped squirming and made my argument for me. The pool around him widened.

Off to my immediate left, a row of doors punctuated the long wall opposite the window side. Two of these had opened in response to the ruckus. In the nearest was Spider Girl, who got the special attention of the Browning. She did a fast fade and slammed the door.

"Any other way out of there?" I said.

"No," said Kleck. "Leave us alone."

"Give me the photographer. Elias, Julian, whatever he calls himself, I want him *now*. Don't wait for me to say *please*."

That was when Gator Guy pushed past a nearly naked normal human in the second doorway, roared like a T. rex, and actually fucking *charged* me.

The firelight edged him in feverish orange. I thought: *That's not a mask.* Real teeth showed inside his mouth, which was open wide—impossibly wide. Flinging spittle, his talons chittering on the marble floor, he charged me.

Rather, he charged the Browning, which was closer by one arm's length.

I disliked shooting left-handed, but at this distance it didn't matter. He took five in the torso, nipples to navel, before he lost his trajectory and crashed into the bar, knocking it over. The racket of the unsilenced Browning meant that palaver was done. The lizard-man rolled amid shattered bottles and pungent liquor but did not seem intent on getting up. He did not seem to possess nipples *or* a navel.

Kleck was pointing mutely at another door, the one I'd seen nearest the window in the corridor.

I moved sideways to maintain cover and gave the door my foot. Too much tough guy . . . it wasn't even locked. But violent, declarative actions would keep everyone else on edge, and therefore transfixed for a few more vital seconds. The frame was cheap crap and the door banged open with a satisfying amount of telegraphed threat.

The whole room was aglow with low-frequency hydroponic lamps, the kind used to nourish plant life. The air was thick and humid. From behind a translucent drape, I saw Elias's now blond head snap up. He was flat on his back on a gauzy canopy bed. Something else was on the bed, too—something with flashing silver eyes, like dog or cat eyes.

I brought both guns to bear and started shooting.

PART TWELVE

ELIAS

My next session at Salon was even more disorienting than the first, and I was supposedly in charge. All it took was a phone call to Tripp Bergin to divorce me from *Vengeance Is* for another day. No celebrities were on set and nobody needed shots of the crew wrapping and striking for a company move.

"You tell me if the heat's off," Tripp had said earlier, from beneath the bill of a cap for *Invisible Enemies*. "You decide to tag along or not. You've turned out to be pretty good at this second career, the whole unit photography thing. But it's one of the first gigs that gets cut as production winds down. Your job is only safe through last day of principal photography. After that, I don't know where to stash you. If there's a problem, let me know now."

"There's still a bad guy out there who wants my blood," I said. "I'm looking over my shoulder every second, except when I'm at the Salon."

Tripp popped three pieces of citrus-flavored gum. "They say this sugarless crap makes you fart. Some chemical in it." He frittered. "Cops are looking for Elias McCabe. That makes me an accessory if you really did something wrong, just so you know. No—I'm not looking for an apology. Just know what you're doing, hear me?"

"Roger that. ID my body if I don't make it."

"Boy, you're just a bubbling fountain of good cheer. You got any kind of fallback plan?"

"Cap's been teaching me to shoot."

"Whoa, stop right there, I don't want to know any more. The only thing you can shoot worth a damn is a camera." He doffed his cap and raked his diminishing crop of hair.

"That's Cap's opinion, too."

"Just make my life easier and don't try to bring a piece onto the set, willya?"

"I already got the lecture."

"Nah, I mean . . . look, we're in friggin New Jersey; anybody here without a gun in their glove box is called a *victim*."

Here was a side of Tripp I had not yet seen. "You have a gun in your car?"

"Shh!" He scanned around for potential eavesdroppers. "I'm just sayin. If I was in your position, I'd be strapped, too."

"Strapped?"

"Packing."

This was fun, in a perverse way. "You mean you would have a gun." I was surprised he didn't call it a gat or a roscoe.

"That would be way illegal."

"Said the master of phony ID cards." I actually cracked a smile. It felt ill fitting and foreign to my face. "Mister 'call me from a pay phone.' Mister 'lose the whiskers.'"

"Ah, who can talk to you when you get this way?" Now he was frittering around in place as though he needed a urinal. "Listen, I told you everything I needed to tell you. I'm your friend, not your keeper."

"Thanks, Mom."

He came in close, mouth to ear: "Just do me a solid and explain it to me when it's all over." Then, more generally: "I've gotta go make sure Hunnicutt can transpo his birds across state lines."

"Is it a bird, or is it a *bird*-bird?"

"This is a bird," Tripp said, showing me his middle finger.

* * *

The first session of Salon photos exceeded my hopes beyond dreams. I had some teaser shots into the bosses at Serpentine Clothing, and early word was that they were ecstatic. Having surpassed the introductory awkwardness of the initial shoot, now I was able to go back with a plan. I knew precisely how I wanted to pose Erik, to light Mejandra, to flatter Kleck and Klia, and to immortalize Davanna. This time, they would all be included—the hypercephalic Lyle, the cyclopean Uno, the Visible Man that was Tabanga.

Kleck was trusting this financial gambit to my good offices . . . because even the darkside lure of the Salon was risky and unreliable, when it came to paying bills. Strict confidentiality. Each member of the Salon owned his or her own image rights and I was the sole designated sublicensor. Kleck appointed me as the deal-maker, the business face of the Salon in this venture. I had done nothing to earn his respect, except maybe not call him a dwarf. Perhaps Lyle had read my intentions and whispered in Kleck's ear.

Empathy was another matter altogether. I was a rank tyro until Davanna schooled me. She had been able to see inside me from the first.

Even for people who have slept with thousands of other people, the memorable moments, the personal bests and frissons, or the rarest-of-all instances of unadulterated romantic fulfillment, cook down to about sixty seconds of flashback images, the kind you store in your personal file until you die.

Being inside Davanna was a once-in-a-lifetime jolt I could never have anticipated, or prepared for, and could never replicate. It ruined me for all other partners forever. And I knew this, as it happened.

It separated me from everything.

In the outside world, people fretted about whether black was back in or not. They invested time in worrying about how to spice up their fall neutrals with bold splashes of color, or must-own handbags that cost more than a car. The age-old Republican versus Democrat circle jerk was still considered to be news, which reminded me of Poe's pendulum—no matter which way it swings, it's always moving down, and eventually it slices you in two. Nobody thought it odd that airport security had become, in itself, terrorism. Everybody was kept at a high pitch of panic about finance, and if that wasn't enough to fog your thinking, there were so many glittering distractions available for purchase that it was a miracle the average citizen remembered to put on clothes before venturing out into the daily fray.

The classic film beauty Gene Tierney had a great line in a movie no one remembers (*That Wonderful Urge*): "The great reading public isn't interested in normal human beings. They want freaks served up with all the trimmings." In her case, it became a self-fulfilling prophecy.

As a steady diet of stomach acid, the freakside had drawbacks normal people would never know.

And now I was serving up the freaks myself. Just as they were using me in return.

The great reading public wanted hyperbolic adjectives and earthy blow-by-blow particulars when it came to sex—that is, mere sexual coupling. This was not that. This was something else, something other. I was only inside of her for a few seconds. In that time she learned everything about me she needed to know, because she was a true empath. In turn she permitted me to see within her, just as profoundly. The contact was electric. It exploded time.

There were myriads of inadequate ways to express it. Hyperbole.

She said she wanted to know about me. With her wings spread, she lowered herself onto me. That was our only point of contact. I could not touch or caress or grab—that would leave marks; that's how sensitive she was. Her translucent flesh caught the light and scattered the spectrum in new ways. I could feel

274

her inside of me, at the same moment I experienced the weird hallucination of looking out through her eyes. At me.

Whatever she saw did not alarm her. That was my deepest fear, to be rendered completely naked in front of another mind, with no succoring darkness in which to hide. She saw me, and I saw her seeing, and the fact that she was not repelled (or taken aback at some sinister motive I had tried to conceal), flooded through me in an amplified echo. This was more than reassurance or safety or love. It was something akin to joy, hard to identify because I had so little experience with joy.

"Oh," she said as I felt myself gripped. As in: *I see now; it is clear; I get it.* I would never find out what that revelation was . . .

. . . because that was when the door to the room was kicked rudely open. Gunshots. I felt the bullets punch through me. The pain folded me up into a fetal ball, and abruptly, I was free of her. Her blood misted my face. She fell toward me. The room seemed abruptly devoid of oxygen.

Only later did I sort out impressions, as though decompressing a complicated file. She divined my reason for exploiting the Salon had changed from usury and my desire for escape from the shadow of Clavius to endorsement and a strange, protective desire to *assist* these invisible people who existed behind their bizarre exteriors. It would have been so easy to be like Mason Stone, to smile with veneered teeth to conceal a deeper sneer, to coast through it all for kicks. The Salon was as socially disenfranchised as I had become, in my new identity. My freak was Elias McCabe, and my aberrations were all on the inside.

She fell forward onto me, almost featherweight, no longer concerned with bruises or marks, and before gravity tore us apart, I felt her die inside.

Sex. Violence. Strength. Contest. What we all use to sell, well, everything, including our own fake ideals of ourselves.

It took a heartbeat and a half for me to realize the bullets had not ripped through me, but through her while our psyches were conjoined.

A thousand things told me the silhouette in the doorway was Gun Guy, back for one more. His stance. His movement. He was so halated in an aura of violence and malignancy that he seemed to leave faint blue vapor trails.

The bloodspray on me had come mostly from a heavy-duty slug exiting her perfect, unique face. Her outside died a moment after her inside.

Then Erik chomped Gun Guy's shoulder from behind with his frightening mouth. I was still on the floor.

They fought, briefly, all snarls and gasps. Erik snapped and missed by an eyelash—his definitive kill timing was off. Gun Guy grabbed his arm and howled, wounded. All in spinning shadows. A stray gunshot obliterated one of the hydroponic lamps used for Davanna's comfort. It spark-arced into a cloud of phosphorescent shrapnel with a bright flash, and suddenly I was blind.

More gunshots, and the unmistakable sound of Erik hitting the polished floor. Another sound—which I now recognized as a clip change, a reload.

Then Gun Guy collected me, as others crowded the entry, time-lapse brave in the face of killing weaponry.

"Hi, Elias, old buddy," he said through clenched teeth.

I was rousted off the floor. The hot muzzle of a pistol cooked a tiny circle into my cheek. *Sssssss*. The hammer was already back.

"I want my gun."

I told him the Kimber was not here. I was ready for him to click me off.

A wave of even greater rage from Gun Guy, like the door of a hot oven opening and closing.

"Then you're going to take me to it. Or every one of your little sideshow fuck toys is going to die while you watch."

Boom—gunshot. *That's all, folks.*

But it was not the gun at my head that had gone off. Gun Guy had two. I heard Klia cry out. Fast shuffle of movement.

"Believe it," said Gun Guy. "There's no time-out. No count-down. You take me to it. Now."

I heard Kleck sputtering in grief. "Please don't hurt us any more!"

"He got bit." Mejandra's voice, talking about Gun Guy.

"He's still got all the guns." Mason Stone's voice. "Back out of the doorway. Clear the way for whatever this nut bag wants."

"What I *want* isn't *here*, you dinky fuck!"

Nobody ever called Mason Stone a dinky fuck to his face. Except . . .

I feverishly hoped nobody said, "Now just calm down," to this man.

The barter was implicit. My life for those in the Salon.

Gun Guy grabbed my head and banged my face into the brick wall outside. Three times. A tooth chipped. I felt my nose try to skew.

He kept muttering "asshole," over and over, while he did it.

"'Julian Hightower?' That's ultracute. That's mega-adorable. That's cost me too fucking much, amigo. Your little butt-buddy in the office? The pasty boy with the video camera? He sold you out. Welcome to Hollywood, sailor. The only reason you're still breathing is my gun. I want it back, you worthless piece of shit."

To keep me malleable, Gun Guy had only permitted me to wear my shirt and trousers. I was barefoot and could feel broken glass and tetanus-laced frags embedding the soles of my feet in the alleyway behind the hotel. My face felt coated in hastily smeared dry blood and terror sweat. Pulsing pain in my cheek, from my fresh branding.

"Did you kill Arly, too?" I asked. My lip had sprouted a fresh bleed.

He shook his head as though he still had not figured out why himself. "No, actually."

He shanghaied me into a characterless rental car. Strapped me in, commanded me to sit on my hands. He was going to take his time killing me, once he had resolved the issue of the MIA Kimber. Pressed to the wall, I knew I would rather be dead fast than dead slow. If I antagonized him the right way, just pushed him a teeny bit, he'd spread my brains and leave me for roadkill, mission accomplished, bye-bye Elias.

But.

I knew something Gun Guy did not. Yet. Kleck and I had discussed it, during the first photo session, when I was finding ways to light Erik's crocodilian teeth so they would pop properly in a photo.

"His bite is mildly venomous, as you may have surmised," Kleck said.

I had tried not to react unseemly. *"Mildly?"*

"A little cocktail of amino acids in his saliva which activates as a threat response," said Kleck.

"It's in my spit," said Erik.

I told him to hold still.

"We did a bit of research and found out that it's called a 'denmotoxin,'" Kleck went on, happy to wax erudite. "Characteristic of chewing reptiles lacking front fangs for hypodermic delivery."

"Like a coral snake," I said. It was the most poisonous snake in the continental United States . . . and the most innocuous-looking. Colorful. Small. Tempting. They had to clamp on to you and chew to get the venom in.

"The denmotoxin in the Southeast Asian mangrove snake evolved to favor birds, which were the snake's principal diet. Perhaps that explains why Erik likes chicken so much."

"I like rumaki better," said Erik.

I told him to hold still again. "So . . . it's still venom, though, right?"

"Yes," said Kleck. "Although you'd need significantly more of it to incapacitate a mammal."

"Erik, is it harmful?" I asked.

"Oh, yeah," Erik said from the back of his throat, knowing

that if he moved I'd tell him to hold still again. The lower register of his voice was creepy all by itself.

"Besides the pain of the bite, you'd experience nausea and vertigo," said Kleck. "If you're sensitive, you might go into anaphylactic shock or stop breathing. Of course, there's a difference between a relatively mild snakebite and Erik. His biology is different."

"Have you ever bitten anyone, Erik?"

Erik's gaze darted to Kleck. Kleck's sharp focus went soft. "Once," Kleck said distantly. "It did not go well."

That was my hole card secret weapon there in the car with Gun Guy, who had sustained a full-contact bite wound all around his upper right shoulder. Blood had blossomed freely through his shirt and he was doing his best to hang tough and ignore it. But I already noticed him favoring that arm.

"Man, you did well," Gun Guy said, almost conversationally. "You played well. Ran me ragged. But you've *got* to be as sick of this as I am."

"You killed my friends." We were headed for the Lincoln Tunnel.

"You don't *have* any friends, sport. Your friends all despise you."

"Not Joey." It still hurt to say his name. About everybody else I'd known, he was basically right.

"That shithead with all the tats? Metal in his face? You probably warned him to stay away from your loft. He went back there anyway, to shoot some porn film, when he knew you'd be gone."

"I wish he hadn't."

The tunnel lights zoomed at warp speed, curving over the windshield. It was the middle of the night; the best time for the tunnel.

"You'd better start getting specific about direction," my captor said.

The only destination I had to give was the location of Cap

Weatherwax's truck. If Cap himself was not there, a Fire When Ready sentry would be on duty. Probably ex-military, like Cap. They did not deserve to die. Neither did the crew members who might be loitering around the other trucks as production was wrapped for the company move.

All beyond my control.

Yet Gun Guy had strong-armed Arly Zahoryin and *not* killed him. He had broken his pattern. Perhaps there was enough of a gap there to save Cap or Cap's men.

It was so late that I hoped personnel was at a minimum. I had no other place to be.

What little I knew of Burke did not extend to whether that was his first or last name. He was just "Burke," a vaguely Middle Eastern–looking fellow who I gathered had logged trigger time with Israeli Special Forces, in another reality. Curly black hair, eternal five o'clock shadow, decisive hawklike eyes, quick to grin.

Burke had his own little way station set up outside Cap's Fire When Ready truck. Standard-issue waterproof folding chair with pockets, the kind the stuntmen always lugged around so they could park anywhere. Camp table, area light, cooler, iPod, and—surprisingly—paperback books. You see a lot more people reading on a movie set than you would at first guess. Stunties, as their Aussie brothers and sisters had christened them, had a lot of downtime between prep, rehearsal, and actual go, because the nature of shots and setups was constantly in flux. You had to be cocked, locked, and ready to rock at any moment. It was similar to combat. Or sex.

"Do you know that guy?" asked Gun Guy.

I asked my evil tormentor not to kill him, please.

"Does he have shome kind of check-in schedule?"

I didn't have the faintest idea. He had said "shed-ule," like the British.

"Even if he does, he'll have some kind of red flag word.

Shomething innocuous. A code word for trouble. No check-in ish itself an alert. So you had better move your assh doublequick, Eliash, when I shay show."

Was Gun Guy slurring his words? Was he aware of it? I wondered what shape Erik was in, back in the city, already a universe ago. He had taken multiple hits from exterminating machinery, both before and after he had clamped his jaws on Gun Guy's still-oozing shoulder. A little less than an hour, since the bite. Erik had held on and grappled, during the time I was practically blind. It had taken more bullets to force him to release. That was pretty much my definition of a full-contact bite.

I wanted to say Gun Guy sounded tipsy. I didn't say anything. It was no time to be ironic or spout off a cool line that might alert him . . . like a code word.

"We shtroll up all friendly," said Gun Guy. I think he heard himself. He hesitated. Jerked his head as though to shake cobwebs. "Hi, how ya doin."

I had stupidly hoped nobody else would be loitering around the truck rally zone in the middle of the night. Now I wished for crowds; circus fairways of warm bodies. Witnesses. But Burke's encampment seemed to be the sole point of light in an otherwise powered-down cluster of tenantless equipment. The trailers here were all grip ordnance, lighting gear, props—locked up tight. More than seventy yards away, there was a security guy in a parked car near the airplane hangar where the sets were being broken down. Some night crew, doing the breaking down. All blocked from view by a herd of Star Waggons–type mobile homes for the cast, shut down, cleaned up, and awaiting Transpo back to the rental place. The distant work lights halated the trailers. The security man would patrol on a one-hour circuit, and besides, what the hell, there was a Fire When Ready man on duty near the trucks anyway. If Burke craved a little conversation or coffee, he'd roll over to the set. Not now.

The arena of my final moments was totally oblivious to my needs. A zillion years ago, a fool in school, I had read Emerson's essay, "Self-Reliance," in which old Ralph Waldo had observed, "Traveling is a fool's paradise. Our first journeys discover to us the indifference of places." My travel had been to escape . . . now look where it had gotten me. I fled from rough handling, and people had died because of it.

"Shtay on your hands," said Gun Guy. Keeping a pistol on me left-handed, he shifted his complicated-looking glasses and dumped eyedrops into his right eye, the one he'd wounded in my darkroom. The glasses seemed to be some kind of compensation for the injury, or protection against a similar accident happening again. They resembled the shooting glasses Cap had made me wear on the range.

My own eyes dialed down to accommodate the darkness. This was not going to end well, but I began to see a way it might end without me dying. I knew where the Kimber automatic was inside Cap's truck. I mean, exactly. The light was crap and Gun Guy's vision was handicapped. My own vision in low candle power might lend me a tiny edge, if it was dark inside the trailer. I knew where the lights were and Gun Guy did not.

I could hear him breathing. I couldn't before. His respiration was becoming more labored. Probably because of Erik. But there was no time for me to wait and watch Gun Guy do a slow fade or do an expository speech as he ebbed; we were already on the move.

"Play friendly. You know thish guy."

And Burke knew my current face. It would be impossible for him not to recognize me, the unit photographer. He looked up from his book at the crunch of Gun Guy's feet on gravel. My own feet were peppered with small stones and already bleeding. Burke was wearing a sidearm in a holster with a thick black thigh strap, as all of Cap's men did.

"Hey, Burke," I said.

He shaded his eyes. "Julian, isn't it? You lose your shoes? Who's with you?"

There was a flat, muffled *crack!* by the side of my head and my left ear felt as though it had just been boxed. All the fluids in my skull lurched to the right. Burke's eye vanished and the light gray truck panel directly behind him sprouted a corona of blood spray that appeared black in the light. Dripping, like fresh graffiti. Burke's hand was not even halfway to his gun. He slumped in the collapsible chair, arms swanning. He looked like a slouching sunbather.

"Keys," said Gun Guy.

I was no longer needed. I saw how the plot twist worked now. Burke dead at my hand, truck burgled . . . and me, dead by self-defense.

All because of a fancy gun.

More accurately, all because I had tried to whip out a little pecker of manhood, against forces whose malign notice I had no business attracting.

Who did I think I was?

"Get it yourself," I said, my voice still cowed. Slightly louder: "If you're going to shoot me, shoot me. Get this over with. I'm done."

"Correction," said Gun Guy. "You're finished. But you're not done." He unsnapped the key bunch from the carabiner on Burke's belt. "I'm not going to ransack the truck looking for my Kimber. *You* are going to get it for me."

He shot me in the thigh, taking marksman care not to sunder the bone. "Or thish ish going to take a very long time, and you-shup a lot of bulletsh."

The silenced shot attracted no one's attention except my own. It felt as though a large screwdriver had been pounded through my leg with a sledgehammer. I fell the way a tripod falls when one leg is unlocked, and landed, as they say in Texas, with my dick in the dirt.

"Ged up, you pushy." He sounded impatient and distracted. I could not see him fighting to focus because my own eyes were spilling hot tears of shock. "It's a flesh wound. Hardball round.

Twenty more if you don't do what I shay." He shook his head to rattle things toward normal, then stretched his jaw. In my blurred view his jaw seemed to elongate, the way I'd seen snakes do it.

Then he said: "Dosh my voice shound *funny* to you?"

Mirth. It sounded like a bad party imitation of Bogart.

"Keyshh. Truck. Now."

There was very little blood on my leg but it was already swelling. He tossed me a kerchief from Burke's gear to tie around it. I could stand, just barely. He made me pick the keys off the ground anyway.

"Do it the way I want," he said, "and id'll be quick. My gift to you."

Burke was dead, and I was next. The end of a long chain of killing, all my fault. I had earned my own demise.

Two big industrial padlocks on the side door of Cap's truck. What a pisser, I thought, if Cap had been working inside the whole time.

Dark inside. No Cap.

"You shtep up first. Lightshh." He tried again, enunciating. "*Light.*"

The first bank of switches near the side door would illuminate several small neon lamps over the principal work surfaces. Next to them, another panel would fire up the interior like Broadway. If the little lights were on, maybe Gun Guy would not think about bigger ones. I clicked two of the five toggles.

He kicked me in the ass as he climbed up, dumping me headlong into the narrow work corridor of the trailer. "Now go for it, you fucking loser."

The rickety dam of my control burst. I scrabbled down the space into the dark like a whipped animal.

Mister Kimber says stay.

It was a replay of the darkroom. I was on the floor again, ready to shit myself, whittled down to instinct and reflex and . . .

. . . *muscle memory.* Just like Cap had said.

Back there, an ordinary person would be pawing around for a flashlight. I could see the steel work drawer containing the Kimber just fine, in gray tones, as though my color input had converted to black-and-white. I did not even need to look at it to know the feel of it in my hand. The weight read as unloaded. The mags with my practice rounds were in the drawer. Load smooth. My fingers remembered. *Do it again. Now do it blind-folded.*

"You got it? Good, good," said Gun Guy from the far end of the box. "About time. Now *take your fucking sshhot,* big man."

He had wanted it to happen this way. That was the answer for why I wasn't dead yet. It was the phony Western shoot-out I had fantasized, but without the fantasy dressing, and strictly per Gun Guy's agenda.

I brought the Kimber up on adrenaline and endorphins. Sight picture. Squeeze, don't snap. Live target. Hot weapon. Erase the bad guy.

One shot wasn't enough. I held rock-steady and fed the clip in Gun Guy's direction, the blasts deafening in the close quarters of the trailer. One shot after another, a purely organic continuance, until the mag was exhausted and the slide locked back and echoes receded and the only sound was me, howling like a caveman.

Gun Guy had not budged.

"You're a lousy shot," he slurred, speaking above the absence of room tone, grinning, devilish. His shooter's glasses seemed to glow faintly blue, an alien visor preparing to unleash a death ray. I thought it was his aura.

He leveled his big, silenced nightmare of a pistol at me and showed me how it was done.

PART THIRTEEN

CHAMBERS

To simply kill Elias McCabe, to overload him with holes and metal as he flailed around like a stymied beast or a terrified child, flapping his hands and crying, would not satisfy. Simply killing him would have been an act of mercy he had not earned. He *owed* me my rage.

The "hot prowl" of my entry to the Salon had my system singing with brain chemicals, akin to an Ecstasy high, but better—a killing high. All systems at full burn. Turban Guy had eaten my shit and died. Gator Guy, ditto. And now it was Elias's turn to blanch before the killing wrath of my weaponry and anger. This is what I did. This is what I was best at.

The monsters in the freak show had nothing on me. Now it was my turn to be the monster. It felt good, and I liked the way it felt.

Still, I needed a half beat for sheer astonishment. More than once.

The first time was when Gator Guy came charging out of his room, nearly frothing, rhino unstoppable, truly a bizarre sight to behold. This was no dude wearing a costume. The teeth and claws seemed brutally real, just as the light in his inhuman eyes told me a swift death was coming to eat me. I cross-sighted the Browning and emptied it into him until he fell, unplugged. But it took five rounds.

That manned up the midget, who gave me what I wanted.

I kicked the door open a bit too aggressively. It turned out not to be locked. Warmth buffeted from the chamber, which was dimly illuminated by hothouse lamps. Ten feet away on a canopied bed was Elias, in flagrante delicto.

Time for surprise number two.

Elias was being mounted by some kind of beige-colored bat-woman, or maybe just a tart in a skintight PVC bondage rig. The large wings were spread wide and catching the chemical light the way moth dust glitters. I had not spied this one from my surveillance roost; it was new to me. My entrance caused it to snap around to glare at me with chatoyant eyes.

No problem. Shoot through it. That was what I had brought the silenced SIG to do.

Elias was completely shielded but a lucky strike might blow through to hobble him. It took four shots to hurl Bat Girl down and clear. I was perilously close to needing a magazine change; the Browning was dry, and there was a whole crowd just outside yet to kill if I didn't get my way.

Elias puled and hollered and fell off the bed. I had him, dead bang.

Before I could squeeze off, a bulldozer rammed me from behind—a dozer with crooked reptile teeth, which it sank into my shoulder, spoiling my aim a wink before I knew I had a fight on my hands.

Gator Guy was still in the ring. Damaged but not decommissioned.

And holy crap, it was just the same as wrasslin' a real, live crocodilian.

I'd heard about the "mouth trick" used by reptile wranglers. You can hold a gator's mouth shut easily, with your hands, with a single strip of duct tape. The muscles that open it are weak. The muscles that close it generate more than 2,000 pounds of crush pressure. Human beings can only manage about 150. It takes about 1,400 to implode a man's skull. You can almost never pry a gator's jaws open once they're closed, and these jaws were trying to marry up through my shoulder, destroying everything in between.

Gator Guy's momentum took us both down. It was stupid and inelegant, a bar fight. My face bounced off the floor and I saw whole galaxies of impact lightning. I lost the Browning. The animal certainty of my assailant's fury rushed into my nostrils, gamey and pungent. I had to sweep him over with my entoothed arm; my SIG and my other arm were pinned under me, and any moment now, Elias would rally and join the battle, since someone else had started it. I'd been attacked plenty of times, but never by a large, wounded, pissed-off monster.

I managed to half spill Gator Guy, whose clamp on my shoulder could only be called a death grip. Once a crocodilian's jaw is closed, you need a crowbar, a tow truck, or maybe explosives to open it back up. I jammed the long snout of the suppressed SIG into the nearest patch of scales and gave him everything the weapon had left. He recoiled as one shot skinned through, ricocheted off the floor, and terminated a large hydroponic lamp inside an aluminum reflector. Apparently there was a knot of vital organs near my blast point, causing him to jerk back as though electroshocked.

My shoulder came alive with release pain, the preamble to a rush of blood. Dizziness, nausea. Gator Guy fell into neutral and I kicked away from him. I could feel the macerated bones in my shoulder grinding as I did a mag change on the SIG as fast as I could manage. It was absolutely mandatory, because any second now the freak show in the next room would get braver.

I half hitched into a stumbling run across the room to nail Elias before he could find the rest of his wits. He seemed lagged or drugged, not quite caught up with the time line yet.

The pain in my shoulder was sparking down my arm like dripping acid. I could not show Elias I was incapacitated in any way. I pressed the SIG's hot muzzle to his face to brand him with a small, circular souvenir about the time the doorway filled up with reinforcements. The midget. The other midget. Mason Stone, playing hero.

I wanted my Kimber back. No way this coward was going to die easy, without my recovering the totem that had somehow started this whole opera.

"It's not here," Elias wheedled. "I don't have it. You're here to kill me, then kill me. I'm ready for that. Just don't harm anyone else."

Amazing—he had finally worked it out. And he still felt as though he was in a position to call shots. I wanted to smash his head until it was no longer a head. Fourteen hundred pounds. But in dissembling, he had given me leverage: the others present, the still-living audience to our conflict. I had enough ammo to kill them all.

The point needed to be made, quickly. I put a round into one of the midgets; child's play at this range. She fell down and everybody in the doorway shied back.

The other midget's voice came out in a bray of loss. "Please don't hurt us any more!" he begged.

The spidery chick was peeking around the door frame. I heard her say, "He got bit." The gravity with which she said it indicated that an encounter with Gator Guy's dentition meant more than just a panic snap.

What if Gator Guy was venomous? That meant I had even less time. Everybody would stand there and wait while I got woozy and tipped over. Then they would all gang up on me.

Unexpectedly, Mason Stone chose that moment to become the voice of reason. He told the group to step back from the door, to clear the way for whatever came next. He called me a nut bag.

What did he mean? Like, a scrotum? A squirrel's food stash? My brain felt dosed with ammonia. I should have blasted him into mixed meat, but my gun was starting to feel like an anvil grafted on to the terminus of my arm.

Elias was my primary. I had to focus on him. Much as I

wanted to bulldog him through the world naked, that would attract the wrong kind of notice, so I had to allow him to shuffle into shirt and pants. No shoes. Barefoot, he would remain more limited and vulnerable. There was blood all over his face. Not his. He mopped it away with a corner of bedsheet, visibly anxious not to incur my wrath further, or amplify the rich mix already fueling me.

We backed out the way I had come, the long nose of the SIG bench-rested on Elias's shoulder. Dick Fearing's corpse was exactly as I had left it in the twenty-sixth-floor foyer. We stepped over it together. Elias barely noticed it, or rather, he failed to lend it the awe or fear that an ordinary citizen would express when confronted with a dead body. Not even fake outrage. He was past all that now, and seemed drugged himself. For the next few moments it would be easier to herd him, but that window would not last.

He was learning.

To refresh his fear and keep him on the defensive, I fisted up his recently dyed hair with my good arm and smashed his face into the wall outside, without preamble. Then I did it again, to surprise him. And again, to make him think I would keep doing it. His face came back sooty and cross-eyed from the bricks, blood on his nose and lips. Good. Let him *feel* what was happening to him. Make him think he was helpless, with no walls of discorporation to insulate him. Asshole.

I made sure he knew Arly Zahoryin was the final link in my trail of squealers. Scared and newly bloodied, Elias assumed I'd mowed Arly down as well.

But I had not, and it still felt odd. Unclean, somehow. Not definitive.

Like a Marine MP with a drunk prisoner, I hustled him across the street to my waiting rental car. My shoulder was already throbbing worse than an abscessed molar. Any moment now, Elias would start jabbering "just kill me," and I had to keep him wobbly in order to recover my lost Kimber. That meant I had to keep him talking during the trip, much as I loathed the idea of conversation.

"Ran me ragged," I said, making it sound accusatory, not complimentary. "But you've got to be as sick of this as I am." I had to hold steady on him with the silenced SIG, left-handed. Every crank of the wheel with my right kicked fresh fishhook pain up and down my arm. I could not let him see it. He might misinterpret it as some kind of advantage to be taken.

"You killed my friends." He sounded five years old.

Good opening. Use it. "You don't *have* any friends, sport. Your friends all despise you." That would cause him to flash-review all the disappointments of his coddled life, and realize it was true. Then he'd bring up his gofer, the amateur porn star with all the tattoos and piercings.

"Not Joey," he said. Sure enough.

"You probably warned him to stay away from your loft. He went back there anyway, to shoot some porn film, after he knew you'd be gone." We were halfway through the Lincoln Tunnel.

"I wish he hadn't," said Elias. Excellent. He was larding himself with guilt over Joey, penitent. I wished he could have actually seen it happen.

Prior to the company move for *Vengeance Is*, the airplane hangar in Jersey was mostly the site of residual breakdown activity. The tractor-trailer truck Elias specified as the location of my Kimber was grouped in a huddle of other shut-down trucks a safe distance from the hangar itself, which offered the complications of warm bodies working, and light. At this distance we could move as shadows and not be overheard.

The armorer's truck, a cache full of weaponry, had its own middle-of-the-night watchdog.

The floor of my mouth tasted tarry, and the fishhooks of distress were starting to flower open and shut all along my spine. I had to Zen this pain away; stash it somewhere else for five more minutes.

I needed Elias as a front to deactivate the sentry. But my damaged eye was yowling, and first I had to hold my gun on my captive while administering Alcaine, the numbing eyedrops. It was a display of vulnerability I did not want him to see.

"He'll have some kind of red flag word," I said, knowing that if the guy checked in on a radio or mobile while we were walking toward him, we'd be made. If he recognized Elias, he would be less alert. "Something innocuous. A code word for trouble. I'll know it if I hear it. No check-in is itself an alert." We had to make haste before someone else's clock doomed us.

Elias looked at me strangely, as though I had given him the lowdown in Yiddish. The SIG reminded him to stick to the task at hand. He would play along for another minute, another two, in the mistaken idea he might be able to save the life of the sentry, whose name turned out to be Burke.

Burke was strapped, but not wearing body armor. Good enough—a single headshot stamped him filed. A nice display to keep Elias rocky. For added distress, I popped off the shot right next to Elias's ear.

It felt as though my lungs were filling up with snot. Or shrinking. I recovered the late Burke's keys and threw them at Elias, which would compel him to pick them up off the ground. Keep him submissive.

I could smell him getting ready to blow. A last act of defiance. He did not pick up the keys.

"Get it yourself. If you're going to shoot me, shoot me. Get this over with. I'm done."

The little bastard had made peace inside his own head. He was prepared to die, or so he thought. All broken and noble, a tarnished hero from some simpleminded movie.

Not.

I hurt too much to endure this pointless bravado. I was only one down on a fresh mag, so I plugged a shot into his thigh to remind him he was not dead yet, and dying could take a very long time indeed. Thighs are meaty—a lot of tissue with a lot of nerves. A flesh wound there could make a point directly. The hardball round rocketed clean through his leg, and I saw the expression I wanted.

He thrashed around a bit, but he picked up the keys like a good boy. My jaw was getting numb and my right ear was flaming hot. Gator Guy had done something to me, all right.

"Does my voice sound *funny* to you?" It was like battering him with words. He flinched. "Keys. Truck. Now." Dead Burke had an engineer's kerchief poking from one pocket; I tossed it to Elias so he could bind his latest wound.

I was fully aware I was letting Elias precede me into a dark trailer full of weapons. This was intentional. I motioned him up the metal steps to the side door. He kept his hands in full view. "Lights," I said. The word went to taffy in my mouth.

We had to hurry.

I came up as he switched on some tiny work lamps and put my boot firmly into his butt to dump him to hands and knees, for crawling, for begging.

"Now go for it, you fucking loser."

He scrambled away toward the darker end of the trailer like a lizard singed by a blowtorch. Back there, he would acquire a weapon—most likely, the Kimber. And I would prove what I already knew.

People who know nothing of weapons waste lifetimes with "if only." If only I'd had a gun, things would have been different. If only I had acted, I could have saved . . . something. If only. All bullshit.

"You got it?" I called out. "Good, good. About time. Now *take your fucking shot,* big man!"

Elias opened fire on me from a distance of about ten feet. By the third shot he was yammering incoherently, which meant he was not targeting worth a damn. He wanted to rinse me from the world in a cauterizing shower of bullets. Armed confrontation is not target practice, not when the target can shoot back. Amateurs think point-blank range is close enough.

Elias missed all seven shots. That is, presuming a jump-load on an empty gun. Call it eight if the pistol was already loaded with a prize in the tube. That Elias accomplished any such functions reliably in the dark, under duress, was admirable—he had been practicing. But it did not matter. He spent his mag and every shot was at least a yard wide of me.

Now I could put him down like a rabid weasel.

I sighted instinctively on his muzzle flash and engaged my SIG. The light in the trailer shifted to a weird bluish tint, and I realized my glasses were . . . glowing.

Glowing blue.

My eyes shifted, just for a fraction of a moment. In that millisecond, they shut down completely. Both eyes. Blinded.

I fired anyway, trusting vector, putting down a pattern that anticipated which way Elias might duck. I'd fired with my eyes shut before. Even blindfolded—it's all part of the discipline.

Just as with the audio on black box recordings salvaged from the wreckage of a plane crash, my penultimate thought was moronically normal. Prosaic.

Oh, shit.

Then something hit me in the side of the neck, with the impact of a rusty nail in the fat part of a ballbat at the end of a home run swing. The opposite side of my neck exploded. Decapitation would have been gentler.

Ballistic force yanked me sideways and earthward in a grand, godlike smite. I had taken bullets before; it had been one of the passage-to-adulthood rites I had in lieu of getting married or having children. Right shoulder rear, dead center back, both arms winged, right thigh, upper chest, most defense calibers. A variety of flesh wounds, to make the list sound more impressive. Not that there was anyone to whom I could brag. A couple of hits—not as many—from knives and edged weapons. But this was different, new, and fatal, so traumatic that most of my nerve endings clicked off and the next thing I knew I was on the floor, my extremities iced into distant uselessness.

Probably a boat-tailed Lapua .338 round, if I knew my snipers.

A full metal–jacketed military round, super-Magnums with a muzzle energy of nearly 5,000 foot pounds. Flat trajectory. It could have been fired from as far away as 1,500 meters.

My eyes were broadcasting static, but I knew Elias was standing over me, probably with a forlorn expression, thinking he had done this.

I had to say something, even through the glottal hash made of my throat. I owed a death, and it turned out to be mine. I had to tell Elias something. Whisper it, as though to a friend or lover. Two words. A name.

Not mine.

PART FOURTEEN

ELIAS

I took Gun Guy's shoes. Dead man's shoes. They fit. I was in no condition to walk anywhere, with my leg gunshot and my feet bleeding. When the *Vengeance Is* overtimers rushed to Cap's trailer at the sound of my gunfire, I was pilfering his first aid box. They were followed by cops, and eventually, Cap himself.

He looked at me as though his own baby daughter had just tried to cut his throat. He stood down when it was deduced that I had not shot or killed anyone. Not yet. He had poor Burke to deal with. When Cap finally left the scene, hours later, I knew I would never see him again. I hoped I had not destroyed anything of value in the trailer with my wild salvo of missed shots.

Elias McCabe came clean to the authorities—so RIP, Julian Hightower—and there came a great many authorities in a fast, frenetic pageant.

The Kimber vanished into evidence, also never to be seen again. I think it was assumed to be part of Cap Weatherwax's inventory (there were photos to prove it), and Cap, as it turned out, apparently never told anyone differently.

Vengeance Is wrapped out to its Arizona location with a minimum of fuss. There were incomplete accounts of a mishap, probably courtesy of Arly Zahoryin. But it had not occurred on-set, involved no celebrities, and was adjudged peripheral to the movie, since nobody was interested anyway, because there was no buzz, no stain.

As far as I knew, the movie got finished. The End.

Which left me doing interviews with investigators. Weeks' worth. During one of these, in an anonymous cubicle in an equally anonymous courthouse, Tripp Bergin rang me on my newest mobile phone and advised me not to talk to him for a very long time.

In essence, my story was so crazy that most of it had to be true. More than one detective said, "You just can't make this shit up." From what I heard, they twigged to Gun Guy's hotel room in the city, but nothing there led anywhere else. The only thing they really had me on was a couple of firearms violations, and I swatted them back with self-defense under duress. I told them I was in fear for my life, not rational, scared shitless, impulsively panicked. Then I told them again, and again, while they assembled puzzle pieces, strange and disturbing, but pieces that fit.

Back on the Left Coast, my loft remained tainted and spiritually unclean. Too many ghosts there, after the spoor of dead bodies and malice had been scrubbed away and repaired. Now the place begged me to forsake it. I took a hit on the lease (or rather, Clavius did), but scored a bargain on a house in the hills due to the real estate crash. "Saved" money is imaginary anyway, if you're still spending.

My new space felt naked and blank, too far white, unseasoned, not broken in yet. Too many windows. Most realtors thought California buyers loved windows and sunlight. I covered half the windows with Dubateen (a trick I had learned from the movie's gaffers, who frequently slept days in odd locations, and used the thick, black metal foil to cover windows as well as mask lighting rigs). More important, I supervised the installation of the security system. I had plenty of time, because I had to wear a house arrest ankle bracelet for four months.

There were a thousand Web sites with advice on how to out-fox it, but I played nice.

I used the time to block out which walls would come down and how my new studio would go up. I drew diagrams on grid paper. I monitored the progress of the Salon campaign begun by Serpentine Clothing.

On the phone, Kleck said, "You bartered your life for us." His voice still held that slight asthmatic wheeze I remembered.

I told him, "I brought it all down upon you." The success of the Serpentine rollout was a better way to give something back to the Salon. A couple hundred thousand dollars, in fact, for starters.

"You saved us," he said, determined to let me off the hook. Good fellow.

"I damned you." Most of our conversations were destined to be like this, for the foreseeable future.

Erik lived, despite stopping nine powerful slugs and spend-ing six months in a wheelchair. Klia survived, too—hit in the left breast, she had needed a respirator for a while. Uno was still dead, as were Davanna, Joey, Varla, Char, Nasja, Dominic Sharps, and Burke. Nobody had any way of knowing what the real tally might be.

Clavius did not return my calls. I was free of him at last.

On my first day as a free citizen, I felt a need to go out into the world, searching for whatever I had lost, although I could not specify what. I wanted to talk to some stranger in a bar. To laugh. To flirt. To feel marginally human. To hang out; some-thing grown-ups almost never do.

I got the first part of my wish.

It was not a sex partner I sought, somebody to batter me silly with fuckstuff. Davanna had ruined all that for me.

But my newest friend certainly was considerable. Five-ten, easy, not counting the boot heels. She could have been one of the endless parade of fashion models, but her face was too stern.

Too much nose for *Vogue*. More compact and contained than willowy. Blond hair in a kind of rag cut; careful disarray that would never get in her eyes. Strong hands, tapered fingers, no jewelry. Eyes of a deep espresso brown that read as translucent black, like onyx. She instantly brought Char to mind.

"Don't tell me—Elias, right?"

My mind stalled. *Searching . . . no files found.*

She had already brought me a refill on my J&B, rocks.

I thought I had it: "You're not a reporter, are you? A law enforcement officer of any kind?"

No and no.

"Law enforcement officers aren't supposed to drink on duty." She sucked on a black electronic cigarette, three puffs of water vapor at 1 percent nicotine. The blue tip lit up when she drew on it. "I love these things. You should be able to smoke them in airplanes, but it makes everybody too nervous. Cigarettes are messy. Before you know it you've got ash in your hair, on your clothes."

She had already seated herself across from me in the green leatherette booth. "Only problem with an electronic cigarette is, they never go out." Her approach was deft, diversionary, but she was inviting my interest.

"And you know me . . . how?"

"I didn't say I knew you." Another puff. A sip. "I just wanted to get another look at you. In the light. See if you were worth all the fuss."

I should have been eyeballing her for a concealed firearm. She seemed to sense this and dealt me a tiny smile, not too much teeth.

"Let's say we had a mutual acquaintance," she said. "Someone who ran around like an insane infant, leaving a poo-poo trail of dead bodies."

I felt my throat and asshole try to swap positions. My vision plunged.

She stayed well ahead of me: "Relax. I'm not here to bother you. I'm not a gal on a mission, or with a grudge. I don't represent anybody. I'm not wearing a wire or anything like that. See?" She shucked her leather jacket, turned out her cuffs, and even pulled the vee of her shirt forward to bless me with an unobstructed view down her cleavage. No brassiere, just wonderful pale skin all the way to her navel, presumably.

I said, "I wonder if the person you're thinking of is the person *I'm* thinking of."

She shrugged. Again the tiny half-smile, which really was a winning one. "Either way. Let's further posit that this person, our friend, let his ego get in the way of business. People died—people who were not supposed to die. Who were not paid for. It's like porn on the Internet: how are you supposed to make money at it when other people are giving it away for free?"

"You want money." I certainly was a dim bulb today.

"Oh, not at all." Puff, puff, sip. "It's just that this . . . our *friend,* was totally unprofessional. Not surgical."

More than ten people dead, and it was amateurish? Char had been raped and carved up and it wasn't *surgical* enough? Slow anger—the deadly kind—began to push up from my gorge like molten lava.

"Don't misunderstand me," she said. "The way he was, our friend, or the way he became, scared a lot of people. You were scared of him."

I felt like saying no, I wasn't, all sullen and teenaged. She already knew this, too, and allowed me some space to decompress.

I could have asked two dozen questions. This woman would merely shake her head. Not relevant. I settled on asking what his real name might have been.

That gave her genuine pause for thought. "Whatever name you might have gotten doesn't matter. None of those people exist. But the people who hired him do exist. And they got scared, too. As scared as you. Even if our friend had gotten all the fish he wanted, that would leave him in the world, and that meant his employer would still be scared, you follow?"

"I'm still scared, right now," I said. "Of you. Did you know this nonexistent person we're talking about?"

Now she appeared wistful, almost. "Yeah, twenty, thirty names ago. We had what you might call a mini-history."

Comrades in arms? Teammates? Lovers, even?

"It's not pretty when they burn out," she said distantly. "It rarely happens, but it happens. I wanted to see if I felt anything when I had to harvest him. Or anything when I told you." She paused to let it absorb past the concrete walls of my thick head. "Nope; I'm good on both counts."

When you have time, alone, inside, cover one of your eyes for about half an hour. Then go to a dark room, or outside at night, and close first one eye, then the other—blinking between your light- and dark-adapted eyes. The difference is startling, in perceptions, shapes, and colors. Ordinary people call this phenomenon "blindsight," but what they're really talking about is human evolution. There are two separate vision conduits in the brain; one for conscious sight and one for more primitive, autonomic visual acuity. Blind sight permits a person who cannot see a thrown object to nonetheless catch or avoid it. And my rhodopsin-enriched rods, my sensitivity to bright light, allowed me to see a black-and-white world where others might have seen only murky darkness.

Once having seen that world, you became one of its tenants.

"Can I ask you something?" I said, gulping half my drink at once. "Strictly hypothetically?"

"Shoot." A trenchant wit, this one.

"What if our, um, friend had not been harvested?"

"Then you, Elias, would be as dead as a shrimp hand roll, and I would be chasing our friend's ass all over the country. Because if I didn't get him . . ."

"Then you'd have somebody after you."

She nodded. Slightly bemused. She had been the pinch hitter, the fail-safe.

"And this is the lull before you blow *my* brains out?"

"No. You're not part of my contract."

My entire skeleton was straining to rip free of my dullard flesh and run away to hide somewhere safe, but I held fast. Where would I run?

"But what if I was?" I said.

"Then this conversation would not be taking place." She puffed some more and I watched the sapphire glow of the LED tip. "Go back to your world, Elias. Bang supermodels. Enjoy your life. Consume and be happy."

That was it: the warning, the threat. The blue glow reminded me of the laser light that had roosted across Gun Guy's face right before his neck had burst in a party popper spray of tissue and blood. Bad guy eliminated; roll credits.

Later I found out that such lasers could be applied to gunsighting, but they were powerful enough to burn and blind. The units depicted online resembled lightsabers from *Star Wars* and were trumpeted as the latest in nonlethal tech.

I thought back to how this ride had started, with Nasja blowing me. Me taking advantage. Me being the world's biggest shit . . . after Clavius. I had been dying by inches. It took Gun Guy trying to kill me to reactivate my brain and make my heart start beating again.

This woman did not need to be told any of that. I would never see her again. Even so, I would spend the rest of my days watching out for that blue light.

"What happens now?"

She almost laughed; I saw her suppress it. If she ever did smile, I suspected it to be a million-watter.

"Okay, sorry I asked," I said. "I only have one more question."

"Shoot."

"Who is Mal Boyd?"

★ ★ ★

Which brings me to the story of my encounter with a totally awesome fellow named Roddy Caperton.

Some months after the murderous debacle on the set of *Vengeance Is*, Roddy Caperton checked in for his job on the night shift at a spa in Brentwood called Sybarite, one of those high-end, private-member ablutitoria where the upper crust could get comfortably mud-packed and plucked and sanded without the lingering downer of paparazzi in the parking lot. After some entry-level janitorial servitude, he had moved up to night shift on the front desk since he was willing to work graveyard, and Sybarite, which did no advertising whatsoever, did its best to accommodate the eccentric schedule waffle of its clients. Roddy had expressed some interest in learning to become a professional masseuse, and ultimately was entrusted with keys and security codes. He never dished on customers, was disinterested in gossip of any kind, and was always game to stay late or do a bit extra. In due time, he became invisible, as all the best practitioners in the service industry should be.

Roddy was not going bald, but shaved his head in accordance with current fashion. The frequently tropical atmosphere inside Sybarite caused workers to sweat, and half of them had shaved heads also. Roddy wore thick-rimmed Buddy Holly glasses, also trendy. He had raised a vague goatee trimmed to a stubble depth of an eighth of an inch, precisely. He felt it lent his profile a more definitive chin.

On the fifteenth of every month, for the past seven years (according to the ledgers), a customer named Mr. Youngman—obviously an alias—booked exclusive use of the spa for an intense, thirty-hour rejuvenation that included purgatives, herbal colon-cleansing, UV treatments, hydrotherapy, exfoliation via "salt glow" plus body wax, a mani-pedi, a scalp massage, and a six-hour detox in an immersion of low-pH "Moor mud" (imported) while wrapped in selected seaweed, kelp, and moss. The mud bath process was akin to leaving soup to simmer, and not recommended for the claustrophobic.

Mr. Youngman was a preferred client who tipped excellently due to his special needs. For one thing, a vegetarian sideboard had to be prepared and maintained for him. For another, he was so obese that the tiled, bathtub-configured tanks would not serve. Especially for Mr. Youngman's immersion wrap, a much larger whirlpool tub was pressed into service. Because of drainage problems, the whirlpool tub had to be cleaned out by hand after Mr. Youngman's monthly regimen.

Mr. Youngman had become a kind of local legend around Sybarite, but Roddy did not get a look at him until several visits had passed; employees tended to vie for the right to serve him. Ultimately, though, Roddy's number came up: second shift, fifteen hours straight, including babysitting the mud-wallow phase from midnight to 6:00 A.M.

Whenever Roddy encountered steam at Sybarite, he had to polish his glasses, which was a minor nuisance. They fogged up now, at about 2:14 A.M. He rubbed off the condensation on his staff T-shirt.

"Everything good so far, Mr. Youngman?" he said to the inert form submerged to the nostrils in the giant spa tub, like a crocodile patiently outwaiting new prey. A languid bubble fought its way up through the dense liquid and took its time popping. The steam taps lent the room the sound of a kettle on low boil.

The occupant of the tub did not reply, but his golden reptile eyes slowly considered the intruder.

"Y'know, I was reading about 'ablutions' in the dictionary," Roddy said, his voice echoing off the tile, yet muted by vapor; a sound booth effect. "It can mean any kind of washing or cleansing, from blessings, to baptisms, to exorcisms."

Mr. Youngman's lips barely moved. "I'm sure that's deeply fascinating to you, but I should prefer you stop talking, please."

"Oh. Yah. Right. Of course. Sorry."

The golden eyes watched Roddy back out, subserviently, to *get right on* whatever little white trash chores enriched his existence. Stupid pillock. He had to be new. A memorandum would be sent, and a gratuity overlooked.

Less than five minutes later, the idiot came back. Without his glasses.

"Mr. Youngman? So sorry to disturb you, but there's one more thing."

Before the tar-pitted fat man could roll his eyes, huff out a sigh, or protest in any way, Roddy dismembered him with five rounds from an AA-12—the Atchisson Assault Shotgun—which made a vast bowl of muddy gruel. At this distance, with this weapon, there was no way in hell he could miss. The gun's roar sounded like Armageddon, but there was no one else present. Lifeblood and therapeutic mud splashed the walls and pooled on the clean white floor, with some of the red stuff following the grout patterns in the tile.

Roddy stripped his latex gloves, which had been specified for dealing with Mr. Youngman. He locked up for the night. Then he ceased to exist at all.

Miss Mystery Date bid me farewell and left me holding the ice-diluted dregs of a drink. My instructions were not to follow her, or even watch her leave.

Beneath her Stella Artois coaster she had left me a folded piece of paper.

The rest, you can guess.

The shotgun came from a rathole apartment in Thai Town, a place so devoid of personal identity that it could have been a three-walled movie set. No computer, no TV, a strictly functional way station. A toothbrush had been left in the mildewy bathroom. Gun Guy's toothbrush. He had brushed his teeth in here, watching himself in the mirror, thinking of how he was going to make me suffer.

Mal Boyd was a fat spider in the middle of a fatter web. My entire rebirth had begun with Mal Boyd. And Mal Boyd was cocooned in security, with the conditional exception of a single day every month, like clockwork.

I considered Roddy's last name: Caperton. I had gotten it from an obituary.

Then I got in touch with a special effects house in Chatsworth, and arranged a consultation for a special hairpiece, exploiting my Tripp contacts. A lionish, good-natured fellow named Greg listened to my lie about having cancer and needing a wig that looked exactly like my normal hair. Pricier this way, but more exact. They did it for actors.

Then I let Roddy shave my head, in honor of Joey. Awesome.

I decided on fake glasses for Roddy. Frames distort memory of one's face. I looked like a used-to-be keyboardist for some nightly talk show band. He maintained a neat—though dyed—goatee to lend his profile more chin. That was what people would remember, if they ever saw him: Bald guy. Glasses. Goatee. The same as thousands of L.A.'s other denizens.

I shot my own photos for Roddy's assorted forms of ID. Bald guy, glasses. goatee, check.

By day I could wear my Elias wig and be Elias. By night I could commence my auxiliary career, working up cred for Roddy, who was friendly and talky and too helpful and not bright enough to piss anyone off.

I had become, in the parlance, a "fake-hair-wearin' bitch."

One who, at night, waited patiently, trading his fake hair for a shotgun.

Limelight is the last thing I want.

Right now there's a billboard in Times Square, eighty feet tall, prime placement; a picture of Davanna that I shot. Kleck was angling for a reality show. New human oddities were already auditioning for him.

Notoriety, fame? Not for me.

Some memories, those compressed files of Davanna's perceptions, can flower open at the vaguest cue. They remain painful, almost physically debilitating.

All of it is information I do not wish to disseminate.

Roddy Caperton vanished from the face of the planet and my hair grew back to normal.

I absolutely do not want to be quoted, anywhere.

I respond to e-mails and texts in the dead of night, a time-delay collaborator. You won't see me much in the daytime anymore.

It's bad for my eyes.

> *To the complaint, "There are no people in these photographs," I respond, "There are always two people: the photographer and the viewer."*
>
> —ANSEL ADAMS, (1902–84)

END CREDITS

Arly Zahoryin attainted Internet notoriety for posting a YouTube video entitled *At Gunpoint,* purportedly footage of a genuine hit man recorded during the filming of the movie *Vengeance Is.* He is currently directing his first feature film, *Cyber-Gator Vs. Tarantulasaurus,* for the Syfy channel.

Tripp Bergin recently threw a party at the Casting Office Bar & Grill in Universal City, California, to celebrate his fifty-seventh birthday . . . and his five hundredth gimme cap, for *Vengeance Is.*

Andrew Collier is currently working with a biographer on a book entitled *When Does It Blow Up?,* about the perils of transitioning from big studio work to independent features after the "tent-pole crash" of 2011.

Clavius (real name: Danko Dyakov) received the BoHo Humanitarian Award in 2011 for his photo series in *Clique* magazine entitled "Ugly Reality: Celebrity Cosmetology Laid Bare." *Clique* transitioned to a digital-only publication in 2011.

Artesia Savoy was sued by Mason Stone following the exposure of several so-called "sex tapes" with the popular action star. Stone won a punitive judgement of $250,000 when it was concluded that the man in the suspect videos "was not demonstrably

Mason Stone." She is presently working in the adult video industry.

Mason Stone's latest summer blockbuster is *Cold Barrel Zero*, for directing team the Suturabo Brothers.

Garrett Torres (second lead bad guy) is currently starring in the second season of his own HBO series, *Sword & Sandal*, about gladiators.

Harry "Boss" Wiley became a successful producer of pay-on-demand adult content for Internet distribution. Some of his projects star Artesia Savoy.

William "Cap" Weatherwax's firm, Fire When Ready, remains the go-to group for movie firearms consultation.

FFF Corporation, the makers of FelineFeast Fancy Cat Foods, suffered a crippling setback in 2011 due to a massive recall caused by salmonella contamination in their product line.

Spooky Sellars (publicist) abruptly left the production of *Vengeance Is*. Her current whereabouts are unknown.

Kleck and **Klia** (real names) are currently cochairs of Salon Fantastique Enterprises, LLC.

Elias McCabe is the reclusive director of McImages and cochair of Salon Fantastique International. He has never consented to be interviewed, and very little is known about his personal life.

ACKNOWLEDGMENTS

Upgunned is not a sequel to *Internecine*, although it takes place in the same general universe as that novel.

Large thanks to Thomas Jane, not only for various heroic step-ups, but for letting me use his face on the cover (again, twice!), and to Tim Bradstreet for rendering the artwork so adroitly and dependably. Several times.

For long—nearly lifelong—advocacy by colleagues, I need to put these names before you once more: John Farris, Peter Farris, Joe R. Lansdale, Michael Marshall Smith, Peter Straub, Duane Swierczynski, and F. Paul Wilson. Read them.

And pick up some Robert Bloch, while you're at it.

Behind-the-Scenes Staff: Charles Ardai of Hard Case Crime; Brendan Deneen, Nicole Sohl, and Thomas Dunne of St. Martins Press/Thomas Dunne Books, John Schoenfelder of Mulholland Books, and John Silbersack of Trident Media Group.

The story of "Mason Stone's Night of Thunder" was cribbed from a production experience I had on the set of *I, Robot* (it was blamed on Will Smith in the papers, and Will wasn't even there). My gratitude goes to longtime pal Alex Proyas and the entire cast and crew of that 2004 film.

On the home front, none of this could have been accomplished without the indulgence of the deeply lovable Kerry Fitzmaurice.

The ready friendship of Underworld denizen Ken Mitchroney

also got me over a lot of speed bumps. Ditto Michael Boatman, Ernest Dickerson, Frank Dietz, Dave Parker, and Sam Witwer.

In the DJS Armory you'll find such luminaries as movie firearms expert Ron Blecker, champion three-gunner Taran Butler, Paul and Jonathan Ehlers, walking ordnance encyclopedia John Fasano, Josh T. Ryan (formerly of Burbank's Gun World and the Showtime series *Lock 'n Load*), Pete Bitar, president of XADS (Xtreme Alternative Defense Systems, Ltd.), and the ever-reliable Ken Valentine—gun men, all.

Needless to say, Cap Weatherwax and his behavior as regards live firearms on a movie set are both complete fabrications, and no connection exists or should be inferred between Cap's doings and the stone-cold reliability and ethics of any professional armorer or firearms expert on any real-world movie set, anywhere, ever.

Atmosphere provided by *You Are Listening to Los Angeles* (http://youarelisteningtolosangeles.com)—LAPD police band monitor veneered with ambient music. It is utterly addictive.

Molly's Charbroiler, on Vine Street, closed forever on June 30, 2011, after being in business for *eighty-two years.*

—DJS